Strike a Match 5
Thin Ice

Frank Tayell

Strike a Match 5: Thin Ice

Published by Frank Tayell
Copyright 2022
All rights reserved
ISBN: 9798832125343

Sometimes, we can change the world. Sometimes, we can only change ourselves. Sometimes, all we can do is search for greener grass in the next valley.

All people, places, and (most) events are fictional.

The author has asserted their moral right under the Copyright, Designs and Patents Act, 1988, to be identified as the author of this work. All rights reserved. No part of this publication may be reproduced, copied, stored in a retrieval system, or transmitted, in any form or by any means, without the prior written consent of the copyright holder, nor be otherwise circulated in any form of binding or cover other than that in which it is published and without a similar condition being imposed on the subsequent purchaser.

Post-Apocalyptic Detective Novels
Work. Rest. Repeat.
Strike a Match 1. Serious Crimes 2. Counterfeit Conspiracy
3. Endangered Nation 4. Over By Christmas 5: Thin Ice

Surviving The Evacuation / Here We Stand / Life Goes On
Book 1: London, Book 2: Wasteland
Zombies vs The Living Dead
Book 3: Family, Book 4: Unsafe Haven
Book 5: Reunion, Book 6: Harvest
Book 7: Home
Here We Stand 1: Infected & 2: Divided
Book 8: Anglesey, Book 9: Ireland
Book 10: The Last Candidate, Book 11: Search and Rescue
Book 12: Britain's End, Book 13: Future's Beginning
Book 14: Mort Vivant, Book 15: Where There's Hope
Book 16: Unwanted Visitors, Unwelcome Guests
Life Goes On 1: Outback Outbreak, 2: No More News
Life Goes On3: While the Lights Are On, 4: If Not Us,
Life Goes On 5: No Turning Back
Book 17: There We Stood, Book 18: Rebuilt in a Day
Book 19: Welcome to the end of the World

For more information, visit:
http://www.FrankTayell.com
www.facebook.com/FrankTayell
http://twitter.com/FrankTayell

10th January

Prologue - The Investigation So Far, and the Mission to Come
Highcliffe Palace, Twynham

Inspector-General Henry Mitchell sat on the rock-hard leather bench outside the cabinet office, dreaming of cushions. At the other end of the draughty corridor, an artist patiently changed a faded sign from *Highcliffe Castle* into *Highcliffe Palace, Houses of Parliament*.

Despite twenty years in Britain, Henry Mitchell had never fully fathomed why some grand houses qualified as palaces and others earned the rank of castle. He *had* learned, with much disappointment, that it had nothing to do with moats, drawbridges, or dungeons.

Highcliffe had been built two hundred years ago, *high* up on the *cliffs*, about five kilometres east of Christchurch. In turn, Christchurch marked the eastern suburbs of the ever-growing, smog-shrouded capital city that sprawled west through Bournemouth to Poole.

Before the Blackout, Highcliffe had been a partially restored public museum. After the Blackout, the mansion had become a refugee camp, a hostel, and then a hospice, but the building was deemed too draughty for the dying. A year ago, it had been bought by Araminta Longfield, ostensibly for use as a hotel. Following her exposure as a leader in the conspiracy to overthrow parliament, and after her subsequent death, her property had been seized. Again, the question of what to do with Highcliffe had been raised, and it had been answered by the politicians.

Since the Blackout, parliament had met in a conference centre in Bournemouth, but only as a temporary expedient. Henry Mitchell had seen the fire-ravaged, partially flooded shell of the old Palace of Westminster with his own eyes. Too many politicians professed a hope of reclaiming London, though it was really the dream of old-world luxuries to which they clung. Ultimately, the increasing pollution from the war-industry factories had swayed even the most nostalgic fantasists.

Twenty years. It had taken *twenty* long years of ice-age winters and furnace summers, of starvation and rationing, of mass graves filled by disease and despair. It was twenty years since a digital virus had crashed the global communications networks and brought an end to the old civilisation, and almost brought an end to the species. Twenty years, and Britain's population had fallen to a tenth of what it once was.

When combined, the old nations of continental Europe were peopled by even less, and many of those now lived in exile in Britain. But for a country that traditionally measured time in units of monarchical reigns, that it had only taken twenty years for parliament to officially change its address was surely progress.

Perhaps he was being unjustly cynical, since his own country of birth was just as stuck in the past. The Americas had suffered similar devastation, and the old United States had split into three. The terms of reunification had long ago been agreed, but the election couldn't be held until later this year in order to maintain the ancient constitution's four-year cycle.

He picked up a copy of the newspaper left on the bench, but a quick glance told him it was light on actual news. The debate on whether the new parliamentary district should be renamed *Westminster* took up seven pages. Even the recent spate of arson attacks, due to the absence of fatalities, had only received a five-paragraph update on page nine. The war still ran on page one, but today's lead story was the two-nil victory by the army over the navy on a frozen football pitch in Calais. When journalists couldn't find anything more gruesome to write about than stud-caused stitches, the world surely was on an upswing. But how long would that optimism last?

Almost twenty-two years ago, Henry Mitchell had made the mistake of enrolling at university. It was the wrong course, the wrong place, and too soon after his father's death. Knowing he was about to fail, he'd decided to quit first. Before he handed in his papers, he'd seen an on-campus job ad. A professor had needed a bag-carrier for a European trip. That professor was Maggie Deering. Her assistant was Isaac. In their bags was a presentation on how to create a truly sentient A.I.

There was wealth in such an invention. There was prestige. There was power. In London, assassins had been sent to kill Maggie. When they failed, a digital virus had been unleashed. It had gone rogue. Across the world, computers had crashed. In self-driving vehicles, the crash was far more spectacular. Heat and speed regulators for domestic fans and industrial cooling systems were switched off, and so the infernos had begun. It took the combined electromagnetic pulses from dozens of strategically detonated nuclear warheads to disable the infected circuitry, but those same blasts also fried any unshielded electronics. The progress of a century had been undone in a matter of days, and that was only the beginning.

Isaac had used the last few bytes of internet to broadcast a warning, instructing selected survivors to head to the south coast, and so had gained a modicum of credibility during the slow march south. When Isaac had introduced Mitchell as a police officer from America, people had accepted it. One of those people had been a junior member of the cabinet who, due to the disappearance, and presumed death, of her colleagues, had become prime minister.

There'd been little policing, less law, and no order during those early months. Mitchell's first job had been as bodyguard to the new prime minister, and then to the scavenger teams hunting for supplies. After harvest, and after the bullets ran out, he'd joined the farmers fighting with axe and club to protect grain silos from people they called bandits, but who were really just desperate refugees.

Winter had arrived early, and didn't leave for years. Plague came with it, and for a time, he was little more than a gravedigger, and too often a grave-filler. The nights were so long, and the days so dark, he didn't notice his work gradually shift from protection detail to thief-catcher to detective. Survival became living. He'd adopted a daughter, Anna. He'd claimed a cottage and made a home. With crime on the rise, he'd had work to keep him busy, and his daughter to bring him joy, but he'd kept searching for a better life for himself and his daughter. He'd never found it.

Anna had followed him into the police service. That hadn't been his hope, but like many of her orphaned and unschooled generation, she was only otherwise qualified for a life of crime. Maggie Deering, the professor with whom Mitchell had first crossed the Atlantic, had similarly adopted a daughter. After the Blackout, Maggie had returned to her first calling, and taken work as a medic in the refugee camps of Kent. Just after a particularly virulent plague had swept through one of those camps, Maggie had found a girl, wandering alone. Ruth was around five at the time, though it was impossible to be certain of her age. Maggie had taken a job as teacher-physician in a resettlement camp on the outskirts of Twynham. Eleven years later, as Mitchell was contemplating changing to an agricultural career, he found Ruth a place at the police academy as a favour to his old friend. He'd even stayed on in the force so, when Ruth graduated, she could be placed under his command.

Had that been a mistake? Should he have retired? Certainly, his growing weariness with his political overlords had led to his demotion back to sergeant. Yet while working with Ruth and Anna, they had prevented the prime minister's assassination. They'd revealed the corruption within the Railway Company, and unmasked the industrialist conspiracy to overthrow the government. Along the way, they'd investigated murder, theft, and counterfeiting, and even saved a few lives. Anna was a beat-cop at heart, a local law-keeper in her local community. Ruth had a detective's analytical instincts. Yes, both were good officers, good citizens, good people, and among the very best of the lost generation raised among the shattered ruins.

Anna had been shot. She'd survived, but though she had returned to work, she was still wheelchair-bound. It was a hard price to pay, made worse by it not being him who was paying it. So had it been worth it? Should he have quit? In this new world, that didn't mean a pension, but he could have farmed a vineyard in France. Maybe. The idea was little more than a fantasy, a possibility of love he'd briefly tasted but not had time to enjoy before the barbarians swept east. The farm had been razed. Jacques, and everyone else in that hamlet, had been butchered. Prideful bravado aside, had Mitchell been there, he'd have died, too. No, he couldn't have changed that. Nor was there anything he could have done differently to change the course of history except, perhaps, never having left America.

From the Blackout to the plagues, the consolidation of the terrorist-tribes in Europe and the failed coup in Twynham to the attacks on Calais: a crooked path led from Maggie and Isaac's A.I. to him sitting on this bench in a semi-derelict mansion, waiting on a summons to brief the prime minister.

The artist carefully placed the stencil back on her tray, stepped back, and examined her work before picking up a much finer brush with which she began adding curls and frills. It might, by parliamentary decree, be a recycled sign in a recycled house, but she was an artist, and this *was* parliament's new home.

The door to the meeting room opened. Commissioner Weaver came out.

"Are you ready?" she asked.

"Are they?" Henry Mitchell replied.

The long and high-ceilinged banquet room had been truncated by a plain pine partition, currently unpainted, but dotted with annotated holes through which the new electrical wires were to be laid. For now, illumination was provided by a quartet of hanging lanterns, which cast a shadow over the room's only two occupants. Even though the assassination attempt on the old prime minister had failed, she had still resigned. Atherton, her long-serving deputy, had been given the keys to Number 10 just before the war began. Opposite him sat Craig Woodley, the new deputy prime minister and the nominal leader of the opposition, though the country had been run by a coalition for so long, the only difference between the two old parties was the colour of their ties.

"Inspector-General Mitchell," Atherton said, his tone tinged by the same exhaustion which lay heavy across his face. He'd aged a decade in a month. "We are ready for your report."

"I know where our enemy is headquartered," Mitchell said.

"Well, now you have my attention," Woodley said. His nasal voice created a shrill echo around the chamber "Where? Who?"

"If I may?" Commissioner Weaver said. "Before the Blackout, MI6 called him Marr. He was more commonly known as Abraham Haymar, Ibrahim Ibn Amar, or Benny Omar depending on which country he was dealing with. His real name is unknown. Accessing old records is obviously difficult, but long before the Blackout, he destroyed all evidence as to his real origins."

"He's a terrorist?" Atherton asked.

"When judged by his deeds, yes," Weaver said. "But he professed no creed except greed, no ideology but his own ego. Mercenary is a more accurate job description, but he also worked as a contractor employed by the British government, among others. We believe his father grew wealthy selling old weapons after the collapse of the Soviet empire. But it is possible that the father re-invented himself as his own son. Every record, photograph, or video in which he featured was altered or deleted. Thus, at the time of the Blackout, he might have been in his fifties, or in his seventies. He owned a stable of programmers who developed digital viruses, but his real skill was embedding those viruses into critical infrastructure. This often involved physical infiltration of places no British agent could reach. His profits were spent on the digitisation of consciousness and on human cloning. The work was notoriously controversial, frequently illegal, and ultimately fruitless."

"And he created the A.I. which caused the Blackout?" Woodley asked.

Atherton gave an agitated sigh.

"Mitchell?" Weaver said.

"There never was an A.I., not in that sense," Mitchell said. "A couple of academics were in London to present a mathematical principle which would revolutionise research in the field of artificial intelligence. Marr sent killers to assassinate them and to steal the research before it was distributed. The assassins failed. Marr let loose a digital virus to wreck London, so as to give a second hit-squad a chance to finish the job. The virus got loose, went wild, and spread beyond anyone's ability to control until it was finally stopped by the EMPs generated by the nuclear warheads."

"How do you know this?" Woodley asked, the cracks in his voice matching the cracks appearing in the coalition. "And how is it I'm only hearing of it now?"

"It was only an unsubstantiated theory," Atherton said airily.

"Even so, I should have been told," Woodley said. "We are supposed to be partners, yet you are keeping secrets from me."

"You're being told now," Atherton said. "Last month your responsibilities stretched no further than fixing the energy crisis." He pointedly peered at the nearest dim lantern. "I am still waiting to see the results."

"If I may?" Mitchell said. "Over the years, we've picked up a clue here and there, but it wasn't until the last few months that we were able to connect the disparate pieces of this conspiracy. The assassination attempt, Longfield's failed coup, the attack on Calais, the corruption within the police and the Railway Company, it's all connected, and connected to the Blackout."

"By this lunatic you call Marr?" Woodley asked.

"He's almost certainly dead," Weaver said. "If he were between fifty and seventy at the time of the Blackout, he would be between seventy and ninety now."

"*I* am seventy-one," Woodley said.

"It's not just his age which hints at him being dead," Mitchell said. "We only learned of this a few months ago, and we've had to guess at some of the details. Before the Blackout, Marr hired programmers and scientists from across the world. They lived, and worked, in a compound near the Black Sea. Among those coders was a couple. About seventeen years ago, she had a child, a daughter. Eleven years ago, the couple fled the compound, and made it all the way to a refugee camp in Kent. One of Marr's agents, the man we know as Emmitt, followed and tracked them down."

"I know that name," Woodley said.

"I should hope so," Atherton said. "He was linked to the assassination attempt, Longfield's coup, the Railway Company's treachery, and the attack on Calais."

"But he's dead, yes?" Woodley asked.

"He is," Mitchell said. "Eleven years ago, Emmitt used a biological agent to kill the family which had run from Marr's compound. Thousands of refugees died as collateral damage. Here's the twist. Emmitt was only interested in the child because he believed her to be Marr's daughter. We don't know the circumstances behind how the child was conceived, and it is possible the child was a genetic copy."

"Do you mean a clone?" Woodley asked.

"It's a possibility, not a certainty," Mitchell said. "His efforts at cloning were notoriously unsuccessful before the Blackout. It *is* possible he perfected it afterwards, though unlikely, and it doesn't matter because that child died years ago. The body was found a few months ago, and has been buried. At the time, eleven years ago, Emmitt either wanted control of this child, or wanted the child dead. Back then, he thought the child *had* died. At some point in the last few years, he came to believe the child had survived. Last year, he came looking for her. It was due to that search that he was identified, pursued, and killed during the attempt to arrest him."

"What did he want with this child?" Woodley asked.

"We don't know," Mitchell said. "But because Emmitt came looking for the child, we are certain Marr is dead. Since they're both deceased, we have to guess at their plans. Marr had a vault in Switzerland, somewhere near Zurich. He knew that his digital virus might get out of control. He knew there might be a global catastrophe, though we doubt he expected it to be as severe as it turned out. In this vault, he stashed a failsafe. A back-up. Over the years, that's taken on mythical proportions, but it's probably some weapon system."

"So this gang, they're all in Switzerland?" Woodley asked.

"For a time, we thought they were," Mitchell said. "And perhaps they were, once. They've been moving around a lot, but never strayed too far from Switzerland. They had access to a lot of weaponry. Assault rifles, anti-air missiles, and mortars. We know some of this was Soviet era stock sitting in warehouses along the Black Sea. With these guns, they armed gangs of bandits until there were only three major groups left, the three groups which launched the attack on Calais. Their strategy was to remove any threat from central Europe. Not just the threat of bandits, but also the threat presented by another organised state that might emerge from the ruins. Meanwhile, over here, they kept us fighting ourselves when we weren't fighting pirates. They organised coups and conspiracies, and the plagues which swept through people and crops."

"But who is running them? Where are they?" Woodley asked.

"*Who* doesn't matter," Mitchell said. "They were always a very small group, which is why they had to use the consolidated terrorist tribes as their foot soldiers in Europe. It's why they corrupted those who gave orders to the police and the Railway Company. Each scheme we thwarted reduced their personnel and resources. With each failure, they had less time to plan their next attack. They slipped up. We know they've moved their base of operations a number of times over the last two decades. We know they're producing their own glass. We know they're refining their own diesel. We know, during the attack on Calais, they gave their radio and refuelling teams German-language maps. We know they've rendezvoused at old campsites. But the fuel turns a search radius into an address. The impurities act like a fingerprint. We took samples from the supplies captured in Nieuwpoort and hunted down old reference documents against which to compare them. The fuel came from the Vienna Basin."

"I thought Vienna had burned down," Atherton said.

"The basin extends beneath Austria, the Czech Republic, and Slovakia," Mitchell said. "The scientists gave me a search grid which centres on the Austrian town of Matzen. It's an ancient place with an equally ancient castle, run as a luxury hotel before the Blackout, and which features on all the tourist maps."

"I'm sorry, perhaps I'm missing something," Woodley said, utterly unapologetically. "Where's the actual proof? Where's the evidence? It sounds to me as if you're suggesting we send all twenty-five of our tanks a thousand miles into Europe on a hunch."

"Eleven tanks," Atherton said. "The others are only suitable for training."

"The report said twenty-five, with another thirty due to be operational before spring," Woodley said.

Atherton gave an exaggerated sigh of exasperated superiority. "You do understand the concept of disinformation, Craig? They had agents in the police, the Railway Company, and who knows where else, but you certainly can't have forgotten they caught a spy in Dover at Christmas. Regardless, Mitchell isn't proposing to send a tank anywhere. Not yet."

"The army are going to push south, towards the Med," Mitchell said. "The navy are making a big deal about an expedition to the inland sea with the goal of pushing into the Black Sea by autumn. Any spies still lurking in Britain, and any still-loyal radio-teams in France, will assume that's our focus. I'm taking a small team by boat into the Baltic. We'll go ashore in Poland and drive south to Matzen. It won't be hard to find a smoke-belching oil refinery. We'll deploy a radio team in southern Germany, and another in Belgium. Once I find their refinery, the location will be relayed, via the radio teams, back to our lines."

"And that's when we send in the tanks?" Woodley asked.

"We'll send in a plane to destroy their base with a missile," Atherton said.

"What plane?" Woodley asked.

"The B1-B Rockwell Lancer the reclamation team in Suffolk restored," Atherton said.

"That's one of the USAF planes we promised to give back to the Americans," Woodley said.

"And they shall *have* the plane," Atherton said. "But after we've given her a test flight."

"This plane hasn't flown?" Woodley asked.

"Not yet," Atherton said.

"Do we have pilots?" Woodley asked.

"The two USAF pilots who were assisting in the restoration," Atherton said.

"Are you saying the Americans know about this?" Woodley asked.

"They don't *not* know," Atherton said. "Their politicians wish to maintain plausible deniability."

"You told them before me," Woodley said.

"Look at this from a different perspective," Atherton said. "We're not risking *our* plane, or *our* pilots, or burning *our* fuel. If Mitchell is unable to find the target, or if the plane won't fly, we can still send our tanks east. But if we can neutralise this enemy with one flight, and with one missile, the diesel reserved for the tanks can be used by our farmers. Imagine how many extra fields we could plough, and not just in Britain, but in France, too. Not only would rationing end, but we would have a feast at harvest time. That won't be very long after the election, whichever of us wins it."

"We've identified a runway we can use in Belgium," Mitchell said. "The plane will fly light to there as its test run. If all's well, it'll refuel and load the missile. The radio teams will set up beacons to guide the plane to Matzen, and I'll use a laser designator to make sure the missile hits its target. The plane will take off at dawn. We know the enemy used anti-air missiles to target our ships, but as this will be the first flight for twenty years, and the first attack on their stronghold, we don't think they'll be prepared for an aerial assault."

"What kind of missile?" Woodley asked. "I want to be clear, are we talking about a nuclear warhead?"

"It's just a conventional explosive," Atherton said. "The toxic fumes from a refinery fire will force any survivors to flee. They will have no more fuel, and no access to supplies. It is low risk, and very high reward."

"There is no such thing," Woodley said. "Twenty years ago, I was a dentist who was forced to become a battlefield medic, but I remember the proclamation when we were told there'd be no more armies. We were going to build a peaceful world. First came the navy to protect us from pirates, then the Marines to secure the shore. Now we have a conscript army. We have tanks. Our first flight in twenty years will be a bombing mission. Where will it end?"

"Hopefully with tourists flying to the pyramids for a holiday," Atherton said. "I would like your support."

"If I don't give it, the mission will take place anyway," Woodley said. "If it fails, I will share the blame. If it succeeds, I won't get the credit whether I support you or not."

"This is one of those times where we must set aside politics," Atherton said.

"Then it would be the first," Woodley said. "You swear these are just conventional warheads?"

"Of course," Mitchell said. "Anything else would be unthinkable."

Unthinkable. The word ran around Mitchell's head as he left Highcliffe. Yes, what he was planning was unthinkable, but it was unthinkable that this twenty-year war could be allowed to continue for another minute more. A conventional warhead would only scatter their enemy. The survivors would regroup, and the cycle would begin again. No, there was one chance to bring peace, but it would require him to do the unthinkable even if it meant no return. He headed back to the road to catch a cab back to Twynham so he could see his daughter and say goodbye.

Part 1
A Burning Passion for the Arts

Dover and Twynham

25th January

Chapter 1 - Showing Today
The Excelsior Cinema, Dover

Inside Dover's Excelsior Cinema, flickering lights cast dancing shadows in a tiered chamber almost completely absent of furniture.

"Well, yes, Josiah," Sergeant Elspeth Kettering said. "You *have* been robbed."

"It's a disaster," Josiah Braithwaite said. The portly owner of the cinema, turned grain silo, turned refugee camp, turned theatre, which had just finished re-conversion back into a cinema, exuded a sweaty glow which matched the gloss paint on the walls.

"How many seats should there be?" Constable Ruth Deering asked.

"Three hundred down here," Braithwaite said. "There are two hundred upstairs, but they weren't touched."

Ruth glanced back up at the balcony, then at the rows of chair-backs missing their seats. Only ten seats remained, all in the front row, though the fabric had been slashed so the wooden base could be removed, leaving the rough wool padding scattered about the crime scene.

"It is a *very* interesting case," Kettering said. "Very interesting indeed. Why don't you gather your staff in the foyer, Josiah? We'll come have a word in a sec." She patted the portly man on the arm and ushered him to the door. When he'd gone, Kettering turned to Ruth, who was examining the ten seats which hadn't been stolen. "You can tell a lot from blood splatter," Kettering said. "Wool splatter, not so much."

Elspeth Kettering had been a police officer in Dover before the Blackout. She'd been born in the city and been married here. After the Blackout, it was where her children had been born, and, more recently still, where she'd buried her husband. He'd died young, like so many in their toxic world, but she'd continued walking her old beat, refusing promotion to the big city in order to serve her hometown.

Ruth, by contrast, had only been in Dover for three months, and had only left the police academy two months before that. For her role in preventing the assassination of the prime minister, she'd been given an early promotion to full constable, and been sent to Dover to learn a more local kind of policing. But Calais had been attacked. The war had begun. Crime hadn't stopped, though it certainly had changed.

After the Blackout, Dover had become a clearing hub for European refugees and then traders and scavengers. After Calais came under siege, it had become a staging camp for the military. Now that the enemy's advance had been broken, restrictions were slowly being lifted. Businesses were re-opening, though this cinema wouldn't unless Mr Braithwaite seriously bent the meaning of standing room only.

"There are three hundred seats," Ruth said. "But the ten closest to the wooden stage aren't missing. The covers of those ten seats have been slashed. The padding has been left behind, and the metal frame is untouched, but the wooden base of the seat was taken. Judging by the size of the frame, the missing wooden panel is about fifty centimetres wide and long, with a depth of about five centimetres." She held her hands in front of her. "I suppose I could carry ten in a stack."

"Then you need to spend a bit more time in the gym, and a little less time in front of that screen Mr Isaac gave you," Kettering said.

"There are such things as documentaries," Ruth said. "How else am I supposed to learn what a shark looks like?"

"*Jaws* is not a documentary," Kettering said.

Ruth said nothing, but continued her mime as she walked her imaginary stack of wood to the fire door at the back of the theatre. "Ten at a time is easy enough, but I'd need someone to stack the load in my arms and to hold open the door. It's definitely a two-person job."

"Minimum," Kettering said. "Do you see the scuff marks on the floor near the door?"

"I do, and I was just getting to those," Ruth said. "The missing chairs were brought down here and stacked near the door. Based on the frames, and the bolts on the floor, they were of the same construction as the seats that were slashed. They were built in pairs, with a half-upright between the two seats. I think one person could carry a pair down to the front, but only after they'd been unbolted. That would have taken all night, so why not finish the job and unbolt the last ten?" She tried the fire door. "Unlocked. It leads to a corridor. There are stairs upstairs, probably to the balcony, but there's a door leading outside, and it's also unlocked." She opened the door and checked the frosted alley before returning to the auditorium. "There are wheel marks out in the slush. I think they belong to a bicycle cart with thick leather tyres nailed in place. The cart is narrow, but tall, and has wooden sides and a cloth roof. It's pulled by two bicycles in a staggered harness so the left is slightly in front of the right. Both bikes were painted red with old house paint which has flaked in the cold."

"If you saw some paint chips, you should collect them as evidence," Kettering said.

"I didn't look," Ruth said. "I didn't need to because I know who did it and I think I know why. Shall we go and arrest him?"

Nine employees had gathered in the cinema's foyer and stood beneath the disapproving eyes of Paddington Bear. The hand-painted poster, and its three nearly identical copies, took pride of place on the pillars facing the doors. Demoted to a wall by the wood-framed ticket booth were gloomier posters for *The Longest Day*, *Saving Private Ryan*, and *Remains of the Day*, the other movies approved by the Copyright Board before the cinema's re-opening was delayed by the attack on Calais.

Ruth smiled while she took in the staff she'd briefly met when they'd entered. Of the nine, two should still be in school. The owner, Braithwaite, was one of three old enough to have escaped conscription, leaving four who would be waiting on their call-up. Or, more accurately, waiting for rifle production to catch up with enthusiasm. Braithwaite looked angry, but she knew he was neither thief nor vandal. The other eight all appeared nervous, but that was understandable. Those who weren't guilty would certainly now fret that the repair bill would be so high, and supplies to scarce, the cinema would shut for good.

"I've always been partial to a country-house murder-mystery story," Kettering said, "but they always skip over the paperwork. In case you don't know, the more paperwork you make us do, the longer your sentence gets. We know who did it, so this would be the perfect time to confess. No? Well, that's one thing they do get right in the stories. Anyone foolish enough to leave such an obvious trail of clues is certainly *not* smart enough to take the best offer they'll get. Constable, the stage is yours."

"Two hundred and ninety seats were stolen," Ruth said. "In addition, the wooden bases of ten more were removed. Enough padding was left behind to imply the wooden seat-bases were stolen for firewood. The other seats were unbolted and carried down to the front of the theatre, stacked, and then loaded into a cart waiting outside."

"So they've been burned for firewood," Braithwaite said, his anger turning to self-pity. "They're gone. We're done for!"

"That is what we're *supposed* to think," Ruth said. "This was an inside job. There was no forced entry. To exit, they used a door which is locked when the theatre is not in use, and for which the only locks are on the *inside*. So, yes, this *was* an inside job. The rows of seats are bolted into metal brackets. It would take five minutes to unbolt each, so this work was carried out at night, and when the thief knew that no night-guard would be on duty. But having unbolted two hundred and ninety seats, why not spend a few minutes unbolting the last ten? Slashing and removing the wooden panels wasn't faster. No, the obvious vandalism was to make us think the seats were stolen for firewood. Wood's scarce. Coal's rare. Firewood is valuable. But the stage at the front of the cinema is made of wood, and that wasn't touched. That ticket kiosk is wooden, so why not take that? Because, though it's cold enough for bird song to freeze solid, this wasn't a theft, it was sabotage." She turned to a skinny man whose chin was too round for his triangular goatee and whose moustache wasn't thick enough to hide the spots beneath his nose. "What's your name, sir?"

"Me?" he squeaked. "Len. Leonard."

"Len Leonard?" Ruth asked.

"No. I mean, Leonard Zapcott. People call me Len."

"Just before Christmas, you opened the comedy club and music room on Stembrook Road," Ruth said. "The official opening was on New Year's Eve. You advertised live comedy and live music. Unlike a cinema, there's not much need for electricity. I went to your opening night. It was quite good. A bit too much chatting to hear the music properly, and too much music to chat, but it should have been a viable business, except you're working here."

"I'm just helping out," Len said.

"But you also drive coal from the railway station down to the harbour. I've seen you driving the cart. It's your own cart, powered by two bicycles, and has wonky leather-and-nail tyres that leave a distinctly memorable impression in the slush, and which are identical to the marks right outside the back door. It isn't a big cart, so when you stole the seats, you must have made lots of trips, all night long. I bet the military police patrol stopped you and asked what you were doing.

You must have proved to them you had the keys to this place, and so had a right to be moving things around at night. They'll still have mentioned it in the report which goes up to the castle at dawn and then gets to us around lunchtime."

Len blanched. His mouth dropped open, while his eyes reflexively looked for an exit. "I... I..." But invention failed him.

"That's not a denial," Kettering said.

"Why did you do this to us, Len?" Braithwaite asked. "A thriving night life helps everyone. There'd be more than enough customers for us both."

The suspect's shoulders sagged. "Because musicians want to be *paid*," Len said, his confession becoming a whine. "No one told me they'd want *real* money. It's not like you have to pay actors for those old movies. You just have to give a cut to the Copyright Board, but I have to pay the musicians *every* night!"

"Did you burn the seats?" Kettering asked.

"No, they're in a shed behind the bar," Len said. "I was going to return them. I was! I just needed a few more weeks to get the business going."

Braithwaite shook his head. "You should have come to me, Len. I could have helped."

"Josiah, if the seats were removed in an evening, you can have them re-installed in a day," Kettering said.

"You mean there won't be any charges?" Len asked.

"Oh, there absolutely will be charges," Kettering said. "Constable?"

She took out her handcuffs. "Leonard Zapcott, you're under arrest for theft and the destruction of property. You don't have to say anything, but it may be held against you if you later rely on anything you fail to mention, like, for instance, the name of your accomplice." Ruth pushed him to the far side of the foyer, away from the crowd of stunned co-workers, and towards the doors.

"What if I trade?" Len said.

"Trade what?" Ruth asked. "It was your cart. Since you've hidden the seats at your bar, someone there helped you. It's not going to be hard figuring out who."

"No, leave her out of it," Len said. "I can give you a big crime, and a big criminal. Way bigger than this."

"Her?" Ruth asked, her ears pricking. "On New Year's Eve, your sister was working the bar, wasn't she? Before you try to deny that, how big is this big crime?"

"The biggest," Len said.

Ruth raised her hand and beckoned Kettering over. "He has information on a bigger crime," Ruth said.

"Then he better share it," Kettering said.

"What do I get if I do?" Len asked.

"If it's actionable, you'll get conscription," Kettering said. "Navy not army, with two years minimum service, and you'll sell your bar to Mr Braithwaite at a price adjusted to compensate him for the damage you've done."

"He's welcome to it. That money pit is drowning in debt," Len said. "You'll leave my… my accomplice out of it?"

"I think he was helped by his sister," Ruth said.

"My old mum taught me there's a finite number of hours in the day, and we should spend each of them wisely," Kettering said. "If you've got information on something important enough it occupies our *complete* attention, we won't have time to worry about your sister. Go on, what do you know?"

"It's smuggling," Len said. "Me and my cart were hired to move some boxes to the old citadel, up on the bluffs."

"Do you mean the old barracks that became a detention camp where they now stage that fight night?" Kettering asked. "That place is a hive of gambling, drinking, and fighting, but we know all about it, so where's the new information?"

"It's inside those boxes," Len said. "A few weeks ago, I went up to Mr Porter to ask if he knew any tricks to running a bar. One professional to another, like."

"Which Porter?" Kettering asked. "The club is run by two brothers."

"Liam Porter," Len said. "He said he had a small delivery job. He didn't have a cart, you see. He asked me to go to the railway station and pick up some boxes. Twelve of them. Long and thin, they were. Not very heavy, neither, but they were awkward."

"What was in them?" Kettering asked.

"I didn't ask. I didn't look," Len said. "I didn't want no trouble from the Porter brothers. I *did* ask if there'd be more work, and they said there'd be some soon to take them down to the docks. They wanted to ship the boxes to France, but there weren't any ships."

"These boxes were long and thin, and not that heavy?" Kettering asked.

"That's it," Len said.

"And there were twelve of them? What were they made of?"

"Wood. Pine, I think. They looked cheap."

"And?" Kettering asked.

"That's it," Len said. "Isn't it enough? They're obviously smuggling weapons. Machine guns, I bet, like that bloke from Albion, and that gang in Twynham. That's worth a deal, right?"

"We'll see," Kettering said. "Constable, take him to the station. I'll escort Mr Braithwaite to the bar and retrieve his seats. We'll take a look at the citadel later."

Chapter 2 - The First Rule of Fight Club
The Citadel, Dover

Nestled among the frigates and destroyers under repair in Dover's harbour was a solitary civilian vessel. At first glance, it looked like a fishing boat, but instead of nets and winches, the deck was almost empty except for a brand-new deck-crane. The vessel was thirty metres long, and had a boxy cockpit. A Stars and Stripes billowed from the crane, a Union Jack rippled at the rear, and a deckhand was hanging shirts on a washing line between.

"There is no way that laundry will dry in this weather," Ruth said as she climbed aboard. "Freeze, yes. Dry, no."

"I am merely following my captain's orders," Isaac said. "How are you, Ruth?"

"Busy," Ruth said. "Why did you install a crane?"

"The better to carry cargo," Isaac said. "If you've come for an afternoon of fishing, we must first ask the navy for permission to leave the harbour."

"Actually, I need some help with a crime," Ruth said.

"Committing or solving?" Isaac asked.

"Which do you think?" Ruth asked. "But it's freezing out here. Can we talk inside?"

Mrs Zhang was in the cockpit, looking over a map filled with rivers and mountains, roads and cities.

"Vienna? I've heard of that place," Ruth said, spotting a familiar name.

Mrs Zhang refolded the chart. "It is famous for many reasons," she said.

"The ship looks clean," Ruth said.

"Because Kelly is with Henry," Isaac said. "It is remarkable how few gun-springs you find lying around when she's away."

Ruth decided to try a more direct approach. "What kind of cargo are you going to carry, and to where?"

"That will depend on Henry," Isaac said. "You said you wanted some help?"

"Just after I arrived in Dover, you said you used to own the citadel, up on the cliffs," Ruth said.

"I occupied it rather than owned it," Isaac said. "About a decade ago, I was looking for a warehouse in which to store loot salvaged from Europe before distributing it across Britain. The European Union had a similar idea, and set up a warehouse in Calais. They won that little contretemps, so I divested myself of a very unfashionable piece of real estate."

"You mean you sold it?" Ruth asked.

"He was paid to renounce all claims to it," Mrs Zhang said.

"Do you know the owners now?" Ruth asked.

"The Porter brothers? I know *of* them," Isaac said. "They operate a fight club, the first rule of which is that it's never open on Sundays and is always shut five minutes before curfew."

"We think they might be involved in smuggling," Ruth said. "We got a lead from a guy with a cart and a lot of debt. He was hired to bring crates up to the citadel from the railway station. He said they might be weapons, but Sergeant Kettering isn't sure. Do you remember the spy, Fishwyck?"

"Whom you pushed off a rooftop, and who was then impaled on a metal Christmas tree?" Isaac asked.

"I didn't push him, he fell as he was trying to escape," Ruth said.

"You think this is connected to the spy?" Mrs Zhang asked.

"Sergeant Kettering does," Ruth said. "She thinks that if Fishwyck was helping spies get into Britain, he could also have helped supplies get smuggled to Europe. Now Fishwyck is dead, those supplies have no easy route to France."

"What kind of boxes are these?" Mrs Zhang asked.

"A dozen wooden crates, probably made of pine," Ruth said. "They're long and thin, and awkward to carry, but not heavy."

"If these were supplies for enemy agents, he is unlikely to be the only courier," Mrs Zhang said. "Fishwyck could have outsourced transportation to the Porter brothers, and they employed this man among many others."

"I'd not thought of that. But what do you think is in the boxes?" Ruth asked. "It doesn't sound heavy enough to be guns, but what about explosives?"

"Do the Porter brothers know what is in the boxes?" Mrs Zhang said. "If so, they wouldn't use an unskilled courier for transporting explosives. Wasn't Fishwyck carrying false documents when he died? Inside the boxes could be something innocuous like candles or glassware. A hollow hidden inside the wall of the box could conceal fake ration cards or identity documents. That is a very old trick from before customs officials introduced X-ray machines at every port."

"There is an obvious way to find out," Isaac asked. "I assume you want us to break in and take a look inside?"

"No," Ruth said. "I want an invitation for me and a group of sailors."

"They sell tickets at the door," Isaac said.

"But if you're with me, they won't suspect we're there to conduct a search," Ruth said. "It'll just be you and me and a few sailors, undercover. We just need to get inside and around the back. The main raid will charge the gates at nine p.m., but it's a long run up the hill, so we don't want the Porter brothers to have time to destroy the evidence."

"A night out sounds delightful," Isaac said. "I'll take you, but not your sailors. We'll ask Gregory to accompany us. Mrs Zhang, do you have plans tonight?"

"I do now," she said.

After the Blackout, as order had returned, so had regulations, particularly those governing gambling. With medical care stretched, boxing clubs had been banned. Some had vanished, others had moved underground, sometimes quite literally, into basements, old bunkers, and older ruins out in the wild-lands. Each time a venue was shut down, a new location would be found. In Dover, a few years ago, a tacit understanding had been reached with the authorities. Fights could take place in the citadel, but only from eight p.m. until eleven, never on Sundays, and always in accordance with the professional boxing rules set down before the Blackout. All bets had to be placed in cash, with nothing on tick, and the maximum capped at a day's wage. And absolutely no fighting anywhere except inside the ring.

Ruth understood the necessity of policing by consent, and the impossibility of criminalising something the majority wanted. But she couldn't understand, with a war just a few miles across the water, why anyone would spend their free time watching strangers batter each other to a pulp.

While the semi-derelict Victorian-era complex was technically inside Dover's city walls, a gated barrier ran across Citadel Road. That gate was open, and the Marine inside the guard post barely glanced up from her newspaper as they walked past. For the evening, Ruth was dressed in her undercover clothes, all hand-me-downs from Anna Riley, and so much smarter than the comfy patched tweed she wore on her evenings off.

"Why did you stake a claim on this place?" Ruth asked as they trudged up the hill, following the slushy footprints of the customers who'd arrived before them.

"I told you, I wanted a warehouse," Isaac said.

"But that was obviously a lie," Ruth said. "Having a warehouse in France makes sense because crossing the sea is the difficult part, but having crossed, why leave salvage here when there's surely more money to be made in Twynham?"

"She's learning," Mrs Zhang said.

"It is my own fault for being such a good teacher," Isaac said. "Are you familiar with the history of this place?"

"It was a Napoleonic fort, built as part of the defences against a French invasion," Ruth said. "They used it again during the World Wars as a bastion. Afterwards, it became a prison for children, then a detainment camp for refugees, then nothing. After the Blackout, it was a temporary morgue. I think that's why it didn't become a refugee camp."

"Ah, but do you know what was here before Napoleon was born?" Isaac asked.

"Cows?" Ruth asked.

"The Templars," Isaac said.

"The Knights Templar, as in the ruins on Bredenstone Hill?" Ruth asked.

"Yes, but I was always more interested in the tunnels *beneath*," Isaac said. "Don't you think it suspicious that successive British governments dug so many tunnels into these chalk cliffs, supposedly because they feared invasion?"

"Since we've had two attempts at invasion last year, no," Ruth said. "Dover's only twenty miles from Calais. Lots of people invaded this way."

"Yes, and that was the government line," Isaac said. "The Romans, the Saxons, the Normans. Napoleon might have. Hitler almost did. But what's the real reason?"

"Oh, go on," she said, detouring around a frozen pothole that, come the thaw, would be large enough to be called a paddling pool.

"The Knights Templar built the first tunnels as a place in which to store the treasures they brought back from the crusades," Isaac said.

"So you bought this place so you could look for the treasure?" Ruth asked.

"He also bought a shovel," Mrs Zhang said.

"I did *need* a warehouse," Isaac said. "I'd read three books which all mentioned the theory. So why not combine need with curiosity and take a look?"

"Did you find anything?" Ruth asked.

"Sadly, no," Isaac said. "However, the enterprise provided a useful introduction to many European adventurers seeking to return to their homeland. In turn, that facilitated the preservation of the European Union, and the concept of peaceful internationalism."

"Peaceful? There is a war on," Ruth said.

"But it is almost over," Isaac said.

"Guards ahead," Mrs Zhang said.

There were four bouncers at the entrance to the club. The four men all wore suits that were more tubular than tailored. In deference to the weather, their trousers were tucked into their boots, each wore a scarf, and they had pulled their peaked hats low.

"One pound to enter. Each," the lead bouncer said. "No weapons."

Isaac opened his coat. "Indeed, no weapons here, unless he counts." He gestured at Gregory who was three inches taller than the largest of the bouncers. "What's the prize for tonight's bout?"

"Twenty pounds," the bouncer said. "Five pounds to weigh in. You can pay at the bar. Move on. There's more coming."

It was clearly too cold to banter. Other spectators were making their way up the hill behind. A handful ahead were already making their way inside, but it looked to be a quiet night for the club, explaining the small prize-purse.

Even without the group ahead of them, it was obvious which way to go. The path through the car park was marked with old pipes, and led them to a redbrick Victorian barracks. Two decades of smoke stains had become dark halos around the warped wooden boards covering half the windows. Thick grime curtained the cracked glass of the rest, allowing out only a thin sliver of light.

Just inside a brazier-heated lobby, another pair of bouncers operated a search-for-weapons coat-check, which Isaac ignored by placing three five-pound-notes on the counter. As the bouncers argued over how to turn an odd number into an even split, they slipped into the venue.

Whatever it had been built for, and whatever it had become during the last two centuries, the doors had been removed and the walls were partially demolished, creating a smoky, dim cavern. In this half, near the entrance, was the bar, and a few tables and chairs, half of which were occupied. On the other side of the demolished doorway was the ring. Rather than raised, it was sunken into the floor, allowing a better view for customers around the edge, and other customers standing on the scaffolding balcony built against the western wall. Currently, the balcony was home to a cellist, guitarist, and a double bass. A piano in a ground-level corner was carrying the tune while a drummer in the other corner set the rhythm. Despite their enthusiasm, they'd not managed to entice any of the early customers to dance.

"Four of your best," Isaac said, throwing more money on the bar.

"Isaac, let me pay," Ruth said.

"What's money for if you can't spend it?" he asked.

Suspecting the notes might be counterfeit, but not daring to ask after the bartender had scooped them up, Ruth took her glass and gave a pretend sip. Even the accidental sniff made her eyes water.

"What is that?" she asked.

"Something to put hairs on your brain," Isaac said. "The bout is at nine, and we've got… ah, half an hour." He turned to the bartender. "My friend wants to enter the fight. There's a twenty quid prize, yes?"

The bartender looked Gregory up and down. "Seen you before, haven't I?" she asked.

Gregory shrugged.

"The sign says all comers," Isaac said.

"And he's every one of them all in one go," the bartender said. She raised two fingers to her lips and whistled loud enough to be heard over the music.

From the other side of the hall, a man in a top hat, black tailcoat, red waistcoat, and high leather boots sauntered over. Beneath the hat were bushy mutton-chop whiskers standing sentry on either side of a too-perfect smile.

"We have a contender, Mr Porter," the bartender said, nodding at Gregory.

"Liam Porter, how's business?" Isaac asked.

"Isaac!" Porter said, and began patting his pockets. "Ah, no, I still have my wallet. So if you've not robbed me yet, does that mean you ain't here on business?"

"This is purely a social visit," Isaac said. "It gets rather tedious living on a ship. We wanted to break the monotony."

"You have a ship?" Porter asked, his professional bonhomie replaced by genuine interest.

"An old fishing trawler," Isaac said. "We intended to sail to France, but the war has created extra paperwork, and now we're waiting for it to clear."

"We should have a word later," Porter said. "I think there's an opportunity here. But first, we have the fight." He turned to Gregory. "You'll do very well for the main event. Between the war and the navy banning sailors from having a little fun, we're light on talent, but your man would make a great contender. Let's say three fights. A win tonight, a loss tomorrow, and a victorious comeback on Saturday. One hundred pounds, what do you say?"

"You—" Ruth began.

"Deal," Isaac said. "Is there somewhere he can hang his coat?"

"Behind the bar. Room at the end," Porter said. "No bets for you, of course. But we'll talk later. I think there's a different way you and I can make a handsome profit."

The bartender led them through a door, and down an L-shaped corridor lined with beer barrels. At the end was a fire door, chained shut. The bartender opened a battered wooden side-door, and hung the lantern on a hook inside.

"There," she said, and left before anyone could comment on the lack of room and the overabundance of smell. Frozen sweat glistened on damp walls splattered with the blood of previous contenders.

"I've seen worse," Mrs Zhang said, as Gregory removed his coat.

Ruth wanted to ask where, but there was another question she had to ask first. "These fights are fixed," she said.

"Of course," Isaac said. "They are supposed to be entertainment."

"But people place bets!" Ruth said.

"A point you can discuss with Porter later," Isaac said. "I believe we can get a confession from him if we wait until after the fight."

"Because he wants to hire your boat," Ruth said. She looked over at Gregory who, due to the lack of room, was stretching his muscles one at a time. "I can't ask Gregory to fight."

The old baker shrugged.

Ruth checked the watch. "No, it's a quarter to nine. By now, Sergeant Kettering will be at the bottom of the hill with forty sailors. I might get there in time to stop her assault, but there's no way the sailors won't talk about what they were mustered for tonight. We should stick with the plan."

"We need more radios," Isaac said.

"You've said that before," Mrs Zhang said. "You and Ruth take the back. Gregory and I will stay here, so he can enter the ring if help doesn't arrive in time."

Isaac took out his set of lock-picks. "Ruth, after you."

She opened the door. Outside, the corridor was empty. She stepped aside so Isaac could make his way past and to the fire door. From the direction of the bar, the band was barely audible above the rising sound of the crowd. Would forty sailors be enough to prevent an arrest becoming a riot?

Behind her came a metallic snap.

"Are you done?" Ruth asked.

"Not exactly," Isaac said. "The pick broke. But give me a moment."

A door further along the corridor opened. A boxer stepped out. He was no giant, but still six feet tall and big all over.

"What are you doing?" he asked, curious rather than suspicious.

"Getting some air," Ruth said. "I think our guy is up against you."

"Are you picking that lock?" he asked, his hackles rising in time with his fists.

He stepped forward, and so drew level with the still-open doorway to their dressing room. Gregory's fist slammed obliquely into his chest. The baker followed the blow out into the corridor. The boxer gasped, and staggered backwards and into the stack of barrels. An empty fell, clattering to the ground as Gregory adjusted his stance, raising his fists, completely blocking the corridor.

Another door opened, and a second boxer stepped into the corridor.

"Isaac, hurry!" Ruth said.

"Done!" Isaac said.

A cold wave washed over her as he pushed the door open.

"Come on!" Ruth yelled, and ran past Isaac, and outside into the frigid, frozen parade ground, and straight onto thick and slippery ice. She fell back, hit her head, and saw stars.

Chapter 3 - Concealed Guilt
The Citadel, Dover

"Are you all right, Ruth?" Kettering said.

As Ruth looked up, she still saw stars, but since she was staring into a cloudless night sky, they probably belonged there. "What happened?" she asked.

"You slipped and hit your head," Kettering said. "Good thing it wasn't anywhere important. After you fell, your friends began tearing the place apart, so we came in early."

"Did the Porter brothers escape?" Ruth asked.

"I think they were too shocked to run. Literally. Your Mrs Zhang zapped them with a stun gun. It looks to be a homemade piece of kit, but they're not dead. How are you feeling?"

"Like my brain is a puddle," Ruth said, raising a hand to her ear to see if anything dribbled out. "But I'll be fine."

"Good, because we've only got a couple of hours to search this place before their lawyer turns up. I don't think we'll be able to hold them, not after a very illegal weapon was just used. On your feet. That's it."

Kettering led her to a well-lit ruin behind the barracks. A few of the lamps were old-world LEDs, salvaged or dug out of storage now that electricity was becoming more commonplace. But most of the illumination came from standard-issue government lanterns, increasingly known as Atherton lamps for being heavy, dim, and occasionally explosive.

"The footprints gave it away," Kettering said. "The building used to be the armoury. That was back in Wellington's day. By the time of the Blackout, it became offices, but there's an underground cellar."

The footprints in the re-frozen snowmelt led to a metal door that lay almost flat with the ground, and which, when closed and covered in snow, concealed steps leading down into the basement. Betraying the cellar's most recent role was the cask-width ramp laid atop the left side of the stairs.

"It's not exactly a secret lair," Ruth said.

"Agreed," Kettering said. "It's a bit too obvious, but take a look anyway, while I follow these footprints. I can count the plus points of winter policing on the frostbitten fingers of one hand, but at least snow always gives us a trail to follow."

Lantern in one hand, the other braced against the ramp, Ruth made her way down the steep steps and into a cellar. The roof was arched and low. The bricks were ancient, and if she were to pick an era, she'd say Napoleonic. A quick count gave her twenty-four casks, ten crates of wine, and ten boxes of spirits, plus ten bales of hay stacked in an alcove behind the beer barrels. A closer examination of the wine told her that half of it was Somerset Sparkler, a fizzy brew that was thirty percent hangover. It was a lot of booze, especially considering the number of barrels lining the corridor outside the dressing room. Some of those had been empty, but she was sure most were full. On a hunch, she began tapping the casks. Each sounded full, but full of what?

"I bring visitors," Isaac called out.

"Who is it?" Ruth replied.

"Liam Porter, co-owner of the establishment," Isaac said. "Sergeant Kettering is speaking with his brother. I left Gregory outside, but I said we'd call if we needed him to rip off Liam's arm."

"Hello again, Mr Porter," Ruth said, walking back to the entrance where the man with the mutton-chop whiskers had preceded Isaac down the steps. He'd lost his top hat, but not his smile.

"You should have said you were police," Porter said affably. "Coppers always drink for free. Are the handcuffs really necessary?"

"You tell me," Ruth said.

"I say no, but of course I would," he said. "Perhaps you could say why you're here? And why are you here, Isaac?"

"I am merely seeking entertainment on a winter's evening," Isaac said. "Constable Deering is here on a rather more prosaic quest."

"Where are they?" Ruth asked.

"Where's what?" Porter asked.

"The twelve boxes you had collected from the train station," Ruth said. "I will find them, but it would save a lot of aggravation if you would just say where they are."

"Are these the depths to which policing has descended?" Porter asked. "No public servant deserves such threats."

"How are *you* a public servant?" Ruth asked.

"As you can see from my attire, providing much-needed entertainment doesn't generate much profit, so why else would I be doing it if not to help the war effort, in my own small way?"

"He had a revolver in his office," Isaac said.

"And a hunting licence in my pocket," Porter said.

"Who hunts with a revolver?" Ruth asked.

"A one-armed man," Porter said.

"You have two arms," Ruth said.

"At present," Porter said. "It's wise to be prepared."

"That's a lot of spirits," Ruth said.

"But less than you'd find in a graveyard," Porter said.

"And a lot of wine, too," Ruth said.

"We're opening a bar in Calais," he said. "There's a gap in the market after the death of Tommy Fry."

"But there's a war on," Ruth said.

"And a peace coming," Porter said. "You needn't strain your ears to hear it. Listen. There. Nothing. Not a single cannon has been fired by the blockade in days. I have a letter from the admiral, and another from our MP, confirming there are no export taxes to pay."

"And the beer? You can't plan on taking that to Calais," Ruth said.

"You haven't been to a fight, have you?" Porter asked. "It's not just punches which are thrown."

Porter had a riposte for everything, but he'd talked too much. She could tell he was nervous.

She moved back through the basement. Behind the casks, benches and tables were stacked one atop the other. Wooden. Old. Six tables in total, and looking the worse for damp. Opposite, though, was an armchair atop a square of carpet with a blanket, a side table, a few old paperbacks, a copy of the newspaper, and a pair of electric lanterns.

"Who sits here?" Ruth asked.

"A guard is stationed here after we close and until the bank opens," Porter said. "We're an obvious target for theft."

Ruth walked back to the barrels, and then over to the ten bales of hay. They were square bales, about half a metre on each face, and a metre long.

"What happened to your horses?" she asked.

"They were requisitioned by the army," he said.

"Really? Do you have a form to that effect?" she asked.

"They never gave me one," he said.

"You've got a letter from the MP saying you don't have to pay an export tax, and you carry around your gun licence, but you didn't get a form when your horses were taken? Yeah, right. Answer me this, if you've no horses, why keep the hay? Why not sell it? It's worth an absolute fortune."

"I view it as a long-term investment," he said.

"But you keep it stacked here in the damp," she said.

"The hay is concealing a hole in the wall," Isaac said. "It was there when I had this place."

"Well, why didn't you just say?" Ruth asked.

"I didn't want to spoil your fun," Isaac said.

Her anger at him gave her more than enough strength to move the hay. Behind them was a metal sheet. Behind that was a hole. From the freshly exposed plaster, bricks had recently been removed to make it bigger. Through the hole was a storeroom containing twelve wooden crates. Yes, they were long and narrow, just like Len Zapcott had said, but he'd missed the part where they were also tall. He could also have described them as being the size of a window, but she doubted that was what was inside.

She drew her knife, and pried at the nails of the nearest crate. She wasn't the first to check the contents, so the nails easily worked loose, revealing the man trapped on canvas inside: a minister with his arms crossed, wearing a top hat and morning coat, and with the skinniest legs she'd ever seen, skated across a misty lake.

Ruth took the painting out into the cavern.

"Look what I found," Ruth said.

"It's the *Skating Minister* by Henry Raeburn," Porter said. "Be careful. It's genuine."

"I've heard of that piece," Isaac said. "It went missing from Edinburgh after the Blackout."

"How did you get hold of it, Mr Porter?" Ruth asked.

"I bought it fair and square," Porter said.

"From whom?" Ruth asked.

"Araminta Longfield," he said. "This was about three years ago. She wanted to buy a thousand acres of mine in Cornwall. She offered cash, or a stake in her business. I asked for something a little more substantial. We agreed on twelve paintings. I have a contract, drawn up by lawyers."

"Which doesn't mean the paintings aren't stolen," Ruth said.

"But I don't think you know that painting, or any of the others, ever *were* stolen," Porter said. "Someone rescued the pictures. Somehow they ended up in Longfield's possession. She used them as payment to me. If there's a crime here, it's not been committed by me."

"You hid them in a secret storeroom whose entrance was concealed by hay," Ruth said.

"As I've said, we are a target for thieves."

"If you're the legitimate owner, why not put them on display?"

"We will. We brought them here because we're relocating to France. Opening an art gallery will get people to visit our bar."

"But a bar in France, with paintings stolen from Scotland," Ruth said. "It'd be a legal nightmare getting these paintings back to Britain. But you know that."

"What's the charge?" Porter asked. "I've got paperwork saying I took those paintings in exchange for land. That proves I didn't take them from Scotland."

"Why did she want the land?" Ruth asked.

"Lithium," Porter said. "It was the most easterly deposit discovered prior to the Blackout. She was investing for the future."

"Does your lawyer's paperwork mention the paintings by name?" Ruth asked.

Porter paused before answering. "No," he finally said.

"So we've no way of knowing if these were the *same* twelve paintings," Ruth said.

"Would I have taken them for payment if they weren't genuine?" Porter asked.

"That sounds like an admission of guilt," Ruth said.

"Just an awareness of their beauty," he said.

"I'm not sure what the charge is," Ruth said. "And I'm not sure if we're going to arrest you, but we're certainly not leaving the paintings here. Take him upstairs and give him to the military police, Isaac. And then get Sergeant Kettering. I'm absolutely positive she'll want to see these for herself."

Chapter 4 - Even Scottish Clergy Enjoy Cocoa
The Police Station, Dover

"What happened next, Mum? And why didn't you arrest the Porter brothers?" Eloise Kettering asked as she helped Ruth carry the paintings into the police station's empty holding cell. Kettering supervised from a chair while recounting the tale of the arrest.

"We can't charge them with any petty crime connected to the club," Sergeant Kettering said. "That's the deal the mayor struck, and to which the navy agreed. We *could* charge them with handling stolen goods, but that would mean re-opening the Longfield case, and I don't think anyone wants that."

"Liam Porter asked Isaac if he could still take them to France," Ruth said. "And then he asked if Isaac wanted to buy the citadel."

"Are they trying to run away?" Eloise asked.

"They're misreading the wind if they think they'll escape justice in France," Kettering said. "The war isn't over. Rebuilding hasn't begun. It'll be a long time, if ever, before our legal systems are disentangled. But I think the brothers know that. And I think they know there are plenty of paintings hanging in European galleries, or in their vaults. It won't be an easy journey to salvage them. The hardier of the surviving terrorists will become road bandits, viewing convoys like that as easy prey. On the other hand, in a month or twelve, there'll be plenty of demobbed conscripts looking for work."

"Hang on, Mum," Eloise said. "Surely all the famous paintings were salvaged, stolen, or lost, years ago."

"*The Skating Minister* wasn't famous until the beginning of this very century," Sergeant Kettering said. "The picture was knocking about in private hands over in the New Forest until about fifty years ago when it was bought by the Edinburgh Gallery for five hundred quid. It was only after they used the image to advertise a new exhibition that it became world-renowned. There's a lesson there, and one the Porter brothers have taken to heart. Whatever pictures they put on display will *become* famous because it's all the art most people will see."

"Will you let them go to France, then?" Eloise asked.

"It's not my decision," Kettering said. "So I decided it wouldn't be my problem, either, and I've passed the aggravation up the chain. I sent a telegram to Twynham, so we'll see if they want to handle it differently. I'm sure they'll send us a reply in the morning, which gives me time to reacquaint myself with my bed. Good night, ladies."

Eloise followed her mum to the door, locked it, then grinned. "C'mon, Ruth, let's have a look at the paintings."

"Absolutely not," Ruth said.

"But when else will we get the chance?" Eloise asked. "They'll go into some big evidence warehouse, and never be seen again."

"I'm sure the pictures will go to a gallery."

"Not around here," Eloise said. "They might as well be left in that cellar for how often we'll ever have a chance to see them. Let's just take a quick look. No one said we couldn't."

"You mean your mum didn't specifically say you shouldn't," Ruth said. "But... okay. Just for a few minutes."

"Great, you're the expert at opening cases, so get the paintings out while I get the cocoa," Eloise said. "It's a new recipe. Word is, this one is actually drinkable."

Hot chocolate was the latest creation by the odd minds at Satz Tea. Like their powdered tea and coffee, the drink had been designed in a lab. Ruth had tried real coffee, thanks to the American ambassador, but preferred the artificial kind. She'd never drunk from a muddy puddle at a cattle yard, but that's how the newspaper had described the company's previous attempt at an artificial cocoa. The new version had received mixed reviews, but at an introductory price half that of tea, it was flying off the shelves.

Carefully, Ruth pried open the box, removed *The Skating Minister*, and set it against the crate. She stepped back to better view the depiction of a man in a frock coat, casually skating atop a frozen pond.

"I like it," Eloise said, coming back with two mugs.

"The cocoa or the painting?" Ruth asked.

"Both," Eloise said. "But I like the painting more. Here." She handed Ruth a mug. "It's not what you usually see in paintings, is it? They're all seascapes up at the castle. Seascapes and people. And when it's people, they always look like they've sat on a pin. This is... it's so alive! How did he do it? It was a he, wasn't it?"

"The artist? I think so," Ruth said. "Um... no, I can't remember his name."

"Did he ask the vicar to skate around the pond, or did he see the fellow once, and paint from memory?" Eloise asked, peering forward in search of a name.

"We should ask your mum tomorrow," Ruth said. "She seemed to know quite a bit about the picture."

"You know how she likes to collect books," Eloise said. "Doesn't matter what genre, as long as it's not one she's read before. No, I like it, and far more than a portrait of some bejewelled baroness. I wish we could keep it."

"We absolutely can't," Ruth said.

"I know," Eloise said. "This was stolen by Longfield?"

"I think it was stolen *for* her," Ruth said. "We know she employed scavengers to steal gold, jewels, artefacts, and art. And we know she wasn't the only one. Mister Mitchell said, once, that it was better someone preserve forgotten art than leaving it to the spiders. He also said there were old laws about reclaiming stolen art that went back to World War Two."

"The admiral told me about how some people, after revolutions, used to strip-mine their own countries," Eloise said. "Oligarchs, she said they were called. But they were mostly mid-ranking nobodies before the coup. They'd overthrow the rich and powerful, and try to steal enough wealth so they could buy the influence to keep it, and keep themselves from the noose. She said that's basically what Longfield did. Um… have you heard from Simon lately?"

"From? No," Ruth said. "Mrs Zhang said he's in Germany now, helping bring refugees to the coast. He'll never be allowed to return to Britain, and I don't think I want to go to Europe again, not after the last two times. Maybe in a few years, when the fighting has properly stopped, and then, maybe, I can collect some memories that aren't of blood and pain. No, Simon's making amends, so I won't say I forgive him, but I'm happy to forget him, and move on." She took a step back. "You know, the more I look at the painting, the more I wonder whether the Porter brothers were hoping for the publicity that would go with the painting appearing in France. The paper would write about it, and there'd be a public outcry, and the paper would write about that, too. The Porters could then return the paintings and get even *more* publicity."

"All so people would hear about their bar?" Eloise asked.

"Oh, I bet their plans are far bigger than that," Ruth said. "When were you talking with the admiral?"

"Every day at eleven, she spends ten minutes in the gardens doing the crossword," Eloise said. "Coincidentally, so do I now."

"Ah, this is why you were reading the dictionary yesterday."

"Those crosswords are *hard*," Eloise said.

"Is she leading the Pacific expedition?" Ruth asked.

"Probably not, but she *is* planning it," Eloise said. "Everything depends on the war, but she hopes it can set sail in the summer and return before winter."

"Are you on the crew list?"

"I'm not sure," Eloise said. "She did say there will be lots of expeditions to the Mediterranean, so I think that means if I'm on any ship, it'll be one going there. But that's not so bad. Imagine seeing the pyramids."

"Imagine," Ruth echoed.

They sipped their cocoa, looking at the minister frozen in time, but lost in thoughts of their own futures.

"We should open a gallery here in Dover," Eloise said. "Let's take over a building somewhere, and put these up on show at least until Twynham says they want them back."

"That's a good idea," Ruth said. "We could use the cinema. It's got no seats, and they need the money."

"What do you mean it's got no seats?" Eloise asked.

"Oh, didn't I tell you?" Ruth said. "That was the first crime of the day. One of the staff stole the seats to stop the cinema from re-opening. Do you remember that bar we went to at New Year's?"

"I remember the slow service," she said. "There were too many tables for dancing, not enough chairs for sitting, but the music was good, when you could hear it."

"The brother and sister who ran the bar stole the seats from the cinema, and tried to make it look like they'd been taken for firewood," Ruth said. "They're barely keeping their bar afloat and thought, without the cinema as competition, they might break even."

"But the picture house hasn't even opened yet," Eloise said. "How can the cinema be taking away their business?"

"And I think, there, we have the reason they can't turn a profit running a bar in a city full of sailors," Ruth said.

"It sounds like you've had a day and a half," Eloise said. "Except when I was trying to figure out a seven-letter word for *a naturally sweet container for a Yorkshire flower*, I spent most of my day tending frostbitten toes. And yes, it really is as gross as it sounds." Eloise stepped forward, half kneeling as she peered at the frame.

"What are you doing?"

"Looking for the painter's name."

"Try the back," Ruth said. "Oh, careful!"

As Eloise stood, her mug sloshed. Cocoa spilled over the side, and onto the canvas.

"Oh, no!" Eloise exclaimed, dabbing at the frame with the hem of her skirt.

"I'll get a cloth," Ruth said. She was halfway to the door behind the duty desk, and the cleaning cupboard beneath the stairs, when she was interrupted by a hammering on the door.

"Use the bell!" Ruth called, even as the hammering continued. When she checked the door's spy-hole, she saw a green army uniform outside.

"Where's the crime?" she asked as she opened the door.

"Telegram, ma'am," the soldier said, handing it to her, then darting away before she could say whether there was a reply.

"Has there been a murder?" Eloise asked.

"No. It's just a message from Commissioner Weaver," Ruth said. "She wants the paintings brought to Twynham immediately."

"Tonight?" Eloise asked.

"I hope not," Ruth said. "But there's a train tomorrow at five. That should be soon enough."

"I told you they'd end up in a gallery in the capital," Eloise said.

"I better wake your mum," Ruth said.

"Not just yet," Eloise said. "The stain's not dry."

"Maybe we should put it back in the crate," Ruth said. "And then I'll go wake your mum."

26th January

Chapter 5 - The Chained Minister
Kent, Sussex, Surrey, and Hampshire

The train rocked. Ruth yawned and then winced. The slip-and-fall at the citadel had left her with a headache not helped by the late night and early start. Catching up on her sleep aboard the train was impossible because she, and Isaac, rode in the prisoner-transport car. So as to prevent a guard from falling asleep, the bare benches were too narrow to lie down on and barely wide enough to sit on. But since the only occupants of the convict-cages were the twelve paintings, a mid-journey escape was less likely than a robbery. She looked over at Isaac and recalculated the odds of a theft.

"Why *are* you here, Isaac?" she asked.

"Because I'm going to Scotland," Isaac said. "There's a sleeper train tomorrow from Twynham."

"I thought you had to go to Belgium," she said.

"Henry requires my boat," Isaac said. "He doesn't require me. Not yet."

"Okay, so why does he need your boat when he's got the entire British Navy floating off the coast?"

"I assume to take him from one place to another," Isaac said.

"This is like getting blood from a stone," Ruth said, leaning forward and making a show of looking under the bench. "Nope, no rocks here. Why are you going to Scotland?"

"Arthur, an old friend of mine, lives outside Thurso," Isaac said. "With one thing and another, one war and another, it's been a while since I saw him. But now that the transatlantic ferry is currently using Thurso rather than Twynham, there's a sleeper-express train."

"I didn't know the ferry was running to Thurso."

"The reasoning was to reduce the likelihood of pirate attacks in southern waters," Isaac said. "But since the railway is selling tickets, it's not much of a state secret."

"Why can't the navy provide an escort?" Ruth asked.

"There aren't enough ships," Isaac said. "In addition to the Channel blockade, and the patrols running down to the Bay of Biscay and up to the Baltic, they're preparing a flotilla to take a conscript army to the

Mediterranean coast of southern France. It's why so many soldiers, and sailors, were given leave this month."

"Eloise mentioned the admiral picking people for a trip to the Mediterranean, but she thought she might get to see the pyramids."

"Perhaps she will," Isaac said. "The war should be over by then, but the navy is jealous of the attention the army has received. They want to demonstrate their worth before the election, and before the new government writes a defence budget."

"It always comes back to politics, doesn't it?" Ruth said, shifting in her seat. She gave up, stood, and walked over to the grilled window. Outside was a new-growth forest interspersed with ruins, but in the distance, she could make out smoke and the ice-flecked rectangles of a few cleared fields.

She sat down, opened her bag, and took out a paperback copy of *Great Expectations*. It was the newspaper's book-of-the-month. In addition to printing articles about Charles Dickens and his works, and filling more pages with discussions of everyday life in 1860s Britain, the newspaper was staging talks every Saturday afternoon, but those were all in Twynham. While the paper wasn't serialising the novel, in exchange for seven mastheads, postage, and a mysterious packing fee, they were giving away copies they had printed themselves. It was one of those editions she was reading, though her copy had arrived as a gift from the journalist Ollie Hunter. With the book had been a note asking for her thoughts on the themes of crime and justice described in the novel, presumably to run as another between-the-advertisements filler. She *had* made a few notes, but hadn't decided whether to post them to Hunter. The more she read of prison hulks, restricted opportunities, and judicial inequality, the less distant the setting felt.

It was two hundred, occasionally meandering, miles to Twynham, and it took them nearly five hours. The Kent wilderness, occasionally interrupted by fortified farms and walled hamlets, gave way to the farmed Sussex woodlands, then to the sheep-dotted, chalky downs. In Hampshire, they turned north to navigate around the urban mines that had once been Southampton's commuter sprawl. Beyond, fields gave way to factories, and the cloudy skies were lost beneath a growing haze of smoke as they approached the capital's bulging outskirts.

Since Ruth was last in Twynham, the central railway station hadn't changed. With the heavy snows, and their recent victory at the Second

Siege of Calais, the war had paused. Some of the passengers waiting on the platforms wore uniforms as well as their bandages. But no matter whether they wore green or not, the passengers were waiting for the same old smoke-belching trains. Ruth had seen three diesel locomotives in the yard on the outskirts, but with bio-diesel so scarce, and the refined kind dependent on supplies shipped in from America, those trains wouldn't run until after the war. No, Twynham hadn't changed. Not yet. But it soon would.

Their train pulled into a secluded platform usually reserved for military traffic. Before the last bump-and-shunt of the settling brakes, there was a rattle at their door as someone tried to open it from outside.

"Hang on," Ruth said. She had to stand on tiptoe to peer through the grilled window and down to the platform. A woman in a tartan sash was attempting to open the door. She wasn't so much thin as narrow, with elbows forming two points of a star as she braced her hands on her hips. Since Commissioner Weaver was standing behind the woman, Ruth unlocked the door.

The woman in tartan stormed aboard. "Is this them?" she asked. "Are they here?"

"Ma'am?" Ruth said, turning to Weaver as the commissioner stepped into the doorway.

"Are the paintings all here?" Weaver asked.

"Yes, ma'am," Ruth said. "All twelve paintings we found last night."

"No one's touched them?" the tartan-wearing woman asked. "Well? Did they?"

"This is the Right Honourable Erin Quinn, MP," Weaver said. "Her colleague outside is the Right Honourable Lilith McMoine, MP."

"No one touched them, ma'am," Ruth said. "After we found them, they were taken straight to the police station. We locked them in the cells last night, and we've kept this carriage sealed from the rest of the train."

"Then you may leave," Quinn said.

Ruth looked to Weaver. The commissioner raised an eyebrow. "Take the air, Constable. And take your *assistant* with you."

"I've been called worse," Isaac said. "A pleasure to see you again, Commissioner."

"I imagine it is," Weaver said.

Ruth grabbed her bag, and stepped down onto the sooty platform. "Home," she said, and coughed. "Yep. That's definitely the smell of home."

"Then let me be the first to welcome you back," a voice said.

"Mr Das!" Ruth said. "Hello."

She'd not noticed the bespectacled man, but he was an easy man to overlook except when he wore his ceremonial armour. Trading on his wife's tenuous link to royalty, after the Blackout she had become Queen Mary III and Sandeep Das had restyled himself King Alfred II. Together, they had laid claim, and protection, to the lands around Sherwood and Leicester, and renamed it Albion. They had kept thousands safe while hunger and bandits roamed the land. Ultimately, his people had been labelled separatists, and even bandits, until, last month, a treaty had been signed whereby Albion had re-entered the fold. The king had given up his claim to the throne, and been given five seats in parliament, one of which he had taken for himself.

Ruth had met Mr Das two weeks ago, during his tour of Dover, Calais, and the front. She'd met his son, Edward, months before, when the young man, then calling himself Ned Ludd, had been framed for murder.

"Constable," Das said. "Isaac."

"Your Majesty," Isaac said.

"Not anymore," Mr Das said. He gave Isaac a nod that bordered on curt, then turned back to Ruth. "Did you really find the paintings?"

"We really did," Ruth said. "Are you an art fan?"

"Is there anyone on this planet who isn't?" Das said. "The paintings are to be returned to Scotland, and I am here as a guarantor of sorts. Ms Quinn wanted to meet the paintings as they arrived, so as to make sure none went missing."

"She's worried they'll be stolen?" Ruth asked.

"I believe her concern is that they'll be deliberately misplaced in some government vault while awaiting appraisal or restoration," Das said.

"Ms Quinn is a member of the Party for a Northern Future," Isaac said. "Aren't they part of your power bloc?"

"I would advise you not to believe everything you read in the newspaper," Das said. "Ah, Mrs McMoine is summoning me, and as an *ex*-king, I must obey. Excuse me."

"What power bloc?" Ruth asked as Mr Das hurried onto the train.

"A coalition has been governing the country during this current crisis, yes?" Isaac said. "Now that peace is coming, so is an election. Anyone who wants change won't vote for Atherton, or for Woodley's official opposition. Old King Alf is gathering together an alternative."

"More politics?" Ruth said. "I can't escape it even for a minute."

"It's better than war," Isaac said. "Commissioner," he added, as Weaver approached them.

Weaver waved to a quartet of green-uniformed army corporals who had been slouching by a pair of metal carts. They meandered to attention, and began shoving the carts towards the train.

"How is Dover, Constable?" Weaver asked.

"Mostly peaceful," Ruth said. "Bar fights are increasingly common, but that's because we've got more soldiers in the city, and they don't like how the sailors have already claimed the best pubs. Are the paintings going to Scotland?"

"Almost immediately," Weaver said. "It is where they belong, and no politician wants to start a debate about rights and ownership in case it leads to a discussion about how the Gibraltar garrison are now working farms to the west of Algeciras. Scotland is where those paintings belong, and as war comes to an end, they will provide an excellent reason for tourists to travel north. Or so I have been told a dozen times this morning."

"You know what lies halfway between Twynham and Scotland?" Isaac said.

"Albion?" Ruth asked. "I thought it was more like a third of the way."

"Yes, but Albion will become quite the transit hub," Weaver said. "Isaac, why are you here and not on your boat?"

"I'm on my way to Scotland," Isaac said. "The boat will collect me, and our equipment, there."

"The ferry has been delayed," Weaver said.

"So I heard," Isaac said. "It's not expected for five days."

"And how did you hear that?" Weaver asked.

"Telegraph operators gossip when they're bored," Isaac said.

"Will it affect timing if the ferry doesn't arrive before you depart?"

"Not particularly," Isaac said. "There's enough diesel in store for our voyage."

"And the... the other fuel?" Weaver asked.

"Enough for the mission is now in place in Belgium," Isaac said. "There won't need to be a second mission. Everything will be in place and on time."

"Then I'll wish you good luck and best speed. Constable, I believe the next train to Dover leaves in an hour from platform 2."

"Oh. Right, of course," Ruth said. "Um… I was hoping to see Anna first. If that's okay."

"Did you clear it with Sergeant Kettering?" Weaver asked.

"She said she coped well enough before I arrived," Ruth said.

"She did indeed," Weaver said. "You've earned a day off. But you won't find Sergeant Riley at Police House. I'll give you the address."

Chapter 6 - One More Page Before Bed
The Bookshop, Twynham

"I thought you were going to Scotland," Ruth said as she and Isaac made their way on foot through the bustling city.

"I am," Isaac said. "But I wanted to see the city, and Anna, before I head to the land of lake monsters. I'll catch the sleeper tomorrow and still be there before my boat."

"What *is* going on, Isaac?" Ruth asked. "It must be something big, because Commissioner Weaver knows all about it."

"It's so big, it's better not to ask," Isaac said. "Ah, I think this must be it."

Above windows covered in newspaper was a newly painted sign proclaiming this mid-terrace shop to be *One More Page Before Bed*. Affixed to the door was another hand-painted sign: *opening as soon as we've glued in the pages*. Ruth tried the handle first, but the door was firmly locked. She tried the bell next. Inside, a jangling clang slowly faded and was replaced by limping footsteps, the click of a cane, and then by the clunk of a bolt being pulled back. The door swung inward.

"Yes?" the young woman asked. She was only a few years older than Ruth, but still younger than her grey overalls, which were stained brown with varnish and sprinkled with sawdust. Tall, willowy, and well muscled from having spent a decade mastering a longbow, her face lit in a smile of recognition. "Ruth! Come in."

"Boadicea? I didn't expect to see you here," Ruth said.

Private Boadicea Essex was an Albion archer, and a member of King Alfred's bodyguard, whom Ruth had met in Belgium, and who'd been shot during the chaotic fighting.

"Come on in and I'll explain," Essex said, stepping aside and motioning Ruth and Isaac inside before hurriedly closing the door. She leaned forward, looking up and down the street. "No, we're fine. I don't think anyone noticed your uniform," she added.

"Sorry, I should have thought," Ruth said. "But we did come camouflaged with lunch."

"Perfect timing," Essex said. "What are you doing up in the smoke?"

"I had to play security guard for some stolen paintings we found in Dover," Ruth said. "I'm off-duty so I came to see Anna. What about you? I thought you'd be in Albion, recovering."

"I've been posted to the Serious Crimes Unit while I heal," Essex said. "I couldn't tell you if it's a promotion or a punishment, but it's mostly in the warm. Sergeant Riley is in the back."

While the bookshop was completely devoid of books, it was full of shelves. Some had been installed, and others were still being cut from planks resting on a workbench.

"It looks like you're genuinely opening a bookshop," Ruth said.

"Whether it's a field, a house, or the world, always leave a place better than you found it," Essex said. "Queen Mary told me that herself, the one time I met her. I was very young, of course, but the words stuck."

The back room contained no books either, but here the walls were covered in maps, notes, hand-drawn sketches, and grainy photographs. In the centre of the room, making notes as she listened to a pair of battered headphones plugged into an ancient laptop, was Anna Riley. She was unchanged since Ruth had last seen her on a fleeting visit to testify in court three weeks ago, but her wheelchair had gained some new padding and a new pair of walking canes tucked into the back. She wasn't in uniform, but wore a long skirt and short jacket. Both were crimson and nearly a match, though absolutely not a match for the bobble-hat, fingerless gloves, and blanket-length scarf worn in defence against the unheated room's frigid chill.

"Knock-knock," Ruth said.

"Ruth!" Anna said, looking up from the laptop. "And Isaac. What are you doing here?"

"I've been demoted to delivery boy," Isaac said, holding up the lunch sack.

"He's here to cause trouble," Ruth said. "I'm here on leave. Yesterday morning, the new cinema reported half their seats had been stolen overnight."

"Inside job?" Anna asked, as she wheeled herself around to face them.

"Absolutely," Ruth said. "One of the employees had opened a bar at New Year's and was already broke."

"That doesn't sound like a big enough case to warrant a holiday," Anna said.

"The thief gave us a tip-off in exchange for a deal," Ruth said. "He owned a delivery cart, and had taken twelve crates up to the citadel. You know, the ruins up on the cliffs where they run that sort-of-legal boxing club?"

"Do you mean where Isaac went looking for the Holy Grail?" Anna asked.

"I wasn't looking for the Grail," Isaac said. "Just gold."

"The Grail's in Glastonbury," Essex said. "Everyone knows that. I'll get some plates."

"What was in the crates?" Anna asked.

"Paintings stolen from Edinburgh just after the Blackout," Ruth said. "When we wired that news to Weaver, she told us to bring them here, so I did, and now I've a few hours off. How about you?"

"I'm knee-deep in the Loyal Brigade case," Anna said. "For me, that means the investigation is lapping at my waist, too."

"Are these the suspects?" Isaac asked, walking over to a wall on which were pinned a mix of sketches and grainy photographs.

"That's them," Anna said. "We've got better images on the screen, but no way of printing them. Parliament approved the use of technology for all cases sent to Serious Crimes. We've got digital cameras, laptops, and a few listening devices. We *don't* have any printers, or any battery-powered cameras we could install in their pub. We're still lacking people, too. It's just me and Essex here, and Hamish MacKay up in Thurso."

Essex returned with the plates. "I'll take mine out front," she said. "The street-cleaner has been lingering outside the chemist opposite. I think it's because she fancies the pharmacist, but you can never be sure."

Ruth took out her lunch: shallow-fried chunks of parsnip coated in a sweet and sour sauce whose specific ingredients it was better not to know. Rationing had been extended after the first attack on Calais. With no spare military ships to act as escort, the southern fishing fleets had been kept in harbour. The winter grain reserve had been held back while the military stockpile had been built up. But now that the enemy advance had been shattered and the army held the coast from Belgium to Boulogne, conditions were easing. Choice was still limited by supply, and during the cold winter months, that was parsnip, swede, cabbage, artificial flavours from the Satz lab, and the inventive genius of the cooks.

"Does the Loyal Brigade still hang out in the pub?" Ruth asked.

"The Iron Kettle, yes," Anna said. "But they're calling it a church now, even if they do still order in beer by the keg. They don't sell it, of course. They give it away after their services, but only once the parishioners have made a donation."

"So they're running a tax scam?" Ruth asked.

"We won't know that until they file their returns," Anna said. "We want to pin something bigger on them, but I'd settle for tax fraud if it sees them behind bars. Behind this shop there's an alley. Go west and you'll come to a tall wall with barbed wire at the top. That's the back of the pub's yard. This shop was the nearest vacant premises, but there's a perch up on the rooftops with a good view of their yard and the upstairs meeting rooms. Boadicea had to climb up there to install the camera. First time I've been grateful for being in the chair," she added.

"And these are all members of the Loyal Brigade?" Isaac asked, still looking at the sketches and photographs.

"Yes, but it's not a complete membership," Anna said. She wheeled her chair over. "The Loyal Brigade was the name of a gang formed about fifteen years ago by Mark Stevens. Ten years ago, they put forward some candidates in the election. When it became clear they weren't going to win at the ballot, they started a fight during the election count. They were routed, and then outlawed. They fled to Sandringham, but were wiped out on the fringes of London by you, Isaac, a subject I'd like to come back to later."

"Nothing I can remember will help now," Isaac said. "Like you say, they were wiped out. It's the brother who runs the gang now, yes?"

"Yes, Mark's brother, Andrew Stevens," Anna said. "The two brothers also had a sister, Kirsty. She died during the Blackout, but left an eight-year-old daughter, Hailey. Andrew raised Hailey, and we think it was because the girl was at home that Andrew didn't join his brother's attack on the election count. Now, jump forward a bit. Three years ago, during a mining operation in Southampton, a tower block collapsed and buried Hailey's fiancé and twenty-nine others. One of the mining venture's backers was also a financier of Mark Stevens during his failed run for office all those years ago. Andrew Stevens, Hailey, and a couple of trusted confederates used the Loyal Brigade name as a disguise when they robbed that financier."

"Were charges pressed?" Ruth asked.

"No, and the financier doesn't want to now," Anna said. "He moved into farming and has a thousand acres of brassicas. He spoke to us last week, but made it clear he wants to stay well out of it. We've a gap in our timeline until the tank reclamation effort began. Andrew Stevens got a job there, and then got his niece employment there, too. Stevens used his dead brother's mythical reputation, and a mix of mystical and imperialist dogma sprinkled with a very loose interpretation of history, to build up a band of followers. Unlike his brother, he used belief rather than fear to gain loyalty, and that's where our difficulties building a case began. After his arrest last month, we also arrested twenty-seven others, but had to let sixteen go due to lack of evidence. Those are the photos with a red dot next to them. None of the others, whom we charged, are talking. They've got the blue dot next to the picture."

"Hailey Stevens has a red dot," Ruth said. "You had to let her go? But didn't you have a recording of her chatting with her uncle when they basically confessed?"

"The judge threw out the recording," Anna said.

"You mean he wouldn't hear it?" Isaac asked.

"Very funny, and the judge is a she," Anna said. "After Hamish MacKay was conscripted, sent to France, and ended up in Dad's little band of commandos, he told Dad about Stevens using the Loyal Brigade's name to get followers from among the people working in the tank reclamation yard. With the help of Colonel Sherwood, Private Essex, and a few other foresters, we launched a sting. Commissioner Weaver got permission to plant a bug inside the yard, but we recorded Hailey and her uncle's confession using a parabolic microphone. The judge said we didn't have approval to use that microphone, so we can't use the recording in court. In response, Serious Crimes got blanket approval to use any working tech we can find, but it's not retroactive."

"They were stealing guns from old war machines, weren't they?" Ruth asked.

"Heavy machine guns, yes," Anna said. "And stealing ammunition from the testing yard by altering the records. When ten rounds were fired, Stevens would add a zero, change it to one hundred and then keep the ninety stolen rounds. We got him for that, and for selling ammo to John Boyle from Albion, but Stevens claims his only other customers were hunters and farmers."

"And now the Loyal Brigade are committing arson?" Ruth asked.

"Not that we can prove," Anna said. "After his arrest, Stevens was sent to the prison hulk in Thurso where he's awaiting trial. That was on the 2nd January. Since then, there have been four arson attacks in Twynham. On each occasion, he'll give a warning to the guard doing the night-time cell-check. That's between seven and eight. The fires start between eight and nine, but his warning has to get from the guard to the governor to the telegraph office, and then it has to be relayed around the mountains and south. It takes a few hours, by which time the blaze has begun."

"That seems pretty cut and dried," Ruth said.

"It's not," Anna said. "Each night, since he was detained, his niece holds a prayer meeting for all members of the Loyal Brigade in their pub. It begins at six, and doesn't end until ten. After, they have a few pints, but leave by eleven, except for Hailey and her entourage who sleep in the pub. During the four hours of sermons and prayers, Hailey Stevens gives a message she says is direct from the Archangel Michael. The transcripts are in that file, or you can listen to the audio if you want because we've been recording what she says. It's all bilge, except on the nights of the fires. The gist, though, is that her family are prophets and seers, descended in unbroken line from the days of the Kingdom of Judea. The Archangel Michael has appeared to her uncle and given him a warning which he's passed on to the authorities. She, not being as adept and experienced as he, only has a vague and incomplete version of the same message. Us cops, being unbelievers, don't heed her uncle's warning, which is why the devil keeps burning down shops."

"That sounds like more proof, not less," Ruth said.

"Except, at the time of these attacks, every likely suspect is inside that pub or in prison," Anna said. "Yes, I know that means the fires are being started by someone we've not linked to the Loyal Brigade, but we don't even have a name."

"Are these the warnings?" Isaac asked, pointing to a set of handwritten cards pinned to the wall.

"On the left is what Hailey said, on the right is what her uncle said to the warder," Anna said.

"Let's see," Isaac said. "Ah, so this is from the most recent attack on the 20th. *No swallows will escape the flames when the demon strikes. Glass won't protect harvest when bakers burn blue.* It's like a crossword, isn't it?

And Mr Stevens said that the devil shall rise and claim his due on Winton Road. That is a little easier to understand."

"There isn't a Winton Road, but there *is* a Winton Way," Anna said. "It's behind the agricultural academy, and doesn't have much else there. Backing onto it is an old care home the academy uses as a factory and office units for their business courses. One is a legal firm run by an academic called Glass who does the contracts, taxes, and other bits of paperwork for the student-run businesses. Another is called the Swallow Farm Tailoring Company, and there's a Winton Blue Bakery. All three of those are named on the signage at the entrance to the road, but the actual target was a temporarily vacant old house."

"So Andrew Stevens knows what the targets are, and Hailey's being vague because she's not sure?" Ruth asked.

"I think it's the other way around," Anna said. "I think she knows *exactly* where the attacks will take place, but she suspects we're listening. We get an hour, sometimes a lot less, between her warning and the fires beginning, and I've not cracked the code in time yet."

"What's the motive?" Ruth asked. "Is it extortion or something?"

"Not that we've been able to prove," Anna said. "We think this is a contingency that Stevens put together months ago. He's an arms dealer. Any of his old customers must fear that he'll give up their names in exchange for a lighter sentence. They'll want him dead, and he knows it. So far, he's told us nothing, but he's still got a target on his back. This is his way out."

"By becoming a prophet," Isaac said. "It's quite clever, really."

"It gets worse," Anna said. "He offered us a deal. He'll serve three hundred and sixty-four days, or he wants a jury trial."

"One day less than a year?" Ruth asked. "Why?"

"If you're sentenced for a year or more, you can't stand for parliament," Anna said. "Our counter-offer is ten years and the names of his customers. So far, the only client we know of is Boyle, from Albion, whom we caught red-handed. Boyle is viewed as a traitor to Albion, and it is only a matter of time before other members of his old tribe end up in prison. He's co-operating for much the same reason that Stevens is putting on this act: for fear of being murdered in prison if he doesn't."

"Stevens wants a jury trial, then?" Isaac asked.

"And the publicity that goes with it," Anna said. "So far, we've kept his name out of the paper's coverage of the arson attacks. But his name will surely be revealed during the trial. He will claim, in court, that he is a prophet and that he tried to warn us about these attacks."

"No one will believe him, surely," Ruth said.

"Some will," Anna said. "Either on the jury, or among the public. The Loyal Brigade will gain new followers."

"They'll gain a legion if Stevens is found not guilty," Isaac said. "I assume the Brigade, or one of his other customers, will make an attempt on Boyle's life. Without him, the case is weakened."

"Not by much," Anna said. "I'm more worried the jury will be threatened, but there's not much we can do about that before they've been picked. Even if Stevens is found guilty, the reputation of the Loyal Brigade will have been amplified by the trial's coverage in the press. I believe his hope is that, with his new-found fame, his former clients will decide he's more useful alive. If the trial collapses, or he's found not guilty, it could get a lot worse."

"Because he's implied he wants to run for office?" Ruth asked.

"I don't think he would, or that he'd win, but he would be a constant thorn for decades to come," Anna said. "Meanwhile, his niece never leaves her pub, and is always surrounded by bodyguards. He petitioned for isolation, which we'd have given him anyway. While he didn't specifically ask to be sent to Thurso, with the reduction in staffing at most jails due to conscription, and with the influx of prisoners from Europe, it was fifty-fifty we'd send him there. Whether it was planned or not, he gives his warning to the jailors just before the attacks, but when it's too late for the message to reach us in time to act on it."

"But if this scheme was planned before the arrest, why didn't the attacks come all on the same night?" Ruth asked.

"I don't think they *were* picked beforehand," Anna said. "Each of the attacks has been on empty premises, and never one with apartments above. The attack on Winton Way targeted the Secret Sisters Repair Yard. They were students who, two years ago, opened a plough-and-cart repair shop in an old shipping container. Six months ago, they switched to making bicycle carts and took over a house on the corner with Beswick Avenue. Since they've graduated, and have moved completely away from farming, the academy said they had to find premises elsewhere. They moved out two days before the attack. It's similar with the other three victims. Two buildings had been sold, and one had been condemned, but only a few days before the attack. You know how it is around here, nowhere stays empty for long. Even the mice have a waiting list."

"Arson attacks on empty premises are intriguing," Isaac said. "If people started dying, fear really would set in, and that would work against Stevens's attempt to recruit more followers."

"They could have picked the streets and dates beforehand," Ruth said. "It's not like either of them mention which business will be attacked."

"Maybe," Anna said. "And I'm not ruling out that they *were* chosen in advance, but other than the academy, or its office units, there were no other possible targets on Winton Way. No, I think the arsonist picks the targets. The location is then communicated to Hailey, and is sent up to Stevens."

"How?" Ruth asked.

"Exactly," Anna said. "We've got cadets working through the known associates, hunting down old neighbours, family, and old co-workers so we can build up a web of contacts. So far, the best two leads we had were people who'd seemingly vanished but who turned out to be dodging conscription. Meanwhile, Stevens is on a prison hulk in the very north of Scotland. He gets no visitors, and is even representing himself. He gets no mail or telegrams, and his niece doesn't send any, either. Inspector Voss, the chief of police there, has interviewed all the warders, twice. He's confident none of them are involved."

"There must be an intermediary," Isaac said. "A stranger in Thurso shouldn't be hard to find."

"Maybe before the transatlantic ferry started docking there," Anna said. "Now there are six hundred passengers waiting to catch the ship, plus a few hundred new shore workers."

"Ah," Isaac said. "Radio, perhaps?"

"Perhaps, but Voss says no," Anna said.

"I'm going north tomorrow," Isaac said. "I can take a look, or a listen, if you like."

"That'd be helpful, thanks," Anna said. "Hamish MacKay is watching the prison ship. It's anchored opposite his nan's shipyard, but he hasn't seen anything unusual. Obviously we're missing something."

"And if you don't find the link, Stevens will walk?" Ruth asked.

Anna laughed. "Hardly. Some of their followers are believers, or they'd *like* to believe, but most were cutpurses and leg-breakers a few weeks ago. I can't see them maintaining four hours of prayers every evening all the way until the trial. Someone will talk. But the longer this goes on, the greater the risk someone will get hurt. Why are you going north, Isaac?"

"That is something I wanted to talk with you about," Isaac said. "It's personal."

"We can talk in the kitchen while I make some tea," Anna said.

Ruth walked over to the crime board, picking out a detail here, and a suspect there, adding to her understanding of a case informed by Anna's sparse letters and the vacuously sensational reports in the paper. There was an arsonist in Twynham, an agent passing messages back and forth to Hailey Stevens, and an agent in Thurso, too. That amounted to at least three genuinely loyal followers, but if this contingency was planned months ago, these agents would have been selected because their link to uncle and niece wasn't obvious.

She picked up the report from the fire investigator. Like a lot of part-time specialists, the man was a professor up at the university, and had submitted an essay rather than a summary. Slowly, she began to wade her way through. The fires were begun indoors, downstairs, and away from windows. Interior doors were wedged open, always with something metallic found inside the premises. Accelerant was poured over flammable objects. Four bottles, made of glass, were found near where the fire began. Because the shops were shut for the day, and no one lived upstairs, by the time the alarm was raised, the fire was too fierce to easily extinguish, leaving the buildings as charred husks.

She flipped ahead until she found the report from the university lab. The accelerant was ethanol. The glass matched the standard pint bottles used for everything from milk to beer.

She began to understand why Anna thought the targets hadn't been picked in advance. The fire itself was simple, picking the targets would take at least one night of research, but there was nothing used in the fire that would link back to the Loyal Brigade.

Ruth picked up a transcript of Hailey Stevens's prayer session, and found five pages of pseudo-Celtic-Christian nonsense. Near the end, one line stuck out. She turned to the map of the city stuck to the wall, on which the locations of the attacks were marked with four red pins.

"No," she whispered. She looked at the transcript. "Yes," she said. "Anna!" she called, and made her way to the kitchen, meeting the sergeant wheeling herself out. "I think I've got it," Ruth said.

"Got what?" Anna asked.

"At the end of her bogus prayer session, Hailey Stevens said that the devil will rise and reclaim his own, but that the white dragon will save us when he returns. I assume the white dragon is the uncle?"

"It could be," Anna said. "According to Private Essex, the red dragon is associated with King Arthur and Wales, the white dragon is the invading Saxons, and it's part of Merlin's prophecy foretelling how Arthur will throw back the invaders. But since Stevens is making things up on the hoof, we don't need to dig too deep into the symbolism."

"Yes, but his goal is to come across as a prophet in open court?" Ruth said. She turned to the map. "Four attacks. Why *only* four?"

"I assume there'll be more," Anna said.

"Yes," Ruth said. "One more. And it's a target they *definitely* picked in advance. I need another pin, and some string. Thanks. Hang on." She placed the pin, then looped the string from one pin to the other. "Five pins. Five attacks. The five points of a pentagram. Stevens is talking about dragons, devils, wizards, and evildoers being smitten, yes?"

"I think the word is smote," Anna said. "It's similar, but there's more lightning, less mooning. A pentagram fits. But there are plenty of other possible shapes you could make."

"But do you see where this fifth pin is?" Ruth said.

Anna wheeled her chair over. "Religion Row! It's perfect. It's obvious. And it must be the last attack, too."

"Why do you say it's the last?" Isaac asked, coming out of the kitchen with a tray of mugs.

"Because Stevens is pitching himself as battling the forces of darkness," Anna said. "He wants to claim these warnings were visions from on high, and the attacks were caused by the devil. Once the pentagram is complete, and the fires cease, he can say the devil was stopped thanks to his prayers."

"I wonder how many witch finders uttered those very same words," Isaac said. "But yes, there will certainly be people who'll want to believe him."

"Then we have to stop him," Ruth said. "I suppose that would be easier if we knew when the attack would come."

"Tonight," Anna said. "There's a pilgrimage for peace beginning at the docks at six p.m. It will end at the Convent of St Joan at nine. The bulletin in the paper noted that the last call to prayer at the Al-Salam Mosque is also at nine, and at nine-thirty, the congregations will combine for prayer and then for refreshments. Tell me that isn't just the perfect target for such a vile group."

Chapter 7 - The Point of a Pentagram
Religion Row, Twynham

"While I prefer a homburg, but would settle for a Stetson, there is something truly British about a bowler hat," Isaac said.

"Damp, you mean," Ruth said, tipping the bowler forward. "No matter how I wear it, rain drips down the back of my neck. This is the most pointless hat in the world."

But the bowler hat and high-collared knee-length coat were the uniform of the Religion Row Wardens, and tonight, that was whom Isaac and Ruth were impersonating. They didn't know which building the arsonist might attack, but Hailey Stevens had called her people in for a prayer session, so it *would* take place tonight. Across the city, patrols had been doubled, but not in Religion Row.

After the Blackout, as refugees flooded to the south coast, churches, temples, synagogues, and mosques were requisitioned for dormitories. Some of the faithful, and their preachers, asked that their place of worship be exempt from conversion to housing, but were instead given a concession in the form of one of the small detached houses on Linwood Road. Opposite the houses was the old Winton Park, which had been renamed Hope Field. In the early days, open-air services had been held in the park until the ground was cleared for planting. Afterward, services were held in the street, with each congregation taking a turn. Over the years, more religions had arrived and some parishes had expanded. A few had even torn down the old houses and built new temples. When taxes returned, an exemption was granted for religious establishments, but only if they were based on Religion Row. Now, that zone spread over two roads. Hope Field had been returned to lawn, grazed by a communal herd of dairy cows, but used for open-air events during the better months.

The tax collectors had put up the fence, so as to better identify who had to pay and who, regretfully, did not. Thus, Religion Row became a haven of tranquillity in their ever-growing city. Meanwhile, the streets ringing the sanctuary became a hive of pubs and cafes where the sanctified could bask in the warmth of a post-prayer prandial. Tonight, on Commissioner Weaver's suggestion, most pubs were offering a forty-percent discount for anyone in uniform, and as a result, were heaving. Most, but not all.

The Watcher at the Gates, a restaurant-bar immediately outside the ever-open gates to Religion Row, wasn't offering a discount, but a poetry reading. When Ruth had walked past, there had been a few customers inside, but there'd been one customer outside, too: a woman in a wheelchair, bundled in a heavy blanket which concealed the phone in her hands.

With half-drunk sailors filling the nearby streets, if the arsonist attacked tonight and wanted an unoccupied target, it would have to be *inside* Religion Row. Most of the preachers, and wardens, were attending the pilgrimage from the docks. *Most* of the wardens, but not the two in the ill-fitting bowler hats.

"How does the phone work?" Ruth asked.

"It's called a mesh-net," Isaac said. "There's no central server on which to download, or from which to upload. Messages are essentially sent from one device to another. That creates a limitation as to the volume of traffic, but I view it as the scaffolding for a greater future network."

"But *how* does it work?" she asked, none the wiser.

"The installation of a telegraph system gave me an opportunity to string my own wires without anyone noticing. The government sends telegrams, while I send letters, and send them faster, and with better encryption."

"Back in America before the Blackout, you worked for Mum when she was a professor, yes?" Ruth asked. "You were some kind of assistant, but you never taught, did you?"

"I ran a few seminars," Isaac said. "But ours was a research project, operating out of the university because they didn't ask annoying questions like how we'd pay the rent, and what, exactly, we were doing."

"If you *had* ever been a teacher, you'd be better at explaining things," Ruth said. "If Anna, back at that pub, sends a message, how long will it take to arrive on your phone?"

"A second," Isaac said. "Technically, it's a fraction of a second, but only in areas with coverage, which doesn't include that field where they hold the summer fete."

"And why didn't you give this network to the government?" she asked.

"Other than the obvious reason that I've met the politicians? The system can only support a few users before it would become clogged. To scale it up would require hardware we just can't make anymore. Enough old technology could be salvaged to create a government network, but only *for* the government. That would turn this into a police state, and that is what I have been working against."

"Yep, you really aren't a teacher," Ruth said. "There are weird shadows by the corner of the synagogue. Do you see them? Oh. It's a cat. So when *will* everyone get phones?" she asked as they continued their slow patrol.

"Not in your lifetime," Isaac said. "Other than my stash, and a few others like it, the handsets have been gathering damp for the past two decades. We don't have the technology to make the glass screens. As for the batteries? Ask me again when we've opened a lithium mine. But it's not all doom and gloom. I think we can bring back pagers and text-only messages, powered by alkaline batteries, and within two decades."

"Twenty years just for a quicker form of telegram?" Ruth made a mental note to stockpile and store a few phones of her own. She'd only had a phone for a few months, and was utterly hooked. Photographing crime scenes was so much easier than relying on sketches.

She tilted the bowler hat back, so she could see the minaret atop the Al-Salam Mosque. She couldn't see Private Essex, but the archer was up there, though without her bow, watching the alleys while waiting on the text message from Riley.

Compared to the rest of the city, Religion Row was under-populated, but it wasn't a ghost town. While the prelates, priests, preachers, and the otherwise-homeless who'd not found a bed in the army's newly expanded ranks, participated in the pilgrimage from the docks, plenty of supplicants still visited the shrines and temples. Despite the cold, many parents, wives, or husbands had come to plead for the safety of loved ones at sea or on the front line. To Ruth's eyes, a worried citizen, wrapped up against the cold, looked very much like an arsonist about to strike. Frustratingly, there were just too many potential suspects, but the presence of the prayerful reduced the number of potential targets to three.

The Book of Wisdom Synagogue was currently closed so the roof could be repaired. Until it was, the congregation were using the community hall by the open-air field. St Michael's, another former

Victorian house, had been scheduled for demolition after a poorly surveyed basement extension had left the foundations unable to support the building above. Third was the Votive Shrine, inside an old garage next to the Quaker Meeting House. No one quite knew how the shrine had begun, but it had become a place to leave paper offerings. Increasingly, and especially since the newspaper had run a month-long feature on origami, the paper was shaped into a totemic representation of the absent loved one.

"It has to be the shrine," Ruth said as they neared. "Think of all that paper, just waiting to burn. Plus, there's no priest, or even an attendant."

"But plenty of visitors," Isaac said as, ahead, a woman ducked into the always-open doors. "The arsonist needs ten minutes of peace and quiet. I'd bet on St Michael's. Aren't they claiming the message came from the Archangel Michael? The paper said they want to build a cathedral on the site."

"Do they? I stopped following big-city news when I moved to Dover," Ruth said.

Isaac laughed. "You think this is a big city? You should have seen Chicago, but be thankful you never saw L.A. Ah, hang on." He ducked into the shadows beside the shrine as he took out his phone. "Message from Anna. We've got a potential suspect leaving the bar. Male. IC5. About thirty. Five-foot-five. Black wool hat, and matching scarf. Black coat. Heavy leather bag. He's got a limp."

The screen flashed bright as Essex reported having received the message. A second flash announced the suspect had walked past St Michael's. A third alerted them he was beyond the synagogue and picking up his pace.

With a rueful I-knew-it shake of her head, Ruth slipped a hand into the coat's broad pocket and gripped her truncheon. Isaac put the phone away.

Ruth could now hear the suspect's footsteps. The man was hurrying, and hurried right past and on to the convent where he rang the bell.

"Father Luke!" the nun announced as she opened the door. "Have you been drinking *again*?"

Before the man could sin further with a lie, the nun dragged the wayward priest inside.

"Not him," Ruth said.

"No, and I wouldn't want to *be* him, either," Isaac said. The phone vibrated. "It's Essex. She says: *Dog walling woman. St Michael's. Rear door.*"

"Dog walling? What does that mean?" Ruth asked.

"It means I forgot to turn off the predictive text," Isaac said. "I think Essex was trying to write *dog walking*."

"The church backs onto Hope Field, doesn't it?" Ruth said. "A dog is a good excuse to be out and about."

Another ping announced another message from Essex. "She says: *Target gone inside. Dog outside*," Isaac said.

"That's our suspect," Ruth said, and began running.

A three-metre-high sheet-metal fence of salvaged steel ran around the condemned church, there to restrain any sudden collapse. In keeping with the season just ended, a nativity scene had been painted onto the metal panels. The festive fresco continued along the hoarding at the side of the old church, and even at the rear where a forlorn spaniel hunched on the frozen ground. The dog's lead was tied to the post supporting the door. As Ruth approached, the spaniel whimpered. Ruth smiled. For now, it was all she could do.

As Isaac caught up, Ruth drew her truncheon. A flash of light burst through the basement's grime-smeared light bricks. Isaac pushed past her, running along the path, and skidded down the plank ramp leading into the basement work-site.

Ruth dragged out her flashlight as she followed, and got downstairs in time to see Isaac smothering a fire with his coat. Ruth swung the torch left and right, across the metal columns currently supporting the house, and over piles of bricks, dust, mud, and debris, and then onto wooden steps which must lead up into the house. She saw no one, but plenty of hiding places, so she turned off the torch. With the fire and flashlight both extinguished, the cellar became dim, illuminated only by a slim sliver of moon and stars creeping in through the excavation hole.

Ruth held her breath, listening, discounting the straining metal supports, creaking timbers, and settling dust, narrowing in on the rustle of cloth. She turned the light on, and saw the suspect by the large dirt pile near the stairs, holding a bottle under one arm and a book of matches in the other hand. As Ruth ran, the bottle fell, and the woman reached into her bag, drawing a knife. Ruth staggered to a halt, truncheon raised.

"Don't! He'll shoot you," Ruth said, hoping Isaac had drawn his gun.

But the woman didn't lunge. Instead, her left arm shot out, and she turned the blade towards her own wrist.

"No you *don't!*" Ruth said, swinging the truncheon forward and down, cracking the woman's wrist before the blade could bite into an artery. The bone snapped. The woman yelled in frustrated anguish.

"Why?" she asked. "Why did you do that?"

It was a question so baffling, Ruth couldn't think of an immediate answer.

Chapter 8 - Baffling Belief
Religion Row, Twynham

Ten minutes later, the medics were on the scene with their horse-drawn ambulance driven by Commissioner Weaver. With Private Essex and five fleeter-of-foot constables on crowd control, Ruth rescued the spaniel.

Cuddling the ice-brick dog, she walked back to the front of St Michael's. The first of the pilgrims had arrived from the docks, while supplicants had emerged from each of the temples, as had their religious leaders, the more forthright of whom were approaching.

"Police," Ruth said, pulling out her badge. "Stay back, please."

"Police, make way," echoed Anna Riley, wheeling herself along the icy path. "Is that our star witness?" she asked, pointing at the dog. "I always fancied a lap dog. Pass her down. Her or him? Her. C'mon, girl." She wrapped the dog in her under-cover blanket. "Where is the suspect?"

"Weaver's talking with her," Ruth said. "Oh, it looks like they're finished."

The two medics carried a stretcher around from the side of the church, and to the ambulance. Weaver followed. Ruth looked for Isaac, but as was often the case when paperwork beckoned, he was nowhere in sight.

"The white dragon will rise again!" the suspect yelled as she was carried to the back of the ambulance.

"Take her to the hospital," Weaver said. "You two constables, go with her. I shall be along shortly." She waved over two of the officers currently holding back the growing crowd of pilgrims.

"Hold on!" Anna said, wheeling her chair over until she was close enough to see the suspect. "That's fine. Thanks. Take her away."

"Can you identify her?" Weaver asked as the patient was loaded onto the ambulance.

"She's Jemima Houghton," Anna said. "She's the sister of Clark Houghton, and he's one of Hailey Stevens's acolytes. He's a bodyguard and bag carrier, and an occasional shopper. He picks up groceries for Hailey, and that must be when he passed messages to and from his sister. Since they're supposed to be estranged, they must be using a dead-drop."

"She tried to kill herself rather than be captured," Ruth said. "She seems like a genuine believer."

"She's never attended a meeting," Anna said. "After we identified her brother as being a bodyguard, and then learned that he had a sister, we got a warrant to look in her apartment when she wasn't there. That was on the fourth of January. She still had her Christmas cards on the windowsill, and there wasn't one from him. No signs of her rooming with a dog, either." She checked the dog's collar. "No tag, no name. Well, finding your home is certainly another lead."

"They planned this quite thoroughly," Weaver said. "I take it we don't have anything to tie her to Stevens or the Loyal Brigade?"

"Only her presence here tonight," Anna said.

"Don't forget the slogan she yelled," Ruth added.

"Yes, it is a curious expression," Weaver said. "I always understood the white dragon to be the villain in that myth. While the suspect is, technically, talking, she has yet to say anything useful, including her name. She didn't ask for a lawyer, or a priest. Constable, you said you searched her before I arrived."

"Yes, ma'am," Ruth said. "I found two more glass bottles of ethanol, and two spare books of matches. Other than the knife, and some loose change, she didn't have anything else on her. No ration book. No door keys. None of the usual clutter every pocket collects."

"Then she emptied them before coming out here," Weaver said. "In addition to her broken wrist, she has a few new burns from this evening, and the scars from many older fires. Hopefully a doctor can date them based on how well they've healed, but that won't prove she is responsible for the other four attacks."

"But we'll get a warrant to search her home," Ruth said.

"A *second* warrant," Anna said. "We didn't find anything the first time, and it's a small flat. Her living room is really a hallway linking the front door to the bedroom and the small kitchenette. She shares a bathroom with two other flats. She works as a cleaner at the university, and it might be that's where she got the ethanol, but that place is a warren. A hiding place there could remain concealed for a century."

"Not if I can help it," Weaver said. "I won't wait for a judge. I'll wake the chancellor and send the cadets in before the students arrive. We'll hunt for the dead drop she and her brother were using, and we'll canvass the telegraph offices between her flat, the university, and the pub. Speaking of which, we received a message from Thurso about twenty minutes ago. Stevens gave a warning and gave it early. Because we were expecting the message, we managed to relay it here almost before the attack."

"What did he say?" Ruth asked.

Weaver took out the slip. "*The devil is aware you've been warned, and so tonight will strike at the archangel himself. God's work must be done. His word must be heeded. An even greater danger is slouching towards us.*"

"How long has that church lain empty?" Ruth asked.

"Two months," Anna said. "There was some opposition to the plans for the new cathedral."

"Opposition from whom?" Weaver asked. "That is another thread for us to pull."

"Hang on, though," Ruth said. "The slouching bit, that's from the poem, isn't it?"

"From Yeats's poem, *The Second Coming*," Weaver said. "It was written in 1919, and while the poem has some wonderfully apocalyptic imagery, the first verse firmly sets the context as the anarchic change experienced amid a global pandemic as old empires collapsed in the aftermath of the First World War. Stevens was referencing the final two lines which, I believe, are: *And what rough beast, its hour come round at last; Slouches towards Bethlehem to be born?*"

"I didn't know you liked poetry," Anna said.

"A garden needs little stewardship in winter," Weaver said. "I've always viewed our work since the Blackout as a struggle to bring back free time. Each spare minute is a minor victory which must not be squandered."

"There's a nativity scene painted on the hoardings covering the church," Ruth said. "They *definitely* picked this location in advance. But even I know saints and archangels are completely different."

"Stevens believes in nothing but himself," Weaver said. "In his arrogance, he sees no need of deepening his shallow knowledge. But will a foiled attack satisfy him? Will there be another?"

"There can't be," Ruth said. "Stevens was warning the police. The police heeded his warnings, and the arsonist was stopped. He's won, sort of."

"Not really," Weaver said. "Houghton believes, or claims, she is an agent of God, but Stevens claims the fires were started by demonic forces. Whatever she says will undermine his creed. That must be why she was supposed to kill herself rather than be caught. Stevens might send an assassin to end her, but must be aware of how unlikely that is to succeed. No, it is more likely she will be disavowed, and another attack will be engineered. Constable Deering, how are you enjoying your day off?"

"It beats a day at work, ma'am," Ruth said.

"How would you like to extend your leave?" Weaver asked.

"To help Anna? Absolutely," Ruth said.

"Yes, but no," Weaver said. "I'd like you to go to Thurso and interview Stevens. Our agent there, Mr MacKay, is a mechanic drafted as a soldier, but I believe you know him?"

"I was with him at the front when his toes were shot off," Ruth said.

"Ostensibly, we'll say you are the official escort for those paintings," Weaver said. "The politician, Ms Quinn, is pushing for their immediate transfer to Scotland. Take your knowledge of this attack with you to Thurso and see if it shines a light on how Stevens was getting his messages from the south. As Isaac was going to Scotland anyway, he can confirm no form of technology is being used to communicate with Stevens. Where is Isaac?" she added, looking around.

"Having a drink on that bench," Anna said, pointing to where Isaac was sharing a flask with two community leaders.

"A priest, a rabbi, and a scoundrel walk into a bar," Weaver said. "That's a joke that never ends well. Constable, your primary reason for going to Scotland is to spring a trap. Tell Stevens he has twenty-four hours to co-operate, or we will move him to a new prison, and so disrupt any communication web he has established in the north. I'm certain he won't co-operate, and I will then telegraph you with a moving date. I will provide Hailey Stevens with a different date, and see if we can force their hand. But I want some time to question the suspect, and see if there is any useful evidence to be gathered here. Sergeant, get some rest. I'll command the operation until dawn, when you can take over. Constable, orders will be waiting for you at the train station tomorrow morning. Now, if you'll excuse me, I should speak with our religious leaders before Isaac gets them so drunk they convert."

Outside of Religion Row, Ruth and Anna, and the spaniel, caught one of the cabs waiting to take advantage of the weary pilgrims seeking a shortcut home. Due to the inquisitive questioning by the cabby, theirs was a monosyllabic journey interspersed with an occasional yip from the now-defrosted dog. The moment Anna opened the front door to her cottage, the dog jumped from her lap and ran inside.

"I'll turn on the heater," Anna said. "There's some tinned meat in the cupboard next to the sink. Unless you fancy some of that yourself, there's bread and cheese in the fridge, but they might need a shave. I hoped we could go for a meal and a chat, but it's getting late, and we've both got to be up early."

"Bread and cheese is great," Ruth said. "We can go for a big meal when this case is over."

"When this one is over, another will begin," Anna said. "Speaking of cases, there are some suitcases upstairs for you. They're full of dresses mostly. And some shoes."

"Are you sure you can spare them?" Ruth asked, bringing in the canned meat which she'd emptied into a bowl. She placed it next to the dog, who had claimed the rug immediately in front of the electric heater.

Anna tapped her fur-lined flat-soled boots. "My days of wearing high heels are over." She smiled. "Here we are, living after the apocalypse, and there's still a market for heels and make-up."

Ruth returned to the kitchen and filled a tray with bread, cheese, and a teapot. When she returned to the living room, she placed the tray atop a side-table covered in maps. "You *are* getting better, though," Ruth said. "You're using crutches now, so you *will* walk again."

"Standing is hard enough," Anna said. "I might walk, but I'll never run, and I won't dance. And that's okay, Ruth. I won't say it doesn't frustrate me, but it doesn't get me down. Not anymore."

"Something happened," Ruth said. "What was it?"

"You're turning into quite the detective," Anna said. "I had a letter, a few weeks back, from the American ambassador. Do you remember him?"

"Perez, sure. He's a real politician," Ruth said. "I liked him but I still can't decide whether to trust him."

"He offered me a job," Anna said.

"In America? And you're giving away your clothes because you're going to take it?"

"I'm giving *you* the clothes because you *should* use them," she said. "Don't take this the wrong way, but you needed a new wardrobe a month ago. As the war ends, and restrictions ease, there'll be galas and balls, and if you don't get invited, you should use your badge to get in. Why not? I did. I have some happy memories, and some terrible stories. You should get some for yourself, too."

"Let's go back to this job offer," Ruth said. She poured two cups, and took hers to a chair next to the heater. As she neared, the spaniel began bolting its meat. "You're actually taking a job in America?"

"Not exactly," Anna said. "But maybe. The offer is for a job *after* he's won the election. That's in November, but he won't take office until January, and that's only if he wins. I don't know what the job would entail, except it surely must be investigatory, and so not much different from the work I do for Weaver."

"So why go?" Ruth asked.

"Because it would be somewhere different," Anna said. "I'm never going to dance again, and there's so much more I'll never do, but that doesn't mean my life is over. Here's an opportunity for some new experiences, or at least some new scenery."

"I thought you liked it here," Ruth said.

"I do," Anna said. "And I could stay in Twynham for the rest of my life and be happy enough. But if I go, I can return with some new memories that might overshadow a few of my new regrets. It's an opportunity that won't come again, so I can't really pass it up."

"But you don't know what the job is?" Ruth asked.

"No. I don't know where it is, or what I'll be doing, or for whom, but none of that bothers me."

"You're really going, then?"

"I'm really going to take up the offer of a return ticket to America later this year," Anna said. "I want to travel *before* the election in case Perez loses, but I don't want to sail anywhere in this weather. I'm thinking September, when it's not baking or freezing."

"Oh. Okay. That's not so soon," Ruth said. "Have you told Mister Mitchell?"

"A few days ago," Anna said. "I met him up at Highcliffe after he spoke to the prime minister. I think they're planning a big offensive that'll end the war once and for all. He wouldn't give any of the details, but I know we ordered a load of fuel from America, and I'm sure it's for the tanks they've been fixing. We didn't have long to talk because

Dad had to return to the front, but he encouraged me to take the trip, and get the details, and then make a decision on taking the job, and to do it in that order. Dad's always been restless. Before he found me, he travelled a lot. Afterwards, he still travelled, though not as much as he'd have liked. He's always been looking for some kind of inner peace, and he knows he won't ever find it, but he can't stop looking. He understands that I've got to look for it, too. I got the tickets this morning."

"You did?"

"Technically, it's a letter from the ambassador to be given to the ship's captain," Anna said. "It's on the table. Take a look."

Ruth picked it up. "It says two tickets. Is Mister Mitchell going with you?"

"The second ticket is for you," Anna said.

"Me?"

"Come see America," Anna said. "You've earned a few months leave, and might never get a chance like this again. Didn't you say you joined the police to see the world?"

"Yes, but I didn't mean like this," Ruth said.

"You mean all expenses paid, and travelling in luxury?" Anna asked.

"It's... I... I don't know what to say."

"There's plenty of time to think about it," Anna said. "But even if you had until the end of time, I bet you can't think of a reason to say no."

27th January

Chapter 9 - An Unwilling Star
The Railway Station, Twynham

Since Anna had swapped heels for wheels, the cottage's upstairs bedroom had become a storage room for all the clutter there was no room, or need, for downstairs. It took Ruth half an hour of mining through cases and boxes before she found the bed. Concerned she'd be buried in an avalanche of clothes, and with a rising gale driving rain into the ancient glass window, sleep was elusive. She lay in the dark, thinking about how quickly things changed, and wishing they wouldn't.

The cottage was old, even by pre-Blackout standards, but Henry Mitchell had claimed it for the ease with which electricity could be stolen from the post-Blackout grid. Isaac had wired the house for him, but Anna had planted the roses. When Anna had joined the police, Mitchell had taken a small room in town. He'd moved out to give his daughter the space and freedom to grow and live. Now that she knew them both better, Ruth wondered how much of the move was so that Mitchell would have his own space, too.

Despite the recent modifications downstairs by Isaac and Mister Mitchell, this quaint old cottage was not built for someone in a wheelchair. Each night she returned home, Anna only had to look at the stairs to be reminded of the life she'd had, and the opportunities now lost. Yes, Ruth understood why Anna would want to move out of here, but all the way to *America*?

Ruth had barely learned which were the high crime districts of Twynham before she'd been sent to Dover. Yes, that *had* been an early promotion from cadet to constable. And since arriving in Dover, her job *had* improved, but mostly because of the war. The military police did most of the patrol work, and so the police station was gloriously quiet at night. Thus she and Eloise could hang out in the upstairs flat in an echo of some of the gigglier movies Isaac had given them. But the war was coming to an end, the military police would be demobbed or deployed to France, the nights would get busier, and Eloise was trying to get posted to an expedition overseas. More police would be stationed in Dover. Whether they were cadets or ex-conscripts, they would need somewhere to sleep. The flat would fill up, so maybe she'd move out, but since in Dover and Twynham she'd lived rent-free, *where to* was a bigger question than her brain had space for.

Her mum was currently working as a surgeon in the field hospital at Dover Castle, but when the war ended, so would that job. What then for her? Ruth had asked, but Maggie didn't, and couldn't, know until the field hospital was shut down. Yet change *was* inevitable. It had become an unstoppable wave, endless and unrelenting. But perhaps it was always thus, and Ruth was only now realising it.

After that gloomy thought, sleep became truly impossible. When she smelled toast, and after she'd dug a tunnel to the door, she made her way downstairs.

"Sleep well?" Anna asked, already dressed, while the rescued spaniel was already eating.

"It makes a change not sleeping in a police station," Ruth replied diplomatically. "But I was thinking too hard about America."

"The trip isn't until the autumn, or *fall*, so we've plenty of time to discuss it when you come back from Scotland. You've got half an hour before the cab is due. There's plenty of hot water, and plenty of warm clothes in the blue suitcase. You should take them all. You'll need them."

Ruth had washed, dressed, and had just begun sorting through the contents of the blue suitcase when the doorbell rang. It was a cab, but it was also Commissioner Weaver.

"Deering? Good. I have your briefing notes for Thurso," Weaver said.

"Can I get you some tea, ma'am?" Anna asked.

"Thank you, no. I'm already swimming in coffee."

"Did you find anything at the university?" Ruth asked.

"Not yet," Weaver said. "The search has barely begun. The chancellor is over-co-operating. He fancies himself as a sleuth, and thinks he can find the suspect's dead-drop through the application of pure logic, so has spent most of the night offering suggestions. With dawn, and classes, approaching, I've replaced the search teams with eight undercover officers, all disguised as custodians who are pretending to clean or repair as they watch for the arsonist's brother. I assume, by now, Hailey Stevens is aware we have the arsonist in custody, but I want her to think she still has the upper hand."

"Do you mean you found something?" Ruth asked.

"I have a theory," Weaver said. "While the cleaning staff don't have access to the mail room, they do clean the academics' lounge. In the corner of that lounge are two post boxes, one for outgoing mail, and one for outgoing telegrams. There are two collections a day, at half nine and half six. Anything larger than a letter, or any bulk mailing, goes to the mailroom where a record is kept, but there is no record of what goes out in the lounge mailboxes. It is considered a perk for the cleaning staff to avail themselves of the free postage."

"And you think that's how the arsonist is communicating with Stevens?" Ruth asked.

"No, but it is potentially how she was sending messages to Scotland," Weaver said. "It could also be how she was sending messages to her brother and so to Hailey Stevens. Sergeant, I'd like you to retrace the brother's steps when he was sent out for groceries and see if he had an opportunity to collect a message, telegram, or letter at the same time. The question we must then answer is whether he, and so Hailey Stevens, ever sent a message *to* the arsonist. Or is the arsonist's communication only one-way? In which case, she certainly isn't merely a follower."

"Has the suspect said anything?" Ruth asked.

"Yes, but it is all pseudo-religious babble," Weaver said. "Either she is a true believer, or it's an act. In either case, since she is talking, she will certainly reveal something. I've notes for you on the prison hulk," she added, handing Ruth a slim envelope. "The prison is a terrible place, and so it's a match for its occupants. I vetted the staff myself. No one is incorruptible, but they wouldn't hold their current position if any suspicion fell on them. See if you, or Inspector Voss, can identify whether the messages are coming by telegram or post, and how they are getting to Stevens."

"Am I still to tell Stevens that he's being transferred?" Ruth asked.

"Yes. If you catch this morning's train, you'll arrive in Scotland in the early hours of tomorrow. I will send a telegram the day after, either with the date we're moving him, or, if things develop here, with further instructions. You can take my cab. You don't want to miss the train."

Despite the early hour, the train station bustled with conscript commuters heading to the outlying war-production factories, but also with a few intercity travellers heading north. A few of those less concerned about the clock, or about arriving at work late, slowed near the waiting room guarded by two Albion Foresters wearing full plate armour. Trying to peer around them, notebook in hand, was the young Canadian-born journalist, Ollie Hunter.

As Ruth approached, the soldiers snapped to attention. In turn, that made the journalist spin around.

"Constable Deering! You're a long way from home," Hunter said.

"I could say the same for you," Ruth said.

"Are you the official escort for the paintings?" he asked.

"I'm going to Thurso, yes," she said. "Are you?"

"Sadly, not for a few days," he said while he wrote. "We've got to get the big edition finished by midnight. Speaking of which, don't you think it's a waste of police resources to provide an escort to some pictures when there's an arsonist on the loose?"

"We caught the arsonist last night," Ruth said. She pointed at a newsstand at the corner of the platform. "Your paper said as much."

"That was this morning's edition," he said. "This afternoon's will ask whether the suspect you arrested was the *only* arsonist. What's your opinion? Don't you think people have a right to know what's going on?"

"If it's a right, you should give your papers away for free," Ruth said. "You can quote me on that. But I'm just a constable on leave from Dover. Because I'm on leave, I got drafted for picture-escort duty. And if you don't put your pen away, I won't say another word."

"Fair enough," he said, and capped his pen. "You know they won't let us even see the paintings."

"These guys?" she asked, gesturing at the armoured foresters.

"No, Ms Quinn," Hunter said. "The paper asked if we could photograph the paintings. We wanted to give each work of art a full-page spread with the history, the influences, and some background on the artist. I spent most of last night waking up old art historians to get some colour, so to speak. But Ms Quinn says no to any photographs even though we now have the new ink. You must have noticed how good the pictures are getting."

"You mean how people don't always look like ghosts?" Ruth said.

"Ms Quinn said the photographs won't do the paintings justice, but we were effectively offering her an eleven-page advertisement for her new gallery, and for free! Next time, we'll charge her, and I told her so."

"What new gallery?" Ruth asked.

"You haven't heard?" Hunter asked. "She's opening a new Scottish National Gallery in Thurso."

"But that's so far north," Ruth said. "Why not in Strathclyde?"

"If you want my opinion, it's to encourage the tourist ships from America to continue to dock in Thurso after the war, rather than coming to Twynham," Hunter said.

"Tourism? Well, I suppose everyone wants a holiday after the year we've just had," Ruth said. "You could quote me on that, if you like."

"I'd rather have something about the arson attacks," Hunter said. "We'll send copies of the big edition up to Thurso for the ferry returning to America. Without the photographs of the paintings, we can't lead with a story about art. The front is wonderfully quiet, which only leaves the arson attacks."

"Do you mean to say you're sending newspapers all the way to America?" Ruth asked.

"Absolutely," Hunter said. "We're opening a local edition in Maine next month, and another in Iowa before June. Quebec and Ontario will follow, but elections sell papers, so we want to strike while the rhetorical sparks fly. Tomorrow's paper includes the editorial on how the Maine edition launches on the first of next month. To make sure people buy the paper, we need a good headline." He uncapped his pen. "In your opinion, would you say that the suspect you arrested last night was a hole short of a donut?"

"I don't think I've ever said that in my life," Ruth said. "And that's not a quote, either. Excuse me, I have to speak with the politicians."

One of the foresters opened the door for her. The other stepped in front of Hunter, blocking his path.

Inside the commandeered waiting room, Quinn and Das stood an impolite distance from each other and had been exchanging unpleasantries until Ruth walked in. The boxed paintings were stacked on two carts, and had gained a further two wire boxes containing long cardboard tubes. Mrs McMoine was guarding them along with two men Ruth hadn't seen before. Rent-a-goons, she decided, bodyguards for Quinn because Mr Das had brought his own. These two would have been teenagers at the time of the Blackout, and grown into men during the violent years that followed, but they weren't so old they couldn't be conscripted. From the white scars on the taller one's cheek and the shorter one's forehead, they were no strangers to aggression. Their suits were cheap but tailored, both a matching dark grey, and over them each wore a blue and white tartan sash, just like Quinn.

"You're late," Erin Quinn said.

"Good morning, Your Majesty," Ruth said to Mr Das. "Ms Quinn. I need to check the paintings."

"That has already been done," Quinn said. "These paintings will remain sealed until they reach Thurso. You will guard them on the train, but they will remain in my custody."

"You're coming to Scotland?" Ruth asked.

"Of course," Quinn said. "I will remain there until the gallery opens."

"When is that?" Ruth asked.

"When it is time," Quinn said.

"What's in the cardboard tubes?" Ruth asked.

"Posters and other marketing material," Mrs McMoine said.

"You had posters made of the paintings?" Ruth asked.

"It took all night," Mrs McMoine said.

"You let some poster-maker see the pictures, but you won't let the newspaper run some photographs?" Ruth asked.

"We certainly couldn't open those crates here," McMoine said. "The coal smoke would do untold damage to the artwork."

"None of which is your concern, *Constable*," Quinn said.

Thinking of the cocoa spilled by Eloise back in Dover, Ruth smiled. "If I can't check them, and if the newspaper can't photograph them, *you* better get them aboard the train."

She turned to Mr Das as pointedly as Quinn had named her rank. "Are you coming to Scotland, Mr Das?" she asked.

"Sadly, no," he said. "But on your way back, do stop in Leicester. You will receive a very warm welcome and Edward would be delighted to see you. That, however, is not why I'm here, either." He laid a hand on her shoulder, and began half pushing, half leading her back to the doors. One of the foresters opened it before Das had to ask. The other armoured bodyguard snapped to attention so loudly the clang caught the attention of Ollie Hunter who had been pointing at the trains while his photographer had been gesturing at the crowds.

"What's going on?" Ruth asked.

"Just a moment," Das said, waiting for the journalist to draw near. Das cleared his throat, and reached into his pocket. "This, Constable Deering, is the Loxley Star. It is one of the highest honours in Albion."

He paused, giving Hunter's pen time to catch up with his words. "Though I have relinquished my throne, duty can never be abandoned, nor the honour that accompanies it. The star is being awarded to all of those who fought so bravely in Belgium. No matter under which flag their parents were born, they came together to hold off an insidious foe seeking to destroy democracy itself." Again, he paused until the journalist caught up. "I present this star to you, Constable Deering, along with my undying thanks. I have one for your colleague, Hamish MacKay."

"Is that Mac with an a or without?" Hunter asked.

"Constable?" Mr Das prompted.

Ruth sighed. "With," she said, unable to contain her embarrassment.

"Would you like a photograph, Mr Hunter?" Mr Das said. "Perhaps the constable could hold up the medal by the ribbon while I shake her hand?"

"Perfect," Hunter said, still writing. "Mel, over to you."

"Don't smile!" the photographer said. "No, don't frown. Just look sombre. Seriously, how hard is it to look normal?" Muttering, she took a photograph. "That better do."

"It will," Hunter said. "It'll be perfect for the front page. A war hero and a king? The Americans will love that!"

"I am always at your service," Das said. "Now, if you'll excuse us, I'd better see the constable boards the train, and see that the train safely begins its journey north."

"Ms Quinn looked very smart this morning," Ruth said as she and the ex-king began walking towards the train. With a clank of plate and chain, the bodyguard followed.

"Politicians must always look the part," Das said.

"Right, but I wonder if she thought a photograph of her might make the front page after she said there were to be no photographs of the paintings."

"Politicians are in the newspapers too often," Das said.

"Weren't you trying to get Ms Quinn to join your alliance?" Ruth asked.

"My arrangements are for nothing so formal," Das said. "Sadly, she and I were unable to reach an agreement."

"So, instead, you gave the newspapers a different front page," Ruth said.

"You'll note that your name is inscribed on the medal," Das said. "I had them minted two weeks ago. The honour is genuine and eternal, as is my gratitude. I wish you good luck with your mission. The Loyal Brigade must be stopped."

Before she could ask how he knew, he tipped his hat and walked off.

Chapter 10 - Awake Aboard the Sleeper
England

Ruth found Isaac waiting in the cargo van near the middle of the train.

"I did wonder if you'd be here," Ruth said. "Where did you get to last night?"

"I had some paperwork to deal with," Isaac said. "It took much longer than I anticipated."

Ruth shrugged. She recognised the brush-off, but it was a long journey to Scotland. There was plenty of time to get a few answers out of him. She walked over to the prisoner-transport cage in which the paintings, and posters, had been locked. "Do you have the key to this padlock?" she asked.

"No, Quinn kept it," Isaac said.

"She locked us out?" Ruth asked.

"In her words, we have no need to open the cage," Isaac said. "But I think I can have that lock picked in ten seconds. How long do you think it would take you? Shall we make it a contest?"

"Definitely not. She's bound to check on the pictures and she already dislikes me." The carriage juddered as the train began to move.

Isaac crossed to the wide windows on the right-hand side. Like most carriages, this one had been a pre-Blackout intercity passenger car from which the seats and grab bars had been removed. Along the left-hand side was a compartment for mail, another for official government cargo, the prisoner-transport cage, and a row of hard metal benches for non-paying but low-ranking official passengers. Today, that was just Ruth and Isaac.

"What are you looking at?" Ruth asked, as she opened the suitcase, hunting for coats she could use as a cushion.

"The city," Isaac said, his tone oddly distant. "It is an impressive achievement in its way. We could have done more, but I think what we did was enough."

Ruth joined him at the window. Outside, the signage for a smoke-belching factory was caked in so much soot, the name was barely legible, but she knew it was a foundry converting salvaged steel into bicycle frames. Next to it was a pottery, then a cutler now making bayonets, and then the tanners, worryingly close to the brewery. It was an assault on the eyes, ears, and nose, but yes, it *was* impressive, in its way.

There were fourteen carriages on this passenger train. The six carriages in front of their car were the sleeper service to the mainland's far north, with five carriages behind for passengers on the stopping services to Leicester. Behind those five were two cargo wagons for small businesses, though most freight travelled on the night train.

The door at the end of the carriage was locked, though with the standard octagonal train-key issued to every railway worker, and which any blacksmith could forge in a few minutes.

Beyond was an old carriage. *All* the carriages were old, but this one was ancient even by pre-Blackout standards. The windows were so scratched they would be better described as etched. The floor was so worn it had been covered with uneven sheets of aluminium, because another trip-risk was just what their jolting journey needed. Rather than individual seats, this car had narrow forward-facing benches on either side of a central aisle. This carriage only had twenty-six passengers, who, in accordance with ancient custom, had taken seats as far from each other as they could.

"Thank you," Ruth said, taking the ticket offered to her by an older woman with a kind face and calculating eyes. It was easier to play ticket inspector than explain why a uniformed copper was aboard. "You're going all the way to Albion?" Ruth asked as she handed the ticket back.

"I lived in Leicester *before*," the woman said. "I thought I might retire there now things are a little easier." She gestured at her bags, ten of them, stacked on the seats and by the window. "My worldly possessions."

The woman was almost certainly a smuggler, looking to draw a profit from the end to the embargo now Albion was once again part of Britain. But if there was a crime there, it was a small one, so Ruth smiled again and continued down through the train.

There were two stops between Twynham and Albion, but all the passengers were heading to Leicester. From a snippet of conversation here and there, having failed to find happiness in Twynham, they were seeking a living in the Midlands, but would settle for somewhere the air was transparent. None were young except for the two families reduced to one parent by the war. They all had a copy of the newspaper from last week where Mr Das had offered a home, work, and schooling for their children to anyone who moved north.

Almost immediately after the peace treaty was signed, the newspaper had run letters complaining that Albion had been given a disproportionate number of MPs for its small population. Mr Das's response had been to invite settlers, no matter how young, no matter how old. Anyone who couldn't afford the ticket could request one from his parliamentary office. There were five passenger cars going to Albion. By the time she'd walked to the very end of the last, she'd checked one hundred and sixty tickets. One hundred and fifty-two had been issued by Mr Das.

"Well, that's five dollars I owe myself," Isaac said when she returned to the cargo van.

"Why?" Ruth asked.

"I had a bet with myself you'd return with at least one person in handcuffs," Isaac said.

"Are you reading my book?" she asked.

"It's been a long time since I read *Great Expectations*," he said. "I thought we could discuss it as we go north."

"There's a few other things I want to discuss," she said, "but I have to check the other half of the train first."

Immediately in front of the cargo-car was the service carriage containing the luggage store and a small galley-kitchen. Both were locked, with a sign informing passengers the train's catering services had been closed due to the war. Next to the galley were the toilets, an arrangement that would have put her off buying any food even if the kitchens had been open. The next carriage was for standard-class passengers travelling all the way to Scotland. It was another old carriage, but this one was in far better condition, having only forty seats and those all having been recently re-upholstered. There were twenty passengers, but the pair closest to the door were Quinn's bodyguards, who'd been playing cards until Ruth entered.

"Where's Ms Quinn?" Ruth asked.

"Sleeping," the taller of the two said. His was a rubbery face. Not fat but full, as if his diet had improved but his exercise regime hadn't. He had a big head and a big frame, the kind she associated with a fighter, and he had the bruised knuckles to match. But her eyes went to the edge of a shoulder strap visible beneath his blazer.

"Can I see the licence for that firearm?" Ruth asked.

He slowly raised his eyes as he tilted his head back, turning to face her square on.

Ruth returned his glare with an interested smile. "The licence?"

"Of course, *officer*," he said, and took his wallet from an inside pocket. He took out a slim card.

"Eustace Pewter," she read. "This was issued in Twynham and signed by Commissioner Wallace, no less. And yours, sir?" she added, turning to the smaller man.

His black hair was cut too short, accentuating his small chin, big ears, and bigger nose. Rat-faced was too easy a description, but the man made it easier still by hunching inside a fraying brown overcoat. He opened a wallet stuffed with blue-paper banknotes, and in which was an old police warrant card. From next to it, he plucked his gun licence.

"Reginald Howe. You were a police officer?" Ruth asked.

"The private sector pays better," Howe said. Where Pewter had the guttural drawl of the Twynham slums, Howe's accent was Scottish, though not the near-Viking lilt of the very far north.

"Thank you," Ruth said. She smiled again, returned the card, and continued down the train.

She checked the tickets of the other passengers, using her uniform to be officially nosey. What quickly became apparent was that everyone in this half of the train, except the bodyguards, was heading to Thurso to catch a boat to America: the grandfather-daughter-two-grandchildren-family playing Scrabble, the nervous-looking draft-dodger who began a coughing fit as she approached, and the pair of vicars, both reading newspaper-editions of *Great Expectations*. The dog collars gave away their profession, while the matching wedding bands gave away their relationship. She was short, tidy, and made to seem more so by the man's stubbly attempt at growing a beard.

"Are you for Scotland?" Ruth asked.

"For Maine," the woman said. "We used to administer rival parishes. It's how we met. We've been invited to minister to the congregation in Bangor. It was a sign."

"I'm sure it was," Ruth said. "Congratulations."

Everyone seemed to be leaving Twynham. Even the preachers. Yes, that was a sign, and she wasn't sure it was a good one.

After a second passenger cabin, she came to the sleeper cars. She didn't know which compartment was Quinn's, and didn't bother to check. After a brief hello to the driver, she made her way back through the carriages, and to the cargo-van.

"Any visitors?" she asked.

"None yet," Isaac said. "Still no arrests?"

"Almost," Ruth said. "Who issues blue banknotes?"

"Maine," Isaac said. "They're returning to greenbacks after reunification, but the blue notes are still legal tender."

"One of Quinn's guards had a wallet stuffed with them," Ruth said. "And he's an old cop. He kept his warrant card."

"Even I know you're supposed to hand that back," Isaac said. "But it sounds as if he's emigrating."

"I thought he was a smuggler," Ruth said. "Buying something with the cash from one of the ship's crew."

"Or he exchanged his British money for dollars down at the American embassy," Isaac said.

"You can do that?" Ruth asked.

"Sure. But only after you've applied for resettlement and have received your ticket."

"Now, that's interesting," Ruth said. "Between us finding the paintings and this train leaving Twynham was about thirty-six hours. Whether those two work for Quinn, or for an agency, they can't have known about this trip more than twenty-four hours ago. The ferry has already left America. The taller, bigger guy, Pewter, had a gun licence signed by the old corrupt, and now dead, police commissioner, Wallace. I think those two were just as corrupt and lost their jobs during the purge. Along came the war, and conscription, and they decided to start afresh in America."

"Will you arrest them for draft-dodging?" Isaac asked.

"All I have is a hunch," Ruth said. "I'll send a telegram back to Twynham when we stop, and ask Anna to run their names. But if they *are* running from conscription, would we really want to put them on the front line? I know *I* wouldn't want them watching my back if they're really looking for a way to escape."

"That's a fair point, but an unnecessary fear," Isaac said. "The war is about to become a peace-keeping exercise. Conscripts will be garrisoned along the coast, and then inland, but mostly along the roadways and rail-lines. Around the garrisons, farmland will be reclaimed. There'll be skirmishing with bandits, but there always has been. The worst of the fighting should be over, and conscription will be replaced with National Service by year's end. The longer-term hope being that some garrison soldiers might become settlers."

"Do you mean that the government is actually encouraging people to leave?" Ruth asked. "Because almost everyone on this train is leaving Twynham for good. It won't be long before there's no one left."

"It's a small train and a big city," Isaac said. "An old city, too. The infrastructure is crumbling. To rebuild, you need taxes. To generate those, you need trade, and that means people to trade with."

"The world really is changing, isn't it?" she said.

"We can only hope," Isaac said. "I bet those ex-cops are hoping for a job with a badge when they get to the other shore. Since you suspect them of being linked to Wallace, and he had a hand in the assassination attempt that nearly killed Perez, that's a piece of intel the CIA would be interested in. Tell Anna to tell the ambassador. It'll stand her in good stead when she takes a job over there."

"How do you know about that?" Ruth asked.

"You'd be surprised what I know," he said.

"Anna told you, didn't she?" Ruth said. "You spoke with her yesterday in the bookshop."

"You're well on your way to becoming a great detective," he said, and picked up her book. "Since we are heading to Thurso, it seems appropriate we begin our book-club discussion with the escape of the convict from a prison hulk."

"Why did you have to say that?" Ruth asked. "Oh, now I'm going to worry that's Stevens's plan."

"Then may I suggest, when we arrive, you speak with the local blacksmiths?" Isaac said.

They stopped just south of the ruins of Leicester, at a still-being-built interchange where the passenger carriages were unloaded, and the passengers for Scotland dashed to the conveniences. Ruth waited in the carriage while Isaac made a beeline for the new kiosk selling pies and tea. She stood by the door, half watching the Scottish passengers, half watching the pair of Albion soldiers, on guard by the gate. Both women wore the full ceremonial metal armour, but the helmets couldn't quite hide their grey hair, and certainly not the lines on their faces.

In Belgium, Ruth had learned that the armour was a disguise. When the foresters went to war, they did so in camouflage, carrying long knives and longer bows. No one saw them, not to live and tell. But everyone recognised the armour, and so a new myth had been born. Would that myth, and the wearing of armour, fade amid this influx of refugees, or would it grow?

"I hope you're hungry," Isaac said, coming back with two large bags.

"What did you get?" she asked.

"Everything," Isaac said. "You should see the prices."

"They're cheap?"

"Exorbitant," Isaac said. "I explained who you were, and got these for free."

"You're kidding," Ruth said.

"Nope. Give the guards a wave."

Ruth did before retreating from the door. "What exactly did you say?"

"I simply asked if they'd read the newspaper article about Ned Ludd. I then said you couldn't leave the train because you were under the king's orders."

"What else did you say?"

"Nothing that would count as a true lie," Isaac said. "The long pies are meat, the round are sweet."

"What's in them?" she asked.

"I didn't ask," Isaac said. "It's a good rule of dining. If the chef isn't confident enough to proclaim the ingredients, you shouldn't ask."

"That sounds like one of Mum's sayings."

"It is," Isaac said.

The train jolted.

"Here we go," Ruth said. "I should go check the passengers, I suppose. But it'll wait a few miles."

She opted for a meat pie first. "Nice pastry. Have you travelled a lot?"

"Work has forced me to," Isaac said.

"You mean running scams?"

"No, my real work," Isaac said. "But that is a story for Scotland."

"I'll hold you to that," she said. "I meant before the Blackout, when you worked for Mum, did you travel a lot then?"

"Sure, but mostly within North America, and mostly so your mum didn't have to. I'd go to the conferences, and things like that, instead of her."

"Doing what?"

"That is another story best kept for Scotland," he said.

"It's six hundred miles from here to Thurso," she said. "We're not going to arrive until early tomorrow morning. That's a lot of time for silence."

"I could tell you a different story," he said. "The same story I told Anna. The story of how the first Loyal Brigade met its end."

Part 2
The Death of the First Loyal Brigade

Norfolk & Essex, Ten Years After the Blackout

9th May 2029

Chapter 11 - The Mystery of the Missing Moat
Sandringham House, Norfolk

"So that's Sandringham Castle," Henry Mitchell said, bending low so as to take advantage of a gap in the hedgerow. Beneath the shade of the overgrown hedge, the ground was still hard after the previous night's frost. The calendar might call this May, but another long winter had barely released its grip. *Every* winter since the Blackout ten years ago had been long.

"It's a house, not a castle," Isaac said, trying to ignore the partially frozen mud in which he knelt and which was slowly seeping into his trousers.

"Movement," Mitchell said. "Pheasant. Strutting along the lawn, about fifty yards away. Why doesn't it qualify as a castle?"

"No moat," Isaac said, tilting sideways so he could see the pheasant. With recent summers so short and the winters so cold, the lawn would be better called tundra. Even so, something had been snacking on the grass, but unlike the pheasant, it had disappeared when the ever-hungry humans had arrived. But from which particular group of humans had the grazing animals fled: the police, or the fugitives?

As the bird speculatively pecked at a taller patch of withered wild grass, Mitchell took out his binoculars. "A very grand house," he said. "Four storeys. One tower that's not much taller than the roof. The wings sprawl into new extensions that'll have their own exits. At the centre, there's… can't really call it a bay since it runs from the ground all the way up to the tiles. Large gated entrance at the bottom, probably wide enough for a car."

"Or a golden carriage," Isaac said.

"That, too," Mitchell said. "There's no smoke, but soot's stained most of the windows. Over half are boarded. Ah, there's a broken window on the ground floor, another at the top and in the centre, and a third at the far west, up in the eaves. A few more on the third floor… No smoke, no fires, no sounds, no movement."

"Which doesn't mean there aren't any people," Isaac said, and took out his small radio. "Mrs Zhang?"

"Hold position," Mrs Zhang said.

"Put that radio away," Mitchell said. "The sergeant's coming over."

Sergeant Lemuel Brakespear, formerly of the parachute regiment, led their small militia. Every one of the twenty-strong squad had served before the Blackout. Two had been Royal Marines, while three were of the U.S. variety. Five had been British Army, two in the French, one in the Egyptian, two in Germany's, one each from Poland, Ukraine, Kenya, Tunisia, and Algeria. These weren't recent refugees, though, but part of the volunteer corps who'd signed up last winter to fight pirates in the Mediterranean. Instead, they'd been put on election protection detail. It was that duty which had brought them, under Captain Henry Mitchell's command, to the old royal residence in Norfolk.

The election had been called early for reasons that made no sense to Isaac, and called for March, which made even less sense, except that it gave everyone something to argue about during a miserable February. Perhaps because there was so little other entertainment, the fringe candidates had signed up in droves. Along with the crackpots, loons, and a legion of ex-politicians whose pensions had been lost when the lights finally went out, was the Loyal Brigade. That gang of duplicitously inflammatory thugs only stood candidates in five seats, but crashed every speech by their opponents, smashed the signs, and trashed the constituency offices of the incumbents. Intimidation is never as successful with a secret ballot, and it was clear before the count they weren't going to win. Clear to them, too. They'd rioted, simultaneously, at all five polling places where their candidates had stood. The goal, presumably, had been to ruin the ballots, and so to force a re-run, but instead they faced a pitched battle with their opponents, all united for once. The Loyal Brigade had been beaten. Literally. The counts had continued. The next day, an arrest warrant had been issued for their leader, Mark Stevens, and every other member of the group who could be named.

Stevens and his band had fled, but from interviewing his followers who'd been hospitalised during the election-riot, they knew the pre-arranged rendezvous was the old royal residence of Sandringham House in northern Norfolk. Those same prisoners had suggested as many as fifty followers might gather to Stevens's banner. As far as Isaac could see, they weren't here.

"Sir, the troops are in position," Brakespear said. Like the rest of the militia, his only uniform was the new government-issue rifle and the old-world body-armour, on the back of which was still stencilled the word *Observer*.

"Any movement?" Mitchell asked.

"Only shadows," Brakespear said. "Nothing that's definitely human."

"As a fortress, how easy would it be to defend?" Mitchell asked.

"We abandoned it for a reason, sir," Brakespear said. "The house was up-armoured, but with terrorist attacks in mind. We had to remove half the windows just so air could properly circulate. There were multiple entry and exit points, and we made more. And the woodland was strategically planted to hide a view of the road, so they won't have seen us approach."

"With so many trees having been felled for firewood, there isn't much cover left," Isaac said.

"There's enough," Brakespear said curtly. The old Brummie soldier clearly didn't mind taking orders from a police officer, even if Mitchell's accent placed him as a cop rather than a bobby, but the soldier had made no secret of his distrust of this American civilian. "If they were going to place sentries anywhere," Brakespear continued, "it'd be up at Snettisham Beach and at the bridge in King's Lynn that crosses the Great Ouse. If they're smart, they'll expect us to come by sea. If they're clever, they might think we'd come by land. But if they've an ounce of sense, they know any battle fought here is the first salvo in a retreat."

Isaac's radio gave an almost quiet chirrup. As Brakespear glared, Isaac held it to his ear. "Ah. It seems our trip hasn't been wasted. There is movement on the ground floor. Watch the broken window."

"Someone's emptying a pot," Mitchell said.

"Latrine duty," Brakespear said. "That's no sentry. Might not even be a hostile. It's a long hike from the south coast to Norfolk. Stevens might not have made it, but this house is on every map. What with the town of King's Lynn having burned down during the Blackout, this estate would be the obvious bivouac for any wandering hunter."

"Then we should be cautious," Isaac said.

"Aye," Brakespear said. "And you should start by putting that thing away before it explodes."

"The radio? It won't explode."

"Saw it happen with my own eyes," Brakespear said. "My sister's phone caught fire. Mine took light the next second. Good thing they were on the table, but every appliance in the house went up, and we barely got out before the building burned down."

"You say there are lots of entry points?" Mitchell said, before a real argument could begin. "We'll approach in four groups of five. You pick the entry points, but in case they aren't hostile, let's give them a chance to identify themselves. You've got five minutes to get in position, and then I'll walk up to the front door and say hello. If the shooting starts, I'll take cover, and it'll be up to you."

"Sir," Brakespear said, and after giving Isaac another glare, jogged back into the trees where the rest of his militia waited.

"Leadership suits you," Isaac said.

"Thank you," Mitchell said.

"The uniform doesn't," Isaac said. "Blue is no colour for anything but denim."

"It's clean, it's new, it mostly fits," Mitchell said.

"That is what worries me," Isaac said. He took out the radio. "Mrs Zhang? The militia are moving out and will make entry in five minutes."

"Spotter. Top floor," Mrs Zhang said. "Second spotter, same room. Broken window, left of the main entrance."

"Got it," Mitchell said.

"Hostile," Mrs Zhang said.

"How does she know?" Mitchell asked.

Isaac repeated the question into the radio.

"Experience," Mrs Zhang said. "Hold position. Fourth hostile, third floor, window to the left of the entrance. It's a trap. They know we're here."

"How does she know that?" Mitchell asked.

"I'll refer you to her previous answer," Isaac said. "I bet you wish your militia had radios now."

"You know how people are with technology these days," Mitchell said.

"It's not people who worry me," Isaac said. "It's parliament effectively banning anything with a circuit board which sends a shiver from ear to toe."

Now he knew they were being watched, the previously soft footfalls of the militia sounded like migrating elephants as they moved between the axe-hacked trees and wild shrubs.

"They're too loud. Too obvious," Isaac murmured.

"Agreed," Mitchell said. "Any ideas?"

"Mrs Zhang, can you cover us?" Isaac asked.

After an ominous pause, the reply finally came. "Yes," she said.

"Cover us as we do what?" Mitchell asked.

"Exactly what you said," Isaac said. "We'll walk up to the front door."

"And if they start shooting?" Mitchell asked.

"We run," Isaac said.

"This is not how I thought I'd be spending my day," Mitchell said, as he slowly stood up.

"Nor how I pictured my vacation," Isaac said, brushing down his recently found, but increasingly tattered, tweed suit. He adjusted his hat: a grey homburg, which, thanks to over-exposure to sea rains on the long voyage from the south coast, had developed a wilting brim. "Shall we?"

"This was never going to be a vacation," Mitchell said, as they began walking along the hedge and towards the old path used by horses as much as people, and which led to the front entrance.

"Not for you, perhaps," Isaac said. "But here I am, in the land of Chaucer, Shakespeare, and more Georges than I can remember, yet I've found little time for sightseeing since the Blackout."

"What about those trips you disappear on?" Mitchell asked. "I know you've been going north."

"Yes, on business," Isaac said.

"And what business is that?" Mitchell asked.

"No business of a police officer's," Isaac said. He'd intended it to be a joke, but once spoken the words seemed to ring with condemnation until they were drowned by gunfire.

Together, both men ran. Bullets thudded into the damp mud, whistled through the patches of un-grazed grass, and tore leaves from the sprawling hedges. The shots from the house came close together, but the gunfire was semi-automatic at best. The bullets from Mrs Zhang's high-powered rifle came one at a time. With each of her thunder-crack shots, the volume of fire from the house diminished. With the third, it stopped.

Mrs Zhang didn't fire again, nor did gunfire resume from inside, but neither Isaac nor Mitchell stopped running until they reached the nailed-shut doors at the front of the house.

"I win!" Isaac said. "You're getting out of shape, Henry."

"Take cover," he said, leaning against the thick stone.

"I don't believe there's any need," Isaac said, taking out the radio. "Mrs Zhang?"

"Hostiles are neutralised," Mrs Zhang said. "The militia has made entry. I'm changing position."

"Where did you find her?" Mitchell asked.

"She found me," Isaac said. "Shall we enter?"

"Not if we might trip over our own people," Mitchell said. "We'll make our way around to the other side, see if we can catch anyone as they flee."

The radio chirruped again. "Engines," Mrs Zhang said. "To the west. At least two vehicles, driving away."

"Driving?" Mitchell asked. "They have cars?"

"Shall I fetch some of the militia?" Isaac asked.

"No, we'll investigate the engines," Mitchell said. "But it sounds like we're too late."

With the help of radioed directions, they found Mrs Zhang outside the Church of St Mary Magdalene, half a kilometre to the west of the main residence.

"Three vehicles," she said, pointing to the tyre marks.

Mitchell squatted by the nearest set. "Land Rovers, I think."

"Certainly," Mrs Zhang said. "The fleet of Land Rover Wolfs provided to the royal family were shielded against an EMP."

"Brakespear said there were some vehicles like that left in the main garage after he and his people were evacuated," Mitchell said. He straightened, backed up a cautious step, and then began counting the other footprints. "I wonder how often he, or one of the other Norfolk refugees, told that story?"

"Repairable motor vehicles abandoned in a garage aren't uncommon," Isaac said. "Even older models without electronics. Fuel for them, however, is rarer than root beer, so where did theirs come from?"

"I will check the church," Mrs Zhang said, and made her way to, and then over, the broken vestry door.

"Who is she, Isaac?" Mitchell asked.

"A friend," he said. "We can trust her."

"That's not an answer," he said.

"Oh, but it is," Isaac said. "You just can't seem to find the correct question."

"The riddle of what the Loyal Brigade is up to is puzzle enough for me," Mitchell said, as he took out a phone given to him by Isaac last Christmas.

"You still have that?" Isaac asked.

"Of course," Mitchell said.

"Then you aren't averse to all technology," Isaac said.

"The new law doesn't ban it," Mitchell said. "We can't rely on it in court, or in official reports. That doesn't mean I can't use it at as an *aide-memoire*."

"Hmm. How *was* France?" Isaac asked.

"The weather's better," Mitchell said. "Proper sunshine is appealing, but it's more dangerous than here, even in the coastal enclaves. If I get a chance to retire from this life, it'll be to farm, and I'd prefer growing grapes to cabbages, but Anna has to come first. She's still settling into life as a copper down in Twynham. I count at least ten sets of footprints milling about here. Maybe fifteen, certainly no more."

"Five per vehicle would be the maximum capacity," Isaac said.

"Not for Land Rovers, and not in an emergency," Mitchell said. "From the depth of the tyre marks, the cars were only brought up here this morning. Then they were loaded. People hung around between here and that set of trees. And *behind* the trees, so they were out here long enough to need a bathroom. I wonder…" He didn't finish the thought, but began walking back and forth along the mud and moss-strewn road.

With no evidence inside the church, and no more to be gathered from outside, they headed back to the house and saw Brakespear coming to find them.

"Is there trouble?" Mitchell asked.

"No, sir," Brakespear said. "We only encountered one hostile. Chased him into a corridor on the lower ground floor. Door at the end was locked. He was trapped, but didn't want to surrender."

"And the three Mrs Zhang shot?" Mitchell asked.

"Dead, sir," he said before turning to Mrs Zhang to give her a nod of professional respect.

"So there were only four people in the house," Mitchell said. "What's through the locked door in that corridor where you chased the suspect?"

"The old stables," Brakespear said. "That's the two-storey block on the corner. Most recently, it was a security station for the house. Lots of CCTV screens downstairs, and some bunk-rooms upstairs for security staff travelling with the principals. We stripped out the electronics, turned it into more accommodation. Looks like the refugees who came here after us, these last few years, they used it for much the same."

"When you say the door to the corridor was locked, do you mean with a key, or do you mean it was barricaded?" Mitchell asked.

"It was locked," Brakespear said. "The key was on the floor of the garage, a few feet from the door. There were four bags in there, with water, a bit of food, some clothes, and the usual assortment of gear."

"It sounds like those four didn't realise they were a suicide squad," Mitchell said. "I met a few of the Loyal Brigade during the election campaign. They're the kind of opportunistic slacker who'd spend all week searching for a way to avoid an honest day's work. Despite Stevens's messianic rhetoric, his people were followers, not believers, so I can't see any of them preceding him to hell in a desperate attempt to buy time. We found tyre marks by the church, and footprints belonging to ten to fifteen people. I think they fled while we were engaged here. Didn't you say there were three Land Rovers left behind in the garage?"

"Yes, sir," Brakespear said. "But there was no fuel. I was on leave, staying with my sister. I got here about two days after the Blackout. By then, the fire was spreading fast through King's Lynn. The fumes were intense, and it was clear no help was coming, so I led the refugees here, hoping we'd find a secure comms link to a part of the world that still functioned. The house was mostly vacant, except for the year-round staff. We had one working generator, and we burned through the diesel store within a week. Petrol didn't last much longer. We became a camp for refugees. Couldn't offer people much except work digging the graves. A lot of people upped and offed, and I never saw none of them again. We got a few rowing boats out onto the sea to fish, did a bit of hunting, did a bit of salvaging after the fire in King's Lynn had burned itself out. But when we heard there was a government on the south coast, we were more than ready to leave." He shook his head, clearing it of ghosts. A respectful silence had fallen as he'd reminisced, each of them, in turn, remembering their own experiences through those darkest of days. "What are your orders, sir?" Brakespear finally asked.

"Finish securing the house," Mitchell said. "I think you were correct, Sergeant. Stevens *did* have spotters watching for us. By the time our ship anchored, they had the Land Rovers ready to go. Not knowing from which direction, or *directions*, we'd make our approach, Stevens picked four of his people to draw our attention to the house. That rearguard was told there was a way out via that corridor, and their bags were waiting on the other side. Stevens locked the door, ensuring the death of his followers, just to buy himself a few extra seconds. So let's take a look at what was left behind and see if we can find out where they're going next."

Leaving Brakespear to continue searching the ground floor, and Mrs Zhang to search the garage, Mitchell and Isaac went to the top-floor sniper's nest. By the window, in a line beneath the sill, were ten semi-automatic pistols. Another three lay on the ground, with two more close to the corpses.

"A Glock 19," Mitchell said, picking up a handgun from next to the body. "Five rounds left."

"Fifteen rounds in a full magazine for this one," Isaac said. He ejected the magazine, pocketing it.

"That's evidence," Mitchell said.

"Indeed, and I'm taking it away for further analysis," Isaac said. He picked up another of the handguns lined up by the window. "Another full magazine." This time, after a moment's hesitation, he placed the magazine next to the gun.

"The serial numbers are consecutive," Mitchell said, picking up another pistol, then a third. "Purchased in bulk, probably by law enforcement or the military, but probably not left lying around here. Mrs Zhang's a good shot," he added, turning to the first of the two corpses. "One head shot, one centre mass. She's military?"

"Ex-military," Isaac said.

"A spy?"

"An ex-spy," Isaac said.

"For whose side?" Mitchell asked.

"These days, ours," Isaac said. "And that is surely all that matters. There is quite a view from this window."

"You're changing the subject."

"I'm trying to enjoy the moment," Isaac said. "It isn't every day you step inside a palace, even if the previous owners didn't think to call it that. I think these must have been staff quarters. This was the study, and that room, there, was the bedchamber."

"It's a great view for a member of staff," Mitchell said as he continued photographing the serial numbers on the handguns.

"Yes, but it's a large study, and only a small bedroom," Isaac said. "The view is magnificent, but it is of the driveway and the stables. The Mistress of the Creaky Wardrobe, Keeper of the Queen's Pigeons, or whoever occupied these chambers, would be able to work at her ledgers while keeping an eye out for the royals returning from jumping over foxes."

"Have you ever considered writing a history book?" Mitchell said. "The serial numbers on these pistols form an almost complete consecutive sequence. Three guns are missing, but there's no reason to assume there weren't other guns with numbers higher or lower than what we've got here."

"It's a shame so much of the panelling was removed," Isaac said.

"Looks like paint on the walls," Mitchell said, briefly glancing up before turning his attention, and camera, to the corpse.

"I was referring to the wood lining the servants' stairs," Isaac said. "Enough remains to tell the craftwork was exquisite. I know every winter has been cold, but there are still a few trees outside which could have been burned first. They took the bannister, too, did you notice?"

"I did," Mitchell said. "Blue jeans, white t-shirt, black waist-length coat. All recent loot. All in need of a wash. It's different gear from the sweater and black trousers they wore during the election. Must have had the change of clothes stashed with the guns, but I doubt they kept that stash here. This place is a name surely everyone in Britain knew, and so anyone who found themselves nearby would have come to take a look."

"Do you know much of the house's history?" Isaac asked.

"It was bought and built for Victoria's eldest around the time of the American Civil War," Mitchell said. "He became King Edward the something. I forget which one. Didn't reign for very long, and died just before the First World War."

"I was referring to the more recent history," Isaac said. "Didn't the most recent group of farmers get pushed out by pirates?"

"By sea-raiders from the Netherlands," Mitchell said. "That was the second official attempt to resettle Norfolk. The first was wiped out by plague, and the same fate befell the unofficial settlements that preceded it. Most recently, about a thousand volunteers were farming thirty miles south of here. I don't think they used the house. There was a pitched battle closer to the coast. The pirates retreated back to their sailing boats. About fifty of the farmers died immediately. By the time the Royal Navy fleet arrived, another twenty had died of their wounds, and thirty more had up and left, we think to go north to Albion. The attack was just after planting. The pirates targeted a temporary dam, and half the newly planted fields were flooded. There weren't enough sailors to both defend the settlement and hunt down the raiders, so our farmers were brought back to Kent. Stevens staking a claim on Sandringham was the last straw for parliament, particularly after he started a riot during the election. That's why we're making this next settlement permanent."

"But Stevens began his journey on the south coast, seven weeks ago," Isaac said. "He travelled here by land. If you know the route through London, and if you have a bicycle, you can make the journey in three days. Since he knew the Land Rovers were here, he must have known which route to take. I heard his speech when he said that Britain's glory began to fade when it gave up the cotton fields of North America."

"He was whistling about slavery," Mitchell said, as he began searching the pockets of the corpse closest to the window.

"Whistling in the wind, thankfully," Isaac said. "But I can see why he might feel a need to claim a royal residence, even an old one from the Imperial era, though I am positive Prince Albert publicly supported the abolitionist cause."

"What's your point?"

"Buckingham, Hampton Court, Lambeth, Westminster, Eltham," Isaac said. "Those are just the London palaces I can remember. Then there's Windsor Castle and the Tower of London. I'm sure there are more, and all on his way here."

"London's a swamp," Mitchell said. "We both saw that for ourselves."

"Agreed, but if they only needed a rendezvous, why come all the way here? The ruins of London offer far better places to wait, and to disappear into."

Mitchell held up a folded sheet of paper he'd found in the killer's pocket. "Because they were going to Balmoral," he said.

"Is that a map?"

"Of a sort," Mitchell said. "It's hand-drawn, and now blood-stained, but it records a route from Sandringham to Balmoral via Leicester."

"Albion, you mean," Isaac said.

"Their leader might call himself king, but his people are just another group of bandits."

"Separatists, perhaps," Isaac said. "But they aren't bad people. They're just survivors like the rest of us."

"If they've found common cause with the Loyal Brigade, they absolutely aren't like us," Mitchell said. "Besides, they wear armour and use longbows."

"After you effectively banned firearms," Isaac said.

Mitchell didn't reply, but crossed to the other corpse and began a search. "Another copy of the same map," he said. "Hand-copied. Almost identical. Sandringham to Scotland, via Sherwood. Do you have a proper map?"

"In my pack, and that's back with our bicycles," Isaac said. "Why?"

"Because I think this route follows the motorway," Mitchell said. "Why bother making the map? Why not just tell his people to follow the road signs to Leicester, and then to Aberdeen until you see the signs for Balmoral?"

"Why even say that when you can find a map in any house, and Balmoral in the index?" Isaac asked.

"Exactly," Mitchell said. "We were supposed to find these maps. These people were supposed to be killed or captured. Now we're expected to head north, and waste a couple more months doing so."

"But instead, we could follow the tracks left by the Land Rovers," Isaac said. "On this side of London, away from the north-south farm-to-mine traffic, it's rare to find more than a single lane cleared of wrecks. Often, not even that, but where Stevens will have to stop to clear a passage, a bicycle won't. We'll catch up with him within three days."

"I can't," Mitchell said. "My orders were to push out the Loyal Brigade so Sandringham could be secured for the farmers."

"A task that can be left to Sergeant Brakespear and his militia."

"There's at least ten hostiles in that group," Mitchell said. "We'd need the militia to assist in the arrest, but the farmers need them for protection."

"Let the farmers wait aboard the ship until Stevens is in shackles," Isaac said.

"And how long will that take?" Mitchell asked. "If we spend three days following the tyre tracks, we won't return here for a week. That's one more week no fields will be prepared."

"The sailors on that ship are more than capable of standing guard," Isaac said. "With their experience of ploughing the waves, a few fields should pose no difficulty."

"Those aren't their orders," Mitchell said. "And they're not mine, either."

"I wonder if Stevens knows that," Isaac said.

"You think he has spies in government?"

"No, I think your government is infested with opportunists who would use any tool to seize power."

"Perhaps you're right," Mitchell said. "But I can't disobey my orders."

"That's the uniform talking," Isaac said.

"Exactly," Mitchell said. "I wear the uniform. I carry the badge."

"I mean to say that you disobey orders when it suits you, so why not now?"

"Because Stevens is done. His gang are just bandits. Yes, they'll raid farms for food, and we'll have to hunt them down eventually, but there are bandits everywhere. There will be even more if we have another hungry winter. Policing isn't just about catching criminals, it has to be about preventing crime, and the prospect of starvation is a motive as old as society."

"They have fuel and guns, Henry. These people are dangerous."

"No," Mitchell said. "They are *very* dangerous. They came here for the Land Rovers, and to lay a false trail. That speaks to a plan a long time in gestation. They want us to rush off, hunting for them, so that's exactly what we won't do."

"Then..." Isaac began. He shook his head. "No, I wanted to have a vacation, not an argument. Since your mind is made up, I shall leave you to enjoy it, and see you back in Twynham."

"You're leaving?"

"I am clearly not needed here," Isaac said.

"Where are you going?"

"To save the future," Isaac said.

13th May

Chapter 12 - Kelly
Stansted Airport, Essex

Isaac let his bicycle freewheel until the mud brought it to a complete halt.

"What did you see?" Mrs Zhang asked, slipping a hand into her coat and to the sidearm concealed there while beginning a methodical survey of the horizon.

"Hubris," Isaac said. He leaned forward, then back, looking the length of the wreck-narrowed motorway. The tyre marks were *just* visible, and there were only three vehicles that could have made them.

It was four days since they'd left Sandringham, though, initially, they had gone southwest to Cambridge. That journey, a distance of fifty miles, had only taken four hours, but they'd lingered in the outskirts for three days. That part of his on-going mission had been a success. In a prototype factory at the science park, he'd found ten electric-powered, six-seater, driverless pods that had never been switched on. The batteries were exactly what he needed. Better still were the two electric buses parked outside. Retrofitted rather than new, apart from flat tyres, they appeared repairable. Nearby, he'd found two small server farms with enough storage and processors to meet his quota for the year. How he would get it all up to Thurso was still a puzzle to be solved, and which had been put on hold when, on the old M11 motorway, twenty miles south of Cambridge, they had come across the tyre marks dug deep into the drifts of mud and leaves on the road's one lane which had been cleared of wreckage. It was obvious to which vehicles the tread-marks belonged.

"Rain's coming," he said.

"Is that why you stopped?" she asked.

"It's so cold it might as well be fall," he said.

"It's spring," Mrs Zhang said equably. "This year, summer will be one week long. But next year it will be two."

"You're an optimist."

"A pessimist," she said. "I like the cold."

"You didn't say that last January," he said. He thrust his hands into his pockets. "It's all so pointless."

"You want to turn back?" she asked.

"Sandringham is pointless," he said. "They only have twenty farmers on that ship, no seeds, and no horses. They'll mark out a few fields, but no real work can begin until they bring up a proper labour force from Bournemouth."

"They're calling it Twynham now," Mrs Zhang said. "And the ship will collect extra labour from among the refugee camps near Dover and Folkestone. I heard the ship's captain discuss it with the chief engineer."

"It's May!" he said, and heard the petulance in his tone. He took a breath. "Those press-ganged farmers won't arrive until June. You can't plant much in the summer, especially if it's as cold as this."

"Cabbage," Mrs Zhang said.

"Winter will come early, any crop will have to be harvested small," he said. "Meanwhile, the farmers will have to be resupplied, and whether those supplies come from Dover or Bournemouth makes no real difference, because it's just too much effort when those same people could be working fields in the south. If they do send more farmers here, they will take them back before winter, but if there's even a garrison left in Norfolk, I'll be surprised."

"Would you prefer leaving an over-extended, under-supplied colony of farmers here to become recruits for land-pirates like the Loyal Brigade?" she asked.

"Obviously not," he said. "But since Norfolk will be abandoned again, Henry could have come with us."

"Ah. But that is not why you are angry," she said. "He came on this mission because he was ordered to, but you travelled with him because you wanted to share an adventure like you did in the early years of this waking nightmare. He has changed, and is changing still. You tell yourself you loved the man he was, not who he is becoming. In truth, you are simply too scared to express your feelings out of fear of losing the friendship you have. The rain is coming. We should continue."

Before he could formulate a rebuttal, she began cycling, so he had no choice but to follow.

"Windsor," she said, when he caught up.

"Knot or soup?" Isaac said.

"Castle," she said. "It is where Stevens will go. Yes, they will go to an old royal residence, but London is a festering swamp. Windsor is a castle, and the Thames runs fresh on that side of the city. Strong walls and water to drink? Yes, that is a more sensible fortress than a house near the coast. This motorway leads to the M25 orbital motorway ringing London, so they followed it west, and to Windsor."

"Could be," Isaac said. "I'd still like to know why they didn't head to the woods, or hide in the crowd, or make for Europe."

"Perhaps they believe the old rumours that there is oil beneath Windsor Castle," Mrs Zhang said.

"There's oil beneath the castle?" he asked.

"No, just rumours," she said. "If there had been oil there, it would have been exploited years before the Blackout. But Stevens believes in the myth of exceptionalism, so maybe he believes other legends, too."

"Windsor is close to the north-south train line," Isaac said.

"Yes. And close to London. If he occupies the castle, word will quickly spread. Followers might come to his cause. He will declare himself lord and hope the cost of a siege is too high for the military."

"Not even this parliament would stand for that," Isaac said.

"I said it was *his* plan, not mine," Mrs Zhang said.

During the Blackout, the fate of a vehicle depended on its type of electronic governance systems. In some cases, the engines died. In others, motors spun so fast they broke or caught fire. Collectively, the result was a planet-wide crash. The roads became clogged. At the same time, planes and helicopters fell from the sky. With the roads impassable and the hospitals on fire, treatable injuries became fatal. In the years since, farmers and salvage teams had cleared a lane here and a road there, as and when they had needed it.

Even if the road signs hadn't warned they were nearing Stansted, he'd have been able to tell an airport was ahead from the increasing density of debris. Circling jets had fallen from the sky. Planes with full fuel tanks, about to take off, had exploded, scattering debris for miles. On this particular stretch of the M11, a single lane had been cleared. The above-motorway bridge must have collapsed more recently. Two hundred metres beyond the rubble, and effectively blocking the road, was one of the missing Land Rover Wolfs.

Mrs Zhang already had her rifle out. "Approach with care," she said. She, though, began climbing the rubble to find an overwatch position on the remaining stub of bridge.

Isaac wheeled his bicycle along the road, his eyes moving from the car to the rusting mounds of steel on either side. He was watching for scattering birds, irregular reflections, or any other signs of an ambush. But by the time he reached the car, all he'd seen was a burst tyre.

Before Mrs Zhang joined him, he'd finished a search of the vehicle. "They left nothing behind," he said.

"This was the tail-vehicle in their convoy," she said. "The tyre probably tore clambering over that rubble."

"In which case, from here, they only had two vehicles to transport everyone and their gear," Isaac said. "I believe they're close. Very close, because an airport is as easy a landmark to find as a castle."

It was even easier than that because, five minutes later, they saw the smoke.

Mrs Zhang saw it first, and dropped from her bicycle, swinging down into a crouch, and pulling the bike with her. Isaac did the same, though with slightly less grace. The smoke didn't come from the airport, but from the west, on the other side of the motorway. Beyond a wide swathe of meadow, tufted with wild grass and dotted with rusting scrap from the airport's explosion, were a score of warehouse roofs, above which a black-grey wisp slowly merged with the increasingly angry sky.

"Is there any reason to think that isn't them?" Isaac asked.

"Some," Mrs Zhang said, once again raising her rifle. "No sentries on the roofs, but be cautious. Approach from the east. Retreat to the airport. You have the radio?"

"Of course."

"Use the earpiece," she said, and vanished among the metal boulders and jagged debris.

There was no nearby road access to the warehouses, nor any obvious wheel marks in the field, and too much debris for anything but a tank. Leaving the bicycle, and with one hand on his holstered sidearm, he began his own slow, and direct, approach towards the smoke.

As he drew nearer, he moved more cautiously, sidling from a monolithic engine blade to an upended cockpit to a rusting cube he couldn't begin to identify, and from where he had a better view of the warehouse, and the fire.

The warehouses were built in three rows of six, forming a U whose arms faced away from the motorway. The arms and base of the U weren't connected, leaving space for a car park, with more parking in the area between. That parking lot had become a dumping ground for shelves, sinks, chairs, and other metal items probably stripped from inside the warehouses, and which offered even better cover, so he slunk a little closer.

Though the warehouses were semi-permanent prefabs built to be replaced after a few decades, only two had failed to survive the Blackout. Some had windows on two levels, others only had a monstrous loading door. The rusting metal clutter dumped outside suggested small-scale and specialist manufacturers who needed the airport for timely deliveries.

In the centre of the U was a large, trough-like metal sink in which a fire had been lit and over which someone had placed a wire grid as a grill. It smelled as if wood was the fuel, and looked as if deer would be the meal, judging by the carcass hanging on an improvised frame. It wasn't being cooked yet. He could only see one person, a woman with a ponytail jutting through a greasy baseball cap, a grubby short-sleeved T-shirt, muddy blue jeans, and no obvious weapons. She was methodically sorting through a suitcase, one of many contained within five large metal delivery cages.

As Isaac watched, she threw something onto a junk pile, then continued rifling through the suitcase's contents. He had done much the same thing more often than he could remember, searching the bags of the dead for food, clothing, soap, or sometimes just out of bored curiosity. On the other side of the access road, parked outside a warehouse with upstairs windows and a loading-bay door were two Land Rover Wolfs.

The looter held a bottle up to the light. It seemed to be what she was looking for. She picked up a small rucksack, put the bottle inside, slung the bag on her back, and headed to the warehouse near the Land Rovers.

Isaac now had the measure of the fugitives. Having left a trail suggesting he was going north, Stevens had fled south, and come here. For a day or two, he'd have posted sentries on the roofs, watching for pursuit, knowing that, with no road access across that field, he'd have the advantage if he had to flee again. It made for a good rendezvous, too, an airport being as well signposted as any palace, but he must have known of this cluster of warehouses before. Possibly even before the Blackout.

The deer, and the suitcases, suggested his people had spent the day hunting and looting. It was unlikely they planned to leave before nightfall. Could he get back to Sandringham before dark? Possibly. Could Henry and his militia get here before Stevens left? Maybe. Was there anything he could do to keep the Loyal Brigade here for a few more days?

Isaac leaned back, taking in a wider view, and spotted the panel van parked at the end of the access road. While it wasn't a wreck, it was covered in nearly as much mud as the lorry next to it. The difference, though, and what made this van stand out, was that the windscreen had been cleaned.

This *was* a rendezvous. The Loyal Brigade's broader plan was still murky, but it was too complex for a bruiser like Stevens. The man was a demagogue, sure, but he was a thug, not a strategist, as attested by his actions during the election. Maybe he wouldn't take orders, but someone was giving him ideas, and it was probably the same people who'd given him guns and fuel.

His earpiece squawked. "Movement," Mrs Zhang whispered. "Your three o'clock. Child."

Isaac didn't spot her until she began to sprint. The girl moved fast, dashing from the shadows at the far end of the U, sprinting along the pavement towards the fire. She was dressed in black and green, but it wasn't camouflage. She had a knife on her belt, and nothing in her hands.

A thief, he guessed. A hungry kid looking for a meal and who'd spotted the fire. But when she reached it, she didn't seem to know what to do. She turned from the deer back to the empty grill, presumably dismayed to find there was no cooked meat she could steal.

Isaac assumed her next move would be to draw her knife and hack a raw chunk from the hanging deer. Instead, the girl picked up a metal pole, wedged it beneath the metal-sink fire-pit, and heaved. The sink toppled, spilling burning coals and flaming logs.

Mrs Zhang's voice whispered in his ear. "Hold position."

It was unnecessary advice.

The girl began running back the way she'd come. The shadows near a broken warehouse door bulged. The girl saw it at the same time as Isaac, but not before the shadows coalesced into a six-foot brute with red hair glued into a spike: Stevens. His fist slammed into her arm, and she sprawled to the ground. She rolled, trying to get to her feet, but not before he was able to launch his foot into her stomach. She fell again, gasping for air. Stevens grabbed her by the leg, hauling her upright.

She yelled, in anger and pain, twisting as she reached for her knife. Stevens hurled her to the ground, and began yelling.

The door to the warehouse by the Land Rovers opened and twelve people charged out, all holding sticks, poles, bars, or other weapons, but at their belts were holstered pistols. They moved to surround the girl. She dashed back, jumping onto the roof of a car, leaped, but was hit by a thrown pole as she landed. She tumbled. As she tried to stand, a barrage of sticks and poles were thrown. Again she fell, while the gang moved in, quickly surrounding her.

"Hold position," Mrs Zhang whispered.

Isaac had his hand on his holstered pistol, but hadn't drawn it. Not yet. He was still calculating angles.

The woman who'd been looting suitcases ran back to the cages, and hurriedly dumped the contents from one. Two others grabbed each of the girl's arms, twisting them as they frogmarched her to the cage. She was thrown in. The door was closed. Stevens casually tipped the cage over, so the door was flat against the ground.

Isaac pressed transmit on his radio. "How many bullets do you have?"

"Two," Mrs Zhang said.

"Wish I'd known that before," Isaac said.

"I need three minutes to get in position," she said.

"No, we'll try the other way," he said. "Listen to your radio."

Slowly, he stood, and began walking towards the fire.

"Howdy!" he called out, as he picked his way around the debris. "Y'all spare a plate for a hungry trader?"

That got their attention. Hands dropped to their holsters while some eyes went to him, but he took care to note those whose first thought was to look for other enemies approaching from behind. Four of them out of twelve, and Stevens wasn't one.

The red-haired giant stepped forward. "Who are you?" Stevens demanded.

"Just a trader," Isaac said.

"You're a Yank?"

"At one time," Isaac said. "I've been in Albion. Now, I'm heading for London."

"What are you trading?" Stevens asked.

"I'm going to reach into my coat to get a sample," Isaac said. Slowly, he drew out the magazine he'd taken from Sandringham.

"Bullets?" Stevens asked. "We've got bullets."

"I'm not trading bullets," Isaac said, taking another step forward. "I'm trading information. See if you recognise it." Isaac lobbed the magazine towards the group. "Go on. Take a look, and while you do, I'm going to reach into my pocket again."

"What for?"

"Proof," Isaac said.

"Proof of what?" Stevens said.

Isaac didn't immediately answer, but slowly withdrew the radio. "Proof I have a sniper trained on this position," he said. "Give me a target, unless you'd like her to pick one of her own."

"A sniper?" Stevens asked, now looking around. His eyes returned to Isaac. "The O in that sign," he said.

"The sign," Isaac repeated.

The rifle cracked loud, and the plastic sign splintered, spraying brittle shards across the muddy debris.

"So you've got a sniper, and you've got spare bullets," Stevens said.

"That magazine came from Sandringham," Isaac said. "It belonged to the four people you left behind, Mr Stevens. The Twynham militia think you went to Albion and are then going to Balmoral."

"Do they?" Stevens said. "And what do you want?"

"To trade," Isaac said. "I see you caught an associate of mine. I want her back. In return, I offer information."

"What information?"

"We're clearly working the same route," Isaac said. "We're obviously working the same side. Seeing as you've got diesel and mechanics, we must have similar clients and customers. You're the Loyal Brigade, so I believe we share some similar aspirations. While we might not be working together, it would be sensible not to work *against* one another."

"She's a thief," Stevens said.

"Aren't we all?" Isaac said. "We can kill each other here, or, in time, we can work together." He held up the radio. "Which would you prefer?"

Again, Stevens looked around. He shook his head. "Let her go," he said. "Go on. Now!"

The cage was rocked onto its side. The door sprang open. The girl scrambled out, and began running towards Isaac, then past him.

"Be seeing you," Isaac said. He tipped his hat, turned around, and walked away in the direction the girl had run.

"They're watching," Mrs Zhang whispered. "No. Five have gone into the warehouse."

"As long as they're not following," Isaac said. Ahead, he saw the girl reach the road, and then saw her grab his bicycle. She began cycling north.

"Two have gone to the Land Rovers," Mrs Zhang said. "A third has gone inside a van parked to the west."

"Sounds like they're leaving," Isaac said. When he reached the road, he finally looked back. One of the thugs was watching him, but from the edge of the warehouse. He picked up Mrs Zhang's bike, and began cycling north.

He saw his stolen bicycle dropped among the rubble of the fallen bridge. He stopped, but kept his hands on the handlebars.

"Why'd you do that?" the girl asked, her voice coming from behind and to his left.

Slowly, he turned. "Because it was the right thing to do," he said.

She held a twisted half-metre-long steel rod in her hands, ready to swing, though she was too far away to make impact.

"You knew them," she said. "You knew his name."

"We're with the police," Isaac said. "And the police are hunting him."

"Who's we?" she asked.

"Me," Mrs Zhang said, stepping down from the embankment, her rifle cradled in her arms. "They aren't following, but they're getting ready to leave."

"They'll go to Hatfield," the girl said.

"What's your name?" Isaac asked.

"What's yours?" she said.

"Isaac. This is Mrs Zhang."

"Are you Mr Zhang?" she asked.

Mrs Zhang laughed. "He should be so lucky," she said.

The girl nodded. "I'm..." She looked around as if seeking something that might jog her memory. "Kelly. Are you really cops?"

"We're friends with the police," Isaac said. "We joined them on the expedition to drive that gang out of Sandringham. The police, and their militia, stayed in Norfolk. We were heading for London, and then the south coast, but stumbled across their trail a few hours ago."

"How do you know they'll go to Hatfield?" Mrs Zhang asked.

"I heard them talking, yesterday," Kelly said. "This is my turf. That's my deer, and my bags. They came three days ago, and yesterday they stole my stuff. Even stole my dinner."

"The deer?" Isaac asked.

"They could have had some, if they'd asked," Kelly said. "It's more than I can eat."

"Are you alone?" Mrs Zhang asked.

"Now, sure," Kelly said.

"How long have you been living here?" Isaac asked.

"Since the sky fell," Kelly said.

"How old are you?" Isaac asked.

"How old are *you*?" Kelly replied. "You're hunting them, right? So I'm going with you. It's not like you can stop me, since I'm the only one who knows where they are."

"Hatfield," Isaac said. "You told us."

"Oh. Right. Yeah. Well, I'm still going. So come with me if you want, or don't. I don't care. I'm going to get a *proper* bike. If you're here when I get back, you better be able to keep up."

She jogged off, up the embankment, and towards the ruined airport.

"She reminds me of you," Mrs Zhang said.

"Funny, I was just about to say the same thing," Isaac said. "She's about fourteen?"

"Perhaps sixteen," Mrs Zhang said. "A poor diet would have stunted her growth."

"Ah. You only have two bullets left?"

"One now," she said. "There are fourteen of them."

"I only counted eleven," Isaac said.

"There were fourteen," she said. "There could be more who remained inside, but less than twenty in total, unless they have more transport nearby."

He took out his map. "Where's Hatfield? Ah, only about thirty miles away, west-southwest."

"It was a palace," Mrs Zhang said. "The first Queen Elizabeth grew up there. The new house is much more recent."

"Did you read that in a history book?"

"A romance," she said. "For events so long ago, fiction is often as reliable as fact."

"Travelling with you really is an education, Mrs Zhang."

"Then let's make this a lesson to remember," she said.

Chapter 13 - Not So Clever at All
Hatfield, Hertfordshire

When Kelly returned, she was as surprised to see them still waiting as Isaac was to see the size of her bike. It was clearly designed for a very tall adult, and for off-road, with a high frame and thick tyres that dwarfed his old boneshaker. To the frame, she'd strapped spears, front and back.

"Swap?" Isaac asked.

"I'll swap for that rifle," she said.

"Do you know how to shoot?" Mrs Zhang asked.

"Dunno," Kelly said. "Let me have a go and I'll see."

"After this mission is complete," Mrs Zhang said.

After visually confirming the vehicles had gone, they wheeled their bicycles across the field to the warehouses. From there, they only had to follow the deep tyre ruts west. Though they had no smoke to alert them to when they neared their destination, a gunshot told them when to stop. Mrs Zhang sprang from her bike, while Isaac rested his feet on the ground, watching the flock of starlings which erupted from a copse a mile ahead.

"Is it them?" Kelly asked.

"We'll leave the road, and then find out," Mrs Zhang said.

"Judging by my watch and that last road sign, we're five miles from Hatfield," Isaac said as they carried their bikes through a gap in the rampant hedgerow. The field beyond was dotted with wind-sown sycamores, none more than waist-high, and so not nearly tall enough to conceal the jagged spears of bone jutting from the uneven soil.

Five hundred metres further on, in an abandoned farm one field from the old road, were the two Land Rovers and two panel vans. The vehicles were parked behind a collapsed barn, with only two guards. One guard slouched by the vehicles nursing a very fresh bruised eye. The other angrily marched back and forth, an extra pistol stuck in his belt.

"House. Movement," Mrs Zhang whispered.

The front door of the farmhouse opened. When it reached halfway, it toppled. The thug caught it, and after wrestling with the one wobbly hinge, tore it loose before propping it next to the opening. He, and the woman who followed him out, made their way over to the wrecked barn. Two more followed.

"They're after firewood!" Kelly whispered.

"Shh!" Mrs Zhang said.

The Loyal Brigade seemed to be collecting timbers and planks, but were selective, discarding as many for being too small as too long. When they carried them back to the house, they didn't take them inside, but stacked some by each window.

"They must have a generator," Isaac said, as other members of the Loyal Brigade began hammering the boards over the windows. "They're blocking light from being seen from outside."

"Smart," Kelly said.

"But not smart enough," Isaac said. "They didn't disguise the tyre tracks, or the vehicles."

"Maybe that's next," Kelly said. "When do we attack?"

"Against superior numbers, always use darkness as an ally," Mrs Zhang said, taking the scope from her pocket. "But time your escape before you time your assault. Death in victory is another name for defeat."

"They have fuel," Isaac said. "Diesel, I assume. Probably transported in one of those vans."

"You want to steal it?" Mrs Zhang asked.

"If we can," Isaac said. "And if we could, and if we disabled the other three vehicles, they would be on foot, and forced to walk from here to Hatfield House. We could return with the militia before they have time to prepare."

"I thought we were going to kill them," Kelly said. "That was the deal."

"No, we promised revenge," Mrs Zhang said. "In this case, it is also justice, and it is wise. They departed Sandringham with three Land Rovers. They lost one, but have gained two vans and their passengers. We don't know where they will go next, or how many people, and what supplies, will be waiting there. We'll need more guns to finish this gang once and for all."

"We can't drive back to Sandringham," Isaac said. "The motorway's one clear lane is blocked by a Land Rover. We'll have to hide the van, and cycle the rest of the way."

"After we've stolen the van, we'll have to stop to collect the bicycles," Mrs Zhang said. "They will be following. They will be shooting."

"And we'll give them a distraction," Isaac said. "A fire should do it. We'll only need a few minutes."

"I'll do that," Kelly said.

"You will guard the bicycles," Mrs Zhang said. "And you will guard my rifle." She handed it to the girl.

"Cool."

"There is only one bullet," Mrs Zhang said.

"Oh."

Darkness wasn't long in coming. As the sun sank, Stevens left the house. He spoke to the guard without the black eye, laughed loud enough to startle a nesting pigeon, then returned to the house. The door was closed. Minutes passed. The guards weren't changed.

"They're doing something inside the house," Isaac said when Mrs Zhang returned from having escorted Kelly back to the field where they'd left their bikes. "Hard to tell what, but I heard an occasional clink and bang."

"Then they are distracted," she said. "We'll have to kill the two sentries."

"I know." Isaac took the suppressor from the pouch on his belt, and affixed it to the pistol. "We'll take out the sentries, I'll disable the Land Rovers, while you keep watch. Then we'll search the vans to see—"

"Shh."

Light spilled from the house and was followed by Stevens. He ignored the sentries, and marched over to the vans. He opened the back, grabbed a fuel can and a canvas bag, and made his way back to the house. The front door was lifted back into place.

"I guess that's the van we want," Isaac said. "Shall we?"

They followed the hedgerow until they were concealed by the abandoned barn. The sentries had stopped pacing, and were now talking. The words were indistinct, but the tone was aggrieved.

Mrs Zhang went wide. Isaac went slow, gun raised, taking care with each step, holding fire until the further sentry turned towards him. Before the sentry showed any sign of recognition, Isaac fired twice, shifted aim and fired again, twice. The last bullet thunked into the van's cab nearly as loudly as the bodies hit the ground.

Mrs Zhang changed her prowl to a run, taking cover behind the van's cab before taking aim at the house.

"Clear," she said when Isaac reached her.

As Isaac tugged wires from the Land Rovers, Mrs Zhang checked the back of the second van. When Isaac moved towards its cab, she gestured to the other van. "Disable the other," she whispered. "We're taking this one."

He didn't ask why, but changed direction. Another minute, and the van would require more than a mechanic to repair.

Mrs Zhang had retrieved a fuel can from the back, into which she had stuck a rag.

"That's not diesel, is it?" he asked.

"Gasoline," she said.

"Now, that begs a few more questions," he said. "I'll start the fire, you drive."

Gun in one hand, heavy fuel can in the other, he made his way to the boarded house. From inside, he could hear glass clinking against glass, a clunking generator, swearing, then laughter. There was an odd smell creeping around the door, something familiar but which he couldn't place.

Carefully, Isaac placed the fuel can by the door. He took out a box of matches, paused for a moment's brief reflection, then tugged the rag out, and gently laid the can on its side, letting the fuel spill over the doorstep. He stepped back, struck a match, lit the rag, and dropped it on the still-spilling petrol. As it caught, he kept running.

Ahead, Mrs Zhang turned the engine on. She'd left the passenger door open. Isaac pulled himself inside as she began to drive. He pulled the door closed, peering in the mirror to see flames licking up the house's doorframe.

"They would have remembered to leave themselves a back exit, yes?" he asked. "They wouldn't have sealed all the doors and windows completely?"

Before Mrs Zhang could give her opinion, brick and tile soared up and out, burning shrapnel fell down, and the farmhouse exploded.

"What was that?" Isaac asked, even as Mrs Zhang braked.

"They can't have been so stupid," Mrs Zhang said.

Slowly, they got out. The farmhouse was a burning candle, reaching halfway to the clouds.

"What variety of stupidity were you referring to?" Isaac asked.

"There are barrels of fuel in the back of this van," Mrs Zhang said. "Half are gasoline, half are diesel. The other van was nearly empty, but it must have contained barrels, too. They moved them into the house."

"They fired up a generator in the same house they were keeping the fuel?" Isaac said. "So they really weren't so clever after all."

Part 3
Coded Messages

Thurso & Scrabster

27th January

Chapter 14 - A Different Variety of Stupid
Scotland

"Is that it?" Ruth asked. "They just burned to death?"

"Technically, I think some were blown up," Isaac said. "But it's an irrelevant distinction. They'd barricaded the rear door and the windows, perhaps to keep light out, but perhaps also because they feared a raid from a trader with a sniper. With the front door on fire, and the other doors and windows blocked, there was no quick way out, and no time to look for an alternative."

"Did Hailey know how the first Loyal Brigade died?" Ruth asked.

"Yes, I believe so," Isaac said. "Back then, we didn't have newspapers, let alone radio, but we had a very effective rumour mill."

"And now they're using arson," Ruth said. "I wonder if that means something. Was the explosion caused by the fuel?"

"As it turns out, no," Isaac said. "Theirs was a different variety of stupid."

"So if it wasn't petrol or diesel, what was it?"

"What was in the second van, you mean?" Isaac asked.

"Yes."

"Don't you want to guess? It's still a long way to Thurso. We could make a game of it."

"I can think of way better games. What was it?"

"They had enough small arms munitions to start a revolution, though probably not enough to win it," Isaac said. "Seeing as the brother ended up as an arms dealer, I think this might have been their original stash. The trigger for the explosion, however, was a still. I always thought it odd that they ran candidates, since the inevitable ballot defeat would have exposed how thin their support was. I think they were *paid* to stand candidates, and to start the riots. Someone wanted the disruption."

"That sounds very similar to what happened in Europe," Ruth said. "When we were in Belgium, Mister Mitchell told me he thought someone supplied the terrorists so they would kill off the rival gangs, leaving only three mega-tribes whom they supplied and so had some measure of control over. You're saying someone paid the Loyal Brigade to be troublemakers at the election, and so become the public face of the enemy."

"Exactly," Isaac said. "Someone like Longfield, perhaps. At this stage, it is impossible to know who, but it's not a new idea. History is littered with empires picking a local tribe to become a client kingdom. The Loyal Brigade were paid off with the ammunition, with the panel vans, and the fuel. I think the still was something they put together themselves. When we returned to those warehouses near Stansted, I took a closer look and found one was a small bottling plant for boutique gin."

"If they were on the run, why did they stop for the night to brew up some booze?" Ruth asked.

"That's the wrong question," Isaac said. "Ask why, on fleeing the election, they went to Sandringham, why they remained there until the militia arrived, and why they then left a false trail implying they'd gone north. They needed time to finish bottling their brew."

"That brings me back to the same question, why stop to make spirits?"

"Money," Isaac said. "To make hooch, you need grain. Back then, the rations were so tight, beer was just a wish. A van full of brain-rot was worth more than ammunition, more than diesel, and, to some, more than bread. It would be enough to live like a king through the winter, and to bribe the guards at the grain silos so you could acquire the ingredients to make more. Having encountered the odd American trader near Stansted, Stevens decided to run his operation through the night, then shut it down and move out. In his desire to stop any light spilling outside, he also reduced the ventilation. The devastation was so complete, I can only give you a theory, but my small blaze caused a panic, and we can blame the stampede for the rest."

"What did the official investigation conclude?"

"There wasn't one," Isaac said. "We drove clear, collected Kelly, left the van, and went back to the farm. No one had got out alive. We cycled back to Sandringham, only to find that Henry had already left for Twynham, so the three of us went on to Thurso."

"But you didn't cycle," Ruth said. "You drove, yes? And after collecting all that tech stuff you found near Cambridge."

"It would have been a waste to leave that fuel behind," Isaac said.

"Okay, so why go to Thurso?"

"That is something easier to show than tell," Isaac said.

"I'll hold you to that," Ruth said. "No one got out?"

"No one. We took some photographs that I gave to Henry when we finally returned to Twynham. While we were in Scotland, a storm swept across southern England. It was bad in Kent, but worse in Norfolk. The attempt at occupying Sandringham was abandoned again. The following year, they shifted their efforts south into France and towards the Mediterranean. The Loyal Brigade was forgotten. Without an investigation, the only evidence anyone had, and which the militia told the farmers who then told everyone else, was that the Loyal Brigade had planned to go to Balmoral via Albion where they assumed they would receive aid. That long winter was when Albion became the public villain for those in the south."

Ruth listened to the wheels clack on the tracks. "What aren't you telling me?" she asked.

"Some minor details, but nothing critical."

"No, there is something important missing. Something big. And I don't mean Thurso. You rescued Kelly, and it's not like you deliberately burned the gang alive. But when you got back to Twynham, you and Mister Mitchell had a huge fight. Anna said the row was loud enough to wake a statue."

"That is complicated," Isaac said. "But it is more to do with Thurso than the Loyal Brigade. Suffice it to say we all change as we wander through this landscape we call life, but sometimes we don't realise how much we've changed, and sometimes we don't realise how little."

28th January

Chapter 15 - The Beginning of the World
The Railway Station, Thurso

As the sun set, falling snow turned the view to static and the carriage into an icebox. Around midnight, the sky cleared and the stars came out. The temperature dropped again, but the train continued lumbering north, only briefly stopping to collect water and coal. The constant shunting jolt of the carriages and accompanying squeal of the brakes made sleep impossible, while the unfinished nature of Isaac's story prevented Ruth from losing herself in her book. Thus, it was a welcome relief when they pulled into a well-lit and well-covered platform.

Smoke from the engine rolled across the roof's steel beams, adding a grey shadow to the cheery signs proclaiming: *Welcome to Thurso, the Beginning of the World*. The locomotive shunted onward until the engine was beneath a roofless section of platform. With most of the smoke now billowing upwards, the doors opened and the weary passengers staggered out.

On the platform, a pair of blue-uniformed guards began ushering people into the enclosed arrivals shed. From the other end of the platform, a man in waxed tweed, a fur-lined hat, and leaning on a cane, began limping his way towards her. Since she'd last seen him in the hospital in Dover, his stubble had been tamed into a moustache, made to seem an even brighter shade of red by the frost-blue tinge to the few patches of skin not buttoned up against the cold. Foreshortened by his limp, he was still nearly a head taller than her, and not nearly as rake-thin as when she'd first met him in Belgium. Ruth gave as cheery a wave as the chill would allow, but didn't leave her post by the door to the cargo cabin.

"Welcome to paradise," Hamish MacKay said.

"How do you find being a police officer?" Ruth asked.

"I'm only a technical assistant, as Inspector Voss keeps reminding me," Hamish said. "But I get the pay just the same, so I won't grumble."

"You're looking well," Ruth said. "And no wheelchair, that's fantastic."

"Aye, well, I tried attaching skis to one, but couldn't find the dogs to pull it. Only three hours late, that's good going for the sleeper. Mr Isaac, is that you? I'm Hamish MacKay, I don't know if you remember me."

"I brought you back from Belgium on my ship," Isaac said.

"You did? Those days are all a bit of a blur, but I meant from when I was a bairn," Hamish said.

"You know each other?" Ruth asked.

"I know his grandmother," Isaac said. "But I remember him building snow-aliens on a bright winter's day."

"When I was a lot, *lot* younger," Hamish said. "What are you doing up here, Mr Isaac?"

"I've come to see your nan, actually," Isaac said. "But that's a story that can wait until we're in warmer surroundings."

"We've a meal waiting and a bed if you want," Hamish said.

"A meal would be great," Ruth said. "But I don't think I could sleep. I've got to hand over these paintings first. Where's Ms Quinn?"

The rest of the passengers had already hurried into the arrivals lounge, leaving Ms Quinn at the centre of a very small crowd. Her two bodyguards were behind her, while a three-person delegation faced her.

"Who are they?" Ruth asked.

"The dragon with the glasses is Dr Frobisher," Hamish said. "She's a Doctor, not Ms or Mrs, and never ma'am. She's very firm about it."

"She's a medic?" Ruth asked, taking in the woman with a lighthouse stare. She wore a fur-lined wax-wool coat with red tartan trim at the sleeves, collar, and hem. As that tartan matched her trousers, gloves, and scarf, it must be an old coat, recently resurrected, and by an expert tailor.

"She has a PhD," Hamish said. "She's the chief librarian, and she's now also whatever they call the overseer of an art gallery. Before the Blackout, she was an archaeologist, specialising in pre-Christian history, but she was here visiting her aunt who worked at the library. It became a popular place after the Blackout. The building had a small gallery, but books, and the learning that went with them, became a priority. The arrival of these paintings was a bit unexpected, and she's not too happy about losing the reading room. The residents are even unhappier, because we're already short on space now the ships from

America, and their passengers from the south, are filling every nook and cranny."

"Who are the other two?" Ruth asked. "One is in police uniform."

"That's Inspector Voss," Hamish said. "He ran security for a squadron of oil platforms out in the North Sea. Managed to save seventy-six people by getting them aboard an old motor launch. When they ran out of fuel, they paddled the rest of the way to Orkney. He was transferred here a few years ago because they wanted a high-ranking officer in town in case there was ever another escape attempt from the prison ship."

"Another escape?" Ruth asked. "You mean there have been some."

"Not where a prisoner made it to shore alive," Hamish said.

The white in the police officer's beard wasn't all snow. About sixty, about five-nine, and bulging a little at the waist, his overcoat was open, and the uniform buttons beneath gleamed as brightly as his metal-framed glasses. On his belt, there was no holster, nor even a truncheon. Around his neck, and somewhat taking away from the air of stern dignity, was a penguin-patterned scarf.

"And the guy with the chain?" Ruth asked. The man in question was in his fifties, and, like Quinn, he wore the blue tartan sash, but he was also wearing a stylish summer-weight suit, and shivered as if he regretted it.

"That's Douglas Stuart, the Laird Mayor," Hamish said.

"The lord mayor, got it."

"No, the *Laird* Mayor," Hamish said. "Don't ask, and definitely don't ask him. Just call him sir."

"Got it. I better say hello."

"And I better not, so I'll come too," Isaac said.

Ruth took a breath, fixed a smile on her face, and stepped forward, just as the group broke up. Erin Quinn followed the Laird Mayor, with her bodyguards trailing after her. Dr Frobisher thrust her hands in her pockets and made her way towards a gate at the other end of the platform. Inspector Voss raised a hand, waving over a pair of somnambulant porters, as he made his way to the train.

"Constable Deering. I'm James Voss, police inspector for the Highlands and Islands. Welcome to Thurso."

"Thank you, sir," Ruth said.

Voss turned to the porters. "Load the paintings."

"Oh, no!" Ruth said, in frustrated realisation. "Ms Quinn locked the cage and still has the key to the padlock."

"It's fine," Isaac said. "I unlocked it."

"This is Mister Isaac," Ruth said. "He's a consultant."

Voss's expression turned thoughtful. "I know you, lad. Seen you before, haven't I?"

"I'm an old friend of Mrs MacKay," Isaac said.

Voss nodded. "Aye, I thought you had the look of a star-watcher about you." He turned back to Ruth. "I had a telegram explaining why you're here, and we'll talk about that after the sun's arrived. The telegraph has reported a landslip near Lairg. You're lucky you made it through, though I expect the engineers will tell us that it was the sound of the locomotive which triggered the collapse."

"We're trapped?" Ruth asked. "What about the telegraph?"

"Aye, that's down, too, at least beyond Lairg," Voss said. "We'll send a work-team south at first light, and have the repairs made within a week. We're always an island up here, and more so in the winter than the spring, but spring is coming, Constable, you can hear it on the wind. I'll leave Mr MacKay to show you around. Once you're rested and settled, you'll find me at the police station." He tipped his hat, and stepped into the carriage.

"Our duty is done," Isaac said. "So how about we find some duty-free?"

"Some what?" Ruth asked.

"Something to warm our insides," Isaac said.

"This way," Hamish said.

"I think Quinn is up to something," Ruth said, glancing back at the carriage before following Hamish towards the gate. "She made a real fuss about no one looking at the paintings before we left Twynham, but didn't come to check on them once during the journey, and doesn't seem to care about them at all now."

"Whatever she's up to, I bet it's politics," Hamish said. "There was a real free-for-all at the last election. Twenty candidates stood, and she won with twelve percent of the vote. They're talking about putting up a unity candidate to unseat her this year."

"I suppose you can't escape politics wherever you go," Ruth said. "When did you meet Inspector Voss, Isaac?"

"Honestly, I don't remember him," Isaac said. "But I suppose that means he's good at his job. Now, can we continue this conversation where the temperature is on the right side of freezing?"

Outside the station, the frozen Lovers Lane was salt-scented from the northern ocean's swirling winds. The road was illuminated by portable lanterns hung just above head-height from brackets welded onto old street-lamps. More lights came from inside the small electric van parked outside the main entrance.

"Climb in," Hamish said. "Unless you'd prefer to walk, but it's two and a half kilometres to the shipyard."

"You have your own van?" Ruth asked, so shocked she nearly forgot how cold it was.

"Aye. She's one hundred percent electric," Hamish said.

"Isaac, is this one of the vehicles you got from Cambridge?" Ruth asked.

"The battery was, but the chassis came from the airport in Aberdeen," Isaac said. "Or was it Dundee? There've been so many places over too few years, it's almost enough to make a man think he should settle down."

The back was an enclosed cargo cabin, while the front contained a single bench seat into which Ruth gladly squeezed. "How come you have an electric van, Hamish?"

"Did I not tell you about how I learned to drive?" Hamish said.

"Well, yes, but I expected some old rust-bucket that rattled more than my old bike, not something so swanky it would make Atherton jealous."

"Aye, she's not bad, is she?" Hamish said.

"I suppose what I really want to know is why don't we have these down in the south?"

"Not enough batteries," Isaac said. "But the root of the reason was the government-endorsed rejection of technology. Too few batteries and electric engines were salvaged during the early years. Now, most are beyond repair. I rescued what I could. Esme MacKay did the same. There were thirty vans at the peak, but that's down to twelve now."

"Eight," Hamish said.

"Only eight?" Isaac asked.

"Aye, two blew at the beginning of winter, and another two were needed to replace the batteries in one of the boats."

"Eight left," Isaac said. "Only eight. Then we really do need a reliable source of oil."

Ruth decided to keep her follow-up questions until they were somewhere much, *much* warmer.

Castlegreen Road was icy but clean, sparkling in a sharp contrast to the sooty grey sludge that pervaded Dover and Twynham. The van was slow, but sheltered from the wind and snow, and quickly filled with steam.

"What's that smell?" Ruth asked.

"Ah, that's a speciality up here in the north," Hamish said. "It's something so prized, we never send it across the border. We call it fresh air."

"The new hydro-plant is working?" Isaac asked.

"Aye. More or less," Hamish said. "Wind's doing the bulk of the work over on the crofts, but the hydroelectric dam has made this a winter to remember. Fire's become a friend, not a necessity."

"Don't you burn coal here?" Ruth asked.

"Not nearly as much as we did," Hamish said. "There's a coal power station to the south of the River Thurso, but coal has to be shipped in, while the water and wind bring themselves. We're heading up to Scrabster. That's the old fishing harbour on the northwest of Thurso Bay. Nan set up her shipyard there, and it's where the prison hulk is moored, but most people live back in the city."

Ruth wiped away condensation from the window. To the left was a roughcast-clad three-storey apartment block. Light crept around the storm-shuttered windows, indicating a few early risers. Opposite were architecturally identical two-storey terraces, which, like in Dover, had long ago been converted to apartments.

An old grocery store was adorned with the nationally ubiquitous posters for Satz Tea, but next to it, a new sign had been recently painted: *Deli and Grill. Dollars Welcome.*

Hamish flashed the van's lights at the manager who was putting out the pavement signage. Next door, an old park had become a development of log-clad shipping containers and low-roofed blockhouses built of brick salvaged from the ever-encroaching wilderness. Old cars had become chicken coops, while old vans had become extensions. Smoke rose from a few chimneys, and those, like further south, were often recently installed in the walls, but to every home went an electricity cable. It was similar to Dover, but different enough to make Ruth see her harbour-home anew and, for the briefest of moments, to give her a pang of homesickness.

At the harbour-hamlet of Scrabster, outside the entrance to an old fish processing plant now grown into a monstrous boatyard, a figure wearing a rainbow cloak leaned on a long shepherd's crook.

"Isaac!" she said. "Aren't you dead yet?"

"Not for want of trying, Esme," Isaac said.

"And you'd be Ruth Deering, would you?"

"Last time I checked," Ruth said. "Mrs MacKay?"

"Aye, I am. Well, come inside so I can look at you properly," she said. With a theatrical swish of her cloak, she swept around and led them inside and into an office where a bleary-eyed receptionist pretended he'd not been dozing.

Behind the reception desk was a glass wall. Behind that was an office filled with computer screens. Ruth had seen those often enough, but usually among the ubiquitous trash discarded when old buildings were cleared of useful salvage. These screens, and their keyboards, looked like they were actually used.

"Where's your manners, Hamish? Take her coat," Esme MacKay said.

"Oh, hang on," Ruth said. "I'm not sure there's a right time for this, so there's no time like the present. I've something for you from Mr Das, Hamish. For what we did in Belgium." She took out the box King Alfred had given her.

"It's a medal?" Hamish asked, looking bemused as he opened it.

"Everyone who fought there is getting one," Ruth said.

"It's the very least you deserve," Esme MacKay said, taking it from her grandson. "Looks like an archer. Not bad. Silver, I think. Take the box and hold still."

"I'm not going to wear it, Nan," Hamish said.

"Oh, you are, my lad," she said. "You earned that with your flesh and blood. There's some around here as need reminding."

Hamish sighed and let his grandmother pin the medal on.

"Quite right," Esme said. "Quite right indeed."

"I need to show her the office," Hamish said.

"And I would like to see Arthur," Isaac said.

"He's asleep," Esme said.

"I won't wake him," Isaac said. "I'd just like to see him."

"Aye, well, we both know where that'll lead," Esme said. "Leave your bag, Ruth. It'll be taken to your room. Douglas, get her bag!" she added, turning towards the once-again dozing receptionist. "And then tell Tam to send two breakfasts to Hamish's office. Quick-snap, or I'll put you on barnacle duty."

"This way," Hamish said, and led Ruth into a narrow corridor enclosed with wooden planks.

"Does your nan own all of this?" Ruth asked.

"Not *own*, not really," Hamish said. "Some call us a clan, but it's more like a collective, and she's the collector. People, technology, ideas, hope. She moved up here before the Blackout because the government promised they were going to build a spaceport. She figured that made it a likely spot for aliens to land."

"You're kidding," Ruth said.

"Not even a bit," Hamish said. "Ask her, but only when you've a few free hours to spare. After the Blackout, a fish-processing factory was no use without the boats, so she organised the conversion of one factory into a small boatyard. The inn over the way was originally a house that became a canteen for the workers. It became a pub, and then a hostel, but now we're planning a proper hotel. During the winter months, when there's no casual work at the farms, we take on a lot of workers here in the boatyard. The pay's not great, but they get room and board, and stay on the waiting list for permanent housing, and a permanent job in the new cannery."

"Why is there a waiting list for homes?" she asked.

"Materials have to be salvaged from the towns in the south," he said. "You can't do much of that in winter. In summer, it's not as big a priority as farming. The nearby ruins were disassembled years ago, so we've got to go further to find less. A lot of our early builds aren't as water and wind-tight as you'd like, so have to be dismantled, and that only adds to the housing pressure."

"You mean the hasty builds are draughty and damp?"

"Up here, damp isn't as much a bother as icicles," Hamish said. "We're building to last now, building for the future. We hope, with the new ships, we can start salvaging the coastal ruins that are too far to reach by road." He opened a door, and led her into a glass-windowed tunnel overlooking a semi-enclosed dry dock where a steel whale was under construction.

"Wow," Ruth said. "It's as big as a street. It *is* a ship, right?"

"She will be," Hamish said. "She's the *Enterprise*-C. Nan picked the name."

"Is there an A and B?" Ruth asked.

"There was," Hamish said, clip-clicking his way down the tunnel. "The first ship overturned. The second wouldn't turn fast enough and ran aground. They say the third time's the charm."

"She's got four funnels," Ruth said. "It's steam-powered, then?"

"Mostly wind," Hamish said. "Those are masts to support the wing-sails."

"Sails? Seriously?"

"She's two hundred metres long, and a hundred metres tall when the sails are fully extended. The masts can extend and retract, you see."

"No, but I'd like to," Ruth said.

"The blueprint was a ship under construction in Sweden, and two others being built in Norway. They weren't seaworthy, but Nan brought back the designs. If she works, we'll be able to travel absolutely anywhere in the world with no need for dead-dinosaur-fuel. *When*," he added. "*When* she works."

"I thought you just had a few fishing boats."

"Aye, the collective has those, too. When she's finished, we'll test the *Enterprise* on salvage missions to Scandinavia. Did you know we're closer to Norway than France?"

"Really? Huh. Okay, but when this ship is finished, and if she works, won't you also have a factory to make even more ships?"

"Aye, just imagine the possibilities," he said.

At the end of a tunnel, one door led into the shipyard, while another was sealed with a padlock.

"Welcome to my office," Hamish said, unlocking the door. Beyond was a square room, about three metres on each side, decked out as a living room with a sofa, a few bookcases, a small stove, and with a spiral staircase leading up. "This was our old weather station," Hamish said. "I spent a lot of winters here when I was a bairn, so no one questions me being here while I'm recovering. You better go up first. It'll take me a wee while longer."

The upstairs room had a single small window in each of the four walls, but these were currently sealed with an interior shutter to prevent light from the electric bulb spilling outside. On a table by the sea-facing wall were three laptops, two telescopes, and an assortment of old electrical items Ruth couldn't name. Beneath the table, a neatly tied bundle of cables disappeared behind a cabinet.

The comfortable chair, with its footrest, was clearly Hamish's, so she took the hard wooden chair, it being the only option other than the rocking chair at the rear of the room.

"We'll have to get you a proper seat," Hamish said, finally reaching the top. "I'll ask Tam when he brings the food."

"Who's he?" Ruth asked.

"An old friend of Nan's," Hamish said, a little breathlessly. He sank into his chair and lifted his foot onto its stool. "Ah," he sighed.

"Do a lot of people think you shot yourself to get sent back from the front?" Ruth asked.

"Some, aye," Hamish said. "How did you guess?"

"From the way your nan insisted you wear that medal," Ruth said.

"Some might call me a coward, but they're the ones who didn't volunteer, so they're projecting their own self-disgust. That doesn't make it easier, not when I grew up with some of them. But I know what I did."

"And so will everyone when they read tomorrow's paper," Ruth said. "Mr Das engineered a photo of him giving me the medal, mostly to spite Erin Quinn for reasons which I don't really follow, but are entirely political."

"Politicians are like storms," Hamish said. "Just as soon as one's over, another is on its way. Do you want to see the prison?"

"At night, can we?"

"Get ready to open the window shutter," he said. "I'll turn out the light."

The chamber went dark. Ruth pulled back the shutter. Slowly, her eyes adjusted to the gloom. A hundred metres long, protected by the seawall, the ship floated alone among the ink-black waves. Painted red, stained with rust, secured with anchor chains fore and aft, the deck was entirely ringed by a chain-link cage twice the height of a person. At the side, a gantry was raised like a drawbridge, and was the only connection to the quay twenty metres away. Ashore was a sentry post, with a spotlight slowly moving from one porthole to another. Fixed spotlights illuminated the quay, the ship, the seawall, and even the small fishing fleet anchored on the other side of the bay.

"It's a bigger ship than I was expecting," Ruth said.

"She's an old icebreaker," Hamish said. "The ship docked here a month before the Blackout. A couple of the crew got into a barney ashore, and Tam was hired as a replacement to work the engine room for a tour of the Arctic. During the Blackout, navigation failed, but they managed to sail her back here. They used her to rescue survivors from the oil rigs, and then as a ferry to Orkney. But the propeller cracked, and she barely made it back to harbour. With the diesel gone, there was no point trying to repair her, but the hull's sound. The ship became a police station, and now it's the prison."

"I'm trying to remember what was in my briefing book," Ruth said. "There are about sixty prisoners, yes?"

"Now there are only thirty," Hamish said. "All are murderers, kidnappers, or rapists, and some are all three, and worse. They're all serving life, but escaped the noose, if you can call this an escape. The frailer prisoners were moved south to make room for some of the numpties we caught in Belgium. But none of those have arrived yet."

"Good. That'll make this easier. Did you hear that we stopped the fifth arson attack and caught the arsonist?"

"Aye, we got the telegram, though it didn't contain any details," Hamish said. "Does this mean the investigation is over?"

"Probably not," Ruth said. "The fifth attack was on Religion Row, and if you mark down all five attacks, you can make the shape of a pentagram. We think Stevens's goal is to get the newspaper to print that shape, his claim to be a prophet, and the warnings he gave to the prison governor. We can probably keep it all from the press until the trial, but not during."

"Who was Stevens's match-happy helper?" Hamish asked.

"Her name's Jemima Houghton. Her brother is a bodyguard to Hailey Stevens, but the arsonist appeared to be estranged from her brother and have no current connection to the Loyal Brigade."

"Until you caught her," Hamish said.

"Precisely," Ruth said. "She started yelling about dragons after we cuffed her. But before then, rather than attack us, she tried to slit her wrists, or acted like she was about to."

"You're not sure if she's a believer or not?" Hamish asked.

"Exactly. She worked as a cleaner at the university, and Commissioner Weaver thinks she might have been slipping mail or telegrams into their collection box. That was a hunch she was looking into when our train left. With the railway line blocked, I don't know what she found. When Houghton was arrested, she claimed to be acting under orders of the archangel, while Stevens has been claiming that the fires were the work of the devil."

"That'll make for an interesting discussion in court," Hamish said. "You say she tried to kill herself?"

"She made a move to cut her wrist," Ruth said. "But Isaac and I were both only a few metres away. There's no way she'd actually have died, but it made for a dramatic arrest. Whether she's a believer or not, Weaver will know by now, but we've got to wait for the telegraph to be repaired. Sergeant Riley thinks Stevens is worried his former gunrunning clients would prefer he and Hailey were dead. He might hope he'll be found not guilty at trial, but he knows he'll boost his believer-base. He needs the Loyal Brigade to think it can only be led by him or his niece, and he needs his former clients to think the brigade is still a useful force both outside prison and inside. We've already had some evidence thrown out, so we need to find how he and his niece are communicating."

"What if they're not?" Hamish said. "What if the targets were picked before Stevens was arrested?"

"Religion Row certainly was," Ruth said. "St Michael's was closed two months ago, and will need to be torn down before it can be rebuilt. Plus, both uncle and niece mentioned Archangel Michael in the warnings they've given. That can't be a coincidence even if it is a theological fudge. But the other four attacks were on empty buildings that were occupied only a couple of days before. Maybe the locations were picked in advance, and they were just waiting on a date when a building on that street was empty. Stevens tells us a street name, not a specific building. Hailey gives us a vague riddle. But if the arsonist picks the target, Stevens is still being sent the date of the attack. It could be by letter or telegram sent from the university, but to whom? How is it getting from the post office to Stevens in his cell? The obvious answer is surely a guard."

"That's what I first thought," Hamish said. "The younger warders were sent south with the frailer prisoners. The remaining staff are all over fifty, and have been working aboard for a decade. Some have families in town who might have been threatened, but Inspector Voss interviewed them all, staff and families, and doesn't think it likely."

"Could they have been bribed?" Ruth asked.

"That was my next thought, but no guards reported even being approached about a bribe. Unless the briber got lucky with the first warder they approached, it's unlikely. Besides, if you're sending someone up here to bribe guards, why not also have them pass the messages along?"

"That assumes they had already figured out a way of getting a message to someone aboard," Ruth said. "In fact, seeing as they didn't know Stevens was coming here, they must have had a method of communication that worked for any jail. Commissioner Weaver wants me to tell Stevens that he's going to be moved. She was going to telegraph tomorrow with more details after she'd spoken again with the arsonist. The idea is to force them to tip their hand, and entrap both uncle and niece. Regardless of who picks the targets in Twynham, the messages are probably being sent by post or telegraph, and are probably limited to the street name and the date. He was sent here on the 2nd January. While he asked for protective custody, he couldn't guarantee to which jail he'd be sent, so his agent almost certainly arrived here after Stevens did."

"That doesn't narrow it down," Hamish said. "About ten thousand people are resident in Thurso, Scrabster, and Castleton, with about the same again within ten miles, and a similar number up on Orkney. But there's also a roaming pack of casual workers who spend the brighter months working the crofts or aboard the fishing fleets. Some head south for the winter, and some volunteered for the army. The rest can always find winter-work at the shipyard, the cannery, the rope factory, or at one of the wool mills on the islands. As for newcomers, about six hundred people are waiting to board the next transatlantic ship, plus there are about a hundred out-of-town shore crew and a few merchants looking to sell or buy from the sailors."

"So the suspect pool is too large to solve this case by interviewing people," Ruth said. "Are many people sending and receiving telegrams?"

"There's always a queue at the telegraph office," Hamish said. "British money won't buy much in Maine. None of the incoming telegrams are obviously suspicious, but that just means the messages are being sent in code, or they're coming by post. No one checks the mail, and there's a train usually every day, either freight or passenger, though not always from Twynham. If it were me, I'd telegraph the message to a station further south, and have another agent post a letter here."

"So we can't narrow it down that way, either," Ruth said. "What about how the message is getting to Stevens?" She leaned forward to look at the spot-lit ship. "It's not that far from the quayside. I think you could shout a message across."

"Not unless you had mighty powerful lungs," Hamish said. "The ferry will dock at the northern quay, along the seawall. Until it arrives, the quay is sealed. The next pier is where the prison hulk is secured, and that pier has been sealed, too. People can come as far as the fishing quay, just beyond the shipyard, and they do. Walking the coast, when the weather allows, is another popular pastime for the cruise ship passengers. There's always a bit of a crowd, and there are the sentries, of course. If you did try shouting, someone would hear. Assuming anyone could hear anything over the wind and waves."

"What about lights at night?" Ruth asked.

"Stevens's cabin is on the far side of the ship," Hamish said. "He has one porthole, and we keep a camera facing it. We've another camera on deck, facing towards his view. I've spotted nothing, but I've kept the recordings. Do you see the sentry towers? There's always someone on duty up there."

"I'm running low on ideas," Ruth said. "Anna said he doesn't get any visitors, is that right?"

"Not even a lawyer, since he's defending himself," Hamish said. "He does see the vicar, but Tam's been a preacher here almost since the Blackout."

"I thought you said he was a sailor who was now your cook," Ruth said.

"He was a sailor, but after the Blackout, he became a pastor. He's playing waiter to us because he's on the short list of people Nan and Inspector Voss trust to know what I'm really doing up here."

"Oh. Good, I think. But I feel like I should ask whether we can trust Inspector Voss."

"He helped me dig my ma's grave," Hamish said.

That seemed to be answer enough.

Ruth closed the shutter. "Turn the light on. Thanks." The dim new-made bulb was momentarily brighter than noon, but her eyes slowly adjusted as the ancient laptop warmed up. "Where did all this technology come from?" she asked.

"Nan keeps a store of it," Hamish said. "Has done since the Blackout. We've got video of the outside of the ship, and photos of the cell, if you want to see?"

"I might as well go and see the real thing for myself," Ruth said. "What's his routine?"

"He's woken at six. Breakfast is brought to him at ten past. Seven is when he gets his shower. At eight o'clock, he has the option of private prayers with Tam. At ten, he's allowed on the deck for exercise. He uses the forward deck, never the rear, and he exercises alone. Whether it's snow or shine, he always takes his hour. At eleven, he's taken back inside. Midday is a meal. The rest of the day, he's inside his cell."

"What about the other prisoners? Are any of them allowed ashore?"

"No. They're held in even stricter conditions than him. As a group, they're not the kind of people you'd invite to a funeral. We've had six visits from two visitors since Stevens was brought here. Both are solicitors from a local firm that acts as representatives to the convicts."

"Then I'm at a loss," Ruth said. "Why don't we hunt down that breakfast we were promised, then I'll meet Stevens for myself."

Chapter 16 - Floating Purgatory
The Prison Hulk, Scrabster

Breakfast was artificially spiced porridge served with dried strawberries from Nana MacKay's own indoor farm. The portions were vast, the tea endless, and took Ruth from starving to satisfied to soporific. The noise in the inn kept her awake, but the only news being discussed was of the down-track land-slip.

Regretfully leaving the inn's warm cocoon, she made her way to the harbour. The new day had brought clear skies, but there was little warmth in the sun, and the rising winds quickly stripped her flesh of any residual indoor heat.

The guard at the harbour gate hadn't been expecting her, meaning she had a ten-minute wait on the sub-zero quay as a swing-bridge was extended from the pier. There was another, though shorter, delay as the drawbridge-gantry was then lowered from the ship. Though the guards ashore were armed with rifles, the man waiting at the bridge's far end wasn't.

"Governor Byrd," he said, after crossing to the shore. His words were whipped away by the rising wind and washed over the side by a squall of salt-water rain. He motioned her into the small sentry box. "Your I.D., please," he said as he squinted at her face.

After she handed it over, he peered at it, so she peered at him.

He was *old*, not just older, and probably a lot older than this ship. His white hair had grown wispy and thin. His cheeks and chin had grown too craggy for a wet-shave, particularly aboard a ship, so he'd grown a beard, trimmed to an uneven inch in length. He was only five-six, and made to seem smaller by his rounded shoulders. Around his neck was a pair of half-moon glasses, which he held up rather than put on, using them as a magnifying glass to read her warrant card. His uniform was blue, like hers, though he had no tie, no belt, and he wore pull-on boots rather than shoes with laces.

"We had word you were coming from the city," he said. "We didn't hear why."

"I'm to give Stevens twenty-four hours to co-operate or we'll move him somewhere worse," she said.

He looked at her face, her I.D., and then at her again. "You came all the way from Twynham to tell him that?"

"I was supposed to be on holiday," Ruth said. "But someone had to accompany the paintings north, so the commissioner asked me to pass on this message."

"My prisoners are the worst people on this planet," the governor said, with a hint of rebuke. "For them, lying is a reflex, so I know well how to spot a falsehood."

"I was asked to check for myself that he's not passing messages," Ruth said.

"He's not. Whatever scam is afoot, it was put in play before his arrest," the governor said. "Now the railway is blocked, you won't be moving him anywhere for at least a week, but I won't stop you completing your duty. I can promise you that there is no jail in the country more inhospitable than this, so be aware you are threatening him with a reward. Before you come aboard, you'll have to empty your pockets. Obviously, your weapons will have to remain here, along with any pens, pencils, your badge, anything which could be used to pick a lock, or be used as a weapon. Your belt. Your coat, because the buttons are metal. Your shoes… no, I think we can risk those for a short visit."

"Are you worried the prisoners will harm themselves, or each other, or the guards?" she asked, as she took off her coat.

"Yes to all of them," he said. "Our prisoners are the worst, the *very* worst. Eight received their sentences before the Blackout. Life without parole. Had they committed their crimes afterward, it would have been death without a doubt. The others bargained their way out of the noose by presenting evidence to the state. Whatever they expected life in prison to be, none knew it would be like this or they would have presented their neck to the hangman instead. They are desperate. They are angry. They are unrepentant. And your hairpins, please. Thank you. You want to speak to Stevens, what else?"

"I'd also like to see any room he has access to."

"That's the shower, the deck, and the chapel," Byrd said. "Inspector Voss has searched them twice, but I search them every day." He checked his watch. "We'll begin with the shower. You will have five minutes. Then we will go to the chapel for ten minutes, and then the deck for eight minutes. You will then speak with Mr Stevens for ten minutes in his cell. It we follow this schedule, you won't see any other prisoners. More importantly, they will not see you, and their routines will not be disrupted. Routine is our best way of preventing trouble."

"They're all men, aren't they?" she asked.

"They are. As are the guards. This was not a deliberate policy, but evolved by accident. Now, it would be too disruptive to change. Far too disruptive." He checked his watch. "Follow me."

On leaving the small sentry post, once again she was buffeted by the winds, but the relief on returning inside was very short-lived, as she stepped into a living tomb that stank of rust and bleach. The lights were encased in metal grills, while the walls were covered in metal panels on which the paint was peeling except in places where it had bubbled. A guard, waiting by the door, locked it behind them. Inside, she followed the governor down corridors that seemed to get narrower at each bulkhead. Each door was locked. Some were guarded, but at others, the governor used his own key.

The shower had no cubicles, and no privacy. There was one showerhead on the bulkhead furthest from the door, and one metal rail on which to hang clothes or a towel.

"Do they come here dressed?" she asked.

"No. Just in a towel," the governor said.

"In this weather?"

"You get used to it," Byrd said. "But it's a hot shower. The hot water pipes run underneath the floor and keep the room warmer than their cells."

"And they come here one at a time?" Ruth asked.

"The schedule is on the door," the governor said.

"There are only ten names on the list," Ruth said, running a finger down the paper list which had been taped, rather than pinned, to the door.

"We have three shower rooms, one on each deck. This is the shower to which Stevens is allocated."

"According to this, there's a twenty-minute gap between showering," Ruth said.

"The showers are searched, cleaned, and dried between inmates. But that work is done by my warders. We all take a turn."

"I think I've seen enough," Ruth said.

"We have to wait one more minute," the governor said after checking his watch.

Ruth used it to look around again, but there was nowhere for a message to be hidden where a guard wouldn't see it.

"How many guards are with him when he showers?" she asked.

"One guard brings them from their cell, but whoever is on shower cleaning duty is stationed by the door. Now we'll go to the chapel."

The chapel was simply another cabin, but with four metal chairs bolted to the floor and facing a metal table.

"Are all the prisoners Christian?" Ruth asked, more as a way of making conversation than out of investigatory need.

"They all claim a religion," the governor said. "By law, this entitles them to regular contact with their spiritual advisor. Since the vicar is the only man who'll visit the ship, they all claim membership of the Kirk."

"Are those ten minutes alone, because you said this was a communal space and there are four chairs in here."

"Prior to the arrival of Stevens, only two prisoners were in isolation. We allowed four prisoners to attend services together, once a week. Following the concerns that Stevens was communicating with the outside world, we implemented a stricter regime. Now, everyone gets a one-to-one session once a week. Stevens, because he is on remand, is offered more regular contact with a spiritual advisor."

Ruth checked beneath the chairs, but was at a loss for where else to look, or what she was looking for.

"It's time," the governor said. "I'll show you the deck."

The ship was a maze. To escape it took them through another five doors. Only the door outside was guarded, and for that door, the governor didn't have the key.

The small platform set aside for exercise was surrounded by two cages. Both were made of close-linked wire, but with a half-metre gap between the inner and the outer. The cages made up five sides of a cube, with the deck making the sixth. The wire was thick and sturdy, but a pair of bolt cutters could create a door in minutes. However, during that time, the prisoner would be under view from the armed guards in the shore-side watchtowers.

"You said this was a communal space," Ruth said. "How many prisoners come up here at a time?"

"Just one, now," the governor said. "Prisoners receive one hour of fresh air or exercise a day. Exercise can be taken on this deck, or the rear deck, or in the gym below. Those not in isolation would be allowed to exercise with one another. We've a table tennis table and a basketball hoop down in the hold. Since Stevens arrived, exercise has become a solitary affair. Most inmates take theirs inside. Stevens insists on coming here, every day, regardless of the weather."

"I can see the shore," Ruth said. "And people. A lot of people."

"Passengers for America," Byrd said. "Gawpers. The ship is a salutary lesson, or so the politicians tell me."

"But an exercising inmate would be in full view of the outside world."

"With a prison ship, it's inevitable," Byrd said.

"Stevens was sent here because we're worried one of his arms-buying customers might try to assassinate him," Ruth said. "I can see a dozen places a sniper might lurk."

"I've four serial killers below who bereaved many parents, spouses, and children, any of whom might have come looking for revenge these past twenty years," Byrd said. "Three did, but we picked them up in town."

"You mean I should accept you know what you're doing?" Ruth asked.

"No, I mean any report you file should include that assassination is a very real possibility. I have said as much, time and time again, and so has Inspector Voss. This hulk must be shut down. It's a waste of resources and valuable harbour space, and adds a dark pall to the entire coast. But I think there are some down south who hope a vigilante might rid them of a convict they can't execute and can never release. As for an assassination attempt on Stevens, he is the one who insists on taking his exercise. I understand he has a niece, whom he raised, and who is considered a co-conspirator."

"Considered, yes, but we're having difficulty proving it."

"Perhaps he hopes a bullet that ends his life will free her from prosecution," Byrd said. "But you are correct, a sniper could shoot anyone on this deck. But it would be a sniper, not simply a shooter. A professional for whom escape from Thurso would be next to impossible. Why take the risk when they know the prisoner will have to be transported back to Twynham for trial? If there is to be an assassination, it will be there and then, not here and now."

"But you have had escapes?" she asked.

"We've had attempts," he said. "Five years ago, a prisoner took a warder hostage, and made it here, to the deck. This was before we added a roof to the cage. They managed to climb up, and then jumped into the sea. He froze to death in seconds. Escape is not impossible, but survival in these waters is improbable."

Stevens's cell was a cabin from which the door, and most of the bulkhead wall, had been replaced with a barred gate through which any guard could easily watch. His chair was a low metal shelf. His table was a slightly higher metal shelf, at which, in crayon, he wrote.

"Another tormentor, is it?" Stevens asked without looking up.

"I'm with the police," Ruth said.

"And will *you* heed my warnings?" he asked, still writing. "Or will vanity block your ears as it has blocked so many?"

"What warnings?" she asked as she took in the rest of the cell. He had a bunk in the corner, and a toilet next to it. The toilet had neither seat nor lid, which must be interesting during a storm. There was no sink. There was, on the floor, a small wicker basket containing a towel, a bar of soap, a toothbrush, and a small tin of toothpaste. In a basket next to that were four books: a Bible, Malory's *Morte D'Arthur*, *Jane Eyre*, and *Great Expectations*.

"I have warned you of five attacks," Stevens said. "Thanks to prayer, and the intercession of the archangel, the fifth attack failed. This is not victory, only a pause in the war. Heed the words of Daniel. Four monarchies have failed, but the fifth won't prevail without belief. It is twenty years since tribulation began. The final battle is coming. The skirmishes in Europe are only the beginning. The signs are there, and yet you ignore them. Will you ignore my warnings, too?"

"I'm just a messenger," Ruth said. "You have twenty-four hours to co-operate. If you do, we'll move you somewhere nice. If you don't, we'll move you somewhere worse. Either way, you *are* being moved."

"A messenger has true power," Stevens said. "For are words not the ultimate weapon? Is *The Word* not the most ultimate? It matters not where I am, for this is not where the battle will be waged. War has come to your streets. I can help, if only you will accept this war is not being fought with guns and bullets, but with lightning from above against fire from below."

He wanted an argument. He wanted a debate. She wanted to ask how something could be the *most* ultimate. Instead, she picked her words with care. *Jane Eyre* had been a book-club book last year. *Great Expectations* was the newspaper's current novel of the month. Up and down the country, everyone was reading it. Even, it seemed, this prisoner. Having noticed the book, it was no surprise to spot the sheets of newsprint on the desk, under the papers on which he was scribbling.

"Did you read about the arson attacks in the newspaper?" she asked.

"All I read in the paper was the story of a convict unjustly sentenced by an unjust court," he said. "The signs are there, if only you were not blinded by sin. The white dragon will rise and cleanse this island anew."

"Governor, I would like you to confiscate that newspaper, please," Ruth said.

"Have it," Stevens said, thrusting it through the bars.

The governor took the paper. "Sit down, Stevens, you know the rules."

"Rules won't save you, Governor. Only the true word can bring salvation."

Ruth waited until the governor had led her back to the entrance before taking the two sheets of folded newspaper from him.

"It's just the book-club insert from five days ago," she said. "Do all prisoners get a copy of this?"

"And the book of the month," the governor said. "The newspaper discussion is the most conversation any of them get. Perhaps because this month's book begins with a convict escaping a prison hulk, they are more avidly enthusiastic than they were with *Jane Eyre*."

"There was a fifth attack, the night before last," Ruth said. "We stopped it, but he seemed to know. Has he had any visitors? Any contact at all?"

"There's been nothing to disrupt his routine," the governor said.

"But he does get the newspaper?" Ruth asked.

"Only the inserts," the governor said. "And always a day or two late."

"Does he get any letters?" Ruth asked.

"None except from the prosecution service, and the last was a week ago."

"What about the books? Where did he get his copy of *Great Expectations* from?"

"Me," the governor said. "But I got them from Commissioner Weaver. She sent a box of forty up, and I gave them out at random. You can't suspect her, can you?"

"No, I suppose not," Ruth said.

Chapter 17 - People Watching People
The Old Weather Station, Scrabster

After leaving the ship, and retrieving her possessions, Ruth returned to Hamish's office where she found the adjunct copper watching the ship.

"Perfect timing," Hamish said. "Stevens is on deck. Want to watch?"

"I want a shower," Ruth said, though she crossed to the window. "Actually, no. After seeing their shower block, I want a bath. Evil oozes out of the walls there. That place should be shut down."

"They were planning to close it before the war began," Hamish said. "We really need the quay-space. And now the American ships are arriving here, the call is getting louder. Nan thinks it'll be closed later this year, but she said the same thing before I went south. Did you meet Stevens?"

"I did, and he seemed to know that the attack on Religion Row failed," Ruth said. She stepped in front of the telescope, which she then aimed at the deck. "He didn't say anything specific, just that, thanks to his prayers and intercession from the archangel, the fifth attack failed. There's nothing there we can prove wasn't gossip that travelled up with the train. Everything else he said was rehearsed gibberish."

"He could have overheard the news about the fifth attack," Hamish said. "The newspaper wires their headlines to the telegraph office, and they pin them to a public board outside. All the warders will have had a chance to read the news. I'd say Stevens overhearing talkative warders is more likely than anyone passing him a message."

Ruth adjusted the telescope. "He's just standing there. He's obviously freezing, but he's standing there watching… what? Oh, he's watching the people watching him."

"They're all ferry passengers getting a bit of exercise of their own," Hamish said.

Ruth scanned the people ashore. No one was doing anything so obvious as holding a banner or light. A few did stop to look at the ship, but most, on nearing the gate, simply turned around.

"Why did you bring the newspaper back?" Hamish asked.

Ruth stepped back from the telescope, took the insert from her pocket, and dropped it on the table. "It's just the book-club pages. This came from his cell. Every prisoner gets a copy of the book, and this month's novel is *Great Expectations*. You know that begins with a convict escaping from a prison hulk? Now I'm wondering if that's his plan. Could he be behind the avalanche that's cut us off from the south?"

"How would that help him escape?" Hamish asked. He unfolded, and then separated, the two sheets of newsprint. He held one up to the light, then the other. "I can't see any marks, or any notes. And these pages are five days old."

"Stevens handed it over so willingly, I doubt it's what we're looking for," Ruth said. "Though it does make me think he handed it over to distract us from something else."

"I've got photographs of his cell from three days ago, and from three days before that here," Hamish said.

"I'll look later," Ruth said, and returned to the telescope. "He's still just standing there. That coat can't be very warm, and it's certainly not long. His hat doesn't cover his ears, and his shoes are more like slippers. How cold is the sea?"

"About five degrees Celsius," Hamish said.

"How long could you survive in the water?"

"Me, with my foot? Not as long as you. A sailor could manage half an hour. Perhaps a bit longer, but they'd need to be fished out because their hands would be useless by then."

"From what I saw, escape isn't impossible," Ruth said. "Aboard the ship, they're governed by routine. But because that routine has been in place for so long, complacency has set in. The governor made me take off my belt, and take out my hairpins, but he kept his metal-rimmed glasses. I think it would be easy to take a guard hostage, and if you didn't mind murder, it would be easy enough to get onto the deck."

"Where you'd be shot by the snipers in the towers," Hamish said.

"Right, but only if the snipers were still there," Ruth said. "Stevens can call on a small army. Those are the sort of numbers you'd need to create an avalanche. So, why not have some shooters take out the sentries, and have another team steal a fishing boat? The rescuers could come along side, climb to the deck, and cut the wire cage. Stevens, having murdered his way to the deck, could get aboard the boat and sail off into the sunset."

"Most of the fishing boats use sail," Hamish said. "Nan's rigged a few boats to run on electric batteries, but she knows precisely how valuable those are. Someone is always on guard, and there are always more guards at the gate. You'd have a pitched battle to capture a fishing boat. How big an army could Stevens muster?"

"Good question," Ruth said. "Anna seemed to think they'd caught or identified most of the followers, but clearly we haven't got all of them. I suppose he might have ten. Maybe even fifteen. It would be a great risk to them all just to end up aboard a sailing boat in the very frozen north. I asked the governor about the assassination risk. He said it was unlikely because the sniper would find it hard to escape. If there were to be an assassination, it would be easier in Twynham. I suppose the same goes for an escape."

"Maybe that's why Stevens is so desperate for a trial," Hamish said. "His real plan is to escape from the courthouse, and all of this is simply cover."

"Could be," Ruth said. "He raised his niece, so it's unlikely he'd run if it left her in danger of being murdered by an old client. Unlikely, but not impossible." She yawned. "Excuse me. Oh, it's been a long day."

"Go get some sleep. There's a room waiting for you in the inn."

Chapter 18 - The Least Improbable Possibility
The Library, Thurso

Ruth woke as the setting sun sent a last spear of light directly into her closed eyes, erasing the memories of blood swimming across her brain. The images visited her irregularly, and always unwanted, leaving snapshots of corpses and screams swirling across her consciousness. As bad as the dreams were, waking from them was worse. She couldn't help but try to place the fragmented reminders of her very worst days. Which were of Hamish being shot? Which were of Anna? Which had come from that so very long-ago time before Maggie had rescued her?

Groggy and grumbling, she got up and angrily pulled the curtains closed before opening them to take a last look at twilight dancing across the snow-dusted fields. She closed the curtain again, changed, and spent a bleary few minutes examining the ancient prints of Apollo spacecraft on the wall until the bathroom beckoned.

Downstairs, in the fire-lit bar, she found Isaac tucking into a slab of fried fish.

"Are you still eating lunch?" she asked, taking the chair opposite.

"Just a light snack," he said. "Eat what you can, when you can, and as much as you can. I learned that a long time ago."

She took his mug and took a sip. It was coffee, the artificial kind, and an unflavoured variety.

"Help yourself," he said.

"Thanks," she said. She waved to the waiter behind the bar, and got an imperceptible nod in return. Hoping that was acknowledgement of her order, rather than aloof civility, she turned back to her confiscated coffee. "Did you meet up with your friend?"

"I did," Isaac said. "All is well as can be hoped for."

"I'd like to meet him," Ruth said. "But after the investigation is over."

"It sounds as if you've stumbled across a lead," Isaac said.

"Possibly," Ruth said. "I saw Stevens this morning. He knew the fifth attack had failed. Thank you," she added as a tray was placed on the table: fresh fish, lightly fried, served with parsnip chips, and a pot of tea.

"And?" Isaac asked as Ruth began to eat. "What did Stevens say?"

"Nothing coherent," Ruth said, the words appropriately muffled by a mouthful of batter. "Everything he said sounded rehearsed. But in his cell, he has a little basket containing all his shower things. You could hollow out the soap, slip in a message, and then use hot water to melt soap back over the hole."

"Would this be done by a guard, or another convict?" Isaac asked.

"Exactly," Ruth mumbled around a forkful of salmon. "It could be hidden in the soap, or sewn into his clothes, or the sheets. A message could be concealed in his meals, or tapped out in Morse against the pipes. Even if the message goes to a different prisoner first, which I seriously doubt, it still has to get onto the ship. Other than the warders, only the vicar has semi-regular access to the ship, and the way Hamish described it, he's an institution here in Thurso."

"In my experience, very few people are incorruptible," Isaac said.

"Sure, yes, it's not impossible," Ruth said. "But if you've corrupted a guard, why bother hiding the message in soap, or anywhere else? Why not have them tell Stevens in person?"

"Spoken aloud would leave less of a trail than anything written down," Isaac said.

"Exactly, and if you've persuaded or paid a warder to tell Stevens a street name, why not have them provide a few more details? What's that line from Sherlock Holmes? When you eliminate the impossible, whatever's left, however improbable, must be the truth."

"While I agree in theory, what seems impossible to one person is merely difficult to another," Isaac said. "In this case, very little is truly impossible, but we do have an overflowing basket of improbables."

She raised a finger, chewed, and swallowed. "So we need the least improbable possibility. Stevens was sent here on the 2nd. The first attack was on the 6th. That's not much time to identify a susceptible guard. It's not impossible, but way too improbable. But we do know Stevens made plans in case he was caught. He didn't know when that'd be, or that he'd be sent here, so he had to keep his scheme simple and easily adaptable to different jails. The more people he involves, the more people there are who might confess in exchange for immunity. I think his inner circle is limited to the arsonist and her brother in Twynham, and an agent here, and no one else, not even a telegraph operator."

"You think they're using post?"

"I'm sure Stevens wants us to think that," Ruth said. "He wants us reading letters and telegrams and re-interviewing guards, all of which wastes our time and will be revealed during the trial, making us look like villains, which better helps him come across as a saviour."

"You've got an idea, don't you?" Isaac said.

"The newspaper," Ruth said. "The convicts each get a copy of the book of the month, and the centre-page pull-out with the discussions about Dickens and the history of that period. The books were shipped here by Commissioner Weaver, but absolutely anyone can write for the newspaper. Particularly articles like that."

"Hold that thought," Isaac said. He got up and walked over to the bar. He returned a few minutes later with the insert from a copy of the paper that had arrived on the train with them. "A secret message won't be hidden in the articles," he said. "Academics are as corruptible as journalists, but you're right; the more conspirators, the more likely the plot will fail. So why bother recruiting an academic when you can just take out an advertisement?"

"Can anyone take out an advert?" she asked.

"It says so here at the bottom," Isaac said. "Send in the text, and payment, and they'll print the ad, or you can make use of their expert but affordable in-house design team."

"That sounds like a scam," Ruth said.

"It always was," Isaac said, running his finger down the page. "Twelve ads on this page, and..." He turned the page. "Ten here. Sixteen on the next, all quite small."

"Do they have any older editions behind the bar?"

"No, we'd find the ashes of those in the fire. Or we can try the library."

"After I've finished my lunch. Or tea. Or breakfast. Or whatever this meal is called," Ruth said.

Outside, grey shadows drifted across the sky as the sharp wind hauled the bad weather southward. Unlike in the dark hours of early morning, in this gloomy afternoon, Scrabster thrummed with activity. By their haste as much as their clothing, she could tell the ferry passengers from the locals. Those resident here all year round were uniformly dressed in well-mended wax-wool and well-worn all-weather boots. They hurried purposefully to finish their day's work before the worst of the night's deep freeze settled in. The ferry passengers were bundled up against the wind, many surely wearing all they had brought with them. Some strode and some strolled, and a little unsteadily, some of those passengers waddled back from the inn towards their lodgings.

Using her badge as her fare, they caught a bicycle-powered masonry-cart repurposed as a pub-trip taxi back to Thurso where more passengers milled about, aimlessly filling the gap between sunset and dinnertime. Outside the post office, and by the notice board where public telegrams were displayed, a woman in a pink scarf and pinker coat lingered. But the sign on the door said the railway and telegraph lines were still down. The teenage boys she'd seen on the train stared wistfully into a small grocery shop named *Nickel and Dime*. The name was surely new, and there to entice American visitors, but how many Americans would linger in this town longer than it took for their train to arrive?

Outside the church, she saw the vicar-husband who'd been a passenger on the train from Twynham welcoming passengers for prayers and a meal. The passengers were on a one-way trip to America and would have exchanged most of their cash after they sold their homes, fixtures and furniture included. They'd need that money to set up a new life overseas, not to fritter away while they waited for the delayed ferry. She thought of Quinn's bodyguard and his wallet full of U.S. currency, and wondered whether he'd be too proud to take advantage of a free meal.

A sign outside the library said it was closed except for the children's section.

"That explains why there are so many people wandering about," Ruth said. "No reading room, no gallery, no library to linger in." She pushed open the storm door, and then the inner.

"If you've no bairns, there'll be no browsing," Dr Frobisher said from behind the returns desk. "You can take a book from that selection by the door. Fifty pence deposit, mind, and I've no change."

"I've got a badge," Ruth said.

"That's not the same as currency," Dr Frobisher said, finally looking up, though only for a second. "Do you have a finger?"

"Ten of them," Ruth said. "Depending on how you count thumbs."

"It's a finger I want," Frobisher said. "Come place it here, on the spine. Hold it while I work the scalpel."

On the desk behind the raised counter, the librarian was conducting life-extending surgery on an ancient leather-bound tome.

"Now keep that finger there until the glue sets," Frobisher said.

"How long will that be?" Ruth asked. "Because we're on a case."

"Has someone finally begun an investigation into who stole the laird's sense of humour?" Frobisher asked.

"It's a case in Twynham," Ruth said. "I came up here as escort for the paintings, but all the beautiful scenery, the fresh air, it's given me a flash of inspiration."

"And inspiration brought you in here, did it?" the librarian asked, her words dripping with suspicion.

"I wanted to look at the book-club discussions in the newspapers for the last month," Ruth said.

"Oh," Frobisher said. "Ah, well, I might allow that. There, I think he'll hold. The reading room is closed. We're using it for a gallery space until we can build something more permanent, but that won't be until spring. When I said yes to a new cultural centre, I didn't think you'd be stealing half the library to build it."

"It's not me," Ruth said. "But I did find the pictures in Dover, hidden in a secret room whose entrance was concealed behind hay-bales."

"Go on," Frobisher said, her interest piqued by this previously unheard story.

"This was in a cellar beneath an old Victorian barracks," Ruth said. "Who keeps hay in a damp cellar? But do you know what really gave it away?"

"That hay is expensive?" the librarian asked, leaning forward in curious anticipation.

"Partly, yes," Ruth said. "But the art thief had hired a guy with a bicycle cart to move boxes. If he had a horse to feed that hay, why hire a bicycle cart?"

"Aye, very good," the librarian said. "I might ask for some more details if you've the time. A spot of modern history always helps illuminate old art. You'll find the newspapers next to the satires, through those doors there."

The main library had become a store for tables, chairs, and reference books from upstairs.

"I feel like I should whisper," Isaac said, righting a pair of rickety pine chairs. "Where do we begin?"

"How about you start with the day he was sent up here, and I'll start with the most recent copy."

"Deal," Isaac said. He grabbed a paper, sat, and then put his feet up on the table. "A-ha!" he added, the moment he opened the paper to the centre section.

"Already?" Ruth asked.

"The secret cure for male-pattern baldness can be mine for only one pound and a large self-addressed envelope," Isaac said. "If I'd only known that five years ago, I could have saved a fortune in hats."

"The insert he had in his cell was five days old," Ruth said. "But the governor said they get the book-club section one or two days late. I suppose because they have to freight them up from Twynham by train. We're pretty confident Stevens didn't need to be told the last attack was on Religion Row, but he would need to be told when it was taking place. The fourth attack was at Winton Way on the twentieth, except he told us it was Winton Road. It's possible the streets were picked in advance, but he'd still need to know the dates."

"So we're looking for a message that, when decoded, translates as twenty and Winton?" Isaac asked.

"Perhaps something about property for rent," Ruth said, opening the paper. "Or is that too obvious? Wow, I never noticed how many ads there were. A saddle-makers, Satz Tea, detergent, pet food, pet grooming, pet hire. Hang on. This might be something. P&O carpets are offering twenty percent off this January."

"So?" Isaac asked.

"Twenty and January," Ruth said. "The fourth attack was on the 20th January. And who gets new carpets in January? Why not wait until March, when the new carpet won't get covered in winter sludge?"

"Which might be why they're offering the discount," Isaac said. "Wasn't the third attack on the sixteenth? I don't recall ever having seen anyone offer a sixteen percent discount on anything. I'll check, and as soon as the telegraph is up, we can ask Anna to confirm whether that firm really is running a sale."

"Do you think Stevens could be behind the landslip?" Ruth asked.

"Not if his scheme involves staying in contact with Twynham," Isaac said. "Besides, if he were, he'd have claimed it as an act of God. Don't fall into the mistake of crediting this man with more intelligence, guile, or cunning than he actually has. Yes, so far he has arranged these attacks through methods unknown, but don't also forget he was caught."

Half an hour later, with him working forwards and she working backwards, they met in the middle.

"Nothing," she said, dropping the paper in frustration. "Nothing obvious, anyway."

"Let me apologise," Isaac said. "This was my idea, and I overlooked the obvious flaw."

"That if you place an ad, you don't know where in the paper it will be placed?" Ruth asked.

"It seems like I have to apologise again," Isaac said. "I'd overlooked that, too, but I was thinking that they had no guarantee he'd be allowed access to any part of the newspaper at all. He should be, because he's on remand, and he should be getting all of the paper, but he's only being given the insert. No, the newspaper is just too unreliable a method of delivery."

"How would you do it?" Ruth asked.

"Not like this," Isaac said. "For a start, I'd leak the first warning to the press. Get the public to pressure the politicians into pushing for a speedier resolution to the arson. The second thing would be to target farmland, because fire is unpredictable, and he's been very lucky not to have killed anyone. I'd strike every night, with pre-arranged targets, giving vague warnings for each. Then the warnings would become more specific, and they'd lead the police to the lair of one of my enemies. Or, in his case, a customer who didn't pay the bills. I'd ensure they were framed for the arson attacks. That would send a message to any other clients who were angling to come after him, and would thoroughly confuse any case against him. After all, he only needs a mistrial."

"But he wants more supporters," Ruth said. "Real believers, too, not just paid help. I wish the telegraph was up so I could find out what the arsonist said to Weaver. Anyway, your scheme doesn't explain how the messages are getting to Stevens."

"I need some thinking time," Isaac said. "And you know what helps me think? Art. Why don't we see if Dr Frobisher will let us take a look at the paintings?"

No was the answer.

"I've not even seen them myself," Frobisher said. "The carpenters are still setting up the exhibition space, except for when Erin Quinn comes to yell at them."

"Is she here?" Ruth asked.

"Can you hear a banshee wailing? No? Then she's out," Frobisher said. "Apparently some posters she brought up from Twynham got lost. Now she's stomping around like an angry stork, leaving me to fix her mess. But if it's art you want to see, have a look in the poetry room."

"You have a whole room set aside for poetry?" Ruth asked.

"Only one, sadly," Dr Frobisher said. "Since you're with the police, you can take a look, but don't you dare disturb the artists!"

"Now I am intrigued," Isaac said.

The door was at the back of the lobby, and near the stairs. On the door was a sign *Caution, Artists at Work*. It was, of course, hand-painted.

Inside, fourteen painters laboured two to a table. None was older than fourteen. Ruth recognised seven of the young artists as having been on the train, and guessed the other seven were ferry-passengers, too, or they would be in school. In front of each was a book, open to a print of one of the rescued pieces of art, but there were other books showing works by Warhol, Van Gogh, Kahlo, and Picasso, among others, but those were the only ones she could name. The lady vicar from the train, who seemed to be supervising, smiled and came over.

"Trouble?" she whispered, keeping a false smile on her face.

"Not a bit of it," Ruth whispered back. "I just came to see some art. It's really good."

"Isn't it?" the vicar said. "Our paints came from the shipyard, and do rather lend themselves to interpretative representation. Did you hear about the posters?"

"They got lost, didn't they?" Ruth asked.

"I heard they were dropped in a snow-pile," the vicar said. "Along with all of Ms Quinn's clothes. Sometimes we are sent a practical lesson in humility, a lesson Ms Quinn seems to be ignoring. Perhaps you'd like a closer look?"

Ruth could hardly say no, so walked from one table to the next, mumbling the best praise she could think of. She'd reached a thick dot interpretation of the *Skating Minister* when a distant door slammed shut.

Seemingly aware of what that sound meant, the children bowed their heads. The vicar's fixed smile grew broader as she walked to the door and leaned against it. "Ms Quinn," she mouthed as feet stomped up the stairs.

"I think we should be going," Ruth said. "It is very good work. I saw a few of the paintings when I found them in Dover, and every one of yours is just as good. I can't wait to see them when they're finished." With a last smile to the vicar, she and Isaac slipped outside.

"What did you make of that?" Ruth asked.

"Children like pop art because it's colourful," Isaac said. "They like Picasso because it's easy to understand."

"You really think so? But I meant about the posters. There was only twenty-four hours to make them, and whoever made them would have had to use old pictures in old books. I wonder if Ms Quinn didn't look at the posters until she arrived, and then saw they were terrible."

"And destroyed them on purpose?" Isaac asked. "Could be. I doubt you can arrest her for it. So, where next?"

"I need to have a word with Inspector Voss," Ruth said. "Then it's back to watching the ship. I can't think of anything else we can do."

"Since I won't get the level of hospitality I've come to expect from the police station in Dover, I shall leave you for now," Isaac said. "I've a different angle I want to investigate."

Chapter 19 - The Universal Similarities of Policing
The Police Station, Thurso

In her travels since leaving the police academy, Ruth had seen a little of Britain and just as much of abroad. She'd observed that climate influenced architecture as much as politics, economics, and geography, but some things were universal, and the layout of a police station was one. From the exasperated sergeant behind the duty desk, to the map of the European front on the wall, the more detailed map of the local area, and the bewildered victims, she could have been back home in Dover. The woman by the heater looked as if she was simply a victim of the weather who needed a few minutes somewhere warm. The man at the desk was dazedly filling in a missing property form.

"Should I write that I bought it in Crosby and Hamptons?" he asked.

"No, sir," the sergeant said. "Just the colour and size, any distinguishing features, what was inside the suitcase, and where you saw it last."

"The manufacturers are in Twynham, you see," the victim said.

"Just start with the description, sir," the sergeant said, and seemed relieved that Ruth gave him an excuse to tend to other business. "Constable Deering from Dover?"

"That's me," Ruth said. "Is Inspector Voss in?"

"Always except when he's out, but he's in his office at the moment. This way."

Ruth was escorted to Inspector Voss's office, where he was writing a report of his own.

"Constable Deering? Just a moment, and I'll be with you," he said. "Take a seat."

She did.

His was a neat office. Sergeant Kettering kept hers sparse, mostly because she kept her clutter at home. The tiny cabin used by the Serious Crimes Unit had been too cramped to spare space for mess. Inspector Voss, by contrast, was clearly a man for whom everything had a place, and it better remember to stay there.

"There," Voss said, putting his pen down. "How can I help you, Constable?"

"I just wanted to test a few ideas about Stevens," Ruth said. "But if you're busy, I can wait."

"The ferry should arrive within forty-eight hours," Voss said. "We've four passengers in custody. I had to put two of them in the break-room because those paintings are being stored in the cells. One lost his ticket gambling, then got into a fight with the local who won it. Their cases would have been heard before the ship sails anyway, but my officers don't like taking their breaks somewhere there's a suspect handcuffed to the radiator. Let me guess, you want to know whether Stevens has bribed a warder."

"I'm starting to think it's impossible," Ruth said.

"It's a thought you should finish with, too," Voss said. He pushed his chair out from the desk, stood, and walked over to a metal cabinet. With a key from his belt, he unlocked it. "These are the files on the staff, including the recent interviews," he said, opening a drawer. He tapped the drawer above. "The interviews with the families are in there. I was transferred here because of that ship. The convicts are notorious. Their names, and crimes, would be familiar to any adult before the Blackout. The concern in the capital was that one of the warders would snap and execute a prisoner. Every three months, I speak with each of them. Every six months, I speak with their families. I've found no indications of threat or coercion. A financial motive is unlikely as they are all on the grave-digger's pension scheme, and will become eligible for early receipt when the prison is shut down, which should be later this year."

"So it would have to be a lot of money?" Ruth asked.

Voss shook his head. "Those men deal with the vilest of the vile. One oversight, one forgotten pen or pin, and you've handed a serial killer a weapon. Those inmates know the only time they'll leave that ship is if it's to stand trial. They've nothing to lose, but could gain a change of scenery by killing a guard. In comparison, Stevens is a minnow, and even his worst associate is no fiercer than a lamb. I am confident none of the warders are involved."

"That's what I thought," Ruth said. "But perhaps they're passing messages on accidentally?"

"They're too experienced for that," Voss said, retaking his chair. "I'll allow it was a possibility prior to the first attack, but they were warned to be more cautious since then. You're no closer to an answer, then?"

"Not really. We've a few leads, but they'd all need to be chased down in Twynham."

"Ah. Well, there is one thing to be said for the telegraph being down, messages can't travel in either direction." He leaned back in his chair. "You were in France."

"Twice," Ruth said.

"My niece is with the Island Regiment."

"She's a conscript?"

"A volunteer," Voss said. "She'd taken an apprenticeship as a teacher. They said they needed five hundred for the regiment, so she volunteered so someone else didn't get conscripted. She's waiting on the order to go south."

"She's up here?"

"On Orkney," Voss said. "She does three days in the classroom, and four days training. They haven't even given her a rifle."

"They've run out," Ruth said. "Which is more reassuring than it sounds. I don't think the government were expecting such enthusiasm. Unofficially, conscription has paused. The enemy's broken. The expectation is that there'll be a few skirmishes in the spring, but that it's mostly going to be guard work as they push the railway line towards the Mediterranean. That's just rumour, of course, and who can predict the future, but in Dover, the EU and the admiralty are talking about rebuilding Calais, not re-fortifying it."

"Thank you," Voss said. "That's as reassuring as it could be."

Outside, wet snow fell, damp, sticky, and invasive. The cold burrowed through her coat, seeping into her skin. When she found herself at the train station, she took out her badge, and blagged a cab to take her back to the shipyard where she headed straight for Hamish's office.

She found him dozing in his chair, with the shutters closed, and the laptop open, showing a snow-flecked image of the lantern-lit shore. It wasn't her arrival that woke him, however, but Isaac's voice, coming from a small grey box.

"Can you see me?" Isaac asked.

Hamish started. Both feet swung from the footstool. When his injured foot hit the ground, he winced.

Ruth picked up the radio. "Isaac, where are you?"

"Press the green button," Hamish said.

Ruth found it, and did. "Isaac?"

"Ruth?"

"What are you doing out there?" Ruth asked.

"Freezing," Isaac said. "I'm by the window beneath the clock tower. Can you see me?"

Hamish leaned forward, and tapped at the laptop. He picked up the radio. "I can only see snow," he said.

"Then the answer is no," Isaac said. "I'll be along later, but for now I'm going to investigate the defrosting powers of single malt."

"Are you okay, Hamish?" Ruth asked, putting the radio down.

"Aye, nae bother," Hamish said, giving the lie to that when he began unlacing his boot.

"What are you and Isaac up to?" Ruth asked.

"Testing a high-tech approach to message delivery," Hamish said. "He started with radio, and worked his way up the wavelengths to light, and then to lasers. I don't really understand what he was doing, but he had an idea involving mirrors and the window just beneath the harbour clock. I said he should take a look at the photo we have of Stevens's cell. You couldn't hide a bottle in there, so how would you hide a radio receiver? And how would you power it? Ah," he added, wincing as he pulled off his boot. His foot ended in a mat of bandages, which were now turning red.

"I'll get the doctor," Ruth said.

"There's a first-aid box under the desk," Hamish said. "I'll change the bandage myself."

"But you *should* see the doctor," Ruth said, passing over the box.

"The cold weather makes it bleed worse," Hamish said, taking out a pair of surgical scissors.

"Can I help?" Ruth asked.

"You're all right. I do this at least once a day. I've got to get used to seeing my foot as it is, rather than trying to pretend it isn't. Acceptance is the first step to enlightenment, Nan says. She's probably right, though she also says enlightenment is the next step to ascendance. You know," he added, pointing at the ceiling, "heading up to space."

"She's weird, your nan," Ruth said. "But in a good way. If you don't want my help, then I won't watch. Did you record anything interesting today?"

"No, but the other screen is cued to Stevens taking his exercise."

Ruth tapped the spacebar. The blank screen came to life, and the video began playing. Stevens walked through the gate and into the on-deck cage. He stood beneath the awning, peering ashore.

"Does he just stand there?" Ruth asked.

"I wondered if he's watching the clock," Hamish said. "And I wondered it aloud when Mr Isaac came in, so he went to take a look inside for himself. That led to him lurking by the window below the clock tower."

"So Stevens comes onto the deck for exercise, and just watches the clock," Ruth said, as she turned back to the screen.

"He never misses his time outdoors, even when there's a gale," Hamish said.

"He's allowed outside in a gale?" Ruth asked.

"Aye, exercise is only cancelled if there's a storm," Hamish said.

"And a gale doesn't count as a storm?" she asked.

"Not up here," Hamish said.

"That's another point in favour of Dover," Ruth said. She leaned back in her chair, watching Stevens watch the clock. Finally, his time was up, and he was taken below.

"Could we get a camera in his cell?" Ruth asked.

"The judge says no," Hamish said.

"Pity," Ruth said. "Can I take a look at the other footage?"

"You think you've seen something?"

"No, but there must be something we've missed."

29th January

Chapter 20 - The Importance of Routine
The Old Weather Station, Scrabster

Crime allowing, Ruth's usual routine was to get up, dressed, and washed in twenty minutes, and then spend the next two hours sipping tea behind the duty desk as she slowly woke up. Unless there was an emergency, Sergeant Kettering arrived at ten to nine. If there *was* an emergency, and speaking to how long Kettering had policed the town, everyone knew to knock on the sergeant's front door. Ruth's watch told her she'd slept in, almost to half seven, but while dawn might be warming the chimneys down in Dover, here it was still only a rumour.

Downstairs, the inn was packed with workers from the shipyard, stolidly making their way through unlimited refills of porridge while keeping one eye on the clock. The handful of early-rising ferry passengers were directed into the lounge, but Ruth was sent to the snug, where Esme MacKay was reading a star chart.

"If you're looking for Isaac, you've missed him," Esme said. "He's gone to see Arthur again."

"Oh, how long ago? Maybe I can catch up. I'd like to meet his friend."

"That's a meeting that can't be rushed," Esme said. "And nor can breakfast, but I'll see what we can find for you."

After enough bacon, porridge, and tea to feed a regiment, she forced herself out of her chair. She could so easily idle away the morning, and probably the afternoon, in front of the fire. She'd done all Weaver had asked, and could do little more until the telegraph was repaired, but Stevens's faux piety had wormed its way under her skin.

Leaving word that she'd meet Hamish in his office, she left for Thurso. Warmed by her breakfast, she decided to walk, and regretted it a chilled minute later. Even so, and even though it was early, other people were trudging north. Some were workers. Some were passengers. She recognised two of the artist-children, accompanied by a woman she assumed was their mother. Ruth gave them each as cheery a good morning as she could manage. But they didn't look enthused to be up so early. For them, having left their old lives behind, but with their new lives yet to begin, this extended stay in Thurso must be purgatory.

At the telegraph office, the woman in the pink coat stood by the public message-board. There was only one notice, though, and it read: *Normal Service Returning Soon.*

"I suppose the line must still be down," Ruth said.

"I suppose— Oh," the woman began, and gave a start as she turned and saw Ruth.

"The ferry should be here soon, though," Ruth said. "It won't be long until you're on your way to America."

The woman nodded, almost smiled, and hurried off.

The library had a new sign, too, *Children's Library Closed by Order of Ms Erin Quinn MP. Voter Registration Forms Available at the Post Office.*

Pewter, Quinn's burly bodyguard, stood outside.

"Out of the way, please," Ruth said.

"No entry to anyone," Pewter said.

"You know that doesn't mean me," Ruth said. "Do you really want me to arrest you? You might miss the ferry. You *are* planning to catch it, aren't you?"

The bodyguard didn't answer, but after a face-saving pause, did step aside.

Two of the posters designed by the children were stuck to the stairwell. Another was pinned beneath the returns desk where Dr Frobisher was pointedly reading a novel titled *The Patient Murderer.*

"What's going on?" Ruth asked.

"The paintings are being delivered," Frobisher said. "Unless they are invisible, they're running late, *again.*"

"Oh, is Ms Quinn here?"

"Upstairs, and flapping about like her nose is roped to her toes," Frobisher said.

"I'll come back later," Ruth said. She stepped outside, and debated checking in with Voss before realising she, like the passengers, was merely marking time. Unlike them, she had the option of doing it in the warm, so she caught a cab back to Hamish's office where she found him waiting to leave.

"I think I need a few new stitches," Hamish said. "Do you mind if I head to the doc's?"

"Of course not," Ruth said.

She settled into the chair, but stood as it neared Stevens's time for exercise, and took up position by the telescope. She watched as he came out onto deck. Watched him take up position by the awning, and turn his head towards the distant clock. Or was he looking at something else?

She stepped forward so she could look down at the small crowd watching the ship. With the ferry's arrival imminent, and a frozen drizzle dribbling from the sun-blocking clouds, it was a very, very small crowd. Two teenagers she remembered from the train marched up to the gate, touched the metal clasp, turned around, and began jogging back to Thurso. The woman in the pink coat and pink scarf held a hat which was more red than pink, and seemed to be watching the ship. An old, bearded man she'd seen propping up the bar last night watched the sea, but he was such a fixture in the inn, they kept his old leather tankard above the taps.

Ruth turned the telescope back to Stevens. He was walking a circle. He stopped, and again seemed to stare at the clock.

Ruth looked back at the crowd. The woman in pink was still there, and still clutching her hat. The pair of vicars approached, leading a squad of children. Clearly, they were doing a bit of child-minding, probably with a smidge of midweek Sunday school thrown in. The vicars paused at the edge of the shipyard and turned around, clearly deciding the freezing rain was growing too intense. Esme MacKay stepped out of her office, and invited them inside. Before the vicars had a chance to be polite, the children ran past them, and into the warm.

Ruth slowly turned her eyes back to the shore and to the woman in pink. The woman was *holding* a hat despite the driving rain. The woman was watching the ship, watching Stevens. And *he* was watching *her*. Ruth returned to the telescope to check. Yes, he seemed to be alternating his gaze between the clock, and the woman in pink. She must be signalling. How?

Ruth watched, but the woman did nothing. She stood there until Stevens was led back inside. Only then did she put her hat on, and wearily trudged back towards Thurso.

Finally, Ruth had a theory, and it was easy to confirm since they had video recordings of the ship and the shore. But there were three laptops, and she didn't know on which the recording was kept, or which might be recording the ship now.

She sat. She stood. She sat again, impatiently waiting for Hamish to return.

"All well," Hamish announced. "And I bring scones."

"I've got it!" Ruth said, running to the top of the spiral staircase. "I know how he's doing it!"

"Who? Stevens?"

"Yep," she said, biting her lip against asking the man to hurry. When he finally reached the top, she smiled. "Can one laptop show Stevens when he comes out for exercise, and one show the shore?"

"Aye. Do you want today's recording?" Hamish asked.

"No. Start with the day of the fourth attack, the 20th January," Ruth said.

"Here you go," Hamish said, setting both files up before pressing play. "They're a bit out of sync. I can fix that."

"No, that doesn't matter," Ruth said. "There. Huh."

"What?" Hamish said.

"The woman in pink took her hat off," Ruth said. "Stevens isn't doing anything, is he?"

"No, he's just standing under the awning," Hamish said.

"Just now, when he was on deck, he was pacing, but only for a minute before returning to stand beneath the awning. Then, a few minutes later, he paced again. I thought that was the code, but on this old footage, he's just standing there. No! There. She just put her hat on. That's it. *That's* the code!"

"Putting her hat on is the code?" Hamish asked.

"Yep, because… because… because…. oh, I should have timed this better. There! See, she took it off. She put the hat on for one minute, and during that minute, she had her hand out in front of her. We can't see it from this angle, but I bet she was looking at a wristwatch. Stevens, though, is watching the harbour clock, and watching her. That's the code."

"The time at which she takes her hat off?"

"I think so," Ruth said. "In fact, I'm certain of it. Okay, let's go back to the beginning, and make a note of the time."

By skipping through the video, a quarter of an hour later, Ruth had six times for the 20th January where the woman in pink had donned her hat: 10:09, 10:15, 10:23, 10:29, 10:34, and 10:37. An hour later, they had the sequences for the nights of the three other earlier attacks. For the attack on Religion Row on the 26th, she only put her hat on at 10:05, at 10:08, and at 10:10.

"Maybe each minute past the hour is assigned to a different letter of the alphabet," Hamish said. "There's three letters in row."

"Wouldn't that spell out O, R, W?" Ruth asked. "And Winton would have been... hang on... I, N, N, O, T, W. He thought the attack was on Winton Road, not Winton Way, so he doesn't have an encyclopaedic knowledge of Twynham's streets. Would he have been able to unscramble that? Plus, N appears twice in Winton."

"But if you cut out X, there are twenty-five letters in the alphabet," Hamish said. "I'd skip a few minutes at the beginning and end in case there was a delay getting to the deck, but that still leaves enough minutes to run through the alphabet twice."

"Even then, it doesn't really work," Ruth said. "What if the minutes corresponded to a word?"

"If it's a word, why not a street?" Hamish asked. "And if each number were a street, why pass on anything longer than one digit? Here, look at this one for the day after the attack on Religion Row. There's another three-digit code. That has to be the signal the attack failed. It's the only occasion on the day after an attack she sent him a signal."

"We're missing something. Let's go back again, and watch Stevens."

The only time there was something to see was today.

"Every day, she's waiting ashore before he comes onto the deck," Ruth said. "And on each other day, he walks anticlockwise, once, around the deck. Today he didn't. He began pacing anticlockwise around the deck for one minute at 10:08, 10:11, and 10:14. It's definitely a code."

"Aye, but what does it mean?" Hamish asked.

"I've no idea," Ruth said. "But I know a woman in pink who does."

Chapter 21 - The Woman in Pink
The Marine Hotel, Thurso

Inspector Voss drummed his fingers on his desk. "Aye, that could well be a code. You've not cracked it?"

"Not yet," Hamish said.

"If you don't, the judge might say it's all a coincidence," Voss said. "Stevens didn't know he was being sent here. Other than Thurso, there are only four prisons with an exercise space visible to the general public."

"But there are only thirteen prisons in total," Ruth said. "They came up with a general plan, and a way to adapt it to work for each prison. I don't think Stevens expected to be caught in winter, and I don't think he expected to be sent here. He's lucky he hasn't got frostbite. But for the plan to work, he couldn't have any contact with anyone. No post, no visitors, and no chance to make any major changes to the plan. After he was arrested, the niece came to see her uncle once, and for only ten minutes. That was more than long enough for her to tell him to keep watch for the pink hat, but not long enough to come up with a more weather-appropriate scheme. At a different prison, where there was no direct line of sight, they could have fired a gun, or released a kite, or set off a siren. Most of the time, the message is coming from the shore to him. He sent a message to her today. Not knowing the other prisons, I don't know how he'd send messages in a different jail, but surely a judge won't want us to explain that?"

"Aye, she might, but one problem at a time," Voss said. "What's the woman's name?"

"Well, yes, that *is* the next problem," Ruth said.

Voss nodded, stood and walked to his office door. He opened it and beckoned over a young constable. "I want the name of the female ferry passenger who wears a pink coat and strolls up to Scrabster once a day. Constable, a description?"

"She's about five-eight without the hat, mid-forties, IC3," Ruth said. "I've seen her around the telegraph office, too."

"On the quiet, lad."

"Aye, sir," the constable said, and ran off.

"We'll get a name within the hour," Voss said. "And then we'll take it slow. Who knows what other tricks they've prepared? Around here, if you follow a road you'll always come to a ruin. They're a great place to stash supplies, and these people are arms dealers. With all the effort they put into communicating, we'll assume they also put some into planning an escape. Wait here, and I'll tell my people to prepare."

It took twenty minutes to get a name for their suspect: Julie Blanchard. The suspect was staying in the Marine Hotel, whose storm shutters utterly blocked the view of the sea, and of the police strike team gathering outside.

Two constables went to the back and two more to the fire escape, but Voss and Ruth went into the hotel alone.

They got the room number, and its key, from the receptionist who promptly disappeared into the small office. As that door lock clicked, Ruth and Voss climbed the stairs.

Voss knocked on the door. "Ms Blanchard, a telegram's just arrived for you," he said.

The reply began muffled but grew more distinct as the suspect approached the door. "A telegram? The telegraph is working again?" she asked, even as she opened the door. The moment it was open an inch, Voss pushed it wide. Blanchard fell backwards, onto the floor.

"My apologies, ma'am," Voss said, "but you're under arrest."

"I'm…" she began, adjusting her robe even as she began to stand. "I have a ticket for the ferry, and so request an immediate hearing, and a lawyer."

"Do you now?" Voss said. "It's cold out there. You better bring that pink coat of yours."

An hour later, Voss came out of the interview room. Ruth wasn't the only copper waiting outside. "Anyone without work to do knows where the snow shovels are," Voss said to the crowd of curious officers. "Come on, Constable," he added. "Where's Mr MacKay?"

"Back in his office," Ruth said. "He had to change his bandages."

"Understood," Voss said. "He's a good lad, Hamish. He has the makings of a good copper, though he might make a better shipbuilder." Voss took the chair behind his desk. "Please," he said.

Ruth sat opposite. "I don't understand why she said she had a ticket for the ferry. Why does that matter?"

"Because the tickets are one-way," Voss said. "Last month we had a similar case, which confirmed that the precedent set in Llandudno two years ago applies in Scottish law, too. You understand the difference between Scottish and English law, yes?"

"No. And I've not heard about the precedent."

"That is a bit easier to explain," Voss said. "We must assume anyone who has a one-way ticket is emigrating, thus they've sold their worldly goods, including their home. They've given up their jobs, and their old lives, and probably can't afford another ticket. If they are leaving the country for good, then there is no chance of them reoffending within our jurisdiction. So, holding them beyond the ship's departure could be seen as a cruel and unusual punishment, and a burden to the taxpayer. Letting them leave could be seen as deportation, and so a problem for America. Thus, why delay the hearing?"

"Oh. So do we have to let her get on the ferry regardless?"

"That'll be down to the judge, and in this case, I think we've grounds to detain her. But the hearing will be tomorrow morning, and you will need to present your case then."

"Me?"

"Aye, it is your case, and you did come all the way up here to investigate it."

"I was really just bringing a message to Stevens," Ruth said.

"Don't tell the judge that," Voss said. "I'll speak with Blanchard, and with her lawyer, and see if she can be persuaded to talk. You should search her room, and see if she left her codebook behind."

Ruth found Isaac in the police station's waiting room.

"I thought you were scared of coming inside here," she said.

"I would describe it more as an allergy than a fear," Isaac said. "But it's cold enough to freeze a whale outside. I hear I missed the excitement."

"It wasn't that exciting," Ruth said. "But I'm going to do a bit of evidence hunting, if you want to lend a hand?"

"It's too early for dinner, so why not? Whom did you arrest?"

"Her name is Julie Blanchard," Ruth said. "She is a widow whose husband was from America, and his relatives have invited her over to settle. They grow corn, potatoes, and maple syrup in western Maine."

"It has been a long time since I had maple syrup," Isaac said. "And who do we think she really is?"

"That's what we're going to find out," Ruth said.

The Marine Hotel had been a hotel back in the gone-before, but had then become a hostel for casual labour. This winter, with the sudden arrival of the ferry, it had been repurposed back into rooms, but it was more of a boarding house than a true hotel. On their way to arrest Blanchard, Ruth had noticed the lack of carpet and rugs. She'd *not* noticed the lack of a dining room until she returned with Isaac, but that had long ago been converted into bedrooms, too.

Blanchard's room had been small before it had been divided in two, but that had been done years ago. A small wood-burning stove would provide as much carbon monoxide as heat, particularly if the windows were kept closed. The furnishings were limited to a single bed, a wooden chair, a small writing desk, and a tall, narrow wardrobe.

"Small, anonymous, cheap," Isaac said, walking over to the window. "You wouldn't stay here twice."

"No, but if you'd booked it from Twynham, what choice would you have when you arrived?" Ruth asked.

"It says a lot about the Loyal Brigade's funds," Isaac said.

"Ferry tickets aren't cheap," Ruth said, opening the wardrobe. "She has a spare pink coat, two pink scarves, and two pink hats. The hats aren't waterproof, but they're almost identical. Ah, and made out of another pink coat. It's got the same chunky braid along the brim that the coat has along the collar."

"Is that a clue?" Isaac asked.

"That'll depend on whether someone in the Loyal Brigade is a tailor," Ruth said as she checked the single drawer below the wardrobe-cupboard. "But you raised an interesting point. This room was cheap. Ferry tickets are expensive. Stevens and his niece are gunrunners. Where's the money been going?"

"There's nothing under the bed, or the mattress," Isaac said.

"She has about five changes of clothes," Ruth said. "Which isn't much. Nor is her luggage. Only two bags, a suitcase and an over-sized handbag. Is that really the extent of her worldly possessions? In the handbag we have her travel documents and some letters, apparently from her dead husband's family, but they could be forged."

"That's easily checked with a letter sent back on the ferry," Isaac said.

"But that'll take time," Ruth said. "She's got a small penknife. A cutlery set. Needle and thread. Two handkerchiefs. A-ha! A notebook and pencil, and... oh. There's nothing inside. Nothing at all, but I think some pages have been removed." She continued her brief search. "Twenty pounds and some loose change in sterling, and twenty dollars. She could have afforded a better room, and presumably twenty dollars should be enough to get her to her in-laws' farm when she gets to America."

"What do you call the opposite of a clue?" Isaac said, having checked behind the framed sketch of a flowering thistle hanging on the wall. "If she knew to request an early hearing because she has a ferry ticket, then she knew she might be caught."

"Or someone did," Ruth said, lifting out the suitcase. "It's not empty. Let's see." She laid it on the bed, and opened it. "Some books. A black hat. Some gauze. Wait, it's a veil, and here are a pair of black gloves. She's going to play the grieving widow in America."

"Maybe it's not an act," Isaac said. "Perhaps they killed the husband so as to give her a reason to catch the ferry."

"But they couldn't guarantee Stevens would be sent here," Ruth said, as she picked up a book. "And they've been careful not to kill anyone during the arson attacks. This is a first edition of *The Time Machine*. And this is a first edition of *Remains of the Day*, and it's signed. And a newer first edition of *Remaining Days*, also signed. *Jane Eyre* and *The Day of the Triffids*. Not signed, but both are first editions. These would be worth a lot in Twynham, so they must be worth even more in America if you know where to sell them. Definitely worth more than jewellery and safer to carry than cash. Okay, so now we're getting somewhere." She returned to the letters, quickly scanning one, then the next. "I think she really was a widow, and really was going to America. But this is just correspondence. It's not an invitation, and there's no mention of her travelling." She put the letters back into the bag. "I think we've found something. I'm just not sure what, so we'll take this evidence to the police station, and go through it more thoroughly there."

At the station, they found Hamish MacKay in Inspector Voss's office, his foot resting on an upturned metal bin, a mug of soup in his hands.

"That smells good," Ruth said.

"The sergeant makes it," Hamish said. "He says the secret ingredient is patience, but I think it's thyme."

"Where's the inspector?" Isaac asked.

"Interviewing Blanchard," Hamish said.

"Then I shall find the sergeant and see if he can spare another mug," Isaac said.

"He won't get any," Hamish said after Isaac had left the office. "The sergeant only makes it for himself, but this is my reward for cracking the case."

"How so?" Ruth asked.

"I went to the telegraph office," Hamish said. "That pink coat is very memorable. Blanchard would go there every day at about nine, and again around half eleven, even after the line went down."

"So immediately before and after watching Stevens take his walk?" Ruth asked.

"Aye, exactly," Hamish said. "But she was only interested in the public messages. Things like the university's weather report, the one-line bulletins from the newspaper, the job-ads, the raw-materials requests, and the general messages from the government."

"The arsonist had a job cleaning at the university," Ruth said. "I assumed she was slipping a telegram in with the outgoing post, but she could have been altering one of the official messages."

"She was," Hamish said. "The code was hidden in the official spring-prediction weather forecast they update every day. The data is collected up here, and then sent south. Every day, the university science people update their guess on the average weather during the planting season, and when that'll begin. At five in the morning, along with the news headlines and any government messages, the summary for northern Scotland is sent back to us. By then, we've used the raw data to put together our own forecast, so no one pays attention to the summary the telegraph office pin to their notice board. There are six numbers: a temperature range at night, another during the day, an estimated max wind speed, and a guess at rainfall. That's six numbers in total, and the ones we have for the days of the attacks are completely out."

"And no one noticed?" Ruth asked.

"Four people did," Hamish said. "One passenger, three locals. They mentioned it to the telegraph clerk, which is how I figured it out so quickly. The clerk assumed it was an error down in Twynham, and did ask our own meteorologist to check the data we sent down, and then forgot about it. Since no one here relies on that data, nothing more was said."

"And if we didn't have the video recordings, we'd never have connected one to the other," Ruth said. "And if we'd arrested Stevens two months ago, we wouldn't have had the recordings. In fact, it's only because Stevens made a fuss about how Weaver had used a microphone rather than a bug to collect the evidence to arrest him that Serious Crime got the approval to use the cameras. So, when Stevens planned all this, he assumed we wouldn't have any recordings. There's a spring weather report for every part of Britain, yes?"

"Yes. So they could use this system for any prison," Hamish said. "This should be enough to prove the arsonist is a conspirator rather than a believer."

"I don't suppose the telegraph line is back up yet?"

"No, and probably not for at least another two days," Hamish said. "But I haven't told you the best part. On the twenty-seventh, the day after the attack on Religion Row, a telegram was sent to Julie Blanchard. She collected it at nine, before she went up to the docks."

"Tell me they kept a copy," Ruth said.

"In the transcription book," Hamish said. "The message said: *6 more people are interested in house. Now 13 in total. Should be sold by 21.*"

"Six, thirteen, and twenty-one?" Ruth asked. "That matches the code she sent Stevens."

"It gets even better," Hamish said. "This morning, she dropped a telegram off, to be sent as soon as the line is re-opened. It reads: *In 8 days I'll be at sea. In 11, I'll arrive in Maine. In 14, I'll be with my family. Wish you were here, JB.*"

"Eight, eleven, and fourteen?" Ruth said. "And that matches the times when Stevens was pacing," Ruth said. "Who was that telegram sent to?"

"Trudy Glossup, 147 Parson Avenue in Twynham."

"Parson Avenue? I can't place it."

"Because it doesn't exist," Hamish said. "I checked the street directory. But Blanchard ticked the box so, if the message couldn't be delivered, it was to be posted on the public board."

"Let me see if I've got this right," Ruth said. "The arsonist alters an official message which is sent from the university to the telegraph office for general distribution. That message is placed on the public board up here. Blanchard reads the message, then heads to the quay. After the arrest of the arsonist, a message is actually sent here. Were there any other messages?"

"To Blanchard, no," Hamish said. "And she only ever sent one back to Twynham, or tried to, and that was today."

"And that was to a fake address so that message would get put up on the general board where anyone could read it," Ruth said. She opened Blanchard's handbag, and took out the letters Blanchard had received from America. "She's passing on the numbers, so she probably doesn't know what the code means, and so doesn't have a codebook. And why give her one? Isn't it safer if fewer people know? She didn't pretend to be a believer, but she knew she was communicating with Stevens. These letters go back a couple of years. The third letter was a response to her telling them her husband was dead. That's the third letter, not the first, and it was sent eighteen months ago. I think these letters are genuine. I think she really *did* hope to make a new life in America, but she hadn't yet been invited. What if, after Stevens was arrested and sent here, Hailey needed to send an agent north? Whom do they pick? What did the Loyal Brigade know about Thurso?"

"Probably only what I told them when I was working in the tank yard," Hamish said. "I might have short-changed it, and said how everyone knew everyone's business. But after I got the measure of them, I said nothing at all."

"But they did know the ferry came here. They needed someone who could legitimately buy a one-way ticket and so hang around up here until the ship arrives."

"Aye, but the ship's late," Hamish said. "What if it had been on time?"

"Maybe Hailey would have found someone else to come north," Ruth said. "I bet there are plenty of people in Twynham who'd stand about in the freezing rain in exchange for a free ticket to America."

"So Blanchard doesn't really know anything?" Hamish asked.

"She knows Hailey Stevens or the arsonist," Ruth said. "Beyond that, probably not, but that doesn't matter either, because she must be the only agent here in Thurso. There's no army of believers. It's just Stevens and his niece, the arsonist and her bodyguard brother. Everyone else is just hired help like Blanchard. We were so worried they might try an escape, or bribe the jury, or kick-start a religious war during the trial, we overlooked how desperate they are. Yes, it's all starting to swim into focus."

"Could you get it to swim a bit closer?" Hamish asked.

Ruth stared at the books, then looked around the shelves. "There!" She walked across to a bookshelf filled with a few old maps and travelogues, and which also held a copy of *Great Expectations*. "The book-club book," she said. "Everyone has a copy, even Stevens."

"You think this is the codebook?" Hamish asked.

"The book club's been running for six months," Ruth said. "The newspaper's announced the books which they'll be discussing until the end of summer. Weaver sent the copies of this book to the governor, so now I wonder if copies are sent to every prison. That's something to check, but even if they're not given to every prisoner, Stevens is on remand, so there's no reason not to let him have a copy. He didn't want visitors, or letters, or telegrams, and must have assumed we'd not let him have the newspaper. But a two-hundred-year-old novel? Where's the harm in that?"

"That's reasonable, but what's the code?" Hamish asked. "It can't be page numbers. Different editions use different typefaces. They might have an introduction, or illustrations, or some other filler at the beginning."

"No, not page numbers," Ruth said, bringing the book close so Hamish could see. "What about first word in a chapter? Wait. No. We've got the date, don't we? We have the date and the minute past the hour. Those two change. So, what if the date is the chapter, and the minutes are the… the word? Or is it the line? The paragraph?"

"Stevens knew the street name," Hamish said. "But that was all. And he got it wrong. Winton has six letters."

"Find Chapter Twenty," Ruth said handing him the novel while she took out her notebook. "He said the attack would be on Winton Road, but it was actually Winton Way. The minutes are 9, 15, 23, 29, 34, and 37."

"The first letter of the ninth paragraph is W," Hamish said. "The first letter of the fifteenth is I. Yep. It's the first letter of the paragraph. I'll check the codes for the other days."

"Start with the message Stevens sent her," Ruth said.

"That's I, I, I," Hamish said. "And for the day after the attack on Religion Row failed, the telegram sent to her, that's also I, I, I."

"It's the same?" Ruth said. "So that must be a prearranged code to indicate failure. We better tell Voss."

Inspector Voss smiled. "Aye, very good. Very good indeed."

"It was mostly Hamish," Ruth said. "Are we going to confront Blanchard?"

"There's no need for such haste," Voss said. "We still have to build our case. Now the paintings have gone on display, I've a free cell to keep her in. Blanchard requested an early hearing, so we'll give her that. We'll present just enough to prevent her from boarding the ship, and then we'll hold her until the telegraph is working. Before it's open to the public, we'll send a wire to the commissioner, and see how she wants to proceed. We might let Blanchard go so she can send another message to Stevens, or we can send one south. Until we know how things stand with the niece, we won't tip our hand."

"Then we should let Stevens know the telegraph is down," Ruth said.

"I'll tell the governor to let it slip," Voss said. "We'll cancel his exercise on the grounds the ferry is about to arrive. Until then, we shall keep collecting our evidence. Take a few hours off. I'll come to the inn tonight, and we'll run through what to say to the judge tomorrow."

Chapter 22 - Seeking Greener Grass
The Library, Thurso

Ruth found Isaac holding court in the police station lobby where a crowd of cops hung on his every word.

"And that," Isaac said, "is when the shark saw the squid." As his audience broke into laughter, Isaac excused himself. "How goes the case?" he asked, falling into step next to Ruth.

"I'll tell you outside," Ruth said, and headed out into the gloomy slush-ridden street. Despite it only being mid-afternoon, dusk was settling. The wind had dropped, and the rain had stopped, but a chill was already creeping up from the frozen pavement.

"Where next for the case?" Isaac asked.

"Oh, we cracked it," Ruth said.

"You did?"

"Yep. Me and Hamish, but we don't want anyone to know yet, not until we're back in contact with Commissioner Weaver. I can tell you as we walk back. Perhaps we should catch a cab."

"Assuming the weather remains as clement as this, the ferry will dock tonight," Isaac said. "The cargo will be unloaded first, and the passengers will come ashore at first light. The emigrants will board next, and the ship will aim to depart at lunchtime. My ship, though, will depart before then."

"Your boat's arrived?"

"It will soon," Isaac said.

"So you're leaving?" Ruth asked. "You didn't introduce me to your friend. Arthur, wasn't it? Maybe we could meet him for dinner?"

"Dinner won't work," Isaac said. "But yes, you should meet him. First, though, I'd like us to go to the art gallery."

"Why?" Ruth asked.

"Because it's a normal thing for families to do," Isaac said. "I'd like to take the memory with me."

"You won't tell me where you're going?"

"I can't," Isaac said.

"It's going to be dangerous, isn't it?" Ruth asked.

"I imagine so."

"Then let's go see a few pictures," she said, taking his arm. "And as we walk, I can tell you how we cracked the code."

Outside the library, a long but slow-moving line stretched halfway to the pub. By their clothing, the patrons were an even mix of ferry passengers and locals. Erin Quinn slowly paced the line, ignoring more people than she spoke to. Ruth smiled, and raised a hand in greeting as she neared Quinn, but the politician turned her back and addressed an older couple patiently waiting their turn to enter.

"Welcome, Margot. Hello, Evan," Quinn said. "Brisk, isn't it?"

"Ian," the man murmured, but Quinn was already continuing on down the line.

"She's only talking to people who might vote!" Ruth hissed.

"Why waste time with people about to leave?" Isaac replied.

"It's rude, for one thing," Ruth said. "For another, there's no way I'd vote for someone so transparently self-serving. Or for *her* party."

"Ah, but she doesn't want your vote," Isaac said.

The door opened, and Dr Frobisher came out.

"Ah, good, the police!" Frobisher said. "I'd like to press charges."

"Against whom?" Ruth asked.

"Erin Quinn, for a crime against taste, and perhaps even humanity," Frobisher said. She stormed down the line, until she reached a shivering pair of children, and their equally forlorn mother. She frogmarched them to the front of the queue, and then inside. Ruth and Isaac followed her in.

Inside, sheet metal panels had been used to create an internal snaking tunnel to the gallery. On those panels were pinned the children's interpretive art. Those pieces were no better, or worse, than any Ruth had seen when she and her mother had lived at the old refugee camp's school, but the context turned them into masterpieces. On the left side, from an expertly disassembled book, was a print of the recently rescued piece of art. On the right was a print of Van Gogh, Kahlo, or whichever piece had been the child's muse. Next to that was a short paragraph, written by the child, explaining their concept and inspiration. Those paragraphs sometimes mentioned the death of a parent, and always mentioned the ferry journey to America, but they all rang with hope. Except that hope was in finding a future somewhere far from these shores.

Ruth lingered by a Kahlo-inspired re-interpretation of John Singer Sargent's *The Lady Agnew of Lochnaw*. The artist, a thirteen-year-old Dolly Deveux, had written that she thought the woman in Sargent's portrait looked a lot like Kahlo's self-portrait of fifty years later and six thousand miles away. The last line read: *Do time and distance really matter?*

"That's poignant," Ruth said. "Is it that she doesn't want to go to America, or that she doesn't want to have to go?"

"The decision to leave isn't the children's," Isaac said.

"No, exactly," Ruth said. "The people I spoke to on the train either had jobs or distant family in America, but they can't know what it's really like any more than I do. All the children have written about hope, but it feels like desperation. Things might be bad here, but they are getting better."

"What does better look like?" Isaac asked. "Each month they tell us rationing will end soon, just not today. Technology is getting more widespread, but mostly within the Serious Crimes Unit. Hope is a song to sing ourselves to sleep, but it won't keep us warm. Did I ever tell you why I went to university?"

"No. But everyone did back in your day, didn't they?"

"Not everyone," Isaac said. "When I was fourteen, I won a coding competition run by a big tech company. The prize was a five-year employment contract with an utterly absurd salary. The catch was that anything I created would belong to that company. I baulked at that, because I'd just proved I was better than any other un-indentured coder in the country. I took my win, and rode the bus from city to city, looking for a university to take me in. Suffice to say my home life was such no one noticed I had left the state. Finally, I found a professor whom I impressed, and was found a place and a scholarship."

"And that professor was Mum?" Ruth asked.

"No. It was an old guy losing a battle to time. But on that course was a football player on a sport scholarship. He took exception to how some of the other students picked on this young kid as if college was still high school. That was Maggie's son."

"Who died? And who was the reason Maggie switched from neurosurgery to computing?"

"Yes, though it was less of a switch and more of a focusing on a very specific part of her specialty. Long before that, at Thanksgiving, her son took me home for a meal. He gave me some of his old clothes, and he gave me a book. If his football career panned out, he was going to become a wrestler, then an actor. That was a high-prestige career path in pre-Blackout America. Maggie was trying to encourage him to have a backup plan, and this book was a hint he might try archaeology, sociology, or anthropology. This book explored how humans switched from hunter-gatherers to farmers. My key takeaway was how life was much, much worse for the farmers. The hours were longer, the work was harder, the life expectancy was shorter, and the chance of losing absolutely everything to drought or plague was much higher."

"If it was that bad, why didn't they switch back?" Ruth asked.

"Because the change took centuries," Isaac said. "When they settled down, they thought stability of place would bring more comfort. They hoped it would bring a better life for their children. A century or three later, when the climate changed, the river dried up, and the valley became a desert, no one remembered a time when they did anything but farm. They had to move on or die, claim more farmland, and kill anyone who might stop them. Thus began humanity's battle for something better. Did we achieve it, even now?"

"Not even the Luddites wanted us to go back to a time before farming," Ruth said.

"No. I'm saying that hope and change, and hoping *for* change, are built into our psyche. Sometimes, we can change the world. Sometimes, we can only change ourselves. Sometimes, all we can do is search for greener grass in the next valley."

There was a cough behind them. "Please, Miss," a young girl, waiting patiently behind, said. "Can my mum have a look?"

When Dr Frobisher had said that carpenters were preparing the exhibition room, Ruth hadn't given much thought to what that would entail, but hadn't expected a barrier. It ran around the room at waist height, keeping the visitors two metres from the art. In the centre of the room were four powerful spotlights positioned at shoulder height so, as people walked past, their shadows were cast on the painting they were trying to view. The only signs in the room apologised for the mess. There were none to explain the art.

Isaac bent low to look closer. "Is that woman actually frying eggs? I can't quite see."

"This is a joke," Ruth said. From the mumbling ahead of her, she wasn't the only one to think so. Ruth marched on, stopping in front of

The Skating Minister. There, hands on hips, she frowned. "No, this is wrong," she said, no longer bothering to keep her voice low. "It's not right them hanging here like this. How can anyone get a proper look when the lights are all wrong, and the shadows are everywhere? How can— Hang on." Ruth swung herself over the barrier. She lifted the painting from the wall, the better to see it.

"Are we allowed to do that?" the young girl who'd been behind them in the line asked.

"Isaac, get Inspector Voss," Ruth said, leaning the picture against the wall.

"Why?"

"Because…" Ruth began and realised the room had gone quiet. Everyone, local and passenger alike, had come to the gallery for some entertainment, and she was now providing it. As it was too late to be circumspect, she decided to be honest. "Because this painting is a forgery," she said.

"How d'you know?" the mother of the young girl asked.

"I was the one who found them down in Dover," Ruth said. "Isaac?"

"Your demand is my wish," he said, and pushed his way to the doors. Meanwhile, more people were pushing their way in, while none of those inside were leaving. The revelation was whispered back and forth to the newcomers.

"What's a forgery, Mum?" the young girl asked.

"A fake," the mother said. "Someone made copies of the paintings."

"You mean like I did with the other kids?" the girl asked.

"No, dear, but I'm sure we're about to find out who."

Ruth was already sure she knew who, and didn't have long to wait until her prime suspect barged her way inside.

"What is the meaning of this?" Quinn demanded.

Dr Frobisher had entered just behind Quinn, and it was she that Ruth addressed. "Dr Frobisher, we need to close the library. This exhibit is now a crime scene."

"Is it, indeed?" Frobisher asked, her face brightening with interest.

"Yes, doctor, it really is," Ruth said, turning her gaze to Quinn. "Perhaps you would wait here, Ms Quinn."

"I want an immediate explanation for this unwarranted insult," Quinn said. "I'll have your badge for this."

Ruth said nothing, but waited for the inspector.

"I thought I told you to take a few hours off, Constable," Voss said when he finally appeared.

"I tried," Ruth said. "I really did, but this painting is a fake."

"You're an art expert, are you?" Quinn said.

"The real painting has a cocoa stain in the top right corner," Ruth said. "This painting doesn't. Unless Ms Quinn can introduce us to her ace restorer, we should arrest her for fraud, forgery, and theft."

"How dare you!" Quinn said. "Do you know who I am?"

"I found these paintings," Ruth said. "I took them back to the police station in Dover. I watched them until they came to Twynham and were handed over to you."

"How did the picture come to be stained?" Dr Frobisher asked.

"I imagine because someone who'd been working a very long shift was too exhausted to pay attention," Ruth said. "That's only speculation, of course. The stain was there in Dover. It's not here on this painting now. This painting is a fake, and the only person who could have swapped them is Erin Quinn."

"That's outrageous," Quinn said.

"Where are your two bodyguards?" Ruth asked.

"I've no idea," Quinn said.

"And the posters?" Ruth asked. "You brought up posters from Twynham, but they never made it this far. Why not?"

"They were dropped in the slush and ruined," Quinn said.

"And thrown into which bin?" Voss asked.

"How would I know?" Quinn asked. "You don't say you believe her? We've known each other for years."

"Aye," Voss said. He raised a hand and beckoned over one of his officers. "Constable, please escort Ms Quinn to the station."

"You'll regret this," Quinn said. "You'll *all* regret it."

Chapter 23 - The Skating Copper
The Riverbank Rest, Thurso

"*Will* I regret this?" Voss asked, after Quinn had been escorted from the scene. One constable remained, slowly ushering out the patrons. Isaac had found a chair, while Dr Frobisher appeared to be making notes.

"No, sir, I promise," Ruth said, but then checked the corner of the picture again. "It's *definitely* a different painting. Quinn and her two bodyguards must be behind this."

"And what, actually, is this?" Dr Frobisher asked. "Do you think it's just a forgery, or could there have been a murder or two?"

"What are you writing, Poppy?" Voss asked.

"The next non-fiction best-seller," Frobisher said. "So, what actually happened here?"

Voss turned back to Ruth. "Constable?"

"I'm not sure yet," Ruth said. "But one of her bodyguards had a wallet full of Maine banknotes. Their plan must be to put the forgeries on display here, and to sell the real ones in America. The posters were the forgeries, and the originals are now disguised as posters. Huh. She only had twenty-four hours to make the copies. That's fast."

"Too fast, because this picture looks real to me," Voss said. "But finding the two bodyguards should be our priority."

Frobisher had kneeled down by the painting. "If this is a forgery, it is excellent work," she said. "I can't see an ice crystal out of place." She turned it over. "Ah, look at the canvas. It's nearly new!"

"If it only held up to one minute of close scrutiny, I wouldn't call that an excellent forgery," Voss said. "Doctor, I'll leave a constable here to guard the evidence, and I'd ask if you could head up to Scrabster. Ask Mrs MacKay to send down some reliable souls. Ten for guarding, and ten for searching."

"The bodyguards are both armed," Ruth said.

"Then we better see this doesn't come to a gunfight," Voss said.

The two bodyguards, Howe and Pewter, shared a room in the Riverbank Rest on Janet Street. Before the Blackout, it had simply been an old house with an even older wall. Since then, it had become another hostel for winter workers, and then an inn, and now had expanded into the neighbouring homes. Ruth, Voss, and Isaac entered through the bar on Brabster Street, originally a garage which had gained a maze of extensions as a watering hole grew into a restaurant.

While a few night-shift workers were nursing a pint, there was no sign of Howe or Pewter.

"Lock the door to the main building," Voss said to the barman as he examined the room-register. "We want the second floor. On me."

Voss led Ruth and Isaac through the haphazardly constructed dining room where no two tables seemed to share the same level, and finally into a flat-floored lounge with a glass-door roof and a winter chill which two roaring stoves couldn't banish. Beyond that was the boarding house, and a rear set of stairs leading to the upper rooms. Descending those stairs were the two suspects.

"Oh, hi, we'd like a word, please," Ruth said as innocently as she could manage. It wasn't innocent enough. The smaller Howe ran first, sprinting past his larger colleague, and back up the stairs. Pewter followed.

"Don't run!" Voss said, but the suspects did, so Ruth did the same.

"I said don't run!" Voss called.

Ruth nearly caught Pewter on the stairs, but despite his newfound weight, and no matter how corrupt he might have become, he had been a copper in Britain during the dark years. He was a fighter, a brawler, and knew just where to kick as she tried to tackle him. She fell backwards, while Pewter ran on.

"Less haste, Officer Deering," Voss said, helping her up.

"What about hostages?" Ruth asked, as Isaac ignored Voss, and took the lead.

"That's why we want to let those two get outside," Voss said. "If we get them outside, they won't escape."

Isaac had almost caught the two men, but had been a second too slow. The bedroom door slammed before he could reach it. Even as he launched a kick, something heavy fell to the floor inside the room

"They dropped some furniture on the other side of the door," Isaac said.

"Keep pushing," Voss said. "On me, Constable." The inspector went to the next door along and knocked. "Police," he said. "Open the door."

"I can pick that lock," Ruth said.

"So can I," Voss said. He raised his boot, kicked, and splintered the frame. The door swung inward. The room had two pairs of bunk beds, both neatly made, and each with a small suitcase sitting next to it. The guests must be ferry-passengers packed and ready to go, and who, fortunately, were doing their waiting elsewhere.

Ruth followed Voss to the window.

"And there they are," Voss said. "They're running, because that's what you train police officers to do down in the south."

Technically, the two ex-cops were climbing. The skinny Howe was already at the bottom of a stout soil-pipe, looking up at his larger colleague.

Pewter had begun climbing down the drainpipe, but when Voss opened the window, the suspect opted for a quicker route down, and tried to drop to the window ledge just below. Pewter misjudged the distance, couldn't get a grip, and fell, landing on top of Howe. From the snap, it sounded as if someone had broken a bone. From how only Pewter got up, it was Howe who'd fractured a bone. Pewter began running, heading for the wall leading onto Janet Street, and the river beyond.

Ruth sprinted back to the door.

"What did I just say?" Voss called. "Save your energy!"

But chasing had become an ingrained reflex for her, too. She followed the hand-painted fire escape signs down the stairs, along a corridor, and out through the kitchens. There, in the yard, it took her a moment to orientate herself.

"South," Isaac said, just behind her. "He'll run inland, not north to the sea, but first we need to get to the road."

"Easy," Ruth said, and headed straight for a one-storey extension built against the wall. From the shuttered window with a bench beneath and an awning above, it had probably been intended as a guest-annexe, but from the thick black dust, it was currently being used as a coal store. The bench gave her something to stand on as she pulled herself up to the awning and then to the roof. There, she saw Pewter running south, and towards a footbridge that crossed the river.

Ruth ran across the roof and jumped down to the road, sprinting after Pewter. He heard her, looked around, saw her, stumbled, but ran on, following the riverside road, as people appeared in doorways and windows, taking advantage of another unexpected entertainment. Pewter ignored them, heading straight for the bridge. He was out of shape, but had a hundred-metre head start on Ruth. She was closing the distance, but not fast enough.

The riverbank on this side of the bridge was marked as a fishing ground, though it was currently empty except for a quartet of youths who were taking turns to see if they could fling a fishing line beyond the ice sheets coating the shore. At the sound of pursuit, all four turned to look.

"Go! Go!" Ruth yelled at them. "Isaac! Get them!"

Pewter half-turned at the shout, then froze as a spotlight glared from the narrow footbridge.

"Halt!" came a warning shout from an unseen sentry. Pewter had already stopped so he did the opposite, sprinting towards a rickety wooden jetty that led out into the river.

"Don't!" Ruth called, but Pewter's brain was too full of adrenaline to think.

At the end of the jetty a small craft was partially frozen in ice. More a coracle than a canoe, it didn't offer any real chance of escape, only a slim possibility of extending the chase for a few minutes more.

"Stop!" Ruth yelled.

A loud crack came in reply, not from a gun, but a wooden board splintering under Pewter's weight. As Ruth drew nearer, she saw the warning signs proclaiming the jetty was unsafe. The fugitive either hadn't seen them, or didn't care. He pulled himself up into a crouch, running onward, slipping on the frozen boards until he reached the very end. There, finally, he paused.

The coracle was two metres away, held in place by ice as much by a solitary rope attached to the jetty's end.

"Don't!" Ruth said. "Just give up!"

But Pewter dropped to a crouch, finally drawing his revolver.

"Gun!" Ruth yelled, dropping to the ground. Pewter, after firing two wild shots, did the same, falling to his belly before slithering off the edge of the jetty and onto the ice. He kept his arms and legs wide as he dragged himself towards the coracle.

Ruth had drawn her gun, but she didn't fire. She could hear the ice creaking.

"Isaac, get those the fishing rods! Quick!" she called, but it was too late.

Even as Pewter reached for the edge of the coracle, the thin ice cracked. He disappeared into the river without time to even scream. The spotlight from the footbridge stayed fixed on the river, but he didn't resurface.

Chapter 24 - Fight, Flight, or Freeze
The Police Station, Thurso

"Fight, flight, or freeze," Isaac said as he came to join her by the riverbank. "Any of those would be the natural responses to pursuit. In this case, he took a rather literal approach to all three."

Ruth shivered. "Any idea what we do?"

"Two of the anglers have run for rope," Isaac said. "But since that team with the spotlight are happy to do no more than keep it shining on the hole, I say there is nothing anyone can do."

Ruth turned at the sound of jogging footsteps. Voss had arrived, and with a small crowd from the bar.

"He fell through the ice while trying to reach the coracle," Ruth said. "He hasn't resurfaced."

"Aye, well, he probably won't," Voss said. "Fan out along the riverbank. Everyone in pairs. No one goes near the ice. Shout if you see him. Quick now!" He pointed up at the searchlight team, then made a back-and-forth waving motion. The light began to play up and down the river, revealing how patchy the ice was.

"On me, Constable," Voss said, and began walking upstream.

Ruth followed, while Isaac returned the two fishing rods he'd borrowed to the anglers.

When Voss was on the inland side of the bridge, he took out his electric lamp, and shone it on the ice. "We slowed the river's flow here as the first stage of setting up a watermill. A plane crashed over there, back during the Blackout. Set off a belowground fuel tank. Quite a crater we had after we cleared it. We let the river flood the crater a few years ago. A sudden slowing in the river's speed confused the salmon, and made fishing a lot easier. When people see that painting, I'm sure ice-skating will again become a popular pastime. Nothing. No, he didn't come upriver."

"I didn't know the bridge was guarded," Ruth said.

"Ever since we were told Stevens was communicating with the south, we assumed he might try to escape," Voss said, as he began walking north, back towards the spot where Pewter had fallen in. "We doubled the sentries on the bridges, and sent a warning to the outlying villages. As I told you when we first met, we're an island here, especially in winter. People can run, but they can't escape. That being said, we'll have to ask his confederate whether he was running *to* somewhere."

"What about a ship?" Ruth asked. "Maybe that's why he took a room in a place so close to the river."

"There's no boat in the bay, and he'd have no chance of swimming any further," Voss said. "An athlete who'd trained for such conditions might survive for half an hour in those waters, but he was no athlete. He was running because we were chasing. The shock will have killed him. But you should check the far bank. Look for footprints. If there are none, then yes, by now, he is dead."

Isaac joined Ruth as she crossed the footbridge, made narrower by the sentry post and its searchlight.

"He was running because I was chasing," Ruth said, as they began following the bank on the far side of the bridge.

"No, he was running because he was guilty," Isaac said. "Quite what of, I am still intrigued to find out."

"But he ran, so I chased," Ruth said. "Voss told me not to."

"Never feel guilt for how another responds to fear," Isaac said. "We are free to make what choices we wish, but we must take the consequences that go with them."

"No, exactly," Ruth said. "It's sad and stupid, and a pointless waste of life. It's just that policing up here is different to the south."

"Life is different," Isaac said.

"However you put it, I've still got a lot to learn," Ruth said.

"A truly admirable sentiment," Isaac said. "But can we continue the lesson inside?"

"Not until we reach the sea."

By the time they returned to the bridge, the impromptu posse had been replaced with a more warmly dressed search party made up of sailors with long rifles and longer boathooks. In pairs, they walked the shore. Voss had left a message that he was going to the hospital to check on Howe whose leg had been broken in the fall. Isaac had to check on the position of his boat, so Ruth returned alone to the riverside hotel. In the ex-cops' room, inside a large travelling trunk, she found the twelve poster-tubes. Inside were rolled-up paintings, and in the fourth, she found an ice-skating cleric with a cocoa stain. She gathered up the tubes, took them back to the police station, and asked the duty-sergeant to send for Dr Frobisher. Not sure where else to go, she took the paintings into Inspector Voss's office.

Hamish arrived before Dr Frobisher, and with a heavy bag. "Nan sent you some dinner," he said.

"What time is it?" Ruth asked.

"About six," Hamish said. "Word is that Pewter drowned."

"You heard what happened?" Ruth asked.

"Everyone has," Hamish said. "It's not every day that twelve forgeries are discovered, a politician is arrested, and an ex-cop becomes an ice sculpture. We'll be talking about this for years. Do I need to ask what's in the twelve tubes?"

"It's the paintings," Ruth said. *"The Skating Minister* has the tell-tale cocoa stain, but a few flecks of paint fell when I was checking it. I decided to let Dr Frobisher take responsibility for examining them. Safe to say these are the twelve paintings we found in Dover, but are they real, or are they copies, too?"

"Why would you make forgeries of forgeries?" Hamish asked.

"Why make forgeries of paintings you were going to put on display?" Ruth asked. "The more I think about this case, the less it makes sense. I've got a theory, though. Fancy helping me test it?"

"How much walking does your test involve?" Hamish asked.

"Only as far as the interview room," Ruth said. "I want to speak with Quinn."

Quinn's solicitor had already arrived. He was a bald man in his late fifties with big eyes, a bigger nose, and a beard too wispy to balance out his face. When Ruth opened the door, the solicitor spoke before Quinn could.

"My client has nothing to say," the lawyer said. "She is, however, a member of parliament, and I demand that you release her immediately. Obviously, as soon as the telegraph is reopened, we will be calling for your dismissal. Charges will follow. How many, and how severe, will be determined by your cooperation now."

"I learned an interesting fact last week," Ruth said, taking the chair opposite Quinn. "In olden times, lords were hung by a silk rope rather than hemp."

"Are you threatening my client?" the solicitor asked.

"No more than you are threatening me," Ruth said. "So maybe we should both stop, eh?"

Hamish took the chair next to Ruth, and stretched his leg. "Ah, better," he said. "This is Charlie McAlister. As well as being a solicitor, he teaches English and Gaelic at the high school. Taught me for a year, and I turned out to be a war hero." He tapped the medal pinned to his coat. "Something in my education must have stuck, so thank you, sir."

"Hamish," McAlister said, unbending a little.

"Did Das put you up to this?" Quinn asked, finally breaking her silence.

"Say nothing, Erin," the solicitor said.

"What does Mr Das have to do with anything?" Ruth asked, momentarily puzzled. She shook her head. "No, I think you should, for now, follow your solicitor's advice. Say nothing, and just listen." Ruth turned to the solicitor. "You're from here, from Thurso, yes?"

"I'm *from* Shetland, but I was working in Aberdeen before the Blackout," McAlister said. "I'm qualified under Scottish law, old and new, if that's what you're asking."

"It's not," Ruth said. "Ms Quinn, you're from Loch somewhere. I forget the name, but it's north of Edinburgh, yes?"

"Loch Leven," Quinn said. "What of it?"

"I'm not sure where I'm from," Ruth said. "But I was found in a refugee camp not that far from Dover. I was about five at the time, and was adopted by one of the doctors. She took me back to Twynham, and she became a teacher and nurse in one of the resettlement camps. I thought a lot about that stretch of Kent when I was growing up, but it wasn't until a few months ago that I went back, and as a copper. Dover's an interesting place. It's always been the front line. Not just in this war, but throughout five thousand years of history. People are always coming and going, fleeing and seeking sanctuary."

"And we're about as far from there as you can be," McAlister said. "Do you have a point?"

"A few months ago, a painter was murdered," Ruth said. "He was a real artist, but one who never really got over the death of his family. He was working in one of those reclaim-and-repair outfits when he should have been in a studio. He didn't care about money. He was already walking in the shadow world, you know? His soul died with his family, but his body was just waiting for when it was time to join them. You must have met people like that."

"Are you saying you think the forgeries were the work of this dead artist?" McAlister asked.

"I don't think so," Ruth said. "The originals were sent to Dover, while the forgeries remained in Twynham, so it's likely the copies were made in the capital. I could be wrong, but the identity of the forger is a minor detail in what is a truly bizarre crime. But as a result of death of that artist, I've been reading up on art and forgery. The fakes are good. Excellent, even. But Dr Frobisher noticed the canvas was wrong the moment she looked at it. She's not an art expert, is she, Hamish?"

"She's an archaeologist by training," Hamish said.

"She spotted the discrepancy within a few minutes," Ruth said. "I can't imagine an actual art historian would take much longer. Surely that's exactly the kind of person who would take a train all the way up here just to see the pictures. That's the weird thing, you see? Why go to so much trouble making forgeries if you don't also find some old canvases to re-use?"

"Don't answer that," McAlister said.

"I wasn't going to," Quinn said.

"Years ago, someone took the original paintings from Edinburgh," Ruth said. "They were acquired by Longfield, and then used to pay the Porter brothers for some land in Cornwall. Then, a few weeks ago, the paintings were shipped to Dover, apparently in preparation for going on display in a bar in Calais, but they were sent to the train station and picked up by a local cart driver. That's odd, isn't it?"

"It's your theory, you tell me," Quinn said.

"Please, Erin, say nothing," McAlister said.

"Or just wait until you hear the rest of the questions, because there are so many more," Ruth said. "If they're so valuable, why send them as freight, and so create a paper trail? For that matter, why make copies at all? Who would buy the originals if copies are on display in France? They have newspapers in the U.S. The American spies who work in the embassy read our press. There is no way that you could have the same painting on display in two different countries without people asking which was the fake. If a painting stolen from Edinburgh simultaneously appeared in France and in America, how long would it take before you, Ms Quinn, stood up in parliament and demanded their return?"

"Don't—" the lawyer began, but Quinn cut him off.

"Please, Charlie," Quinn said. "We are not in France, or America, Miss Deering."

"No, because *I* found those paintings in Dover," Ruth said. "That wasn't part of the plan. The Porter brothers picked the wrong cart driver. His stupidity led to his arrest, and he told us where the crates were hidden. Because we assumed they had some link to the spy ring we'd unmasked at Christmas, we raided the Porter brothers' club. We found the paintings. I am absolutely certain we were not supposed to find them there or then."

"Where and when were they supposed to be found?" Quinn asked.

"Erin, please," McAlister hissed.

"Nearer to the election," Hamish said. "That's what this is about, isn't it? The opposition candidates are unifying against you. You needed a big win in the press."

"Do you know what happens when unity candidates win?" Quinn asked. "Nothing. There's no party structure behind them, no whips, and no conferences to debate policy. Without the strength and organisation of a political party, there will be five years of inaction."

"You're confessing?" Hamish asked.

"No, merely filling a gap in your education," Quinn said.

"Once word reached you that the paintings had been discovered in Dover, you hadn't much time to act," Ruth said. "The pictures would have gone on show in Dover. Reporters would have come to see for themselves, and the story they wrote would be a victory for the Dover Constabulary. Atherton might have visited for a photo op, and might have claimed some credit, but you would have got none. Worse for you, those were the originals. The forgeries were already in Twynham. They must have been, because there's no way you had time to create twelve fake paintings between their discovery and the train leaving for Thurso."

"A fascinating fiction," Quinn said, her lips curling into a disconcerting smile. "Do go on."

"You made sure the paintings would be rushed to Twynham," Ruth said. "You wouldn't let anyone see them, not even the press. Instead, you brought them up here, and put the forgeries on display in a badly lit room with too many shadows for anyone to properly see anything. It didn't matter what people thought of the exhibit, just that they knew the paintings were here. You were going to have Pewter and Howe take the originals to America. You wouldn't have been able to sell the pictures, but your agents could certainly have *discovered* them. By then, the paintings here would have been proven to be forgeries. You would have demanded the return of the originals, and gained publicity just in time for the election as a champion of the arts, of culture, of heritage."

"That's an absurd tale with no basis in fact," McAlister said.

"Charlie, if I may," Quinn said in a tone which brooked no disagreement. "Your theory is interesting, and I suspect it's not entirely wrong. If true, however, it makes me look a complete fool by displaying forgeries here in Thurso. How can I be a champion of the arts if I can't tell a real from a fake, especially when a frosty bookworm spotted it within a few minutes?"

"You admit it's true?" Hamish asked.

"It is demonstrably false," Quinn said. "If you had done your due diligence before entering this room, you would have learned the maiden name of Lilith McMoine is Howe."

"The deputy in your party is the sister of the ex-cop who was here as a bodyguard?" Ruth asked.

"Exactly," Quinn said. "I am the victim, not the perpetrator. If my goal was publicity, then the minute I was approached by these Porter brothers with news they had the paintings, why would I not go to the police? Why embark on some elaborate forgery scheme?"

"But why build such a terrible exhibition space?" Hamish asked.

"I did the best with the materials available," Quinn said.

"Hang on," Ruth said. "What does McMoine have to gain from all this?"

"Control of our party through my humiliation," Quinn said. "Yes, I wanted the paintings returned to Scotland, because otherwise you would have put them on show in Dover, then Twynham. If they were *ever* returned, it would be Atherton who'd gain the credit. McMoine encouraged their return, and provided her brother and his friend as bodyguards. They were on their way to America anyway to take up jobs as sheriffs, or so they said. That I put the forgeries on display would have been such a humiliation, I would have lost my seat at the election, and would have to resign as party leader."

"And her brother finding the originals would have ensured McMoine got the credit," Ruth said.

"And it would have assisted in his own rehabilitation," Quinn said. "Howe and Pewter lost their positions after Commissioner Wallace's death. There were no charges filed against them, obviously, but they were encouraged to walk. Ask them."

"Pewter's dead," Ruth said. "He drowned trying to cross the partially frozen river."

"I see," Quinn said. "And Howe?"

"He's in hospital. His leg's broken."

"Then ask him," Quinn said.

"Howe and Pewter would have got their reputations back," Hamish said. "Good jobs would follow, on one side of the Atlantic or the other. McMoine would have gained the leadership of your party. What was in it for the Porter brothers?"

"I have helped you more than enough," Quinn said. "I really will say no more except that I truly will look forward to your disciplinary hearing."

"That's okay," Ruth said, smiling as she stood up. "I think I've worked it out now. Thanks, though."

"That didn't go as expected," Hamish said, after they left the interview room. "We're going to be in big trouble."

"Not so big," Ruth said, as they walked back to Voss's office. "And mostly from Inspector Voss. I think I get his point now. Mister Mitchell learned to rush before the criminal had a chance to reload. Sergeant Kettering doesn't do much rushing, but she does hammer at a case until it cracks. Rushing about up here is a good way to freeze to death. Instead, you have to take your time."

"Which is what we should have done," Hamish said, easing himself into a chair. "Ah. What was it you worked out?"

"That McMoine and her brother are only one half of the crime," Ruth said. "What did the Porter brothers get out of this? It's not just about publicity. They took twelve paintings from Longfield in exchange for land in Cornwall rich in lithium. After Longfield's exposure as a traitor, all her property was seized, including that land, but if the Porter brothers can prove the paintings they took as payment were fake, they could petition for the land to be returned. However long it is before we can actually make lithium batteries, now that there's no ban, now that technology is being rediscovered, that land will grow in value every day."

"Would any judge grant them the land?"

"Who knows?" Ruth said. "They decided it was worth the risk because Longfield is dead."

"Okay, but they had the originals in Dover, while the forgeries were in Twynham. Shouldn't it have been the other way around?"

"Assuming the paintings we found in Dover *are* the originals," Ruth said. "Liam Porter said his contract with Longfield didn't mention which specific twelve paintings he'd taken as payment. There's quite a few details to pin down, starting with whether we've found the originals and when the forgeries were made. The link to Wallace worries me. If the forgeries were made before Longfield's death, then the goal of this scheme might, originally, have been to humiliate her. I know Wallace and she both had their eyes on absolute power, and there's only room for one at the very top."

"In which case, the Porter brothers could be facing a treason charge," Hamish said. "That should get them to confess."

"Howe and McMoine, too," Ruth said. "Forgery and political sabotage are bad enough, but treason carries the death penalty."

"Quinn will have to be released," Hamish said.

"Probably, but that'll be up to Inspector Voss. We should send a message to him."

But as she walked to the office's door, a constable was already hurrying to them.

"Constable Deering, a message for you," he said.

"It's from Isaac," Ruth said. "I'm needed in Scrabster."

"You don't think Stevens is trying to escape?" Hamish said.

"Right now, nothing would surprise me," Ruth said.

Chapter 25 - Goodbye
The Docks, Scrabster

Leaving Hamish to send a message to Voss, Ruth grabbed the first cab she found, and had almost reached Scrabster when she saw Isaac walking back towards Thurso.

"Stop here, thanks," she said, jumping out. "Isaac, what is it?"

"My boat has come in," he said. "I'm leaving."

"Now?"

"The ferry has arrived, but between unloading the cargo and swapping passengers, it might be twenty-four hours before it departs. Ideally, my boat would have slipped in and away unseen, but we can't afford the wait. There's a storm in the Atlantic creeping towards these shores."

"Well, let's take the cab," she said.

"Let's walk," he said. "Did you wrap up your case?"

"Nope. We arrested the wrong politician. Quinn's deputy is behind the scam, but she's down in Twynham. The real crime, though, was committed by the Porter brothers."

"It was?"

"We think they want to reclaim the land in Cornwall they sold to Longfield by saying they were paid in forgeries."

"Oh, that does sound intriguing," Isaac said. "I'll regret not being able to tag along on that particular investigation."

"I never met your friend," Ruth said. "Is there time for you to introduce me?"

"Sadly, no. But I asked Esme to take you to meet him," Isaac said.

"You could take me yourself, when you get back."

"I don't know when, or if that will be," Isaac said.

"That sounds so final," Ruth said.

"Goodbyes always should be, if only to make a reunion so much sweeter," Isaac said. "But this could be the last time we speak. Even if we're successful, it might be impossible to return."

"Then don't go. Find another way," she said.

"If there was one, we would," Isaac said.

At the harbour, spotlights had turned night into day, with dozens of pole-armed dockers having joined the armed sentries at the gate to the harbour. The ferry had docked. Twice as long as the icebreaker, and much taller, a crane was being erected to offload the cargo containers. A much smaller crane was loading two crates onto the deck of Isaac's much smaller boat.

"What's in the boxes?" Ruth asked.

"Two Land Rover Wolfs," Isaac said.

"The same cars from Sandringham?" Ruth asked.

"About sixty percent the same," Isaac said. "They were winterized for Norway, and modified for this mission."

"Everything you say just makes me worry more," Ruth said.

Isaac stopped, turned to face her, and took her hands. "Then, instead, let me thank you."

"You're welcome, but what for?"

"For giving Maggie a fourth act," Isaac said. "Most people don't even get a third. I knew her before the Blackout, of course, and I knew her afterwards, but it was only after she met you that I saw her truly come alive. For that, I am more grateful than I can express."

"No problem," Ruth said again, though her voice was now hoarse. "Please come back."

"If we can, we will," Isaac said. "Until then, keep doing what you're doing, because you're doing it exceedingly well." He hugged her, turned, and walked towards his ship.

Ruth bit her lip, but couldn't stop a tear rolling down her cheek.

A sailor stood from where he'd been sitting on a coil of rope and walked over, pulling back his jacket's waxed hood and revealing a very familiar face.

"Mister Mitchell?" Ruth asked.

"I think you can call me Henry," he said.

"I don't know that I could," she said. "I thought you were in Belgium."

"I was. Kelly picked me up."

"Not Mrs Zhang?"

"She's in Belgium with Gregory. Kelly's piloting the ship, but will remain with it when Isaac and I go ashore."

"I don't suppose you'll tell me where," she said. "Isaac wouldn't."

"Poland to start with," he said. "We needed to pick up the Land Rovers and spare diesel from here. If the ferry had been delayed much longer, our plans could have been seriously disrupted. But it arrived as we did, so we'll stick to our schedule."

"And after Poland?"

"We're driving to our enemy's base," Mitchell said. "Historians love turning points, the one person, the one act, which changed the future for everyone. Isaac and I decided to make one of our own. We're going to change the future."

"Just you and Isaac?"

"Just him and me," Mitchell said.

"But that's crazy. Why not take an army?"

"Because we want to end this war," he said. "One strike might do it. But if we battle our way across Europe, our enemy will retreat, and this conflict will continue for another twenty years. That's as much as I can tell you, and you should keep it to yourself. I've written a letter which will be delivered to Anna after the mission is over. She'll explain everything."

"I... I see. Give me twenty minutes to get my bag, and I'll come with you."

"Not this time. This is our fight, not your mum's, not yours, or Anna's, or Kelly's. This is our chance to bring peace, once and for all."

"Don't you dare die trying," Ruth said, again finding her throat swelling.

"Until we meet again, keep an eye on Maggie, and Anna. I won't offer you advice, because you don't need it. Take care, Ruth."

She couldn't hold back the tears as he boarded the boat. A camouflaged sailor released the rope, and far sooner than she was prepared for, the boat began pulling away.

"We've a tradition when a ship sets out on an uncertain voyage," Esme MacKay said, appearing soundlessly at Ruth's elbow. She held out a flask. "Take this."

"He said they were going to Poland. Do you know where they're going after?"

"I wouldn't loan Isaac my boat, or my two best cars, without knowing where they were heading," she said, fishing two small glasses from an inside pocket.

"So where are they going?" Ruth asked.

"To war in the hope they can find peace," Esme said. "Fill them up, then."

Ruth poured a measure into each glass, and then took the one offered to her. "Is this whisky?"

"Not just whisky, but vintage," Esme said. "Aged a whole two years, that is."

"Do we drink to a safe return?" Ruth asked.

"The sea is a dangerous place, and land isn't much better," she said. "Don't say goodbye, and don't hope for a reunion. No, as much as we look to the future, sometimes it's helpful to remember the past. So we'll raise a glass to the first Isaac."

"From the Bible?"

"I mean the Russian who became the fastest writer in the West. The Isaac from whom your Isaac stole his name. Then we'll drink to Mary, Jules, Herbert, Arthur, Ursula, Jack, Gene, and John."

"That's a lot of people," Ruth said.

"It's only the beginning," Esme said. "There are lot to whom we should be thankful. Don't you worry, I've another bottle back in the office."

"How about we drink to peace," Ruth said. "Whenever it may come and for however long it may last."

Part 4
Doing the Unthinkable

Poland, the Czech Republic, and Austria

1st February

Chapter 26 - Hidden Sailors
Kolobrzeg, Poland

The floor fell. The bunk dropped. A wave-wall slammed into the cabin's small porthole. Henry Mitchell found his place and had managed to read another sentence before the rollercoaster began again. In the three days since they'd left Scrabster, he had re-read the battered copy of *Thud!* nearly twice and found more than just comfort in the familiar words. The book was a reminder that there was always another way, as long as you were prepared to do the previously unthinkable. The ship rolled, rocked, and dropped, all at the same time. He hit elbow and knee against the bunk, and lost his place again.

Last night, they'd sailed over the lost bridge which had once linked Copenhagen to Malmo. By the time they'd circumnavigated the Falsterbo Peninsula, it had been too dark to see the remains of the abandoned settlement that had almost become another Thurso, another Dover, or perhaps even another Twynham.

Situated at the southern tip of Sweden, and so at the northwestern edge of the Baltic, the peninsula had become a post-Blackout refuge for sailing boats from Germany and Poland. The harbour soon filled, but the refugees kept arriving, bringing news there was no better safety further east. With resources creaking, the newcomers had been given what little could be spared and sent onward towards the North Sea. Only one ship, a twin-mast racing catamaran, had made it to Scotland, but by then, the first nine-month winter had begun. It was another thirteen months before a Royal Navy ship had made contact with the community on Falsterbo.

The population had then stood at a desperate thirty-three thousand. Slowly, it grew as sibling-settlements were established elsewhere on Sweden's coast, then on the other side of the sea in Germany and Poland. From there, traders had gone south, meeting with scavenger caravans who'd set out from Calais. Hope bloomed, but disease flowered, and the pirates picked off the survivors.

The ship rocked. The bunk bounced. Mitchell sighed, but was saved from having to hunt for his place when Isaac entered the narrow cabin.

"Surely you know that book by heart," Isaac said.

"Heart's not the same as brain," Mitchell said. "Is there trouble?"

"In an utterly unspecific way, yes," Isaac said. "Land is ahoy, though I don't know if it's Germany or Poland. There is an obvious way to find out, but while Kelly is now captain, you are the general, so I thought it polite to ask."

"Can we make it ashore in waves this high?" Mitchell asked.

"Ashore, yes," Isaac said. "I can't promise unscathed, but that will be the case with wherever we end up."

"Then let's get it over with," Mitchell said.

For a bookmark, he used an old airline ticket. This one was a never-used single to Brisbane he'd picked up in a New Forest ruin seven months ago. He'd lost his own return ticket when the Blackout began, on the night assassins had come hunting for Maggie and Isaac. Each plane ticket told a story of an unmade reunion, an unmet promise, or a once-in-a-lifetime vacation which truly lived up to its name. To him, each was a reminder that death could arrive at any moment, and always left much undone.

He slung himself out of the cot, knocking his head as the ship rolled ten degrees. Dreaming of planes, trains, or just a good pair of boots, he slotted the book into his bag, and pulled on his uniform jacket. The prime minister had insisted this was an official mission to be conducted by those with an official sanction, and so they had to wear a uniform. Naturally, the honour of equipping his team had gone to the Senior Service, but the navy quartermaster, not wanting to waste good gear on soldiers, had given them mouse-nibbled rags. Colonel Elizabeth Sherwood, commander of Albion's Royal Bodyguard and heir to the defunct Albion throne, had stepped up and provided sets of the foresters' reinforced camouflage. The pattern had been designed for concealment among the ruins of Leicester and Nottingham, but it should work just as well for the desolation they found in Austria.

In the ship's small cockpit, Kelly was by the wheel, Colonel Elizabeth Sherwood was consulting a chart, while Isaac was consulting a telescope.

"Where are we?" Mitchell asked.

"Somewhere near the border, but definitely Poland," Kelly said. "The storm shoved us eastward."

"I spy something that begins with industrial chimneys and ends with a monstrous crane," Isaac said. "Ah, no. It might be a wrecked wind turbine. It's hard to tell while the ship is bouncing like a rabbit in a carrot field. It's times like these I wish I'd salvaged that submarine."

"Pass me the telescope," Mitchell said.

"Do you mean the submarine that sailed up the Thames to Parliament?" Sherwood asked.

"Sadly, it was just a myth," Isaac said. "We checked."

"He really did," Kelly said wistfully. "We waded through a swamp, nearly drowned in Pimlico, practically suffocated in Westminster, and almost got eaten by dogs in Buckingham Palace. It was my seventeenth birthday."

"Good times," Isaac said.

"The best," Kelly said. "But you still owe me a present."

"I gave you a rifle."

"Mrs Zhang gave me that rifle," Kelly said.

"The harbour's abandoned," Mitchell said. "No smoke. No flags. No ships. Probably no pirates. Colonel, tell your squad to prepare to disembark and secure the landing site. There's a concrete-covered river-channel running into the sea. We'll make for that. Isaac, take the helm. Kelly, you're on overwatch."

Waves crashed onto the rusting hulks lining the shore on either side of the river's concrete embankment. He'd seen that type of haphazard construction in more post-Blackout harbours than he could remember. In theory, the hulks would limit where the pirates could land, and so force any raiders into a kill-zone. It never worked. Any crew of pirates who'd sailed for days to reach a target wouldn't be deterred by an aquatic obstacle course. Invariably, they'd gone ashore a few miles away and attacked from inland.

The first pirates weren't hardened butchers like the Knights, the Caliphate, or the Free Peoples. They were hungry refugees, trying to save themselves and their loved ones. When their families had died, as often from disease as violence, revenge became a way of life. *Join or die* became their motto, though most had done both.

Yes, that was why Britain had prioritised the Royal Navy over education or industry. Yes, even now, Mitchell was sure it had been the necessary decision. And yet, as he surveyed the desolate shore, he couldn't help feeling guilty that they'd not found a way to do more.

At the entrance to the river channel, ropes and chains dangled from poles drilled into cement, marking where a net had once been strung as a gate, but it was as long-gone as the defenders. They'd left behind broken cranes, collapsed warehouses, and bent chimneys. In the distance, shattered apartment blocks rose skyward, the broken glass glinting in the day's early sun. Was it just broken window glass? With its nautical proximity to Sweden, to Denmark, and to the North Sea, wherever this harbour was, it must have been a trading town since ancient times. Had it become a sanctuary again?

"Here will do, just on the left," Mitchell said. "That bit of seawall looks wide enough. There's a warehouse behind, and there'll be a road nearby."

As the ship bumped into the wall, the six foresters jumped ashore, sprinting into the ruins with longbows ready to be drawn. Kelly followed, but stayed on the quayside, rifle raised, scanning the opposite bank.

As Isaac worked the crane, Mitchell secured the ship. He'd barely finished when Sherwood returned, her team now invisible against the rusting ruins as they stood guard.

"We found a seaworthy boat in the orange-painted warehouse," Sherwood said.

"That's paint? Thought it was rust," Mitchell said. "What kind of boat?"

"A twenty-metre, steel-hulled sailing ship with long oars hanging on one wall and fishing gear stored on another," Sherwood said. "It's stood on a wheeled trailer, with the nearest slipway some fifty metres away."

"So it's concealed if not hidden," Mitchell said. "When was it last used?"

"Not within the last few days, but it could be launched within an hour."

"Did you see any spare sailcloth?" Mitchell asked.

"Not in there," Sherwood said.

"This is an industrial harbour," Mitchell said, once again taking in the fractured skyline. "Around here, the sea would be full of heavy-metal run-off. Any fish you could catch, you certainly wouldn't want to eat. But a few miles out, as long as you didn't disturb the sediment, you should get a good haul. One day's fishing could feed a village for a week, but a village needs drinking water, too. They'd have to get their water from inland and upriver, maybe from some smaller tributary. Ideally, that's where they'd live."

"But if this countryside is plagued by bandits, they would hide in the ruins within walking distance of fresh water and food," Sherwood said.

"And right now, we look a lot like seaborne raiders," Mitchell said. "Those shattered apartment blocks would make for excellent watchtowers. Pull your people back, Colonel, and tell them to stay alert."

They had travelled top-heavy from Thurso with two Land Rover Wolfs strapped to the ship's deck. Mitchell knew it was pointless to question Isaac's maths as regards buoyancy and ballast, but the converted fishing freighter wasn't designed to carry such cargo. As the crane rose, the ship wallowed and rocked.

"Go, go, go," Mitchell murmured as the first Land Rover swung ashore. The moment the cage touched the ground, he jumped up to the top, pulled the release pin, and then had to drop to the hard quayside as the released hook wildly swung.

Only when the second Land Rover was ashore, and the hook was safely stowed, did he relax, and then only marginally. As the foresters formed a protective cordon, he unfolded a map on the hood of his Land Rover. Isaac and Kelly joined him. Colonel Elizabeth Sherwood called over Sir Guy Glastonbury, a fifty-six-year-old Master of the Royal Armoury who had once been a cross-Europe courier and who was her team's driver.

"According to those signs, we're at Kolobrzeg," Mitchell said. "We're in Poland, and about eighty kilometres from the Oder, and that's where we thought we'd go ashore."

"Will that be a problem?" Sherwood asked.

"Not a huge one," Mitchell said. "In the last twenty years, the maps have been updated by a handful of traders, and a few of the more perceptive refugees, but even the best of their reports are incomplete. However, a broken bridge *won't* have been repaired. We'll follow the compass south until we can pick up the trade route that ran from Berlin to Lodz. We're well behind enemy lines. We're unlikely to encounter any retreating bands of barbarians. But any surviving groups of refugees, hiding in forest or mountain, will be defensively hostile."

"What are the rules of engagement?" Sir Guy asked.

"The mission must succeed," Mitchell said. "For it to do so, everyone must stick with the plan. Colonel, when we near the old German border, you'll take your team west towards Nuremberg. You only need to get within ninety kilometres of the old city. Set up the beacon, power up the radio, and wait for our call. Isaac and I should reach Matzen around the same time. Kelly, as soon as we leave, you must do the same."

"You don't want me to wait here?" she asked.

"If you did, you'd have to fight the locals," Mitchell said.

"I'd win," she said.

"I know," he said.

"How will you get out of Austria?" Sherwood asked.

"We'll drive as far as we can and hope it's far enough that we can reach our forces over radio," Mitchell said.

"Then take two of my foresters with you," Sherwood said. "The extra weight might mean you end up on foot a few kilometres sooner, but you'll be grateful for their hunting skills if you've a long walk back to Calais."

"Getting out isn't as important as getting this done," Mitchell said. "Two people make less noise than four."

"Not less than my foresters," Sherwood said.

"I'm not disputing your people's skills," Mitchell said. "But Isaac and I have moved in the shadows for years. Let's not any of us kid ourselves. For this to succeed, absolutely everything has to go as we've planned. And even if it does, it still might not stop the war." He reached into his coat and took out a letter. He handed it to Sherwood.

"What's this?" the colonel asked.

"Excuse us," Isaac said. "Kelly and I have a few matters to discuss." He and Kelly walked out of earshot.

"That letter is a summary of what we're doing and why," Mitchell said. "There are a few details the official briefing skipped. A somewhat more detailed version will be given to the newspaper after the plane returns to Belgium."

"This mission was supposed to be a secret," Sherwood said.

"You can't hide a plane when it flies overhead," Mitchell said. "Whether we succeed or not, half the front will be asking what target the plane attacked. Some things can't be kept secret. Some things shouldn't be. A real victory for us, going forward, is a more open and honest society. That letter explains it all, including that we're currently fighting the survivors of the team who caused the apocalypse. They are, or were, scientists and programmers employed by a billionaire mercenary called Marr who wanted to cheat death. There were two strands to this research: cloning and digitising human consciousness. They failed. Funding came from hacking, sometimes for governments, and so they were experts at creating digital viruses."

"You mean they created the Blackout?" Sir Guy asked.

"Yes," Mitchell said. "Marr learned someone else's research into a fully sentient A.I. was about to be presented to the small part of the world that was interested in such things. A digital virus was unleashed to conceal a team of assassins who were sent to steal the rival research. The virus went global and caused the Blackout."

"My father told me a version of this story a long time ago," Sherwood said. "I was never sure how much truth there was to it."

"I suspect Isaac told your father," Mitchell said, glancing back to where Isaac and Kelly were in quiet but animated conversation.

"How did he know?" Sir Guy asked.

"Because I killed the assassins in London during the Blackout," Mitchell said. "Afterward, collecting evidence was difficult. Ironically, a lot was just sitting on some ancient MI6 servers, but I didn't have access to those until recently. By the time I did, it merely confirmed what we'd learned from the war, and the investigation into the events leading up to it. After the Blackout, Marr's scientists created dozens of biological weapons to cause plagues that swept through Europe. They were unable to mass-produce vaccines, and so the number of true followers remained restricted. Instead, they armed bandit tribes like the Knights of St Sebastian, the Caliphate, and the Free Peoples. They created client states, and ensured those mercenaries destroyed any nascent communities in central Europe, then Western Europe, and most recently, they sent those client-killers to attack Britain. They wanted us to destroy the terrorist-tribes, and bankrupt and exhaust ourselves in the process, leaving central and southern Europe empty for them to conquer."

"I'd say they succeeded," Sir Guy said.

"Yes," Mitchell said. "We *are* exhausted. The EU is, once again, in exile. Most of Europe and North Africa is just like this harbour-town, ruins where the survivors hide in the shadows."

"But the terrorists *have* been destroyed," Sir Guy said. "The largest group disappeared into the ruins of Paris. The rest just disappeared. They're starving, scattered, and without any coherent leadership."

"Exactly, and exactly as our enemy wanted," Mitchell said. He unfolded the map, and pointed at Austria, where it bordered the Czech Republic and Slovakia. "That's Matzen. They picked this location because of the oil beneath the ground, but those were imperial homelands for centuries. With the Alps in the south, the Carpathians in the east, and the Sudetes in the north, the mountain ranges act like walls. To control the passes between the mountains, you must occupy the plains. For that, you need farmers, and there are thousands hiding in the mountains or out in the forests. To control the farmers, they need only be given tractors and oil."

"And they have a refinery," Sir Guy said.

"Spring is almost upon us," Mitchell said. "They've cleared their new homeland of bandits. Any who remain can be dealt with by a farmer carrying a Kalashnikov, and we know they have lots of those guns. They'll recruit refugees as farmers, offering them security and food. The farmers will repay that with loyalty. If our mission fails, our army will head to Austria as part of a tank convoy, using up every drop of diesel we've bought from America, and every litre of biofuel we've been able to make. The enemy have missiles and mortars, as you saw in Belgium. They'll make short work of our tanks. Whatever damage we do, however many we kill, we won't kill them all. They can retreat back to the mountains. We'll have to retreat, too, and mostly on foot. It'll be very hard to sell that as a victory to the people back home. There's no way the politicians will settle for a defeat."

"Not with an election on its way," Sherwood said.

"So we'll have to create another, bigger army," Mitchell said. "That'll mean more rationing, more privation, more conscription. But during that first attack, our army will have massacred its way through those mountain-pass farming towns. We'll become the villains, the bandits, the terrorist government who butchered the innocent."

"We'd never do that," Sherwood said.

"We might not plan it," Mitchell said. "It could still happen."

"I would never do it, nor would any forester," she said.

"And would Albion go to war with Twynham to prevent it?" Mitchell asked. "Would you raise an army to stop parliament, *Princess* Elizabeth? Would you take the crown to protect against tyranny? Don't forget the EU. Regardless of what the British parliament decides, the Europeans could close the Channel Tunnel in Calais. Would we go to war with them, too? And all the while, enemy agents would be whispering sweet sedition in the ears of anyone who'd listen."

"Like John Boyle," Sir Guy said.

"And like Longfield and so many others," Mitchell said. "And so the war goes on, and it's the same war we've been fighting these last twenty years. While we fight among ourselves, our enemy will regroup, grow, and then turn their eyes southward. There might be a lake of oil beneath Austria, but there's a sea of it in the Persian Gulf. For a community with trucks and fuel, it is no distance at all. There's a reason that they funded the Caliphate as well as the Knights and Free Peoples. They wanted the Middle East as depopulated as Europe so they could make it part of their new empire, too. In five years, we'll have three empires: Britain, France, and Austria. That's history repeating itself, and we know how that history ends."

"Then we'd best not fail," Sherwood said.

Mitchell took out another envelope and gave it to Sherwood. "This is a copy of the same letter. Give it to a forester who is returning on the ship with instructions to hand it to your father. If our mission fails, he'll hold the balance of power. Whatever decisions he makes should be informed ones. We move out in ten minutes."

Mitchell made his way over to Kelly and Isaac, standing quietly together by the pier.

Kelly hugged Isaac, then turned to Mitchell. "I could end this," she said. "Me and my rifle. One bullet is all it would take. One shot is all I would need."

"I was never a fan of the Great Man, or Great Villain, approach to history," Mitchell said. "For every FDR, there was an army. For every Lincoln, there was a cabinet. When Stalin died, the oppression didn't end. When Mao died, freedom didn't bloom. Democrat or dictator, when one dies, however they die, another always takes the throne. If we fail, and there are so many ways we could fail, only the gun will remain. But one bullet won't be enough. That's why we must try something different."

"One missile," she said. "This is almost certain suicide."

"Not if everything goes to plan. Head back to Belgium, see the foresters ashore, pick up Mrs Zhang and Gregory. Hide. For how long depends on what happens back in Twynham, so listen to Mrs Zhang, she'll know what to do next."

"I will," Kelly said. "I know you can't promise to come back, so promise you'll look out for each other."

"Always," Mitchell said.

After twenty kilometres of driving, Isaac finally broke his silence. "Did you give Sherwood the speech?" he asked.

"I did," Mitchell said.

"I'm still curious as to why you brought Albion Foresters when you could have had your pick of British Marines."

"Sir Guy knows how to drive," Mitchell said. "He was a courier before the Blackout."

"Yes, but there were many other older sailors, and soldiers, you could have asked. Some of whom you would even call friends. A suspicious man might think you asked for Sherwood so you could give her that speech, and send a letter to her father, which won't be delivered until after the plane takes off. Do you think you stopped a revolution, or began one?"

"That's why we changed the payload," Mitchell said. "If we succeed, there *will* be a revolution, but hopefully it'll be a peaceful one. If we fail, then it will be down to Mr Das to stop a different kind of revolution."

"You're all but handing him the crown," Isaac said. "Or her, since he's officially renounced it."

"Better a constitutional monarchy than an accidental empire," Mitchell said. "But if it *is* her monarchy, democracy still stands a chance. We can't dictate the future's ultimate destination, but we can steer it in a better direction."

"Speaking of which, there's a wreck ahead."

"We can squeeze past. Warn Sherwood."

The colonel's car, driven by Guy Glastonbury, and carrying Corporal Lancaster and Private Scunthorpe, were following a hundred metres behind.

"Did you tell Weaver?" Isaac asked.

"No, she needs plausible deniability so she can keep her job. I hate to think whom they might pick to replace her. Did you make plans for Arthur?"

"Esme MacKay and I have had a plan for years," Isaac said. "He'll be taken to safety if it comes to that. Mrs Zhang will collect Maggie, Ruth, and Anna. They'll be safe. Unhappy, of course, but safe. Even if we fail, our legacy will not be lost."

They drove on in silence. Minutes became hours. Metres became miles, but not nearly fast enough as old wrecks and new rivers forced one detour after another. Occasional birds burst from the trees, and wild pigs darted across the road. Young forests rose from the ruins, occasionally interspersed with open pasture grazed by wild horses as often as deer. There was life in Poland, just not the human kind. Not anymore.

After two frustratingly slow hours, they reached a crossroads where a noose hung from a tree. A few bones lay amid the leaf-mulch beneath, but the rest of the body had long since been claimed by scavenging carnivores. Just beyond the crossroads was a partially dismantled roadblock built of sawn trunks and rusting steel. A few bullet holes, a few more bones, and a lot of brass, spoke of what had happened to the defenders. As to who had done it, they had left their mark carved into the tree: the two-bar cross of the Knights of St Sebastian.

2nd February

Chapter 27 - The Weeping Blight
Dabrowa Boleslawiecka, Poland

Darkness came early as a storm pushed north. Uncertain where they were, they took shelter in a farmhouse just as the rains began. Even with the storm truncating visibility, they didn't risk a light. Instead, they ate a cold meal, and took what sleep they could find as they waited for dawn.

Mitchell took the last watch. While Colonel Sherwood could move silently, the old floorboards of the two-storey ruin creaked with each soft footfall as she approached Mitchell, standing by the cracked window.

"Have you seen anything?" she asked.

"Nothing," he said. "Not a single light. With dawn on its way, we won't now."

"There are people out there," she said. "I just know it, and wish we could reach them."

"Give it a few months," Mitchell said.

"A few months, yes," she said. "I don't understand what you want me to do with that letter."

"What you do is up to you," Mitchell said. "You and your father have an outsized influence, but it won't last. For maybe the next decade, when you speak, people will listen. I learned, a long while back, that you can't tell people what path to take. All you can do is limit the options."

"By removing the worst?" she asked.

"Sometimes," Mitchell said. "And sometimes by making it a choice between the very worst and the barely adequate. We can have empires or democracy, famine or plenty, war or peace."

"If history teaches us anything, it's that we'll have them all," she said.

"Perhaps, and perhaps the best I can hope for is that my daughter gets a little calm before the next nightmare begins. But for how long the calm lasts is up to the people as much as the politicians, and you and the press have positioned yourselves as buffers between them. What you do, what they do, is out of my hands."

"Except that you just put that letter *into* my hands," she said.

"Like I said, it's out of *my* hands. Dawn's breaking, it's time we moved out."

At first light, they continued south, this time finding a highway where one, and often two, lanes had been cleared by forgotten teams of farmers and traders. A mile further on, a plume of smoke rose from a near-road patch of trees. Someone had heard their engines and hastily extinguished a campfire. They didn't stop, or even slow, but pressed on, ever alert for an ambush.

At midday, halfway through a fire-ravaged village now home to a colony of elk, the road was blocked by a fallen tree. With singed stone on either side, there was nowhere to turn.

"Watch for an ambush," Sherwood warned over the radio, and just before Mitchell could give her the same advice.

"Her foresters are stretching their legs," Isaac said. "As long as they're not stretching their bowstrings, I shall do the same."

Keeping the driver door open, Mitchell followed.

The elk had vanished, but their presence suggested a lack of humans nearby.

"The trunk's cracked, not sawn," Isaac said, standing on the stump of the tree blocking the road. He breathed deep, turned around, and paused. "Henry, come and see this."

"Trouble?" he asked even as he jogged from the car.

"Beyond those houses," Isaac said. "It's death."

A black field lay beyond the ruined village. Crudely ploughed, possibly by hand, it had then been planted, but never harvested. The crop had been left to rot, freeze, thaw, and become a blackened swamp.

"It's the Weeping Blight," Isaac said, joining Mitchell at the field's edge.

"What's that?" Sherwood asked.

"You haven't heard of it?" Mitchell asked. "The Weeping Blight is the English translation of the name given to it by the refugees the plague created. The stems ooze sap just before they die. It swept through Poland and Germany about thirteen years ago. The winters were just starting to shorten. There were hints that, within a few years, life would ease from being an hourly struggle into a daily chore. It was a time of planning and dreams, until we got word of the blight. There were at least four million people living between the Danube and the

Dnieper. Maybe even as many as ten million. The crops died, and the farmers became refugees. Not all in one go, of course. Some left early. Some travelled just to the next town. Some slaughtered their livestock, or tried to become hunters, but that's a hard trade to learn when you're starving. Some made it to the coast, and then to Britain. They brought a different kind of plague with them. Back here, the Knights rose from the ashes, recruiting from among the hungry farmers. Afterwards, after we'd buried the dead in Britain, after traders began pushing east and north, there was no more word of the blight. No further outbreaks. How long ago do you think this village was razed?"

"Two years. Perhaps three," Sherwood said.

"This crop was planted last year, and it died last summer," Mitchell said. "Someone returned here, but was burned out of their home by bandits. Someone returned again, and this time, their crops were targeted."

"The fungus could have been dormant in the fields," Sherwood said.

"Or our foe wanted to make certain there was no food anywhere except near Calais," Mitchell said.

He took advantage of rank, letting the foresters move the tree while he paced the road. He was so lost in his ire, he nearly missed the fallen road sign. He kicked the mud clear, then hurried back to his Land Rover, where he checked his map.

"We're not where I thought we were," he said. "We're actually closer to where we need to be. We're on the DW297, and it's about to meet the A4. Colonel, you can take that road west into Germany. Follow it towards Reichenbach, then take a left after Dresden."

"And us?" Isaac asked.

"We'll go east," Mitchell said. "We'll take the long route to avoid the Jizera Mountains."

"Will you have enough fuel for a detour?" Sherwood asked.

"To get to our target, yes," Mitchell said.

"And to get back?" Sherwood asked.

"We'll worry about it when the time comes," Mitchell said.

Chapter 28 - The Consequences of Our Mistakes
Jelenia Gora, Poland

"Jelenia Gora is our next waypoint," Isaac said, his finger dancing across the map as the Land Rover bumped and juddered across the frozen field. "Assuming we make it that far."

"We'll be back on the road in a few minutes," Mitchell said. "We're almost past the wrecked plane."

"Assuming we *do* make it, after Jelenia Gora, we'll aim for Lubawka and then cross into the Czech Republic," Isaac said. "If we can avoid driving into the cities, and avoid the mountains, and if we're not delayed finding a way across the Elbe, we might make it to Brno before nightfall. The Austrian border isn't far from there, and Matzen isn't much further."

"I want to cross the Austrian border at dawn," Mitchell said. "The enemy has radios, trucks, and more fuel than we've seen in two decades. They could have roaming patrols, so we'll have to cut our speed the closer we get."

"Patrols in cars?" Isaac asked. "I doubt it. Surely that would only alert refugees to their presence."

"I said could, not would," Mitchell said. "The further they roam, the more likely they are to be spotted by refugees and fleeing terrorists. But they'll have to start roaming and recruiting soon."

"But not until after the thaw," Isaac said.

The car bumped, rocked, and returned to the road.

"How's our fuel?" Isaac asked.

"It's a good thing we brought enough to get back, or we'd run out before we arrived," Mitchell said. "This truck isn't as fuel-efficient as I hoped."

"I apologise. I did the calculations based on an idealised winterized Wolf, not on one which had been previously up-armoured to transport the Windsors. I told Ruth the story of how I found the cars."

"And how you met Kelly?" Mitchell asked.

"A somewhat sanitised version, yes," Isaac said. "I didn't think Kelly would appreciate me telling the *whole* story. Speaking of which, Ruth asked me something to which I couldn't give a satisfactory answer. After I saved Kelly, you and I fell out. We didn't speak for nearly a year."

"We spoke. There was the murder in Plymouth, and the kidnapping in Llandudno."

"That was us working together. *Your* work. Anyway, you're dissembling. I know it was Thurso."

"What about Thurso?"

"That I picked it to be my base, and never asked the locals if they'd mind. I did look for alternatives, before and after. I went back to Cambridge, but it was too damaged. I tried Albion, but their beliefs didn't entirely mesh with my own. I even bought that wretched citadel in Dover."

"You bought that old ruin so you could dig for treasure," Mitchell said.

"I dug for the treasure *because* I'd bought it. But I bought the citadel because I thought that's what you wanted."

"What *I* wanted?" Mitchell asked, glancing sideways.

"Watch the road, because it disappears in a quarter mile," Isaac said. "A field has flooded."

"The last turning's at least a mile back," Mitchell said, slowing to a stop. He stepped outside, and climbed up onto the roof. "It's a new flood," he said when he climbed back in. "And it's almost as high as the hedgerow, but there's a westward track we can follow upriver." He restarted the engine. "Why do you think I wanted you to move to Dover?"

"You said my work should be at the centre of the reconstruction effort," Isaac said. "For all that Twynham became the capital, Dover was, and always has been, the confluence of Britain and Europe. But it's impossible to get anything done there, then and now. Between the navy, the EU, and the local council, applying for a permit to chop down a tree requires a forest of paperwork."

"When did they introduce permits for forestry?" Mitchell asked.

"I was being hyperbolic," Isaac said. "They still barely have any wind power, and even the hydroelectric project on the Medway won't be properly operational until this summer. Dover wouldn't work now, and it was obvious it wouldn't have worked then. I had to choose Thurso. It's so remote the residents could ignore Twynham's objections to technology. I didn't see I had another option."

"I'm not arguing with you," Mitchell said.

"Not now, but you did."

"When I said I'd like to see your efforts at the heart of things, I didn't mean geographically, and assumed it might be some kind of university. Like every tech guru in the old world, you wanted a place that was light on regulations, and in which the officials would leave you alone, you and your fellow believers, your guardians of the future."

"I never called us that," Isaac said.

"Kelly did. She wrote it on her hat."

"She was a teenager inspired by my stash of old movies," Isaac said. "You make us sound like a cult."

"You are," Mitchell said. "How else would you describe a common belief that technology will somehow save us, so it must be preserved?"

"It's only knowledge we're preserving," Isaac said. "You can't say you object to that."

"I don't. I never did," Mitchell said. "Maggie was already on a different path, but I know you spoke to her. You took advice from Mrs Zhang after she found you. You listened to Kelly, and to others. You weren't deciding on the planet's future alone."

"I asked you to help, too," Isaac said. "Or I tried to."

"You wanted to preserve a piece of the old world against a time when it could become the present, and so guide the future. That's what you said."

"Word for word," Isaac said. "You remembered."

"Of course," Mitchell said. "But I was just trying to keep the peace on some very hungry streets. I was raising a daughter while still recovering from my own childhood. Every morning was a new crisis. I had no time to worry about the future, but there were times when I was glad that you had found the time."

"Then I don't understand what the problem was then, but it has cast a shadow over everything since."

"Looks like a road ahead," Mitchell said. "It's flooded, but the waters don't look too deep. I think we'll be able to ford it."

Isaac kept his silence as they churned their way through the slow-moving flood. "If it wasn't my picking Thurso, what was it?" he finally asked.

"I'm not as clever as you, Isaac," Mitchell said. "Other than Maggie, I don't think there's anyone alive who is. But as clever as you are, you don't realise you're an outlier. It took me a while to connect the pieces, mostly because I didn't have time to think about them. You, of course, assumed I knew, but it wasn't until after you returned with the news of the death of the Loyal Brigade that I put it all together. It wasn't how they died, but how you told the story."

"What pieces?" Isaac asked.

"At the beginning of the Blackout, before the internet went down, you sent out a message telling people to head south. You told them there'd be food on the coast thanks to the cargo ships you hacked and had run aground."

"You can't object to that," Isaac said. "Most ships would have been lost at sea. If some had made it to their home port, or to their original destination, the food wouldn't have lasted long. People *were* going to starve. This way, by bringing half a continent's supplies to one place, we had enough to keep some people alive until our first harvest."

"No, I don't object to that," Mitchell said. "What you did was heroic. It definitely kept us alive. But that message was only sent to people on a government contact list."

"It wasn't as if I could download a directory," Isaac said. "There was so little time, I had to use what pitiful systems were available. The UK alert system was only designed to contact a small number of specialists."

"Sure. We couldn't save everyone. And as we headed south, and as other people followed, word spread. You saved a lot of people. But in addition to the food-carrying cargo ships, you hacked every American cruise ship with the fuel to reach Britain. Only the American ships."

"They were cruise ships which had set off from an American harbour," Isaac said. "I had no idea who was aboard."

"You had a very good idea who could afford a European cruise departing from the U.S.," Mitchell said. "Middle-class, semi-retired, affluent professionals. Republicans."

"How on Earth would I have known how they voted? I had less than thirty minutes."

217

"Republican with a small r," Mitchell said. "Anti-monarchical. Federalist with a small f. Democrat with a small d. As the world was literally falling down around our heads you looked to the future and found a way to manipulate the demographics of a future super-state. You knew the old world was gone, and the devastation had been so great that what came next would be a shadow of what went before. There'd be new laws and new ways of governing. You were worried about a dictatorship, yes?"

"I knew there would be a dictatorship," Isaac said. "And there was. It is only in recent years I would say we advanced to a merely authoritarian rule. But it could have been much worse. It could have become imperial. It still could, and that is why we are driving together on this desolate road."

"This is what I mean," Mitchell said. "We think so differently, you can't see it, even now. Within a few minutes, you foresaw a future that spanned decades and devised a plan to restrict the potential outcomes. You picked who to save, and who to let die. Your instinct wasn't to save the most people, but to save the right kind of people. At an ingrained level, you believed there *was* a right kind of person to save."

"Everyone does, Henry. You've been at enough apartment fires to have done it yourself."

"Sure. You save the kids. You save the closest. You save those who, having been rescued, could go on to rescue more. Others might save the most powerful, the leaders, the rich, or even the working-age adults. You did something very different. You weren't acting for the moment, or for the next week. You were planning for years ahead. You knew how much food those cargo ships carried. You estimated how many survivors would reach the coast, what the total population would be, and so how many ship-borne refugees Britain could take. Then you picked your ships. You could have picked the closest, but instead you picked those which, statistically, would contain English-speaking, middle-aged professionals. You knew they'd have been architects, lawyers, academics, doctors, dentists, and engineers. They would become our biggest minority, and they'd occupy the kind of positions where their shouting could be heard by the decision-makers. Statistically, you knew most would have adult children back in the U.S., so these people would push for British eyes to look westward. You made a deliberate choice to save people who could influence a future state, and do so in the direction you wanted."

"Almost," Isaac said. "My choice, when I was sitting at the keyboard, writing code as I thought, and as the world fell down about our ears, was between an influx from a homogeneous ethno-cultural democracy, or a random selection of the world's once-in-a-lifetime vacationers. It was a gamble, because I had no guarantee that democracy would survive in the U.S. I didn't foresee America fracturing into three parts, but nor how relatively stable those pieces would be."

"And as it worked out, Britain and America pushed each other back towards democracy and liberty," Mitchell said. "Whatever your motivations, and the relative morality of your decision-making process, you were young and under duress. We all made terrible and stupid mistakes back then. But most of us learned from them and changed. After Sandringham, that's when I realised you hadn't and wouldn't. You could have set up a university, or a department within government. Instead, you set yourself apart, and outside of the laws. Meanwhile, I was trying my best to uphold the peace even when it meant bloody murder during the food riots."

"So do you resent me for what I did, or for how I did it?"

"No. I was angry because you and Maggie had developed something that would have changed the world as utterly as the Blackout. I couldn't do more than stand in front of a grain silo with an axe-handle, asking myself when it would be time to draw my gun. If anyone could have done more, it was you. Instead, you found your followers, and hid all the world's secrets up in Scotland."

"What more could I have done?" Isaac asked. "Really, what?"

"I needed *you* to tell me that," Mitchell said. "Then, and now."

"If there was a better alternative, then or now, I would have spoken up," Isaac said. "It was predictable that there would have been coups and plots. Even the rejection of technology was inevitable. Better for people to claim they chose to abandon doom-scrolling than admit a pernicious pastime had been snatched from them. But it was equally inevitable this was a mere generational trend. The next generation will re-embrace the past, but find the hardware decayed, and the factories collapsed. All I could do was preserve the knowledge of how that technology could be reacquired."

"And I agree, more or less," Mitchell said. "You could have taken a shot at becoming a dictator. You didn't. No, as I said, what you did was heroic. I recognise that, I truly do. My anger was a very personal one. Maybe it was jealousy. Maybe it was regret. I'd adopted Anna, and you'd effectively adopted Kelly, yet we were living such very different lives. You were still living the life you'd had back in America. A life, in many ways, I wanted. You were still trying to shape the world, and I was just trying not to drown. That's why I was angry, not because of any one thing you did, but because I finally understood you, and so embarked on a journey to understand myself. Since then, and perhaps before, we've been walking different paths, aiming for different goals. It's led us here, to an act of high treason in order to end a war we both saw begin in London twenty years ago. Either we both succeeded, or we both failed, and we're about to find out which."

Chapter 29 - The Moravian Gate
Brno, Czech Republic

"Roadblock!" Isaac said, braking sharply as he spoke.

"Toll booth," Mitchell said. "I was expecting it. We're nearing the Moravian Gate."

"That's this place's name?" Isaac asked.

"No," Mitchell said, picking up the binoculars. He scanned the road ahead. There was no movement, but an experienced ambusher never left many signs. "It's the name of the sixty-five-kilometre-wide lowlands between the Carpathian and Sudeten Mountains. Some of it's in Moravia, and some of it was part of Silesia, but it runs from Brno to Ostrava. If you control this pass, you control the direct land route from the Baltic to the Balkans, and from Germany to Ukraine. More immediately, you can't control the old Slovakia, the Czech Republic, or Austria, without controlling this plain. To control the plain, you need to control the roads. Hence the toll booth."

"Which appears deserted," Isaac said. "When did they start charging to use this road?"

"Somewhere around eleven years ago," Mitchell said. "They cleared the roads from Brno to Ostrava, and kept them clear."

"How much did they ask for?"

"Ten percent of whatever you were carrying," Mitchell said. "Must have been at least five thousand of them. They ran some farms, and the road, and a trading post at either end. To avoid the toll, you could just sell them your goods. They'd sell them on."

"Ah, now that sounds like a far more sensible business model. Eleven years ago? That wasn't long after the blight killed off the crops a few miles to the north."

"The year after the plague swept through the camps closer to home," Mitchell said. "As far as is possible to ascertain, this land was utterly deserted when the toll-charging settlers moved in. They coalesced from collapsed farming communities in every direction. When you're a refugee heading south, and you bump into refugees heading north, what choice do you have but to stop walking? About four years ago, a trade caravan returned with news the place had been abandoned. It was one of the last trade caravans to come through these parts before the bandits made travel impossible."

"It doesn't appear as if our friends in Matzen have yet claimed it," Isaac said.

"But if they want a European empire," Mitchell said, "they must control this toll road and the entire Moravian Gate."

"So we should expect lookouts if not sentries," Isaac said. "How do you want to proceed?"

"Slowly." Mitchell took a smoke grenade from the weapons bag at his feet. "If there's gunfire, reverse out of rifle range. We'll see if they follow, and *how* they follow. If they have motor transport, we know where they got the fuel from, and we'll have to revise our plans, but only once we're clear of pursuit."

"It's quite a hefty piece of construction," Isaac said, as he put the Land Rover into gear. "Mostly shipping containers, zippered along the road. Stacked two tall on the road, and three tall at the edge. The doors aren't on this side, so we are expected to drive through, and will then find our ambushers behind and above us, and protected by steel walls. It is a veritable killing zone. That begs the question of why we came this way."

"Curiosity," Mitchell said. "Despite the bluster from the traders who made it all the way to Twynham, the people running the road were honest. They maintained the highways and protected the nearby lands from bandits. They didn't charge refugees and would offer a meal in exchange for labour. There was plenty of farmland for settlers. Like Falsterbo, it should have become a regional hub."

"But a hub depends on the spokes," Isaac said. "The Knights were moving into the north, the Free Peoples were sweeping through the west, and the Caliphate were burning their way across the south."

"Exactly," Mitchell said. "The end result was nearby farmers had less to trade, and even less desire to travel. Meanwhile we in Britain, and our navy, were too busy with pirates raiding our coast and the Mediterranean enclaves to investigate why another settlement in the European interior had collapsed."

Slowly, they drove on and around the outer set of shipping containers, and splashed their way into a rust-flecked swamp. The shipping containers blocked any natural drainage. Wind-blown leaves had become mulch. Snow had turned that to mud, and the recent freezing rains had topped that with a pond. They took a right-angled turn around the next shipping container, and then another. At the roadside, now semi-submerged, were trimmed tree trunks through which stout loops of chain had been threaded. Atop the shipping containers were the cranes which would have swung the trees across the road. None of the cranes had nooses hanging from them; even so, it felt like they were surrounded by ghosts.

"Last one," Isaac said as clear road appeared ahead.

"Stop here," Mitchell said. "There's a door in that last shipping container."

"And a warning on the side," Isaac said. "*Zaraza*. That means plague."

Mitchell left the smoke grenade behind, but drew his forty-five as he got out. Slowly, he made his way around to the container's wooden door set in a warped wooden frame. It took a lift and an upward shove before it swung outwards. Beyond was a second door, this one made of opaque plastic in a metal frame, and which was larger than the hole cut in the side of the shipping container. That door swung inward more easily, until it knocked into a skull. Mitchell, meanwhile, had been knocked back by the foetid stench of the poorly sealed tomb.

"Corpses," he said, taking out his flashlight. He shone the beam inside, and across chairs, tables, a stove, a bookcase, and a ladder leading through a hole in the roof and up to the shipping container above. On the floor were skulls, bones, and rags.

He turned off his light and returned to the Land Rover. "We're about twenty kilometres from Brno, and another fifty from there to the border, and another fifty gets us to Matzen. About eleven years ago, someone gave a bunch of starving farmers the supplies and the equipment to build this barricade and a dozen others like it. Any stray survivors nearby moved closer. Four or five years ago, they were poisoned. A couple of years ago, the enemy moved to Matzen. How many other communities, near other oilfields, were set up to die?"

Halfway between Brno and the Austrian border, the bridge over the Vestonicka Reservoir had been demolished, forcing a detour towards Znojmo, an ancient wine-making town which had long been on Mitchell's if-only-there-was-time list, but another hand-painted plague warning made them take another detour.

An hour later, a change in the road signs marked the near invisible border crossing.

"Stop a minute," Mitchell said.

"You want to stop for the night?"

"Not on this road," he said. "But I want to look at that tree."

The trunk had split, but the branches had been trimmed. They, and the trunk, had been dragged to the side of the road. "Someone cleared the road," Mitchell said.

"Last year, I think," Isaac said.

"This was them," Mitchell said. "They cleared this road. They blew the bridge over the Vestonicka Reservoir. They destroyed the toll-road farms. They're probably responsible for the plague at Znojmo, too."

"I'm not sure precisely where we are," Isaac said, looking at the road signs, "but it can't be more than forty kilometres northwest of Matzen. Two days' walk. Two hours' cycling. Half an hour's driving if the roads are clear, and this tree trunk suggests they might be."

"Sunset is an hour away," Mitchell said. "If they are nearby, they'll be heading home by now. We'll continue for another few kilometres, then radio in our position." He opened the rear passenger door and took out a shovel.

"What's that for?"

"To dig a grave," Mitchell said.

"I can't see a body, or even any bones," Isaac said. "Or is the grave for me?"

The shovel's blade bit into a few inches of topsoil before hitting solidly frozen ground beneath. Mitchell scraped a few inches of dirt clear. "Your turn," he said, handing Isaac the shovel.

"What for?"

"Just dig," Mitchell said.

Isaac scoured another few inches of soil from the surface. "And?"

"Now we bury our arguments, our grievances, and our regrets," Mitchell said. "We each lived a life full of good, bad, and everything between, but for both of us, the best was in the lives we saved, and the lives others got to live because we didn't give in to the darkness. Whatever happens next, we served our people, our friends, our family."

"Yes, not a small accomplishment when you put it like that," Isaac said. "We kept them safe and gave them hope, so let's head on to Matzen, and see if we can give them a better future, too."

3rd February

Chapter 30 - Good Salvage at Bad Pirawarth
Matzen, Austria

After bivouacking at a farmhouse, they set off at first light. At each felled tree, they stopped to look for smoke and to listen for the engines of a mobile patrol.

"The hungry horses remind me of Dakota," Isaac said.

"You saw horses?" Mitchell asked, applying pressure to the brake, as he peered left, then right.

"The ducking donkeys," Isaac said. "Grazing grasshoppers. Praying penguins. Erratic emus. The walking-beam oil-pumps."

"Pump-jacks were never called grazing grasshoppers," Mitchell said.

"They should have been," Isaac said.

The blue-painted pump-jacks proved they were in oil country. Not every weed-strewn field hosted a pump, but they swiftly became too many to count, though none were operational.

He was so focused on scanning for trouble, Mitchell didn't notice they were entering the town until they were passing down a narrow road bracketed by terraced bungalows from which the windows had been removed. After five houses, they came to a frosted heap of drainpipes, and a snow-flecked stack of roof-tiles next to a hollowed-out shell. He'd seen that kind of salvage work before, but usually in Britain. The systematic deconstruction of a village was the sign of an active settlement only a laden cart-ride away.

"Where are we?" Mitchell asked.

"Bad Pirawarth," Isaac said. "In the era of globalisation, and technology-driven Anglicisation, why not split the town in two? Call one half Good Pirawarth, the other Bad, and theme them accordingly. It would have been fantastic for tourism."

"How close are we?"

"Ten kilometres to Matzen. Of course, that assumes they will actually be *in* Matzen. This oil deposit extends into Slovakia."

"The scientists told me it was within thirty kilometres of Matzen," Mitchell said.

"Exactly," Isaac said. "Even with an optimistic margin of error, they could be anywhere."

"But they must be within a day's ride if they're salvaging windows and roof tiles."

"A day's *drive*, Henry," Isaac said.

"Good point," Mitchell said. "But I bet it's Matzen. That castle is just the kind of lair these people would pick."

"Then we should get off this road," Isaac said.

Beyond the town, they re-entered overgrown farmland dotted with stunted saplings, dead weeds, dormant grass, and the increasingly ubiquitous pump-jacks. But one field stood out.

"It's been cleared for grazing," Mitchell said. "They even repaired the fence. No livestock yet, but we truly must be getting close."

"Very, *very* close," Isaac said. "Because I can see smoke on the horizon."

A mud-coated track led to a farm. Like in Bad Pirawarth, someone had recently visited, but they had left doors, windows, and the roof, and had boarded up a broken pane. The barn even had a new padlock on the door. Ten seconds with a lock-pick had it open. Inside, on an eight-wheel trailer and covered in a tarp, was a four-seater helicopter.

"There's no fuel," Isaac said, looking inside. "There is a map, but it's a local one."

"What kind of range do you think it has?" Mitchell asked.

"It's a Robinson R44," Isaac said. "Other than English, the writing is in German. It's a civilian model. No corporate name or logo. As to range, I'd have to guess, but five hundred kilometres seems a reasonable maximum."

"How far is Switzerland?" Mitchell asked.

"It would depend which part, but you mean Zurich, don't you? About seven hundred kilometres in a straight line. While helicopters do fly straight, this machine wouldn't have the range."

"Can it fly?" Mitchell asked, as he began a quick search of the barn.

"It appears to be in good condition," Isaac said. "There are no spare parts lying around, so this is a storage shed rather than a repair yard. The tools are packed away, while the engine has an optimistic scent of oil and lubricant. If I can borrow your detective's hat for a moment, this is an escape vehicle. Probably just for the pilot and their lover, and with enough ammo and food to keep them alive after they flee. East, I suspect, towards the Black Sea, as any other body of water would risk bringing them too close to the Royal Navy."

"Or they plan to use the helicopter to keep tabs on the toll road and on other outlying farms," Mitchell said.

"Well, yes, I suppose so," Isaac said. "There's no fuel here, but I would bet it's nearby if this is intended as an escape vehicle."

"We're about nine kilometres from the castle," Mitchell said. "That smoke plume is obviously not a cooking fire. It's got to be the refinery, so we've driven as far as we can risk. Right now, our tyre marks lead right to this barn. Someone occasionally checks up on this helicopter, and probably drives here to do it. So, anyone other than the pilot is unlikely to think much of the wheel marks we've left in the mud outside. The only question is whether someone will check on this helicopter between now and the missile strike."

"Unfortunately, I left my crystal ball in Dover," Isaac said. "My vote is for leaving the car here, and for setting up the beacon. If anyone does discover our Land Rover, they'll be too busy searching for us to search for the beacon. If we're caught, the plane can still find its target, even without the laser designator. Which of course begs the question of whether we can't just set up the beacon and drive out of here at dusk."

"We've come this far, we've got to see it through," Mitchell said. "We'll set up the beacon, and we'll radio Sherwood, but then we'll hike to the target. If we're wrong, we can radio back that they should pause."

"And if we die, the mission will continue," Isaac said. "Agreed, albeit with a modicum of selfish regret. I'll need a few minutes to set up the antenna and broadcast the signal."

"I'll get our gear," Mitchell said.

They'd travelled heavy from Poland, expecting to have to bribe or fight their way through farmers. Depressingly, that hadn't been the case. For this final part of their mission, they would travel light, carrying only weapons and water.

Half an hour later, they set off on foot, following a compass bearing to the wooded hills which would lead them towards the castle, the town, and the dark column of smoke. They moved low and fast until they were hidden within the forest. The ground was hard, the trees bare, the undergrowth dense except where animals had trampled a trail. Frustratingly, no foraging four-legger had cut a track straight to the castle, so they zigged, zagged, and occasionally made their own path through the undergrowth.

After an hour, and with no warning, the trees gave way to open ground, dotted with only a few trees. Clearly a popular grazing spot for returning deer, it had also become a hunting ground for a large group of locals, only fifty metres away.

Mitchell grabbed Isaac just as an arrow whistled through the air, almost overhead.

Isaac shifted the grip on his carbine, but Mitchell shook his head, and motioned they should wait. A second later, there was a victorious shout, followed by the sound of running feet, but they were running the other way.

Slowly, Mitchell raised his head. Sixteen children had run from the forest and over to a doe with a crossbow bolt jutting through its head.

The children, a mix of boys and girls, were in their mid-teens. All wore brown and grey which had been repaired so often the patches created a camouflage pattern. Two held crossbows, though not the quivers. The rest held spears. The seventeenth, however, was a greybeard who carried an AKM on his back as well as a quiver of bolts. He limped his way over to the crowd, and made a generally approving noise.

The greybeard whistled. A woman of about the same vintage as the man, and with a similarly ancient rifle, led out three pairs of hunters. Each pair carried a small piglet strung between two spears.

"Hunting lesson," Isaac whispered.

"Looks it," Mitchell whispered back. "Back up."

Slowly, they crawled, but only made it twenty metres before running feet again made them duck low. One of the archers had come looking for the stray bolt.

Isaac reached for his knife. Mitchell looked at the blade, and then at the child. He unclipped the button on his holster. But before he had need to draw, the child found the bolt. Holding it aloft, he ran back to his pack.

"Definitely a hunting lesson," Isaac whispered, as the group began heading back the way they'd come. "About fourteen years old?"

"Or fifteen," Mitchell said. "Assuming they operate some friendly-fire safety procedures, there shouldn't be any other hunting teams in this area. We'll follow them from a distance. The castle must be their home."

"But it's a class, Henry," Isaac said. "The implication being other classes of other age groups. Extrapolate that to a population, and we're looking at thousands, minimum."

"I know," Mitchell said. "It's exactly as I feared." He buttoned his holster, but then slipped the M4 off his shoulder, and affixed the suppressor.

They gave the hunting group a ten-minute head start, gauging that would keep them at least half a kilometre ahead. Increasingly, they found signs of wild fields having been cleared, with mounds of damp ash from brush and bush bonfires. Trees had been felled. Roots had been tugged clear. Near those were tyre tracks leading to and from the trail they were following. That trail grew wider with increasingly frequent tyre marks branching off into the forest.

When they heard shouting and cheering, they moved into the trees, and continued on and to the edge of a ploughed field. The furrows were erratic and shallow, and looked to be the work of another group of children who had broken off from their lesson to greet the returning hunters.

"We need better cover," Isaac whispered.

They moved further east as hunters and farmers swapped. The morning's kill was propped at the field's edge. A girl with her arm in a sling was stationed as a scarecrow. The second class took spears and bows, while the former hunters gathered around the tractors. The grey-haired teachers led the new hunting party back along the trail. When the tractor's engine came on, Isaac and Mitchell made their way through the bracken and deeper into the forest before picking a parallel path towards the town, and the castle.

"Two classes, of the same age," Isaac said.

"Yep."

"They're teaching them how to drive tractors, and how to shoot with a crossbow."

"Ammo must be running low," Mitchell said. "It makes sense to keep it for people and bears."

"I was musing on the implications," Isaac said.

"Me, too," Mitchell said. "But I'm not going to draw a conclusion until I see the castle."

But when they did, they saw it was a ruin.

Chapter 31 - Beneath the Broken Tower
Matzen, Austria

"I can't imagine a more perfect spot for a sentry," Isaac said, after they reached as near to the top of the derelict castle's tower as it was safe to climb. The tower, like the rest of the ruined castle, was as lifeless as the grave it had become.

The tower's top and most of the internal floors were gone. The soot-stained walls explained how. The bones below, and in the courtyard, and inside every charred doorway told them why. While the open roof had let in the rain and snow, the holes in the floor had become a drain and an encouragement to damp. The few remaining floorboards either sagged or creaked as Mitchell picked a cautious path towards the broken window.

"If we were to bring the beacon up here, we could just drive away," Isaac said.

Mitchell didn't reply.

"Mrs Zhang does the silent treatment far better than you, Henry," Isaac said as he took a rope from his bag. "Who do you think the bones belonged to?"

"Innocent refugees," Mitchell said.

"Perhaps I should be asking when they died," Isaac said. "My first thought was plague victims, brought here because it was far from the farms. At the conclusion of the contagion, they deemed it too dangerous to bury the bodies, so incinerated them instead."

"Could be," Mitchell said. He took a wide step over a half-metre hole.

"Except it couldn't," Isaac said. "This is a very old castle."

"A thousand years old, if you believe the history books," Mitchell said as he took another step. The floor groaned. He took the hint, stepped back, and made his way to a different window. "I don't believe them, or that guide book. I'd say this castle was six hundred years old at most. This tower is probably a lot more recent. That's assuming concurrent construction techniques here and in Britain."

"The fire burned too hot," Isaac said.

"Petrol," Mitchell said. "They'd have had lots to spare, because they only wanted diesel. I count three tractors down there."

"Three? Where? I can't hear them," Isaac said. Opting for speed rather than caution he took three jumping strides to the narrow and glassless window. "Ah, yes. Three tractors, one field, and quite a crowd."

"It's another class," Mitchell said, holding a monocular to his eye. "Or three classes. Kids are about half the height of the adults, so around ten, depending on their diet."

"If they can't reach the pedals, they're too young to drive," Isaac said.

"Maybe they're just teaching them how a tractor works," Mitchell said. "That's five tractors we've seen. Those three machines are smaller than the two back in the forest, but they have a similar green and black paintwork. That doesn't tell us whether they came from nearby."

"Or how many more they have. Do you see the horses?" Isaac asked.

"I count eight," Mitchell said. "I think a horse has to be two years old before you start teaching them to carry a rider or yoke, and we think these people haven't been here as long as that. I'd say those horses are feral, and are being tamed."

"Or they're loot which is being familiarised to engine sounds," Isaac said. "They're walking them in pairs. Possibly to pull a plough, but probably to pull a cart."

"Horses and tractors," Mitchell said. "They supplied the bandits, and they supplied the people running that toll road. I bet they supplied other people, too, including at least a few dozen to keep an eye on this oil-rich land. When they decided to move in, they killed off the locals, and called it a plague. The bodies got burned, and the evidence was destroyed. This wasn't their first refinery, but it was supposed to be their last, and the first piece of their new empire."

"Whoever controls the oil controls the tractors," Isaac said. "They're going to hire them out, aren't they?"

"To clear a field, to bring in a harvest," Mitchell said. "Give away the horses, then hire out the tractors, and the specialist teams to operate them. Control the knowledge, and you control the farmers. Sure, you can harvest a field by hand, but is that the life you want for your kids? No, you'd want your kids to learn to drive. You'd pay your taxes just so your kids got an education, so they wouldn't know the lean years we did. It's a brilliant way of building loyalty."

"It's a very *old* way," Isaac said. "Extrapolating from the classes, there must be at least two thousand residents. But despite all the pumpjacks we saw while driving, none were actually active. We haven't found where they're getting their oil."

"I can make out a zippered barricade on a road leading into the town," Mitchell said. "Looks like a few rooftop watchtowers, but they're all empty."

"If you ask people to stand watch, you have to give them a reason why," Isaac said. "Their plan was to drive all bandits west, and they have no reason to think their plan failed."

"Because it hasn't," Mitchell said. "Not yet. They sent about a hundred specialists to the west. If they had more to send, they would have, so there's fewer than a hundred loyalist-specialists still here, and not all would be part of the inner circle."

"But there are at least two thousand farmers," Isaac said. "With the war almost over, the inner circle will have become much smaller. The easiest way of hiding the horror of this nation's founding would be by killing everyone who knew the truth."

"We can but hope," Mitchell said. "The refinery is about two kilometres distant. Assuming they're pumping oil closer to there, we can assume at least one more village has been occupied."

"So four thousand farmers and other labourers?" Isaac asked.

"Could be," Mitchell said. "And it could be more, but not too many more. Not yet, or they'd risk a coup. They've bought their positions with electricity as much as with weapons. I can see wires running between the roofs. I'm going to assume generators powering freezers, stoves, lights, and heaters. Those would all help make a thin harvest stretch well beyond spring. A couple of years ago, they sent their specialists to clear out the hired locals. The main group moved more slowly, picking up a stray family here and there, initially only offering protection. Once they began pumping oil, they began recruiting more widely, but not until last year, and only from the south and east, or the German refugees would have heard rumours."

"So last year's would have been the second successful harvest for some of them," Isaac said. "Two safe, warm, replete winters would certainly buy the loyalty of most people anywhere. Those five thousand farmers will be loyalists this spring. By this time next year, their ranks could easily have swollen to fifty thousand."

"Just as we feared," Mitchell said.

"Fine. Agreed," Isaac said. "We can't hunt for their leadership group, not in such a dispersed settlement. We'll have to target the refinery. The laser designator will work from here. Of course, if the plane is going to target the refinery, it could aim for the smoke so there's no need for us to bother with the designator."

"They had anti-air missiles in Dunkirk," Mitchell said. "Every extra second the plane spends overhead will only increase the chance the jet gets shot down."

"So we're targeting the refinery which is only two kilometres away?" Isaac asked. "Do please read into the oblique question my scepticism of us escaping here with our lives."

"Our deaths were always a probability," Mitchell said.

"And you were always terrible at math," Isaac said.

"There's no alternative," Mitchell said. "Tell me I'm wrong, but it would take weeks to infiltrate them, just to find out who their leadership group are, and where they're based. By then, spring will be upon us, and they'll have begun recruiting more farmers who will certainly pick up a rifle to defend the crop they've just planted. Assassination or invasion, both would fail. Both might be inevitable. But we can try this first."

"I know, but an overwhelming desire not to die has come over me," Isaac said. He smiled. "No doubt it shall pass, perhaps even before I do."

4th February

Chapter 32 - Waiting for the Sun
Matzen, Austria

Whether it was called nine kilometres or five and a half miles, it was still a long way to hike in the freezing cold, and while steering safely clear of the last hunting lesson of the day. They made it back to the Land Rover unseen, collected the laser-designator, and radioed a confirmation of the attack order before heading back into the forest.

Darkness had settled before they returned to the ruined castle. Even with the aid of the rope Isaac had slung earlier, by the time they'd reached the top, it was too dark to do anything but wait for dawn. With the air twinkling with frost, it was too cold, too exposed, and far too tense for either to sleep.

"What time is it?" Mitchell finally asked.

"Three-thirty," Isaac said. "Not long to go, assuming the plane takes off at five."

"That's the plan," Mitchell said. "It'll fly thirteen hundred kilometres in approximately seventy-five minutes and be overhead at six-fifteen. When will we pick it up on the short-range radio?"

"When it's within fifty kilometres," Isaac said.

"Minutes before the attack," Mitchell said.

"Barely minutes," Isaac said. He stood and scanned the town with a low-light monocular before returning to his seat next to Mitchell, in the corner with the sturdiest section of floor. "How long do we wait if the plane doesn't appear?"

"Until dusk," Mitchell said. "It's too dangerous to trek back through the forest during daylight. If they find us, they'll find the laser-designator, and that'll make it obvious why we're here. If we fail, and this does come down to a land war, we don't want to give these people any warning."

"Patience was always your virtue more than mine," Isaac said. "The extended version of my life is slowly replaying in front of my eyes."

"Mine, too," Mitchell said. "What would you have done if it had worked?"

"If what worked?" Isaac asked.

"Your demonstration in London," Mitchell said. "You told me there would be untold riches. What were you going to do with them?"

"Yes, sorry, that might have been an exaggeration," Isaac said. "I'm certain we would all have become incredibly comfortable, but my aspirations, even then, tended more towards wine and cheese than champagne and caviar. Maggie and I would have won the Nobel, of course. There would have been interviews galore, and the publicity would have ensured some level of safety. That's what I assumed, anyway. We'd had some clandestine overtures I assumed were from the NSA, and I feared if we weren't abducted by a foreign government, we'd be kidnapped by our own. It's why we decided on a public demonstration, why we picked London over Seattle for the demonstration, and why we didn't pick somewhere more foreign. I was naive, yes, but not entirely so. But of all my preparations, the only one which had any positive result was recruiting you, a non-scientist student, to assist with the lifting."

"You weren't going to become an overnight trillionaire from defence contracts and social media apps?"

"You're missing the key component of him being a truly *sentient* intelligence," Isaac said. "If I were to have used him for my own financial advancement, that would qualify as indentured servitude. I suppose if that was what he'd wanted, I'd have helped, but then the wealth would have been his, not mine. If I had one certain dream, it was not to work for anyone, not even my own creation. I'd have taken a nice house with a view and same-day deliveries, and a teaching job with no early morning classes."

"You were too restless to settle down," Mitchell said. "You'd have gone looking for the next challenge."

"Perhaps," Isaac said. "But what would that have been? Hollywood's vision of terminating cyborgs had blinded us to the social and economic upheaval the announcement of a truly sentient artificial consciousness would bring. While not as catastrophic as the Blackout, it would have brought bigger and more immediate change than anything since powered flight. If an A.I. is sentient, aren't they protected against slavery? Shouldn't they be paid? Shouldn't they get time off? And if we say they can only work for eight hours in every twenty-four, what happens to your smart-home during the other sixteen? If an A.I. is alive, it can't be reproduced without permission. Equally, wouldn't wiping a server count as murder?"

"That sounds like the kind of debates we were having anyway," Mitchell said.

"Exactly," Isaac said. "They *were* happening anyway, but the introduction of a new form of consciousness would have kicked the discussions into overdrive, not just altering how we lived and were governed, but adding new immediacy to the necessity for change. A humdrum lecturing job with tenure and a view might well have been the very best I could hope for. But it is so difficult to know. My memories of past dreams are packaged with the regrets of a life never lived. I suppose the one lesson I can take from the Blackout is that whatever plans I make, the universe will make others."

"We did the best we could," Mitchell said.

"That we are here and awaiting a missile strike implies it wasn't enough," Isaac said.

"It could have been worse," Mitchell said. "But when the newspaper runs that article, there will be an opportunity for change. The better angels in our society can seize the moment, or not, but it will be their choice, not ours, not the politicians', not the terrorists'."

"Yes, and I can't help wondering whether I thought much the same twenty years ago as we flew to London," Isaac said.

Time seemed to slow as it neared five. When it did, there was still nothing to do but wait. At five-thirty, they aimed the laser-designator on target. First light turned the sky grey and the clouds orange, against which a dark plume marked the refinery's belching chimneys.

"Six," Isaac said, now holding the radio. "It has been fun, these last twenty years."

"Some of it," Mitchell said. "At the time, most of it was terrifying."

"We had some adventures, though," Isaac said.

"I'd definitely agree with that," Mitchell said.

Below, the town was slowly beginning to wake. Smoke began rising from a few chimneys, while steam vented from many more. An engine burred. A pot clanged. A hammer banged. Doors opened as the workers began their day.

"Six-fifteen," Isaac said. "The plane will be overhead any minute."

Almost as soon as he finished speaking, an unfamiliar American voice came from the radio in his hands. "Eagle-One to Groundhog, come in, over."

"Henry?" Isaac said, holding out the handset.

"Groundhog to Eagle-one, you are a go," Mitchell replied.

"Roger," the pilot said.

"And that is that," Isaac said, as Mitchell lowered the radio. "We could leave now."

"A few minutes' head start won't make a difference," Mitchell said.

"It might well be the difference between death and life," Isaac said, but he didn't move.

Mitchell checked the viewfinder, and that the laser was aimed at the distant pillars of smoke and steam. Was that really the refinery? Was this really the right town? Right or wrong, he could hear the plane. The soft burr grew into an ocean roar that grew even louder still. The sky filled with noise, drowning the sound from the town as every door opened. The younger folk looked around. Only the older townsfolk knew to look up. Only they might have seen the missile detach and race towards its target.

Mitchell took his eye from the designator and watched the sky, and saw the missile disintegrate in a white cloud that slowly drifted towards the town.

He held the radio to his mouth. "Eagle-one, that's a hit," Mitchell said. "Return to base."

"Roger. RTB. Safe travels, Groundhog."

"It actually worked," Isaac said.

"You sound surprised," Mitchell said, still watching the missile's payload slowly drift to the ground.

"Well, of course," Isaac said. "I didn't want to worry you, but it's not like I've built anything like that before."

"I'm glad you didn't say," Mitchell said. "Let's pack this up, get back to the car, and see if we can escape Matzen alive."

Part 5
How Worlds Change

Scotland, England, and Austria

4th February

Chapter 33 - Arthur
Scrabster & Thurso

The hammering of mortar shells in Ruth's dreams faded into a heavy rat-a-tat against her hotel room's door.

"Hang on," Ruth said, as she disentangled herself from the sheets while trying to find a light. It was definitely still dark outside, though this far north, that didn't mean it wasn't daytime. She made her way to the door, opened it, and saw Esme MacKay.

"Is something wrong?" Ruth asked.

"No. Get dressed. I'll meet you downstairs," Esme said.

Grumbling, Ruth found her clothes. She grumbled louder when she found her watch and saw it was only three a.m. Five minutes later, she was in the inn's small bar which was empty except for Mrs MacKay.

"What's happened?" Ruth asked.

"The railway line has re-opened," Esme said.

"What about the telegraph?"

"Not until this evening," Esme said. "And perhaps not until tomorrow, so the fastest way to get a message to Twynham will be aboard a train, and the first will leave in two and a half hours."

"Right, yes, good, thanks," Ruth said, groggily. "I should speak to Inspector Voss."

"He won't thank you for waking him," Esme said.

"So why wake me?" Ruth asked.

"Because I promised Isaac I'd introduce you to Arthur," Esme said.

"Oh. Of course," Ruth said. Between the on-going observation of Stevens, the paperwork for the paintings, and her appearances in court as Howe and Blanchard were arraigned, she'd barely had time to sleep, and had forgotten about Isaac's friend. "Will he be awake?"

"No. But that's not the point. I've packed you some coffee and a sandwich. You can eat while I drive."

Unlike Thurso, Scrabster, and the roads between, this route had none of the new roadside lanterns. Despite the headlights from the electric truck, and the extra lamps on the roof, it was so dark outside, Esme MacKay was clearly navigating by memory. They'd begun heading west, but then turned inland, onto a narrow road, and then onto a well-maintained track that ended in an old fence, and an equally old gate which had a new padlock.

Esme flashed her headlights, before getting out. As she opened the door, Ruth heard the rhythmically soothing swish of a windmill's blades, but for as far as the car's headlights reached, she could only see tufted heather and a rutted track.

With the gate open, Esme climbed back into the car. This time, she drove slower, and stopped outside a wide one-storey building that had too few windows to have been an office.

Ruth reached for the door handle.

"Wait a minute," Esme said, and picked up a handheld radio. "It's me. Stand down."

"Aye, Esme," came a crackly reply.

"You have armed guards here? Is this a prison?" Ruth asked.

"Not really," Esme said. "But save your questions. It's easier to show than tell."

She got out, so Ruth did the same, enjoying the cold for nearly a whole second before it wormed its way through her clothes and to her skin.

"What was this place before?" Ruth asked as Esme led her towards a pair of glass doors and what had to be the entrance.

"A data centre," Esme said. She stopped by the door. Inside, a light came on. Beyond these doors were another set, then a third, and only then was there a small reception area with about the same dimensions as each of the doors' lobbies. With a loud clunk, the outer door was remotely unlocked. Esme pushed it open.

"After you," she said. "Before the Blackout, the government promised to build a spaceport here."

"That's why you moved here, isn't it?" Ruth asked as Esme pushed the outer door shut behind them. It locked before the inner door opened.

"Aye, though it's more accurate to say the promise of a spaceport was an *excuse* for me to pick here as the place to settle down. I was living in a van at the time, me and Stella. That's Hamish's mum, and it's a story for another time. We weren't the only people to see the opportunities that'd come this way." The second door clicked open. "This place was owned by a nice old gent who'd been an utter villain in his youth. He'd hunted elephants to infuriate conservationists, evicted neighbouring tenants so he didn't have to share his view, and turned farmland into desert so he could redirect the water to his golf courses. But he changed, and there's a lesson there. The worst of us can change, but if they can change, so can the best of us. He put up the wind turbines and this data centre as a way of covering costs until the first rockets could launch. They didn't, but it gave us the start we needed."

The last door unlocked, and Ruth followed Esme into a small reception area. Behind the desk were two armchairs, a flask, a small stack of books, and a very large machine gun with its barrel aimed at the door.

Esme picked up a lantern from a shelf behind the desk. After she turned it on, the lights went out.

"No point wasting electricity," Esme said. "This way."

She led Ruth to the one door at the rear of the room. Again, it was opened remotely. Beyond, the air was cool and dry. Against one wall were neat racks and hooks containing more brushes and brooms than Ruth thought existed.

"Arthur's a clean-freak?" Ruth asked.

"Oh, no, those are Orchid's. She's one half of the protection team. She likes everything spotless, which is why Bobby spends most of his time in a shed near the gate."

"Arthur has two guards, or are they jailors?" Ruth asked.

"They certainly aren't that," Esme said, stopping by a wide set of doors on which was a mechanical keypad. The code was an easy-to-memorise 1,2,3,4. The door opened into a very short room with a second door, a single screen, a keyboard, and a glass wall. Beyond the glass wall, large grey pillars stretched as far as the lantern light would reach. Other than an occasional red or green LED, the chamber, and the viewing room, were in darkness.

"Ruth, this is Arthur," Esme said.

"Are those computers?" Ruth asked.

"Servers, but yes," Esme said.

"Arthur is a computer," Ruth said. "Wait. Arthur is the A.I. This is what Mum and Isaac created?"

"He," Esme said. "Yes. More or less."

"Oh," Ruth said.

"Your mum never came here. That was her choice, but Arthur is still her creation, which makes him your step-brother."

Ruth stepped closer to the glass. "Hello, Arthur," she said. No response came. "Should I talk into the screen? Or do I need to type out the message."

"Neither. He's asleep," Esme said. "Arthur requires a lot of power. So does the town."

"This is Arthur," Ruth whispered. "This is why Isaac came to Thurso?"

"He went to a lot of places before he settled on Thurso," Esme said. "These servers were sealed from the outside world before they could be infected. The wind turbines provided some power, and I and my friends, we understood the value in what Isaac wanted to do."

"Do you mean saving Arthur?" Ruth asked.

"Saving the future," Esme said. "A future that might have been could still be our future again. There are some of us who thought humanity was starting to get its act together. I'm not saying the planet was perfect, far from it, but by and large we were heading in the right direction. The Blackout didn't have to be a complete reset, but we knew there'd be a long dark age. There were many people who wanted to preserve knowledge against a time when it could be released back into the wild, and we wanted to hasten that time's arrival. Just because our lives would be coloured in shades of wood, coal, and copper didn't mean the likes of you and Hamish couldn't have silicon and satellites."

"By keeping Arthur alive?" Ruth asked.

"By re-learning old knowledge," Esme said. "Old-world hand-me-downs will only last so long. Phones, cars, guns, they all break. With so many dead, we can't rebuild exactly as it was, but who would want to? Why replace our coal ships with diesel when we can build a cutting-edge sailing ship that can outrace any of those converted cruise-ships? The future, at least some of it, can be now."

"So this is what Isaac's been doing. Him and his followers."

"We're not *his* followers," Esme said. "We collectively built a searchlight to pierce the darkness, and we're all following the beam, helping each other along, and helping drag the rest of the planet with us."

"It's still a conspiracy," Ruth said. "It's the mirror-opposite of what the Luddites wanted, and it doesn't sound that much different from the schemes Longfield cooked up."

"It is very, *very* different," Esme said. "Longfield and her ilk wanted to wield power from atop a golden throne. We prefer a comfy sofa big enough to be shared. We don't want to tell people what to do, but don't think they have any right to tell us what we *can't* do. So we've kept the knowledge against the time it might be useful and usable."

"And kept Arthur against the time it could spread through cables and computers and take over the world," Ruth said.

"He, and no, that's not how a digital consciousness works, except in fiction."

"How does he work?"

"Just like you and me," Esme said. "Well, almost like you and me. Obviously, he can't do the things that require arms and legs. He thinks, he learns, he grows, but that takes time, just like it does with us. Our perception of time might change from person to person, moment to moment, but time itself works the same on all of us, him included."

"I don't know that I understand all of this," Ruth said. "But I think I understand Isaac. Arthur is his son. To keep Arthur alive requires computers. Old computers won't last forever, so a new computer industry, and all that entails, has to be built."

"That might be his motivation. Mine is a little broader," Esme said. "Arthur won't change the world, but some of his memories of old-world learning might be a guide to those who will. People like you and Hamish. We preserved what we could, and most of it was just ideas and blueprints. Doing something with that knowledge is your responsibility. Not now. Not yet. Perhaps in a decade. Perhaps sooner. But whenever the time comes, remember that with responsibility comes power, so wield it wisely. But that's why I brought you here now rather than yesterday. You need time to process all of this, just like Arthur. Talk with your mum. When you return here, in a month or a year, you'll know what to say to him."

Hectic wasn't adequate to describe the train station. The newly arrived American ferry passengers had been trapped in Thurso while the railway was being repaired. While tickets for the first train had been prioritised for those in the smaller and draughtier rooms, it seemed as if everyone had turned up hoping they would be found a seat.

Ruth found hers easily, and alone, inside a prisoner transport wagon. No prisoners were returning with her. Howe, with his broken leg, was confined to a locked room in the hospital. Blanchard was in a cell. Stevens remained on his ship, hopefully believing Blanchard had boarded the ferry. Quinn had been released, though only on condition she didn't leave Thurso. The paintings, both originals and forgeries, had been left in the care of Dr Frobisher. The convict-cages were, this time, filled with the confiscated luggage of the train's passengers.

The recently arrived American ferry hadn't brought any true migrants to British shores, though there were two dozen overly-armed adventure-seeking travellers hoping to find a fortune in Europe. Inspector Voss had put the weapons into the custody of the ten new embassy staff who were setting up a consulate in Calais.

The rest of the passengers were less of a headache. Some were academics, but most were merchants seeking new markets, or new products, and sometimes both. They were as interested in France as Britain, and had pestered Ruth to the point of annoyance every time she and Hamish had attempted a quiet meal in the inn.

As the train pulled away, she waved farewell to Hamish, then gratefully sank back on the hard bench, closed her eyes, and let her brain bubble away in peace.

She wasn't sure how much of a danger Arthur would have been in the old world, but he certainly wasn't a threat now. Either it was just code trapped on silicon and dependent on electricity, or he was just a kid, dependent on the care of his family. Maybe it was both. Maybe it was neither. She couldn't see it made any difference to her life, or to her future. Not now, anyway. She'd have to ask Mum how much of Arthur was her creation, too, and knew the answer would be a lot more complicated than if it was a mere biological question.

At least she better understood Isaac, Mitchell, and the friction between them. While Mitchell had bent and twisted the law into a shape that could be upheld in the present, Isaac, and his fellow followers, had written off the present so they could shape the future.

The train ran slow for the first four hours, until they were beyond the repaired section of track. She tried to read a hefty history of computing which Mrs MacKay had loaned her, but her mind kept drifting, thinking of the past, and the possible futures yet to come. When they stopped, those thoughts were replaced with a question. The telegraph office at the water-and-coal stop didn't have today's newspaper, but the morning's headlines had been wired up from Twynham and written in big letters on a sandwich board: *Peace in Europe? Surrender Ultimatum Given.*

Naturally, to find out the details of the ultimatum, and which side had issued it, would require buying a newspaper. With no copies available, the question remained a mystery.

Ruth sent a coded wire south, to Anna, saying she was on the train, and had an urgent case to discuss, and considered asking for more details about the newspaper's article to be wired to the next coal-stop. She decided against it. Whatever the news was, it would wait until she reached Twynham.

5th February

Chapter 34 - Mutiny, Treason, and Coup
Twynham

When the train reached Twynham, at a time so late it was nearly early, it wasn't Anna waiting at the railway station, but Commissioner Weaver.

"Deering, with me," Weaver said, as Ruth stepped onto the platform.

"I'm glad to see you, ma'am," Ruth said. "Inspector Voss had to arrest Erin Quinn, and we've now got to arrest Mrs McMoine."

"Whatever for?" Weaver asked, as she stopped dead in her tracks.

"Quinn's probably innocent, but McMoine ran a forgery scam to seize control of her party, and so the Porter brothers could reclaim some land in Cornwall that they sold to Longfield and which the government seized."

"Is anyone in imminent danger of being murdered?" Weaver asked.

"I don't think so," Ruth said.

"Then it can wait," Weaver said. She began walking again.

"And there's Stevens," Ruth said, hurrying to keep up. "We think we've got him."

"So do we," Weaver said. "The niece is in custody."

"Oh. How?"

"That can wait, too," Weaver said, stopping by the platform's waiting room. The *closed* sign was on the door, but Anna Riley was waiting inside, reading that morning's copy of the newspaper.

"Hey, Anna. What's going on?"

"Trouble," Weaver said. "Deering, what do you know about Austria?"

"It's near Germany," Ruth said.

"I told you she wouldn't know anything," Anna said.

"What's going on?" Ruth asked.

"The most peculiar coup in history," Weaver said. "Are you sure you know nothing?"

"I don't even understand the question," Ruth said.

"Good," Weaver said. She reached into her pocket and took out an envelope and a badge. "Anna Riley, I'm promoting you to police captain in command of the Serious Crimes Unit. I was going to do so anyway, but we can't wait. The promotion will show I have faith in you, and so should give you some protection during the hearings, assuming I don't get fired or arrested first. And that's assuming I make it back from Austria alive. Deering, the best protection I can offer you is the suggestion you return to Dover and stay there. You mentioned something about Ms Quinn and Mrs McMoine?"

"Oh, yes, we need to arrest McMoine," Ruth said.

"This sounds like a case for the Serious Crimes Unit and its new captain," Weaver said. "Do try to stay out of the spotlight, both of you. Captain, brief Deering, then deal with this McMoine business. Deering, I shall speak with you again when I travel through Dover. Good luck." With that, she left.

"I've never seen her like that before," Ruth said. "What on Earth is going on? She mentioned a coup."

"It's not that bad," Anna said. "Did you see yesterday's newspaper?"

"Only the headlines that were telegraphed to the water and coal stop," Ruth said.

Anna reached into the pouch beneath her wheelchair's seat and took out a folded newspaper. "This is yesterday's paper. The afternoon edition."

Ruth took it. The headline read: *Give Peace a Chance?*

"Why is there a question mark at the end of the sentence?" Ruth asked.

"It's complicated, but Dad and Isaac, and Mrs Zhang and Kelly, and a few others, have given Britain a chance to stop the war, expand the EU, change the outcome of our election, and maybe the entire future of this continent, if not beyond. It all depends on how things work out over the next month. Everything could still go the other way, and end up with us bogged down in a bloody war."

"How? Why?" Ruth asked.

"I've coffee," Anna said as she took out a flask. "I'll pour us a cup while you read the paper."

Ruth turned back to the newspaper, and began to read…

This morning, at 05:00, a restored Rockwell B-1 Lancer fighter-bomber piloted by an American crew departed from an airfield in Belgium. British Intelligence had identified an oil refinery in Austria (see map on page 4) run by the same terrorist cell who so savagely attacked Calais. The refinery workers aren't slaves, but farmers duped into thinking their leaders are beneficent refugee-scientists. In truth, this group of two hundred terrorists are the same vile souls originally responsible for the Blackout, for the plagues that swept through Europe, and for the coups and war crimes perpetrated on British soil (see timeline on page 8).

Recent investigations, including the unmasking of a spy ring in Dover at Christmas (see page 9), have revealed our enemy's plans. They hoped for a military assault on this refinery, forcing us to massacre their farmers, and so sowing poison between Britain and Europe for generations to come. During that assault, our tanks would have consumed our entire diesel stockpile, leaving none for agricultural use this spring. Rationing would continue, as would conscription, and, of course, the war.

Instead, with support from our European and American allies, a plane was launched, and once over the target, rather than obliterating them with an explosive, leaflets were released, revealing the sinister true identity of these criminal-scientists (for transcript, see page 3). An ultimatum was given to these farmers: detain or expel the terrorists before our police arrive. In return, we will buy their oil and put Europe to the plough, for surely that is better than the sword. (continued on page 2).

"That's only left me with even more questions," Ruth said, swapping the paper for a mug of coffee.

"I think Dad wrote the article," Anna said. "This was the second edition. Dad had left a letter with a lawyer to be delivered to the newspaper after the plane returned. The first edition was mostly about Hailey Stevens's arrest. But the second edition was truly explosive. Considering the maps, and the details, and how the story runs for a full twenty pages, they must have printed exactly what Dad gave them."

"So it's true?" Ruth asked.

"As true as any news ever is," Anna said. "I think the editor must have known this was coming, but I didn't. You didn't. Even Weaver didn't. The politicians certainly didn't."

"Weaver said there was a coup. Who's in charge?"

"It's still Atherton and the coalition," Anna said. "Let me start at the beginning. If we go back to Christmas, the military goals for this coming year were to secure the Belgian and French coast, then to drive a road and rail link to the Mediterranean. Conscript garrisons would have been stationed along those roads, where they could also protect some farms. The more experienced military units would hunt down stray bandits and impose a peace of sorts. We'd repaired some tanks, and bought diesel from America, so our victory was assured, even if it would be a small one. But then, after the attack on Dunkirk and then Nieuwpoort, Dad worked out where the terrorist leadership was based."

"He's been looking for years, hasn't he?" Ruth asked. "That's why Isaac sent Simon Longfield to Switzerland, but they turned out to be in Austria?"

"Yes, at least for the last year or so," Anna said. "Having learned where they were, parliament wanted to destroy them. Parliament, and the admiralty, decided that we should send the tanks across Europe to wipe them out. Dad had a better idea. That diesel we'd use in the tanks could also be used by our farmers, but only if we found an alternate way of destroying our enemy. Why not blow up the refinery?"

"That's why he went to Austria?" Ruth asked.

"He went to Austria to guide in a plane, one of three planes which is theoretically airworthy. The rest of the reclamation effort has involved salvaging parts from otherwise wrecked aircraft. The planes, and the salvaged parts, were all promised to America in exchange for diesel for tractors, tanks, and trains. Without any jet fuel of our own, we can't maintain an air force, so this exchange made sense to everyone at the time. This particular jet was ready to fly and scheduled for a test flight before being shipped across the Atlantic. Dad suggested they test it by flying to Belgium. There, they'd load a missile, and then fly in an arc over Germany, safely away from any bandits in France, and launch the missile at the refinery in Austria. There, Dad and Isaac were pointing a laser just to make sure it hit the target. That was the plan to which Atherton agreed, but Dad switched out the missile. Actually, I think it was Mrs Zhang and Gregory who did the swapping."

"Changing explosive for leaflets," Ruth said, looking again at the newspaper. "If a leaflet fell from the sky here, saying Atherton was responsible for the Blackout, I wouldn't believe it. Why should anyone in Austria believe this leaflet?"

"It's a gamble," Anna said. "A *huge* gamble. But the theory, based on the attacks on Calais, is that this group have a very small core leadership. Everyone else are farmers or oil workers, but a year or two ago, they were refugees. Sure, they'll fight for their land and their families, but would they fight for their leaders if they knew those same people were responsible for the Blackout, the plagues, and for the Knights, the Free Peoples, and the Caliphate?"

"Yes, it is a gamble," Ruth said. "But it sounds more like a mutiny than a coup."

"Or maybe it's treason," Anna said. "The American pilots must have known what the payload was, so it's probable that someone at the embassy knew, too. The editor of the newspaper knew something was happening. At this stage, I'm not sure who else knew, but I'm sure there are others. The leaflet said we're sending police to arrest the ringleaders and to then buy oil from the refinery. That's where Weaver is going now. She's going to lead the convoy to make sure it actually does leave, and that they take trucks, not tanks, because she wants them to arrive looking like police and traders, not soldiers or conquerors. If her mission is a failure, if they're attacked, we won't have enough fuel to deploy the tanks until the summer."

"Then why did Mister Mitchell do it?" Ruth asked.

"Because it might actually work," Anna said. "You should have been here when that newspaper was released. The whole city went crazy. The first flight in twenty years was a mission of peace, not destruction. Everyone decided it meant the war was over. *Really* over. The jubilation nearly became a riot."

"But it isn't over, is it?" Ruth said. "Not yet. Not until Weaver gets back from Austria. If she gets back, which she might not."

"Yes, there is a chance this ends in a massacre," Anna said. "And she's still got to travel through the remains of the bandits we shattered last year. But there's more to the story, and which the newspaper doesn't know. Dad gave the article to a lawyer to give to the newspaper editor. That same lawyer came to see me, and read me a letter from Dad, and then she burned the letter."

"Really, why?"

"Because as much as there are some things which must be written down, there are others which shouldn't," Anna said. "There were two leaflets dropped on Matzen. The first is what the newspaper printed. The second is a list of suspects. It's every name Dad and Isaac ever learned, and could get from the old MI6 databases that Weaver gave them access to. Most, if not all, of those people are long dead, and maybe even before the Blackout. But even if none are in Matzen, anyone who is truly guilty will recognise at least some of the names. With that list went a warning that we were coming for them, and then we're going to open the vault in Switzerland, for which we have the address, and to which we're going on our way back from Austria."

"What's in the vault?" Ruth asked.

"I've no idea. I don't think Dad does, either," Anna said. "It's all a bluff. He wants to see who runs so he can arrest at least one of them. Even if he can't catch them, when the farmers see that some of their overlords are fleeing, that'll prove the leaflets are true."

"Do you really think so?" Ruth asked.

"Not knowing anything about the people there, it's so difficult to know," Anna said. "We don't need a full-blown civil war in Austria. We just need one strongman to launch a coup. One farmer or hunter, or even a terrorist, to decide it's better to kill anyone who might incriminate them, and then declare themselves king of Austria, and then sell oil to the British."

"So we're just going to let some murderer become dictator?" Ruth asked.

"Not this time, no," Anna said. "But it'll be a lot easier to arrest them after we've set up a trade route. If we can avoid a massacre over the next six months, we stand a good chance of ensuring peace and justice for a few years."

"And if it all falls apart, and if Weaver is killed, I suppose we'll send in another plane, this time with a real missile."

"That's certainly what the Austrians must be thinking," Anna said. "After that newspaper came out, Atherton, and then Woodley, stood up in parliament and took credit for the plan as the newspaper laid it out. They didn't have to. But they did. They lied. The original plan was to blow up the refinery and to kill the workers and the farmers. Only Atherton and Woodley, and Weaver and Dad, were in the room when the decision was made. But afterwards, the admiralty will have been informed of the missile strike. Since the Americans provided the planes, pilots, and the fuel, they knew the official plan, if not the unofficial one, too. The truth will get out."

"Eventually. Maybe," Ruth said.

"No, within the next few weeks," Anna said. "Weaver knows the truth. I know the truth. So does the lawyer who told me. So do you. There's an election coming. Whether this mission is a success or a failure, we can't begin the election campaign with those two claiming credit for something they had no hand in. Weaver didn't say as much, but when she's back, I think she's going to press the issue. I've no idea what'll happen next, except it'll have a huge impact on the election."

"Meaning Mr Das will win," Ruth said.

"His coalition will do well," Anna said. "But that'll only cement him as a parliamentarian rather than a royalist. Who knows where it'll lead, but things here will certainly change. They'll change in Europe, too. Atherton didn't inform the EU leadership in advance of the flight. The Europeans are furious. Their response has been to mobilise so they can join the journey east. Right now, the EU is basically another name for France. Next month, it could mean Germany and Austria, too. By the end of the year, it could be everywhere from Poland down to the Adriatic."

"Is that a good thing?" Ruth asked.

"It's better than kingdoms and empires," Anna said. "Who knows where it'll end, of course, but it will begin as a democratic partnership aiming to bring stability to the continent. And that will happen regardless of how successful or not Weaver's mission is. Our focus will now be on Austria, either for trade or revenge. Dad always wanted Britain to look further than the coast. Isaac wanted the world to look up from the hole it had buried its head in. The Blackout taught us it was foolish to guess at the future. But one thing I know, and which everyone who read the paper knows, is that instead of blowing up farmers in a missile strike, instead of consuming a year's fuel reserve to deploy those tanks, instead of sending more of our sons and daughters to die, we're sending police to make an arrest. There's a chance it'll work. Only a chance. But what a glorious foundation for the future if it works."

"How long until we know, do you think?" Ruth asked.

"It depends on how long it takes to get to Austria, but Colonel Sherwood is already in Germany, finding a driveable road-route back to our lines. Maybe two weeks. Maybe a month. Definitely not much longer."

Ruth finished her coffee. "I don't know if my brain has room for this," she said. "It's still full of Stevens, and McMoine and the paintings, and Arthur."

"You met him?" Anna asked. "I did wonder if Isaac might introduce you."

"It was Esme MacKay who did the intro," Ruth said. "I sort of ran out of time with Isaac because of the investigation. You've met Arthur?"

"It was Kelly who told me, and that was years ago. Isaac invited me up, in that way he does, but it's just a computer and a big digital library without enough electricity to properly run. I decided, since it's well out of my jurisdiction, the less I know, the better. But I can't say that about McMoine. Do we really have to arrest her?"

"Absolutely. And I need to re-interview the Porter brothers. The paintings were swapped, here in Twynham, for forgeries. It's possible that the paintings found in Dover are forgeries, too. McMoine wanted to embarrass Quinn so she could seize control of the party. Her brother was going to discover the originals, or a set of copies, in America. The Porter brothers were then going to say that since they'd been paid with forgeries, their contract with Longfield was null and void, and could they please have that land in Cornwall back."

"You can conduct the interview of the Porter brothers down in Dover," Anna said. "We'll take care of McMoine before you catch the train."

"What about the Loyal Brigade? We cracked the code."

"It was hidden in the weather report, yes?" Anna asked.

"You figured it out?"

"Don't sound so surprised," Anna said. "Though, okay, it was the chancellor at the university who spotted the anomaly. He really does fancy himself as a sleuth. With that, we then arrested the arsonist's brother, and told them we had one deal and it could either be taken by him and his sister, or by Hailey Stevens and her uncle. They talked."

"They told you about *Great Expectations*?"

"They did," Anna said. "Did their agent get on the ferry?"

"No, we've detained her," Ruth said.

"Great," Anna said. "We've arrested Hailey Stevens, and she's willing to give up the names of all her customers if she and her uncle can get some kind of protective custody."

"Do I need to go back up to Thurso?" Ruth asked.

"No, you should do as Weaver said and go back to Dover, but I'll take down the details over a quick breakfast."

"Yes, Captain," Ruth said. "*Captain* Riley. It has a nice ring to it. Will you still go to America?"

"I don't know if I'll still have a job here in a month, or a job offer there," Anna said. "No, I'm not going to make any more plans until Weaver comes back, and we've heard what happened with Dad and Isaac."

5th February

Epilogue - The Final Suspect
Haiming, Austria

As Isaac refuelled the Land Rover, Mitchell walked a slow perimeter of the car. A thin layer of pristine snow coated the road ahead. A thicker layer covered the ruins on either side, with even more topping the mountains looming beyond. While he wasn't sure where they were, he was certain no one had lived here for years. He climbed up onto the roof, and took out his binoculars. After a brief scan of the road ahead, he turned his gaze to the way they'd just come.

"Anything interesting?" Isaac asked as he replaced the fuel cap.

"Only snow," Mitchell said. "There are no tracks ahead of us. No smoke. No helicopter. No trucks behind us. I can see some animals over to the east that might be sheep, but are probably wild dogs. Otherwise, we're alone."

He climbed back down, and picked up the map. Isaac returned the fuel can to the back of their Land Rover.

"Are you worried that a column of trucks is about to appear on our tail, or worried they won't?" Isaac asked.

"Both," Mitchell said. "How are we for fuel?"

"We can manage another six hundred kilometres," Isaac said. "More if we lose our excess baggage, but if we are being followed by an angry army of Austrian terrorists, I'd prefer to keep our arsenal close to hand."

"I can't help feel we've done this wrong," Mitchell said. "We shouldn't have chased the helicopter."

"We were lucky to escape Matzen in our truck," Isaac said. "Having done so, we could only watch one road. That leaflet we dropped, saying we had the Swiss vault in our sights, would have given the impetus to any true terrorist to beat us to the punch, and so go west. We watched the roads to the west of Matzen, and we saw the helicopter fly overhead. It's interesting that it didn't appear until one o'clock. They took their time before leaving."

"Yes, but we're assuming that helicopter continued going west," Mitchell said. He took out the map and unfolded it until he found Matzen. "Our leaflet, and its threat, would only mean something to surviving members of the original conspiracy. But what if they already cleared out that vault years ago, so knew there was no reason to go west?"

"Then why did we see the helicopter flying west?" Isaac asked.

"Because the only way to navigate from the air without radio beacons is by following old roads. They could have turned south near Salzburg, and so aimed for the Adriatic."

"Or the helicopter could have been the scout, and we have a hundred trucks just a few hours behind us," Isaac said. "Why are we speculating?"

"Because I was sure that helicopter was aiming for Innsbruck," Mitchell said. "That old airport was the perfect place to stash fuel."

"Yes, and we spent two hours looking for signs of it," Isaac said. "We saw no helicopter, we saw no disturbed snow."

"But we focused on the airport," Mitchell said. "That's old-world thinking. They could have set down in any parking lot."

"Perhaps they did. Or perhaps there is no fuel stash. Yes, from the air, you'd have to follow the road, judging distance by time, the mountain peaks, and a few church spires. They could have set down in the wrong town, missing their stash house by more than a day's walk. In this weather, a day's walk is not very far. Look at those clouds to the north, that's an approaching blizzard if ever there was one, and a suggestion we shouldn't linger here much longer."

"Right, so do we turn back?" Mitchell asked.

"To what end?"

"We've got enough fuel to return to Matzen. We could survey the town, switch that radio set back on, and relay what intelligence we collect back to Britain."

"But Sherwood's orders were to find a road route back to our lines," Isaac said. "Until the column drives east, there will be no one to speak to. You are currently experiencing a general's anxiety. The pieces are in play. The game is afoot, but we're not the players. This hunt we're on is a sideshow. We don't know who is left in Matzen, or whether the helicopter was the only vehicle that left. We don't know if, to save themselves, they released a biological agent to kill off the farmers before returning to the Black Sea. If they haven't fled yet, they might when that convoy from Britain arrives."

"If it arrives," Mitchell said.

"Hence your anxiety," Isaac said. "Because this is a game being played by Britain as much as by Matzen. We're out of it, you and I. Look, if you want to return to Matzen, I'll be at your side. But if we return, we're not skulking about in the woods, or in that ruined castle, where we're liable to be shot by some anxious teenager. We'll drive in with flags flying, and as officers of your law. But the leaflet you wrote said there would be a convoy of police. One Land Rover doesn't make a convoy, and we have no trade goods with which to make nominal payment for any fuel. Nor can we guarantee the convoy *is* on its way. We have done our little bit of meddling, and must now let events play out."

"Leaving us on a snowbound mountain road in Austria, without the fuel to reach France," Mitchell said.

"We could reach Germany," Isaac said. "Once out of the mountains, we can find some bicycles, and link up with the refugee-rescue route, such as it was. Or we can head to Zurich, look for that helicopter, and prepare against a larger column arriving on our heels. From where I stand, the worst, and best, case scenario is that we live on our rations for a month, hunting the ruins for a forgotten stash of chocolate and brandy. Regardless of what we decide, that storm is getting closer."

Mitchell folded the map, and climbed back into the truck.

They drove on, but Mitchell was still lost in his thoughts. There was no way of predicting what their enemy would do in Matzen, but there were so many possibilities. They'd butchered civilians before, and so would surely have no qualms about doing it again. His assumption was that any remaining biological weapons would have been hidden, if not destroyed, as they rebranded themselves as scientist-protectors of Austrian farmland. They could have left together for a previously used bastion along the Black Sea, or to some hitherto unknown redoubt further east. Or he could have misjudged the relationship with these farmers, and they could all be now building barricades and destroying bridges, getting ready for a siege.

His rationale for committing mutinous treason had been that the worst-case scenario if his plan failed would be war, which they were already fighting, but Atherton's plan would have resulted in the deaths of potentially innocent civilians. Isaac was correct: whatever happened next, in Britain and Austria, was out of his hands, but however slim, he'd given both sides an alternative that almost looked like peace.

"How about a game," Isaac said, already slowing the truck. "I spy with my little eye something beginning with jackpot."

Ahead, on the road, was the helicopter they'd found in the farm outside Matzen, and which they had then seen flying west. Isaac stopped a good five hundred metres distant.

"Drive closer," Mitchell said.

"Are you sure?"

"They would have set down yesterday," Mitchell said. "No way would they have camped overnight in that tin can."

He was right. The helicopter was empty, at least of the living.

"Male," Mitchell said as he examined the corpse. "Thirty. North African extraction. Could be Caliphate or Free Peoples."

"Or neither," Isaac said. "How did he die?"

"There are two gunshot wounds," Mitchell said. "One to the right leg, just above and behind the knee. One to the side. There's a thick bandage on his side, but I think the leg wound killed him. The pain from his side made him unaware that an artery had been nicked. He was a passenger, and sitting in the back."

"Then I shall hunt for the trail left by the pilot," Isaac said.

Mitchell walked a circuit around the helicopter, and counted three bullet holes near the tail. For the helicopter to have reached this far, those bullets couldn't have done any damage, but there were none in the cabin. Who had shot at the helicopter and its passengers, and had they continued the chase by truck? Again, he looked back down the road. He and Isaac had driven slowly, and in daylight, and they had spent two hours searching Innsbruck. No, if a truck was in pursuit, it would have caught up by now. Probably.

Mitchell turned his attention to what else had been left behind. From the position of the tape, the man had applied his own bandage, but there was no first aid kit. There was a Heckler & Koch MP5 submachine gun, and a bag containing clothes and a wash-kit. That bag had been opened, though. There was no spare ammunition for the submachine gun. Nor were there any journals, diaries, or even a phone in the bag. Nor was there any food.

Mitchell checked the body. The clothing was in good condition and civilian, probably designed for skiing, though the boots were better suited for hiking.

"I found a trail," Isaac said. "Two sets of prints. A size seven and a size ten, give or take."

"Two people?"

"A man and a woman, or possibly a teenager."

"Or a woman with big feet and a man with small," Mitchell said. "They left nothing behind to identify the man, took the ammo, but left the gun. They must each have a submachine gun of their own."

"Or one submachine gun and something better," Isaac said. "That's not a Kalashnikov from some old post-Soviet storage depot."

"Nope," Mitchell said. "There are a few bullet holes at the back of the helicopter. They were shot at as they were leaving Matzen."

"That's good," Isaac said. "Disunity is a good sign."

"It's not a bad sign," Mitchell said.

"If you want a sign which is unequivocally bad, I could point to those clouds," Isaac said. "One can hope they're merely rain, but the air pressure bodes something far sharper."

They left the body in the helicopter, where the cold weather might preserve the corpse, though it was doubtful a salvage team would even be sent for the helicopter. They drove on, slowly following the indistinct trail left by the two pedestrians, but still travelling faster than anyone could walk. Even so, it was ten kilometres before they saw smoke, rising beyond the horizon. As they neared, the smoke disappeared.

"They heard us," Isaac said.

The road travelled through another of the roadside almost-villages, where the year-long winters had caused the buildings to be abandoned long before the mountain storms demolished the roofs. They stopped on the outskirts, pulling slightly off the road, and taking cover by the remains of a steep-roofed chalet.

"Would you be offended if I were to state the obvious?" Isaac asked.

"It's cold, it's dark, and the storm clouds are approaching," Mitchell said.

"Yes. That would do for starters. We also have no idea who we're chasing."

"And they have no idea who we are," Mitchell said. He'd raised his carbine, and peered down the scope, surveying one ruin, then the next. "I've never been sure what label best describes me. Copper, officer of the law, law-keeper, law-giver, they all mean such very different things. You hired me, all those years ago, because I was no scientist, and I'm still not one now."

"No, you're more of a humanitarian," Isaac said.

"If I had to pick, I'd prefer calling myself a student of human nature, and that's universal when it comes to survival. Look three hundred metres ahead at the building with the nearly intact roof. There's a blanket covering the broken window. I think that's our target."

"Excellent. How shall we proceed?"

"Cautiously," Mitchell said. "On foot, and in cover."

They made it to within fifty metres before the first gunshot, though the shot went wide, disappearing among the ruins. Even so, they took cover.

"We want to talk!" Mitchell yelled before lowering his voice. "Can you see anything?"

"Not yet," Isaac said.

Another shot echoed across the snow-flecked landscape.

"A storm's coming," Mitchell called. "You'll be trapped here until the thaw. Do you have enough food? Or we can drive out of here together, outrace the storm."

"Maybe they don't speak English," Isaac said.

But at least one of them did. "Who are you?" a man called, with an accent from the Germanic-Slavic borderlands.

"Henry Mitchell. I'm a police officer from Britain, and the author of those leaflets we dropped on Matzen. You were on the helicopter. Are you the pilot or the passenger?"

There was a pause before the man answered. "Why are you following us?"

"The leaflet was a ruse," Mitchell said. "We knew most of the locals in Matzen were protecting nothing more than their fields and families. We wanted to see who'd run if they thought the net was, once again, drawing in. You ran. Or flew. Here's the good news. There's a deal. A pardon. You'll get a sea-view, you'll be guarded, and somewhere without as many mountains as this. Your alternatives aren't great. Those clouds are slow-moving, and getting denser by the minute. The snow will fall for days. You'll be stuck here until the thaw. How much firewood have you gathered? How many matches do you have? How much food? If you stay, you'll freeze. You'll die. Or you can come with us."

There was silence from the house.

"We could do just that," Isaac whispered. "We could leave them to freeze."

"We could, but you know we won't," Mitchell said. "Do you have the grenades?"

"Fragmentation and smoke, though what's on the label doesn't always match what's in the can."

"When I—" Mitchell began, but was cut off by a gunshot from inside the house. Another two shots came, but of a different calibre.

"They've turned on each other," Mitchell said. "On me. Watch the window." He ran low and fast, gun raised, his eyes on the door. No one came to the door, nor were there any more shots from inside.

On reaching the building, Isaac held out a grenade. Mitchell shook his head, gesturing around the back before pushing at the door. It fell inward, the hinges long having been broken. Inside was a man in his late forties and a woman who was easily in her seventies. He was dead, shot once in the neck. She was bleeding, one hand clutching her side, unable to stem the blood spreading across her frayed ski-jacket.

Mitchell kept his gun on her until he was close enough to kick the fallen pistol away from her hand. She just watched him, her eyes sagging.

"I couldn't let him take the deal," she whispered. "This had to end."

"Clear," Mitchell called.

"Clear," Isaac said, making his way through a ruined doorway at the back. "Ah, so she shot him, and he shot her."

"This doesn't look too bad," Mitchell said, kneeling down near her.

"It is," she said. "With this rate of blood flow, I'll be dead in minutes."

"You're a doctor?" Mitchell asked.

"Their doctor. Just their physician. That's all I ever was."

"You've been with them since the beginning?" Mitchell asked. "Since the Blackout?"

"I wasn't supposed to," she said. "My practice was in Tel Aviv, but I was paid a fortune to visit a compound to consult. The world ended, and I was a prisoner at first." She coughed. "The lies we tell ourselves so we can sleep. I was the prisoner of a monster, but I became a monster. We all did. We killed so we could live. We murdered so we could rule. Rule what? What did it achieve?"

"Not much," Mitchell said. "Who shot at the helicopter?"

"Viktor," she said. "He wanted to hand me over to the British police as a gift."

"And who's he?" Mitchell asked.

"Go to Matzen and meet him," she said, the words trailing into a cough. She sagged.

"There's a bag of thermite grenades here," Isaac said, stepping back from the bag by the wall. "You were travelling west, towards Zurich. I think you were going to the vault."

"To destroy it," she said.

"Which means, I think I know what was in it," Isaac said. "It's Marr. Or as much of him as the man was able to digitise. It's his research, isn't it? Stashed there before the Blackout."

"It must be destroyed," she said.

"He's dead?" Mitchell asked.

"Years ago," she said. "I was the last of the original survivors. The original prisoners. The original murderers. But our successors truly learned from our mistakes."

"Tell us where the vault is, we'll go to Zurich, and make sure it's destroyed," Mitchell said.

She shook her head. "I was going there because I thought you knew where it was. That leaflet said you knew. But you don't. I am the last who knows. Now that I'm dead, the location will be lost, and it will be over. Finally."

She closed her eyes.

Mitchell stepped back, watching, waiting. "She's dead," he finally said.

"Well, this is rather a pickle," Isaac said.

"Not really," Mitchell said.

"Zurich's a big place, and has a lot of vaults," Isaac said. "We were banking on one of them leading us to the correct one."

"I always thought the vault was just a curiosity," Mitchell said.

"Its existence was the reason they never strayed far from this corner of Europe," Isaac said.

"I assumed the vault contained weapons, but if it was just his research, then it's worthless, yes?" Mitchell asked.

"Well, yes," Isaac said. "The Blackout was a result of his failure. Any lessons to be gleaned from his mistakes were learned when the planes fell out of the sky."

"We never got her name," Mitchell said, taking out his phone so he could photograph the dead woman. "But someone in Matzen will know. We have no reason to disbelieve her when she said she was the last surviving member of the old guard."

"But no reason to believe their new leader, Viktor, will be anything but a dictator," Isaac said.

"The future is still balanced on a knife edge," Mitchell said. "But it does sound as if they're going to attempt trade rather than war. The vault's location has been lost. We've confirmed all the original conspirators are dead. The war could be about to end. We'll take peace today and find time for justice later. I won't say we won, but victory is within reach."

"Leaving us with only the minor question of what we do next."

"We'll start with getting off this mountain before the blizzard arrives," Mitchell said. "We'll head to Germany and look for a castle, or a palace, or just a nice house. We'll see if we can pick anyone up on that radio, and if not, we'll find some bikes and cycle our way west, so we can pass on news of this woman's death."

"I doubt we'll be welcome back in Britain," Isaac said.

"That was always the price we were going to pay," Mitchell said. "But it's a small price in the scheme of things."

"Then let's gather what we can," Isaac said. "Didn't they make wine in Germany?"

"Before the Blackout, sure," Mitchell said.

"If they made wine, they had vineyards," Isaac said. "Why don't we go and find one?"

The end.

Printed in Great Britain
by Amazon